GLASS THORNS

BOOK TWO
ELSEWHENS

D1147306

Also available from Melanie Rawn and Titan Books

TOUCHSTONE

GLASS THORNS

BOOK TWO
ELSEWHENS

MELANIE
RAWN

TITAN BOOKS

ELSEWHENS
Print edition ISBN: 9781781166628
E-book edition ISBN: 9781781166635

Published by Titan Books
A division of Titan Publishing Group Ltd
144 Southwark Street, London SE1 0UP

First edition: February 2013
1 3 5 7 9 10 8 6 4 2

This is a work of fiction. Names, characters, places, and incidents either are the product of the author's imagination or are used fictitiously, and any resemblance to actual persons, living or dead, business establishments, events, or locales is entirely coincidental. The publisher does not have any control over and does not assume any responsibility for author or third-party websites or their content.

Melanie Rawn asserts the moral right to be identified as the author of this work.
Copyright © 2013 by Melanie Rawn. All rights reserved.

No part of this publication may be reproduced, stored in a retrieval system, or transmitted, in any form or by any means without the prior written permission of the publisher, nor be otherwise circulated in any form of binding or cover other than that in which it is published and without a similar condition being imposed on the subsequent purchaser.

A CIP catalogue record for this title is available from the British Library.

Printed and bound in Great Britain by CPI Group (UK) Ltd, Croydon, CR0 4YY.

Did you enjoy this book? We love to hear from our readers.
Please email us at readerfeedback@titanemail.com or write to us at
Reader Feedback at the above address.

To receive advance information, news, competitions, and exclusive offers online,
please sign up for the Titan newsletter on our website:
WWW.**TITAN**BOOKS.COM

For Bradford Blaine
Wilbur Kitchener Jordan Professor of History, Emeritus
Scripps College
(muchly beholden)

PROLOGUE

There was no control, no escape. No mercy. Cayden knew that. The Elsewhens were part of him. Sometimes they provided only a brief glimpse into a future (of his making, of his choosing), sometimes—as now, with thorn firing his veins—a whole, long, intricate story to be viewed as if it all happened onstage. He was only the audience to this version of himself, a Cayden Silversun who was the sum of all his decisions, all the choices that mayhap had not even seemed to be choices at the time. Watching himself, not knowing how he'd got there or why he'd become that, but knowing that this future was possible. It was all possible.

{Ten years on the Royal Circuit. Ten years of performing classic plays with inventive twists. Ten years of kicking the droops out of stale old comedies, of transforming (some said perverting) standard dramas with fresh insights, of shocking audiences with original works. Ten years of shattered glass.

Touchstone was unprecedented. Touchstone had owned every stage in the Kingdom for ten years.

Cade had given up fighting a long, long time ago.

When Mieka married the girl, Cade stood back and

smiled and wished him well—and kept his mouth shut about the Elsewhens.

When Mieka told him he was a fool if he didn't marry that elegant, brilliant noblewoman who loved him, he had to agree, and Mieka stood back and smiled and wished him well, and was the life of the considerable party afterwards.

He found and threw out more thorn than Mieka ever knew—it was so easy to fool him, he was always at least half drunk, and when Cade told him he must've left his thorn-roll at the last inn, or forgotten it in the tiring room or on the coach, he was always convinced.

But it was only postponing the inevitable. He knew it, and raged, and wanted to resign from the Circuit and take Mieka someplace warm, quiet, safe—get him sober and healthy, find again the laughing, beautiful boy he used to be.

But he didn't. That boy was gone.

Now, seated in a hard wooden chair in a memorial garden, staring at his own hands, he realized it was the violence that had undone them. Not in the way he'd anticipated, but it had been violence all the same. By now, of course, it was much too late.

What he couldn't identify was the turning point. Perhaps it had been the first time Mieka showed up so drunk that he could hardly hold the withies. He'd been drunk during shows before, of course. But that one night, that first time he'd been unable to go onstage until they'd doused him with cold water— that had been different. Jeska screamed at him. Rafe was remote and contemptuous. Cade slapped him. Several times.

Or perhaps it had been the glass basket Cade crashed over Mieka's head. It had been an accident. Mostly, anyway. Mieka had refused to speak to Cade for a week.

Or did it go back as far as that very first Winterly Circuit, the time Jeska threw Mieka's thorn-roll into the fire and, when the Elf dared come at him with both fists, knocked him out cold?

Touchstone had long since stopped meeting for tea or dinner or a few beers in the Threadchaser parlor, the Silversun kitchen, Blye's glassworks, the river garden of Wistly Hall. Jeska showed up for rehearsals and performances, and that was all; after a while, Rafe adopted the same habits. Once they made the Royal Circuit, they demanded separate rooms at every inn. They worked together, and that was the only time they were together. They had nothing to say to one another that didn't involve the theater. Everybody kept saying these were obviously four young men who didn't like each other much. But their work was superlative, so nobody—especially not the four of them—delved very far into the inner workings of the group.

At times Cade had hated Mieka for not experiencing the same anguish he did. He *knew* about Cade's Elsewhen dreams—hells, he was the one who'd put a name to them. Mieka *knew* that all manner of futures depended on each decision he made or didn't make, and yet he did exactly as he pleased with no thought to anything but immediate pleasure. It was as if Mieka considered himself completely free from any rules or consequences at all—not because he was superior, or because his talent absolved him, or because he was the Master Glisker of a wildly successful theater group and could do as he bloody well liked, but simply because he didn't care what anyone thought. He did what he did, he sought the sensations that pleased him, he was greedy about thorn and drink and food and women, and he didn't give a shit about the futures.

Cade hated him for that. He hated himself even more for not being like him, for anguishing himself halfway to madness. For not being able to accept what was real and true without wanting to take it apart if only to find out how it worked. How to control it. The anger was a living thing inside him, frightening in its power. He couldn't control it. It wasn't the physical violence, though that was a part of it; it was the ferocity of his emotions that scared him. He hated having to feel so much rage, so much fear. He punished Mieka for it, and for much else besides. The night he gave Mieka a black eye that lasted a week was the night he knew he was completely out of control. But he couldn't seem to stop any of it.

It was the violence that defeated them, in the end. He saw that, seated on a hard wooden chair in a memorial garden, staring at his own hands. There had been so few moments when there was peace, when Mieka was gentle and calm, whimsical and warm, when Cade could be as happy as it was possible for someone like him to be.

Touchstone married, fathered children, bought elegant houses and fine carriages, created lives apart from one another. They worked on Cade's inspirations and performed for thousands. They were befriended by royalty and celebrated by the populace, and it began to be said that Touchstone was the greatest theater group in the Kingdom's history. They toured the Continent three and then four times, and made more money than any of them had ever dreamed existed. But somewhere, amid the fear and the ferocity, so much went missing. Not dead. Never dead. Just... misplaced. Like an Elsewhen for which Cade had forgotten the unlocking words.

At the very first Royal Theater Festival one summer at Castle Biding, someone gave Mieka what he thought was greenthorn that turned out to be laced with dragon tears. Sometimes fatal to Elves, Mieka had told Cade once, boasting that he had enough other kinds of blood in him to be able to take anything. Not this time. He staggered out from behind his glisker's bench before the first magic had spread across the huge crowd, stumbled off the riser, and collapsed into

Jeska's startled arms. Rafe carried him off, barely breathing. There came then the ultimate humiliation: having to ask Pirro Spangler of Black Lightning to fill in. They were *Touchstone*, for fuck's sake—and they had to ask their only rivals for a favor. Pirro did the work competently, but competent wasn't what people had come to see. They wanted the best theater group in the Kingdom of Albeyn and they wanted the best glisker and that glisker had been taken off the stage barely breathing. He survived it. Mieka always survived.

Cade stared down at his hands and tried not to think about the first time he saw the imagings of Mieka in black leather that cinched his slowly thickening body... imagings of him in auburn wig and purple velvet gown, Guards uniform, Good Brother's robes, the wild tatters of a Woodwose... imagings meant to shock, to provoke. What they meant to Cade was that whatever still tethered Mieka to reality was fraying fast. He didn't know who the person in those imagings was. He didn't want to know.

He was so tired of fighting. It was so useless. He drank. He no longer used thorn of any kind, not even blockweed for dreamless sleep. He drank. It muddled his thinking and played bloody hell with his writing, but he needed it. Especially while writing *Broken Doors*. It was a work of immense importance, four separate plays done on two consecutive nights, and the performances on their third Royal Circuit would prove it—but the piece was too complex for most audiences to understand (that was what Cade told himself, anyway) and they ended up returning to their standard folio.

And then there was Alaen—brilliant, tortured, gutted Alaen—and the horror of helping him overcome his thrall for dragon tears. On the nights Cade woke to the sound of Alaen's screams, more than once he thought it was Mieka's begging voice he heard, Mieka he would find huddled frail and frightened in a corner, Mieka he would soon be bracing against shivering sickness—

No. They were nothing alike. Alaen's need for dragon tears was nothing like Mieka's need for alcohol and thorn. Cade drank, too—sometimes as lavishly as Mieka did—and he knew it was different. It had to be different. Didn't it?

They rehearsed and set out on the Royal Circuit for the sixth time. Mieka actually cut back his consumption of alcohol. He got through the Circuit, and vanished for the winter into Wistly Hall, restored by his earnings into the grand residence it had been long ago.

Not so grand as this place, this ancient stone pile called Clinquant House, built by some long-ago Windthistle Elfenlord, with its massive towers and three little half-sized houses at the bottom of the garden "where the Faeries sometimes stay" (though Cade didn't believe that) and the memorial garden beside a pond, where they all sat in hard wooden chairs and watched the flames burn and wondered where the years had gone.

Cade knew where they'd gone: into brandy bottles. So many years now. After he bought the town house, he set up his library in the attic and told his wife and children to leave him the fuck alone while he was working. He worked constantly. He called a meeting of Touchstone at his house shortly after Wintering to prepare for their seventh Royal, and gave them the scripts for a new play cycle. Mieka read through *Window* quickly, flung down his brandy bottle, threw his arms around Cade, and burst into tears. The piece was that depressing, that raw with despair. When it was first performed in Gallantrybanks, a shocked Tobalt Fluter called it "Cayden Silversun's suicide poem."

The girl left Mieka for a lord's son and took her children with her. Mieka left Gallantrybanks for a house by the sea and took his entire cellar of liquor and his entire cabinet of thorn with him.

Cade found a balance of sorts. He lived with his wife and children, though he knew he was a rotten husband and not much better as a father. It was the work that really mattered. It was all he really had.

He saw Mieka at a Namingday party for Prince Ashgar's third son. The Elf didn't look ill, exactly, but he didn't look strong, either. It was as if he was being used up, all the energy and laughter and wild brilliance burning away. Cade hadn't even been able to speak to him. Had there ever been a time when he could? Not in this life. This life; there was none other. Why did he choose to open this door every morning before he woke? What was it that could possibly make him want to be here?

He didn't want to be here now, with the wind in his face as he stared down at his own hands and waited for the Good Brother to finish with the fire.

Just before their ninth Royal Circuit, Mieka showed up out of nowhere with a gorgeous blonde and no money, twenty pounds heavier, with lines on his face and silver threading his hair and terror in those eyes and an uncontrollable tremor in his fingers. He was fighting the alcohol and the thorn every moment of every day. The sad, desperate gallantry of it ripped Cade's heart open. He watched in helpless agony as Mieka struggled through rehearsals, shook so cruelly that he couldn't hold his withies, started drinking again, went back to bluethorn, and at last reached a precarious equilibrium that let him learn the new set of plays. *Bewilderland*, Cade had named it: a long, nightmarish piece of warped landscapes and grotesque assaults on the senses. Jeska's transformations were abrupt, jarring, as the world around him changed, and changed him without warning: trapped, no escape.

Audiences were shocked. But they came back time and again to be terrified by Touchstone's nightmares. With renewed success came renewed bank accounts, and Mieka's cravings for liquor, food, and thorn remained ravenous—as did his appetite for women, to judge by the rapid replacement of the blonde for a redhead for another blonde for a dark-skinned girl from the Islands for yet another blonde.

She'd been there, that night less than a week ago. That final night. Eleven years after the original Downstreet burned to the ground, Touchstone opened the new Downstreet: a real theater now, not a tavern. The place was thrice the size of the old one and packed to bursting. They did a short version of *Bewilderland* and then "Sailor's Sweetheart" for memory's sake. They finished, exhausted, and Mieka, in a loose long-sleeved yellow shirt that failed to disguise his paunch, clambered up onto the glisker's bench to leap to the stage. Cade hardly heard the screaming crowd, scared to death as Mieka wobbled and almost crashed into the glass baskets. Cade lunged, barely in time to catch him as he staggered on landing. Mieka laughed, those eyes glassy and mad. The face turned up to Cade's was blurred, damaged by thorn and liquor and desperate unhappiness. As he threw back his head and laughed again, there was something bleak and broken in those eyes, something hopeless. Cade smelled the acrid sweat on his skin, in his thinning hair; he was soaked with it, exhausted in a way he never used to be, his face gray beneath an unhealthy flush of exertion.

He wasn't even thirty years old.

Jeska came over, helped keep Mieka upright. Rafe joined them, his face impassive, his blue-gray eyes dark with disgust as he looked at Mieka. Cade cast about frantically for something to say, anything. Jeska spared him the effort by shouting over the tumult at Rafe.

"Oy—good work tonight, especially the tricky bits of *Bewilderland!*"

Cade looked at Rafe, then Jeska, and saw his own thoughts in their eyes: that the fettler's prodigious skill had been tested tonight to its limit by the unpredictability of Mieka's performance.

Cade waved expansively to the crowd as if trying to shove them all into the Ocean Sea, shouting at Rafe, "Let's get the fuck outta here!"

Backstage in the tiring room there were imagers hoping for a sitting, reporters hoping for an interview, girls hoping for a fuck. Cade rudely deflected them all. He accepted a big silver goblet of brandy and ice, resented the presence of the ice, downed the liquor in three gulps, and hated himself for worriedly looking around for Mieka.

A beautiful girl with blond hair and kagged ears wandered up to the stocky little figure over at the drinks table. Her scrawniness and her not-quite-dead eyes told Cade that she was hopelessly thorn-thralled. Abruptly sick, he wondered if that was why Mieka wore a long-sleeved shirt tonight, if his arms were reddened with thorn-marks as Alaen's had once been, streaked with tainted veins.

He didn't want to know. He just didn't want to know. If he knew, he would have to feel. And he'd given up feeling a long time ago.

Alone in his carriage, he finished his third brandy and thought about exactly nothing. Then he was trudging up the steps of his house, opening the door, glancing at the framed imagings on the wall: his wife, his children, all sleeping upstairs, never waiting up to welcome Da home from another wildly successful show. It was nothing to do with them. It was just the way Da paid the bills.

He slogged upstairs, careful not to wake anyone on

the way to his attic library. His sanctuary. There were more imagings here, the ones his wife didn't want elsewhere in her house. Rafe and Crisiant and a family sitting in a garden; Jeska and a family sitting in a sitting room; Mieka sitting in the open boot of a Royal Circuit coach holding a little boy with his mother's iris-blue eyes and his father's elegantly Elfen ears. They were all so normal, so conventional... wives, children, homes... lives separate from Touchstone, ordinary lives that had nothing to do with the extraordinary work that was *his* life—

He'd been right, all those years ago, about Touchstone being a knot of four people, a singular thing they made together. Touchstone was the rope knotted round all their necks.

A fresh bottle of brandy on his knee, he stared at the display of Trials medals: one Winterly, one Ducal, and ten Royal, all framed in gilded wood by Jedris and protected by Blye's finest beveled glass. All were accompanied by an imaging: Touchstone through the years. He watched himself change, his hair longer, his face bearded and then clean-shaven and then bearded again, his cloud-gray eyes—he wondered if a Gorgon's eyes were gray like his, cold like his when she turned anyone who dared look at her to stone. If her eyes glinted with his sort of madness because she knew she was helpless, too.

He stared for a time at his younger self, back when he'd been *Quill* and knew how to laugh; at the young Mieka, back when he'd been clear-eyed and quick and clever and beautiful. Their fifth year on the Royal—that was the one where the hate really started to show in Cade, the coldness. The proverbial heart of stone. The seventh Royal, though, that was the worst, the one he loathed most.

The imager had posed them wearing black clothes and oversize white silk roses in their jacket lapels, sitting one behind the other: Jeschenar cross-legged on the floor, Mieka on a footstool, Cayden on a chair, Rafcadion on a barstool. Cade had to dig his fingers into Mieka's shoulders to keep him from falling over. The imager called out adjustments in the pose and their expressions until at last she got what she wanted. Rafe: cool, sardonic. Jeska, looking like a fallen Angel. Himself, grimly smiling, daring anyone to interpret that smile. And Mieka, playing the sweet innocent, a mockery that made Cade want to slap him when he saw the finished imaging.

But there'd been another imaging, quickly done without their knowledge a few minutes later. The woman had had only a few moments to capture them with her magic inside the withie, but capture them she had. Every time he saw this seventh Royal medal, it was that other imaging he remembered, and that was why he hated it so much. Jeska, stiff and weary, had closed his eyes. Rafe was stretching a cramp from his neck, grimacing. Cade had no expression on his face at all—for Mieka had hunched a shoulder and turned his head to rest his cheek on Cade's fingers. What he hadn't seen until the finished imaging—and thank the Lord and Lady and all the Gods it had come to him first—was the look in those eyes: lost, hurt, miserable, the genuine innocence still at the core of him all too clear in his face.

Cade had torn the imaging to shreds and ordered that there be no engraving of it ever made so that no one else could ever see it. But he remembered it every time he saw this Trials medal.

"It was only some redthorn, Cade! I had to sleep!"

"And you had to wake up, so you took—"

"Fuck off! You self-righteous snarge—like you never pricked thorn in your life?"

"Not three and four at a time, while drinking a bottle of brandy! You're turning into a thrall, Mieka! You can't sleep without redthorn and you can't get out of bed without

bluethorn! Look at your hands shake! You're more likely to stab yourself with the withies than—"

"What the fuck do you care? You can just have me stitched up again like after you crashed a glass basket over me head!"

"I already apologized for that a hundred times—and you're the one we're talking about, not me! Look at yourself! You can't hardly function—and the liquor is making you fat, Mieka. You're slower, and heavier, and you're getting sloppy, and by the end of a show you're completely knackered—"

"I'm as good as I ever was—I'm better! I'm Mieka fuckin' Windthistle of Touchstone! I'm the best glisker in the Kingdom and I don't need you tellin' me how t'live me life! I don't need you!"

Had it really been only a week later that he'd turned his head to rest his cheek against Cade's hand, his heart in those sad, soft eyes?

When the bell sounded downstairs, he flinched so violently that he almost dropped the bottle. Who would be coming round at this hour of the night? He took the bottle with him. The steps seemed to have multiplied. As he passed his wife's bedchamber door, he heard an impatient rustling, and knew he would hear about this tomorrow at coldly condemning length. Hurrying, lurching a bit, he made it down before a fourth ring could wake the children, and yanked open the door.

Lord Kearney Fairwalk had exquisite taste in footmen. One of them stood there on Cade's doorstep, gasping with exertion, his plum-colored livery jacket unbuttoned at the throat to show the deep blue shirt beneath. Cade didn't recognize this boy; he never did. Kearney hired them and sacked them with dedicated regularity, almost as quickly as Mieka went through women.

"Do you know what the fuck time it is?" Cade demanded.

The boy flinched, then held out a piece of paper. "I ran all the way here—His Lordship's orders—"

He focused his eyes with difficulty on Kearney's scrawl, cramped and hasty below the oak-leaf emblem.

Mieka was taken to the Princess's Sanatorium tonight.

"Again?" Cade muttered, and took a pull at the bottle.

He collapsed at the Kiral Kellari. When the physicker arrived, he was barely breathing.

It had happened before. He'd had messages like this before.

The physickers sent word to me, and I was there within the hour.

Nice of His Lordship to interrupt whatever he'd been doing with this pretty young boy and see that Mieka's name didn't get into the scandal broadsheets. Again. Yes, he'd seen all this before. But what came next—that was something he'd never seen before.

I sent for his parents.

The bottle slipped from his fingers to the carpet at his feet. Silently. The silence was suddenly so huge, so powerful.

Mieka died a few minutes after midnight.

The horror was cold and raw and completely sobering. Into the silence his own voice said, "But I'm still here."

He shut the door in the boy's face, went into the drawing room, found a chair. He could hear his wife's voice raised in irritated demand from the top of the stairs. He sat, staring at Kearney's words, at his own scarred fingers. Wondering why, on this night of all nights, the blood didn't show.

He stared at his hands again, there in the memorial garden of Clinquant House, while Mieka's ashes were placed into an exquisite glass urn. Blye had made it: swirling black and green and brown and blue and an elusive flash of gold, all the colors of those eyes. The urn was then buried and the carved marble headstone placed atop it. Surely that little hollowing of earth was too small to contain a spirit as vast and wild as Mieka Windthistle's.

He couldn't face any of the family. He got back into his carriage and told his driver to find him a tavern. An hour later, he was seated in murky corner, drinking himself stupid.

Mieka—oh Gods, I'm sorry, I'm so sorry—

I know, Quill. Stop blaming yourself. I know you tried.

Not hard enough. I got tired of fighting and then I stopped. How could I do that? How could I just give up like that? This isn't the way it should've been. I–I wanted so much for you to be happy—

You gave me your words and your magic—trusted me with them—and that made me happy. And you were always there.

I should've done more, I should've done anything to keep from losing you—"When Touchstone lost their Elf, they lost their soul"—I tried to dream it better, Mieka, I tried to make the Elsewhens better—

Shush. Not even you can make dreams real, Cayden.

You did. You made my best dreams real—everything I am, everything I've written—it wasn't until you showed up that first night—

That was a night, wasn't it!

None of it would've happened without you—believing in me, making me want to be the best because you're the best—it was only after you found me that I even dared think I could—

You bloody great fool. Whatever you are, you would've been, no mater what. It was always in you. And you made me part of it. To be dancin' behind me glisker's bench with you watchin' me durin' a show meant all the world to me. I guess I just ran out of time before I thought I would.

I miss you. I don't want to be here without you, Mieka. There's no place I want to be if you're not—

Shut up! Don't you dare even think it!

There's times when I can't think of anything else.

Well, don't! You stay here and raise your children and write your words and make two thousand people scream every time you walk onstage—and you bloody well better behave yourself when the King gives you that knighthood—

Are you still on about that? You silly little Elfling!

You haven't called me that in a long time. But I guess I haven't been your Elfling in a long time, have I? I'm sorry, Cayden. I'm the one as should've tried harder. But I promise I'll be waiting—at the end of it all, I'll be waiting. Now, go sleep this off. And one day write me something—nothing big or grand, just—write me happy, Quill.

"Time, me lords! Time now, gentlemen!" called the barmaid. He opened his eyes, and pushed himself to his feet, and went to sleep it off.}

And woke up weeping.

This future was possible. It was all possible.

Elsewhen.

1

He couldn't breathe. His chest was tight, his head aching. His hands shook as he rubbed his tear-streaked face, terrified that he might have cried out and woken someone—

By the Lord and Lady and all the Angels and Old Gods, please let him have cried out and woken someone in the vastness of Fairwalk Manor.

By the time he recovered his breath and his heart stopped thundering, he knew he had stayed silent. There was no one to knock on his door, call out his name, come into his room, exclaim with shock at what he knew must be in his eyes. There was no one.

Brishen Staindrop had promised him dreams to fire his imagination and make his writing richer, deeper. He ought to've known. Blockweed hadn't worked on him the way it was supposed to; neither had this, whatever it was. All he wanted was a few hours spent someplace beautiful that danced and sparkled, someplace safe. What he got istead was horror.

And he would have to remember it, wouldn't he? It was part of him now. To tuck it all away and forget the words that unlocked it would be to lose something of himself. If he was true to his own arrogance, he would have to keep this Elsewhen as he had kept all the others.

Pushing himself to his feet, he made his slow, aching way to the hearth and half-fell onto his knees, reaching for logs to stoke the fire. There was no clock in the bedchamber—Kearney Fairwalk forbade clocks at his residences, with the splendid disregard of a very rich man for such mundane concerns as being anywhere on time. Cade might have lingered in bed and rung for a servant to replenish the fire for him, but the frantic need to see another living being had faded. He didn't want anyone to see him like this.

To be in possession of a suite of rooms at Fairwalk Manor was a privilege not accorded many. Touchstone had been invited for the fortnight preceding Trials. After their first gruelling Winterly Circuit and dozens of shows in and around Gallantrybanks, all four young men were in need of time off. But rather than visit Fairwalk Manor, Jeska had chosen instead to escort his mother to a seaside town where he'd taken a month's hire on a cottage for her, and stay for a couple of weeks. Rafe and his new wife, Crisiant, had accepted His Lordship's generosity as a welcome escape after the strains of putting together their wedding celebrations. Cayden, determined on other forms of escape and certain that Fairwalk Manor was precisely the location for them, hadn't blushed a single blush when he got into a carriage the morning after Rafe and Crisiant's wedding and betook himself to Fairwalk Manor. In fact, he hadn't seen the couple at all. Not only was the tall, sprawling house gigantic, but orders had also come down from Lord Fairwalk to his servants to give his guests whatever they wanted whenever they wanted it, and do this as unobtrusively as possible. What Rafe and Crisiant wanted was exactly what Cade wanted: privacy.

Cade knew exactly how they were spending their time. He spent his exploring the library, the grounds, the stables, and the little blue leather roll of thorn he'd purchased from Mieka Windthistle's Auntie Brishen.

He'd always thought Mieka would be with him when he did this. *Don't worry about going too lost, Quill, I'll always come find you,* he'd written in the note accompanying that first little green wallet of blockweed. But Mieka was in Frimham, pretending to stay at a seaside inn while really staying with the girl whose existence made the thorn necessary.

Cade was supposed to be working on various playlets, polishing those that Touchstone might have to present at Trials and crafting his own ideas into performable shape. He arrived at Fairwalk Manor fully intending to do his duty by his group and his talents. Instead, the afternoon following his arrival, he took a long walk about the sculpted grounds, ate an early dinner, and told the servants to leave him alone. And they had done so; even if he had cried out, no one would have come. He got out the roll of thorn and stared at it for almost an hour before deciding which little packet of powder to use.

He hated what was in his mind. He had to find some way of enduring what he knew was to come. If thorn helped, then he'd use it.

Elsewhens, Mieka called them: visions while he slept and sometimes when he was wide awake of futures that might come to pass. Cade had neglected far too long the orderly categorizing of what he'd foreseen. The memories of things that hadn't happened yet were crowding his head, and he knew he had to discipline them or run mad.

The Elsewhens about Tobalt Fluter in the Downstreet, talking to some reporter about Touchstone—those didn't count now, not since the tavern had burned. He didn't have to worry about them anymore. He didn't have to think about hearing Tobalt say, *"His mind's cold, but his heart's colder"* or *"Touchstone is still together after twenty-five years."* Whatever futures Tobalt had referred to, they would be different. Cade could rid himself of the despair of the first—and the determination not to let it happen.

He had to let go of the joy of the second—and the fear that now it would never come true. The futures would be different, and those dreams didn't count.

But as he went through each in his mind, reviewing them before locking them away, he noticed something strange: the lutenist in the second vision. With a soundless bark of laughter he suddenly recognized Alaen Blackpath—twenty-five years older, his reddish curls turning silver—

—just as he'd seen Mieka's black hair silvered in a single tantalizing flash, lines framing his mouth and crossing his forehead; older, yes, but still bright-eyed and laughing and beautiful.

He wanted so much to hold on to that one. It was still possible, wasn't it? Just because Tobalt could no longer sit in the Downstreet and say that Touchstone was still together after twenty-five years, it didn't mean that Cade would never see Mieka like that.

No. He had to be ruthless. He couldn't keep that one just because it made him smile, because it comforted him. He had to get rid of at least some of these Elsewhens crammed into his brain. Not that he'd ever done it before, except the once.

"Once you've learned it, the technique will in all probability save your sanity," said Master Emmot. *"If only by convincing you that there is an order to things, an order that you may impose upon them. Organization is a desirable thing. When we can accomplish it, in whatever area of life, it is to be cherished and defended. To impose order on the chaos of living, on the potential chaos of your own mind—what else is language, and the division of the world into separate nations, and even the ordering of time itself into hours, weeks, months, years? Thus, too, it must be with your foreseeings. And just as words are used to identify time, places, things, you may use a series of words to classify each separate dream."*

To think he had actually been intrigued: learning how to select a couple of words or a phrase that encompassed a particular foreseeing, how to think of his mind like a trunk with an ever-increasing number of locks, each giving access to a little compartment where a dream was kept.

"It's very like what men used to do when they wanted to memorize large quantities of information, such as the solar or lunar calendars, or an epic poem cycle. They would construct whole houses in their minds, and furnish them from front doorway to attic roof with items that prompted memory of a particular thing or things. The four vases on a table in the vestibule, each containing flowers of a different season, might be reminder of the dates of the phases of the moon. Perhaps the railings of the staircase each depict a particular tree, like the old poem that describes the attributes of each. Yes, I know you've read it—but could you memorize it in perfect order and then tuck it away, to be brought out again when you look into your mind and see those railings? In our day, we are a literate society, so we don't have to use these techniques to remember and pass along information. We have only to go look it up in a book. There are those in this world who still practice this method of memory with images as their keys. But you are, as we both know, someone to whom words are of paramount importance, so the only image you will use is that of a large locked trunk. Make it as plain or as ornate as you wish. The keys will not be made of brass or iron, but of words."

To think that he had actually found it interesting: creating the trunk, dividing it into sections according to subject (one of them pretentiously labeled THE KINGDOM OF ALBEYN), choosing a primary word for each section and then more words for specific identification. He'd actually enjoyed it.

"Remember the whole of the experience, as I've taught you. Assign your key to it. Then lock it away until you wish to review it again. Or until you wish to be rid of it forever."

But he'd done that only once, just to prove to Master Emmot that he could indeed do it. His reasoning had not sat well with the old Sage.

"You tell me, Cayden, that if a man is the sum total of what he has learned and experienced, then to rid yourself of even one foreseeing would be to take away a portion of who you are. But did you hear what you just said? What a man has learned. *What he has* experienced. *Those things are in the past. What you see is the future. Once a future becomes impossible, for whatever reason, you would be doing yourself and your overactive mind a favor by getting rid of it. Right now you are fifteen. What if you live to be eighty or ninety? Moreover, what if your turns as you get older become more frequent, or lengthier, or more detailed? They might do, you know. The brain grows and changes, and does not fully mature until the age of twenty-one or -two, perhaps longer for one of mostly Wizarding blood. My advice is to clear your mind of things that are no longer possible. Don't clutter up your life with irrelevancies. But the choice is yours, of course."*

Irrelevancies—perhaps every dream he had ever dreamed was now irrelevant. Perhaps he ought to treat them as if they were.

He wanted so much to keep the one where he'd seen Mieka with those laughing eyes and that silvering hair.

But what of the others concerning him, others about him?

Watching the moonglade on a river: *"Whatever I give you, you give back to me better than I could ever imagine it. You always do."*

Watching the girl and her mother discuss their plans to tame him.

Watching himself slam Mieka against an icy lamppost.

Watching his own hand slap Mieka again and again and again.

Watching Mieka beat his pregnant wife.

Watching his own scarred fingers (when and how had those scars happened?) holding a note, reading the terrible words scrawled on it, hearing himself say, *"But I'm still here."*

He couldn't rid himself of any of it. Each of those foreseeings, and a hundred more—they were part of him. They were his memories, even if they hadn't happened yet, even if they would never happen. If he lost them, he would lose parts of himself.

"Don't worry about going too lost, Quill, I'll always come find you."

To lose himself for at least a little while seemed a very good thing. But the thorn hadn't done for him what it was supposed to do.

"I don't have the sort of dreams most people have…"

This new one had come in grim sequence, like a play. Or a fire set by a professional arsonist. The scene set and surveyed. The vulnerable points identified. The progress, inevitable and devastating, to the final taste of ashes: *"Write me happy, Quill."*

Perhaps it was his own instincts, his tregetour's brain, that had given him that long plotline instead of mere glimpses. Perhaps there had been a dozen separate dreams that his trained mind had organized into a whole. Perhaps it had been the influence of the thorn. Perhaps he simply didn't dream the way other people did.

As if any of that mattered.

He'd tried to fight his way out of it, truly he had, but the thorn was powerful in him by then and it was much too late. It would *always* be too late. If he saw a possible future, it meant that something had already happened that made that future possible. He couldn't change it. He was helpless. He couldn't control what other people did or said or thought or felt.

So why bother anguishing himself about it? Things would happen the way they would happen. He had no power over futures decided by other people's choices. Yet it seemed he was constructed inside in ways that compelled him to try. If a voice sounding remarkably like Master Emmot's whispered, *"How?"* he refused to hear it.

Over the next nine days at Fairwalk Manor, he used all the different thorn packets in the roll, daring them to do what they were supposed to do. Recklessly he gave himself over to the thorn, sometimes using just before he went to sleep, other times spending the whole day lying on a deep padded sofa in the shade of an apple tree, aware that anyone seeing him would think he was drowsing. He wasn't. His eyes were closed so that the view of serene pasture and green hillside could not compete with the scenes inscribing themselves on his brain.

Always it was the same dream, with variations that never made any real difference and occasionally with elaborations that gouged pieces out of his heart. The Elsewhen infected him like a wound gone to poison, suppurating into his every conscious thought. He knew why there were no significant changes. None of the decisions that would change it were his to make. He had no choices, none at all.

But Sagemaster Emmot had always said that if he had no choices to make, he would see no futures. He'd seen this one, over and over again; therefore he must have made a decision that caused it.

On the tenth night of his stay at Fairwalk Manor, having run out of thorn, he got drunk instead. The next morning he wrote a brief letter to Brishen Staindrop, asking what other sorts of thorn she could suggest. He spent that day and the next writing "Doorways." He told himself that by calling it that, and keeping it a single play instead of the series of plays that *Broken Doors* had been in the dream, he was beginning the changes that must be made in order to render that future impossible. And as for *Bewilderland*—he vowed never, ever to write anything even remotely like it, nor use the title or any variation thereof. Senseless word, anyway.

That last night at Fairwalk Manor, he had the dream about Tobalt Fluter again.

{The office was strut and brag from the carved door to the wide widow overlooking the river. The walls were thick with books on shelves, and copies of important front pages and broadsheet articles framed under glass, and imagings of the famous with their signatures, all inscribed to Sir Tobalt Fluter. Little trinkets glinted on every shelf, some of them the symbols of various clans—Pheasant, Lion, Scorpion, Elk—some of them punning on the names of those who had given them: an apple made of oakwood, a circle of braided gold, a bent bow, a green glass lily leaf from the guilds of that town. A very important personage was Sir Tobalt, his influence coveted and his interest courted by anyone who was anyone or wanted to be. He sat at his desk, angled so he could see the door and the window view, and arched his brows at the young man who hunched in a severe wooden chair before him, pen and notebook at hand.

"I must've written dozens of pieces about them through the years," said Sir Tobalt. "But I'd never talked to the people around them at such length before. Gods and Angels, what some of them are saying—"

"Which people? The wives? Parents?"

A shrug and a thin, shrewd smile that crinkled the corners of his eyes. "Don't think I'll tell you my sources. All you're here for is a tickle of what the chapbook biography will contain."

"So make me laugh," the young man invited brazenly. "Set me positively howling. How much of what everyone's saying is true?"

"Nobody wants to admit to anything, especially concerning the Elf. You can't print that, by the way." He ran a fingertip along the trinket that had pride of place on his desk: a glass basket about the size of his cupped palm, with a little silver quill and a green glass withie propped inside along with a selection of the finest gold-nibbed pens. The gesture was lazy, at odds with the sudden vehemence of his tone. "Damned I'll be, though, if I include all those lies Mieka's wife told me. I hear enough of that muck from Cade." He snorted. "*Bewilderland*—that's what he'd like all of us to live in, some insane fantasy where his lies are the only truth."

"I don't understand what lying gets him. I mean, after all these years, to keep telling the same stories that nobody ever believed the first time he told them—"

"Got no choice, has he? He'd go mad, otherwise. Because he knows. He'll never admit it, but he knows. When Touchstone lost their Elf, they lost their soul."}

No, Cade thought when he woke, he could never rid himself of any of the Elsewhens. They were part of him.

At last came the morning of departure for Gallantrybanks. Cade nodded to the servants, thirty of them, all lined up to bid him and Rafe and Crisiant farewell. But he didn't look directly into the eyes of any of the maids, footmen, cooks, grooms, gardeners, and sundry other staff standing there in the gauzy spring rain. He still felt too guilty. Cade's parents rarely accepted invitations to stay at noblemen's houses. His mother always begged off with the excuse that her husband's duties at Court did not permit his absence from it, and she simply couldn't think of going anywhere without him. In reality, the Silversuns hadn't the cash to spare for tipping the servants as was expected at all the great houses. Lady Jaspiela had reminded Cade several times before this trip that he must do so, especially at the home of so exalted a lordship as Kearney Fairwalk.

The housekeeper hadn't let him. "Oh no, Master Silversun, no! 'Twas our privilege and delight to serve yourself and Master and Mistress Threadchaser! We've so few truly distinguished guests, not at all like in His late Lordship's day—" She bit both lips together, as if she had said too much, then gave him a swift and sincere smile. "'Twas our pleasure, every one of us."

As he settled into a sprightly little carriage drawn by two high-stepping grays, waiting for Rafe and Crisiant to join him, he mused on the implications of what the housekeeper had said. So he was *truly distinguished*, was he? And comparable to those who had visited in Kearney's father's time? What sort of guest did Kearney invite down to Fairwalk Manor, that a tregetour and a fettler and the daughter of a man who built chimneys for a living were *distinguished*?

The carriage door opened and Rafe handed his wife in. Cade smiled. Crisiant settled facing him, Rafe soon at her side, and as the coachman chirruped to the horses, they both looked at him for the first time in almost a fortnight.

"Too weak to shave, were you?" Rafe asked.

"It would probably be good manners to apologize," Cade said, "for not even once joining you for dinner. But I can't think of a single reason why I should. It's not as if you missed me, is it? And I knew for certain sure you wouldn't appreciate catching whatever illness I brought with me from Gallytown."

"We did wonder where you were," Crisiant said. "The servants mentioned that you seemed to like the gardens—"

"When I wasn't yarking in the garderobe," he lied with perfect glibness. He knew what he looked like: the haggard face that hadn't known a razor in a week, the circles beneath his eyes. "Kearney's people took good care of me, though, and now I'm well and ready to work." He smiled again, and winked at Crisiant. "You can have your husband from curfew bell to lunching, but there's Trials coming up so I have to steal him the rest of the day."

Rafe nodded slowly, still not quite convinced but, as usual with him, not pressing the point. "Jeska's due back home tomorrow. Mieka—"

Crisiant interrupted. "You may have to hire a regiment of retired guardsmen to drag him back from Frimham and—what was her name, again?"

"Well," Rafe mused, "the family name is Caitiffer, whatever that means."

"I thought she had a bit of a foreign look about her."

Cade glanced out the window and bit his lips against laughter. In a Kingdom where Wizard, Elf, Gnome, Goblin, Giant, Piksey, Sprite, Fae, and who knew what all else had all contributed their distinctive features—facial and otherwise—to the general bloodlines, it took a Gallybanker with Crisiant's decided views to proclaim that anyone could actually look *foreign*.

"But I don't think Mieka's ever mentioned her name," Rafe went on.

Cade said, "That's because he doesn't know it." When they both stared at him, he grinned. "Jinsie told me at your wedding that her clan is fanatically conservative, and only the immediate family ever knows anyone's given name."

Crisiant mulled this over. Rafe said, "Wouldn't make much difference in bed, I'd expect—in my experience, a *dearling* here and a *sweetheart* there usually suffice—" His wife clouted him in the arm and he laughed. "—but it seems a bit much to have to marry a girl before you find out her name."

"Mayhap that regiment can threaten it out of the mother," Crisiant said, "while they're peeling that silly Elf off the daughter."

"No regiment required," Cade assured her. "I'll just send his brothers after him."

"If you can peel Jed away from Blye," she retorted.

"I've been wanting to ask how all that happened," he said, and like every girl in possession of a happy and successful love story of her own, she was eager to detail the progress of a friend's romance. Why was it, he mused as he listened—and kept track of each incident, because he really did want to know—that when people paired off they wanted to see everyone else paired off, too? He assumed it was a generous impulse, but all he could think of was that Elsewhen that had repeated over and over, and the unknown faceless woman who would become his wife and the mother of his children, and her total indifference to the fire that had begun by illuminating his soul and could end by destroying him.

He spent so much time being afraid. Two afternoons later, when Touchstone gathered in Mistress Threadchaser's sitting room, just like always, and Mieka bounced in as blithe and laughing as ever, he began to think that perhaps he hated the Elf for not even knowing what fear was.

He sat back to watch and listen as news was exchanged. Jeska sported an enviable sun-browning from his weeks seaside; Mieka did not. This brought the inevitable teasing ("Why, whatever could you have been doing to keep you indoors all that time?"), which only made his grin all the sleeker, all the more smug, as if he'd done something very clever. Cade, sorting withies, wondered if the girl was already pregnant. Amazing, really, that she'd yielded her virginity more readily than her name. But he supposed that might be much of the attraction: the mystery of her, the wanting to possess everything about her. He banished the insistent vision of that sad-eyed little boy from another Elsewhen, grateful when Mieka turned to Rafe with mischief sparkling in those eyes, the look he always wore when about to tease.

Rafe knew what was coming. Pointing a long finger at the Elf, he said, "Make a start with me, and I'll tell Crisiant every word of it."

Mieka pretended to cower back in terror. "Gods, not that! Anything but that!"

"Can we get some work done?" asked Jeska, fidgeting with the new pages Cade had given him.

"Not before you tell us how many adoring ladies you left languishing behind you," Mieka retorted. Then, to Rafe, in aggrieved tones: "Cade was there with you at Fairwalk Manor, so he already knows everything! Won't you even tell me—?"

"We didn't see him the whole time."

"Oy, Quill! What's her name, then?"

Cade looked up from the glass basket. "Whose name?"

Mieka was making a sly, smirking face. "The lovely birdie as kept *you* busy!" Then he fell back into his chair with a look of horror. "Holy Gods—don't tell me you spent the whole while *working*?"

"Not all of it." He manufactured a smile, complete with suggestively arched brows, and tossed over a primed withie. A quick glance at Rafe showed him a frown, and too late he recalled that he'd said he'd been ill. Suddenly resentful that he was having to tell all these lies, he asked himself who cared what Rafe thought, or knew, or thought he knew?

"Speaking of *working*," Jeska said pointedly.

Mistress Threadchaser entered then, carrying a teapot and four glass mugs. The familiar little ritual of pouring out occupied them for a time. When they had settled once more, Cade wondered if they'd ever recover the easy banter, the comfortable mockery they'd known on the Winterly Circuit. All those months when they'd been far from home, with no one but each other to talk to and rely on—it might have been expected that the intensity and exhaustion of performing and the long days of boredom in the coach would have had them at each other's throats, but instead they'd grown even closer. Not a plural, like the Shadowshapers or the Crystal Sparks, but a single thing: Touchstone. A knot of four ropes that became tighter with every show they played.

Yet he'd felt that connection loosening, once they had returned home to Gallantrybanks. Onstage it had been the same. The bookings at the Kiral Kellari had been brilliantly successful. But offstage, other people began to tug. Now, after a scant fortnight apart, Cade felt the difference in the mood and it scared him. It was as if they all had other places they'd rather be: Rafe with Crisiant, Mieka with his girl, Cade with his thorn… of them all, only Jeska was determined to get down to it, get some work done.

So they started. A bit rusty at first, but things slowly came together. Cade had them run through bits of half a dozen pieces to introduce them to changes he'd made. When Mieka proclaimed himself hopelessly confused and threatened to smash the glass basket over Cade's head unless they were allowed to do one playlet all the way through, Cade's temper blew up like an exploding withie.

"Which particular piece of rubbish would you like to do?" he snarled. "It's all equally shitty! I hate every word of it! There's not an idea in any of it that means anything at all!"

Jeska's fists clenched as if throttling his own temper. "It's *your* writing, ain't it? It's what we've been doing for more than a year now—"

"That's the whole fucking point! It's stale and it's boring—"

"So write us something else!"

"Keep feeding the beast? I put my guts into something new and original and you suck it dry, all of you, and then the audience does the same, like a whole belfry of fucking Vampires—"

"What in all hells is wrong with you?" Rafe shouted. "This is what you've wanted since you were fifteen years old! Now you're telling us it's meaningless?"

"Yes." Mieka's voice was lethally soft. "As pointless as searching for nipples on a chicken. He's seen us work these pieces too many times. They don't mean anything to him anymore. He's not there inside them, working them the way you and me and Jeska work them. And he's not the audience, neither. *They* don't think it's rubbish."

"Audiences," Cade sneered. "What do *they* know?"

"They know enough to know we're good. Gods damn it all, Cade, we're great and everybody knows it!"

"Excepting him," Rafe growled.

"Why not join in one night?" Mieka taunted. "Watch us perform, be part of the crowd. That's what you were telling

Tobalt in that interview, innit? That men want to be part of a shared experience?"

"I'm already part of something." All at once all the anger left him, and he smiled. "Touchstone. I'm part of something worth being part of."

Mieka glared at him, then collapsed back in his chair, laughing helplessly. "Oh, Quill! You're such a fraud!"

Jeska looked bewildered, but Rafe was slowly succumbing to a grin. Cade shrugged, hands spread wide in the Wizardly gesture that meant *You may trust me*, and the fettler gave a complex snort before rapping his knuckles on the table beside him.

"All right, children, that's enough. Now that we're all agreed that the three of us are brilliant and Cade Silversun is a shit-wit with delusions of intelligence, may we continue?"

And after that, everything was back to the way it used to be. Not that Cade had intended his little tirade to produce that effect—he was still wondering as he walked home just how it had happened, in fact, but was too grateful to do much analyzing. He had his group back. He was part of Touchstone, and Touchstone was well worth being part of. This *was* the life he wanted to be living.

Elsewhens and all.

2

Every stitch of clothing Cade owned could not be stuffed into one small and one large satchel, but he was giving it his best try. The Winterly Circuit had taught him that laundry service on the road was dodgy at best. More than once he'd had to wash his undergarments himself—on one memorable occasion with the contents of a pitcher that Mieka had used the previous night as a piss pot. It had been nine in the morning and barely light in the room, and he'd had a hangover; how was he to know that damned Elf would set the pitcher on the windowside table instead of on the floor where it belonged? Cayden's roar of outrage as he realized what he'd poured into the basin with his smallclothes had sent Mieka into gales of giggles. Only then did he realize that it had all been deliberate, and Mieka had been feigning sleep in his corner bed, waiting for Cade to use the pitcher one way or another. Threats to dangle him by the tips of his ears out the nearest window only made him laugh harder. The incident had taught Cade something about Mieka's sense of humor that he hadn't previously known: The Elf would prolong a joke far past anyone else's paltry imaginings. For, that very next morning, Cade discovered that every other set of underwear he owned was gone, and in their place was a pair of knitted lamb's wool short pants, soft as a cloud, wonderfully warm...

lurid green and frilled at the hems with bright purple lace. He could only stare at them, fascinated in an appalled sort of way, and wonder where in the name of everything holy Mieka had found something so revolting. A desperate application to the innkeeper's wife assured him that all his smallclothes were in the wash and would be clean and dry by nightfall. That day he also learned that whereas Mieka's japes went several steps beyond what anyone else would ever come up with, he also possessed a nice sense of compassion. More or less.

This year, even for Trials, Cade intended to pack as many clothes, especially underthings, as he possibly could. It wasn't just that now he had a much more extensive, and expensive, wardrobe; he was part of Touchstone, and Touchstone must be seen to be a raving success. Kearney Fairwalk had said so, and Cade agreed.

Besides, he liked dressing in flash clothes. It meant people noticed what he wore, not what he looked like.

That afternoon before the journey to Seekhaven, whilst he was sorting what he wanted to take with him from what he absolutely must find room for, his fifth-floor aerie was invaded without warning. Mieka had taken to flitting in and out of the Silversun house at Number Eight, Redpebble Square, as if he lived there, but rarely did he venture all the way up the wrought-iron stairs to Cade's room. Today he did, waving a freshly printed broadsheet.

"Only you, Quill," he announced, tossing the pages atop the clothes strewn across Cade's bed. "Only you!"

"What?" he asked, eyeing Mieka warily. "What've I done?"

The Elf grinned and made himself comfortable in Cade's desk chair. "And here I thought what you said about women at performances and onstage was scandal-making! Little did I know!"

Cade picked up the copy of *The Nayword*, unfolded to an article by Tobalt Fluter.

"Of course," Mieka went on, "the chavishing from that has

died down, so we owe Tobalt a drink or three for putting our name back out there again."

"But I didn't give him another interview. What's he—?"

"Read it." When Cade only stared at it, Mieka snorted and snatched it off the bed. "I'll do the honors, shall I?"

UPCOMING AT SEEKHAVEN: TOUCHSTONE

Last year, the Ninth of the Thirteen Perils, the one about the Dragon, was performed at Trials by Touchstone: Tregetour Cayden Silversun, Masquer Jeschenar Bowbender, Fettler Rafcadion Threadchaser, and Glisker Mieka Windthistle. Whichever of the Thirteen the group may draw this time, count on surprises. This is a group that thinks.

Cade frowned. "That doesn't sound scandalous."

"Dead chuffed with yourself, is that it? P'rhaps His Lordship ought to have that printed on our placards from now on: 'Theater for the Thinking Man.' And bless his ink-stained balls, old Tobalt, for getting all our names right! But listen on, old son." Holding the broadsheet to catch the early afternoon light through Cade's window, he went on, "Let's see… we're impressive, we're innovative, we're clever—ah, yes, here it is."

Yet for all his novel ideas about allowing women into theaters and even onstage (see this journal, issue Number 16), Silversun's feelings about women as expressed in last year's Trials play are curious indeed.

"Oh Gods," Cade muttered, and sat on top of the shirts Mistress Mirdley had finishing pressing just that morning.

"It gets better," Mieka told him.

The Prince was real, and the Dragon was real—uncomfortably

so. The Prince had honest doubts, and by the end of the battle was honestly exhausted. The Dragon breathed flames so realistic that many of the audience flinched with fear (a tribute not only to the power of Silversun's magic but also the brilliance of Windthistle's glisking and Threadchaser's stupendous control).

"You're powerful, I'm brilliant, and Rafe is stupendous—Gods, he'll be six different hells to live with from now on, won't he? But poor Jeska! Nary a mention!"

"Keep going," Cade ordered.

Both the Prince and the Dragon were real. But the Fair Lady remained a shadow, an unreality. Even though she was the reason for all the striving and agony, she was never seen. She was not real. She was not even an ideal of what to strive for. Her commentary on the battle was nervous, self-centered, even whiny. She was nothing like the perfect lady of a man's fondest imaginings. Indeed, the audience never even found out whether or not she was pretty. She was never seen. Her loveliness was assumed—and assumptions are evidently dangerous, with Cayden Silversun.

"Oh Gods," he said again, this time in a moan. Mieka went on reading aloud, with indecent relish.

To him, the importance of the play, and by extension the importance of life, is the struggle. The battle with oneself, with one's personal dragons, with the world's expectations, with doubt and fear and exhaustion, the conflicts that go on inside a man's mind or body or spirit—the important thing is fighting through to win. What's won doesn't really matter: it is a shadow, unseen, insubstantial, even unreal. The Fair Lady, or whatever she represents, is not the goal. The battle is what matters: not to give in, not to give up. Moreover, through the battling, to discover truth.

When Mieka fell silent, Cade stole a glance at him. "Is that all?" he asked feebly.

"Well, there's more. He can't wait to see which of the Perils we'll draw this time, expect to be surprised again, and so forth. But he missed something, y'know. Women *aren't* quite real to you, are they? They're more of a concept."

"Do you have any idea what you're talking about?"

"Have you ever known me not to? Individual women, you're fine—Blye, Crisiant, the mothers of your friends—the luscious Lady Torren of the lavender-scented pillows at Seekhaven last year—but as for whatever birdies you've dallied with from the flocks outside our shows—" He paused. "Do you remember any of their names, by the bye?"

Stung, he retorted, "Of course I do!"

"You're lying, Quill." Mieka shook his head sadly. "I've told you and told you, your eyes will always give you away. What I'm saying is that to you, there are women who are people, and the rest of them are just ideas. They're a concept, like money."

Thoroughly bewildered now, he could do nothing but stare. Mieka wore a half smile, those eyes glinting merrily. "Money?" he echoed.

"You get it, you use it, it's gone."

He could think of no reply to this latest outrage. Mieka didn't seem to expect comment, having warmed to his theme.

"Y'see, there's seven types of women. There's mothers—mine, yours, other people's, and I include Mistress Mirdley and Croodle in that category, women like them. That sweet old lady where we spent Wintering, f'r instance. And me Auntie Brishen. That sort. Then there's sisters—kind of the same category, just younger. Maybe Croodle should be put in with them, what do you think? Then there are women who have to be treated as men. That's Blye. She does a man's work, she doesn't expect anybody to take care of her—"

"Jedris had to get used to that, didn't he?" Cade asked with a smile. "Oh, didn't he just! You don't mind about her and him—"

"Of course I don't!"

"—because you see her the way I do. She's a friend, we love her forever, but she's not a woman like other women. All right, then, next we come to women who are women but we don't want to bed them. You know, the ones who're available enough, and sometimes even rather pretty, but there's no spark. You know 'em when you see 'em—just like you know the next kind, which is the women who're women and you'd love to have 'em, but they're somebody else's property. Wives, girlfriends, that sort. Have to leave them alone, no matter if the sparks are flying all over the room!"

"I've seen you flirt with—"

"Have to let a woman know she's attractive, don't I?"

"And you're the only one who can, is that it?"

"I consider it one of my matchless contributions to the happiness and well-being of the Kingdom," Mieka announced blithely. "Where was I? Oh yeh—whores. One must be nice to them, poor darlings, unless they forfeit the privilege one way or another."

Cade recalled a night last spring, when a street trull had insulted him and Mieka had been, in his own matchless way, hilariously rude. "That's six sorts of women. I bet I can guess the seventh."

Mieka nodded. "Women a man wants to fuck."

"Which in your case is the entire population of young, pretty girls."

He smirked, wiggling his eyebrows.

Too late, Cade remembered the girl in Frimham. Amusement

slipped away like a knife from a dead man's hand. Quickly, he said, "What you mean is that I don't categorize beyond women who are real to me and the general concept of woman."

Mieka was abruptly serious. "What I mean is that you hold yourself back from *everybody* until you know them as people. Women and men both. Oh, you're perfectly willing to bed a girl for the pleasure of it, but she's not real to you, none of them are. You accept what people want to show you of themselves, but you don't give anything back until you're sure it's reasonably safe."

"Safe!"

"Well, yeh. It's one reason why you don't remember their names." A broad grin, a sudden swerving into humor again; Cade told himself he really ought to be used to it by now. "There's a good little comedic playlet in that someplace, Quill—wakin' up in the morning next to some girl, tryin' to recall her name, wonderin' if you've caught somthin' awful from her—"

"Is this me we're talking of, or you?"

Mieka laughed. "I'm careful, oh-so-very-careful! How about you?"

"Isn't that more the girl's responsibility than the man's?"

"Holy Gods, don't ever let Jinsie hear you say that!"

Reaching for the broadsheet, he read the last paragraph for hi self, relieved to find it was just as Mieka had implied: a tease about what Touchstone might do with others of the Thirteen Perils, speculating that great things were ahead. He liked Tobalt Fluter, and was grateful for the mention in this increasingly influential broadsheet, but he wished the man weren't so perceptive about what Cade himself hadn't even seen until it was pointed out to him. It was the sort of thing that could inhibit one's writing, if one weren't careful—or if one actually cared what people thought.

"This is new," Mieka remarked all at once. He'd left the desk and was fingering through Cade's closet. The shirt he picked out to admire was one Mistress Mirdley had stitched, tucked away for him to discover as a surprise belated Namingday present. Mieka held it up to himself, stretching out an arm with the sleeve lying along it. "More my color than yours, but—Quill? What's wrong?"

"Any color is your color, you frustling little fop," he managed to say. He also managed to look directly into Mieka's face and smile.

He'd have to get better at it.

"You just saw something, didn't you," Mieka said flatly. "Don't bother to lie. Damn it to all hells, Cade, don't *lie*!"

"I'm not. I didn't see anything just now."

"Then it's an echo of something. Tell me."

"Mieka—"

"Why won't you tell me?" he cried. "What's so bloody horrifying that you won't tell me? If it has to do with me, don't I have a right to hear it?"

"No." Pushing himself to his feet, he crossed the room and took the yellow shirt from Mieka's hands. "Listen to me—can you shut it and listen? Who do you want living your life? You, or my Elsewhens?"

"What did you see, Cade?"

Defeated, he stared down into those eyes, watching them darken to brown with Mieka's mood. He'd never seen eyes like these, so passionately changeable, so instantly responsive. "I saw you in a dream, wearing a shirt almost this same color. We'd finished a performance and Jeska had to hold you up when you stumbled onstage, you were that drunk. We were all of us older, but we were still Touchstone—Lord and Lady alone know how, because none of us liked each other much anymore. I don't know what happened to us, Mieka, I only know what I saw. I don't know how we got to be that way. I think I hated you."

For two breaths, then three, Cade thought he might have

been wrong about not telling Mieka, not warning him. That he could change what must change simply by sharing his foreseeings with this Elf who was Touchstone's soul. That Mieka would somehow understand, would make the decisions that would preclude future horrors. That they could talk it all out, solemn and honest, and everything would be all right.

He ought to have known.

An insolent grin decorated Mieka's face. "Well, then," he said, "I'll just have to remember never to buy a yellow shirt."

Cade started laughing. He couldn't help it. He heard the note of insanity, but he couldn't stop laughing. "Only you," he gasped out, "only you could say that and expect everything to be all right! Never buy a yellow shirt! As if that's all anyone would have to do—"

Still mocking, but with an edge to his voice now, the boy said, "If you're telling me never to take a drink again, forget it!"

"I can't *tell* you anything! That's the whole fucking point!" Collapsing into his desk chair, he hauled in a deep lungful of air, then another. "I'll tell you a story, shall I? How I know that what I see is possible. The very first time it ever happened, my father was waiting to see if he'd got an appointment to the Prince's Household. He—"

"I know this one," Mieka interrupted. "Blye told me."

"Then I'll tell you one Blye doesn't know—and if you ever breathe a syllable to her, I'll take you apart and put you back together inside out. I didn't remember dreaming about her mother, but when she was run down and killed by a noblewoman's carriage it was like I'd already heard about it, I already knew. The lady blamed her maids for taking out the carriage when they weren't supposed to, and swore to all the Angels that she hadn't been there at all. But I saw her, upriver by a boathouse, and just as the carriage pulled away a man came out, a man who wasn't her husband. I could smell the fish in the stalls nearby, and hear the boatmen calling—" He broke off, took another breath. "When the constable's runner came to Criddow Close, and asked at our kitchen door where Master Cindercliff could be found, I knew. I remembered. I knew what had happened and whose carriage it was and that the lady had been with her lover."

"You never told anyone."

"I told Mistress Mirdley. I said that if people wanted to know what really happened, they should ask if the lady smelled of fish." He hesitated, then shrugged. "Sometimes my father's not all that bad a person, really. Mistress Mirdley told him she'd heard a rumor—not that it came from me, she never let on about what I said to her—and he saw to it that the lady paid for Blye to attend the same littleschool as me and Rafe from then on, even though crafters' daughters aren't supposed to go to the better schools. And she put together a dowry, too—though that all got used up when Master Cindercliff became ill. *He* thought she was just being kind because it had been her carriage. But my father could have ruined her with just a few words here and there, and he let enough hints drop that she knew it."

"But—"

"It must've driven her mad, wondering how my father knew. He had this choice little piece of information—oh, not that her carriage had run over and killed Blye's mother, that sort of thing happens all the time, nobody cares. But she'd been out that day when she said she'd been at home, and she thought nobody but her coachman knew, and he and the maids were her creatures so they'd never split on her. But for years she danced to whatever tune my father cared to whistle."

"Murder doesn't count, but having a lover does?"

"That's the Court."

"Who was she?"

"Let's just say that the next Wintering I was allowed to serve at her private celebrations."

Mieka caught his breath. "Princess Iamina?"

"The very same. Mistress Mirdley told me never *ever* say anything about it to anyone else—not just because of the Princess, but because it was the kind of Wizardly gift that could get me strung up from the nearest tavern sign."

Mieka chewed this over for a while. Finally he said, "I have to trust you. I have to trust that it's more than simply not ever buying a yellow shirt."

"Buy one if you want. It's your choice. Your life."

"You said you hated me."

He nodded wearily. "I'm sorry, Mieka. I don't know how we got there. I don't know how it happened."

"We won't get there. It won't happen. We won't bloody let it."

"It's not up to me."

"So the truth of it is that *you're* the one has to trust *me*. And you don't."

"I do, though. I really think I do. But there's other people involved. They have choices to make as well."

Again the Elf was silent. Then, briskly: "I'll still never buy a yellow shirt. Come on, Quill, finish packing. Or did you forget that you're spending the night at Wistly Hall?"

He had indeed forgotten. Much closer to the Palace courtyard whence the coaches for Seekhaven would depart, the Windthistle residence wasn't the quietest place to spend the night, not with all those scores of relatives hanging about, but it was the most convenient.

Cade and Mieka took a hire-hack to Wistly Hall. The driver, who turned out to be a theater enthusiast and knew their faces from the placards all over Gallantrybanks, helped them pile the luggage in the front hall. Up three flights of stairs, down another and a half, around several mazy corridors that would have had Cade completely lost had it not been for the glimpse of the river every so often—new windowpanes, he noted with a smile—at length, Mieka took him up yet more stairs and led him to a door that opened into a turret.

"Take a look at the view—but have a care," the Elf warned. "It's got a bit rickety over the winter, and the floorboards aren't what they ought to be in places."

Once the door had swung closed behind them, Mieka shoved aside a few planks and boxes, flung back a moth-chewed carpet, and opened a trapdoor.

"This," he said, gesturing grandly to the room revealed below, "is the only place in this whole great barn I can be completely by meself. Nobody knows about it, not even Jed and Jez. Nobody comes up here but me."

"I can see why," Cade told him, eyeing the rotting joists, the rusting bolts. "Is this held together with magic, or just wishful thinking?"

Mieka laughed. "It's been here so long that it stays tacked onto the rest of the house by habit! C'mon, follow me."

He did, gingerly, through the narrow opening down onto another wooden floor. Looking round the little room, lit by the setting sun through very old, very bubbly windowglass, he began to smile. If the view of the Plume from the chamber above was spectacular, from here it was like floating over the river.

"It's wonderful, Mieka."

"I knew you'd like it." He gestured to the pillows strewn about and flopped onto several of them.

Cade sat cross-legged, and the change in altitude let him see all the little bits and bobs Mieka had tucked away in corners and on makeshift shelving. One of this spring's Touchstone placards leaned against the back wall, and pride of place was given to the framed list of Rules (each one crossed through) from the Winterly Circuit coach, and just in front of it were two of the three candleflats Blye had made for him last year on his eighteenth Namingday.

"I gave the other one to Jinsie," Mieka said, following Cade's glance about the lair. "And that remembers me. I missed your Namingday this year, Quill. Here." He reached up to a shelf and took down a little paper twist. "I thought we might give it a try tonight, after dinner."

There was no ink mark to indicate what type of thorn it was. Thus far in his experimentations, Cade had used various combinations of green, purple, blue, and red. "What is it?"

"Auntie Brishen got your letter."

"Oh." The one where he'd told her that things didn't work on him the way they did on other people, so could she suggest something else? "What is it?" he repeated.

"Damned if I know," Mieka said with a cheerful shrug. "She just said that you and me might find it interesting."

Cade pocketed the thorn. "After dinner. Beholden."

Rafe, Crisiant, and Jeska showed up with piles of gear in time for the meal, which tonight was strictly immediate family—Mieka's parents, three brothers, and four sisters—in a small dining room overlooking the river garden. Master Windthistle confided to Cayden that this was his favorite place to eat dinner, for the view was soothing and the table sat only fourteen.

"Not like that bloody great cavern on the other side of the house," he sighed, plucking from a wire basket another of the feather-light bread rolls that Rafe had contributed to the feast. "Three trestles and a high table, as if we were Royalty—and I dare swear that the King himself doesn't regularly sit down to almost a hundred, the way we do."

"A hundred?" Cade's fingers slipped a little on his spoon. "I thought maybe fifty people lived here."

"If only! Mieka's told you something about the family, I suppose. My six uncles and four aunts had thirty-seven children amongst them, and at last count there were seventy or so in the next generation, not counting my eight. Then there's my wife's relations—she was the youngest of seven—and all their progeny—Mishia, love," he called down to the other end of the table, "what's the count of nieces and nephews on your side these days?"

"Too damned many!"

"That's what I thought!" Hadden Windthistle grinned a familiar grin, his third son's mischief dancing in his dark brown eyes. "Most of 'em twins. Piksey blood in her line, y'see. Mayhap in mine as well, no matter what Granny Tightfist might pretend. Mieka will have said about her as well." He arched a questioning brow and Cade nodded. "Uncle Barsabian—I know you recall him—"

"More Elf than the first Elf, Mieka says."

A look of swift fury crossed his handsome face. "We threw him out after what he said to Blye last spring. A small army of relations I'll tolerate, but not that sort of muck. He's gone to live with the old miser at the Clink—Clinquant House, and don't ask me how or why it was named that—and I've not a doubt he's convincing her that we're even more Piksillated than she believes us to be. So it's likely she'll leave him the Windthistle treasury. If she ever does the world a favor by dying, that is."

"You don't seem concerned," Cade ventured. "About the money, I mean."

"Not a bit," he replied cheerfully—and honestly, which Cade found incredible. "For one thing, Mieka's contributing quite a bit these days—your doing, and don't argue with me, boy," he warned, shaking a finger at Cade's nose. "He's good, and what's more he knows it—but he'd be playing for naught but tavern trimmings if you and Rafe and Jeska hadn't found him."

"He sort of found us." Cade grinned.

"There's Jed and Jez as well, with a business starting to thrive. A few assorted cousins and nephews are advancing in their careers—and advancing out of my house is only a matter of time. Alaen Blackpath, the young man as played at the Threadchaser marriage and after, it's three lutes he's bought from me now, and there's a cousin who's coming by next fortnight, said to be as good as Alaen. We'll see, of course. I'm told the King has it in mind to send musicians as well as players over to the Continent when they get this artistic exchange sorted, so there's another few instruments."

"But you sell only to those with real talent."

"I can tell with a look. You've no music in you at all, by the bye."

"I know. I can hear it, but I don't really understand it."

"And how many people can say much the same to you about how you work your art? Where Mieka got the glisking, I've not a clue. There's never been a Windthistle or Staindrop or Moonbinder or any of our other Names anywhere near the theater."

"My grandfather was a fettler."

"I know. I saw his group a few times."

"Did you? Were they good?"

"Yes, but not like Touchstone. Not like Touchstone at all. Traditional things, nicely played, that was the Summerseeds. They had a good run—ten years, I think it was, on the Ducal, after a few on the Winterly. Always good value, they were."

And after the tenth year on the Ducal, Cadriel Silversun had met and married the wildest and most beautiful of the Watersmith daughters, and it was from her that the Fae heritage had come to give Cade his Elsewhens. He didn't mention it. Because it was this same Fae blood that had driven her half mad, and his Uncle Dennet entirely so.

"Now, tell me," said Hadden Windthistle in a low, serious voice, "as you've known her from childhood—do you think our Jedris will be able to make your Blye happy? Is he what she needs in a husband?"

A few hours later, up in Mieka's bedchamber, Cade put both

hands on the Elf's shoulders and grinned down at him. "I *love* your family!"

"Things are much nicer around here," he agreed, "with Uncle Breedbate gone."

"That's not what I meant." He shook Mieka playfully, then sprawled onto the threadbare sofa that would be his bed for the night. "Anybody else would ask if a girl is right for his son. Your father wanted to know if Jed will be a good husband for Blye! I *love* your family!"

"Then he's asked her? She's accepted him? Why, that miserable cullion! The whole morning I spent with him—his own brother!—and he never said a word!"

"I don't know if he's asked, but she'd be mad not to accept him."

"He did say one thing," Mieka mused as he flopped across his bed. "I didn't understand at the time, but now it makes sense. He wanted to know if he was too tall!"

Cade was still laughing over that as he brought out the little paper twist.

"The others didn't do what you wanted, did they?" Mieka asked, watching as Cade prepared the powder for the glass thorn. "You're a huge puzzlement to Auntie Brishen, y'know. She wants your kinline chart to find out what you've got in you that makes you such an anomaly."

"Where'd you pick up a word like that?"

"I *can* read, Quill."

"And the last time you opened a book was…?" he asked pointedly.

"The one I snupped for you at the Castle Biding Fair."

Cade returned his attention to the thorn. In another moment they'd be talking about the girl, because the day Mieka had bargained down the copy of *Lost Withies* was the same day he'd met her. Cade had avoided this particular conversation with the devotion of a Nominative Good Brother studying sacred ritual. He certainly didn't want it to intrude now.

"Ready," he said. "You first?"

"No, you. I'll make me own."

Cade settled back into the pillows and stared at the cracks in the ceiling. "Come sit beside me, and tell me what you're seeing."

"Right now, just a lazy lumpkin of a tregetour." Mieka left his bed and sank cross-legged onto the floor. "But wait a little while, and you'll be singing hymns with naughty lyrics."

"You've got me confused with Jeska." Things were growing hazy now, and he could feel the familiar flush of warmth across his cheeks.

"Did I tell you I learned a new one?"

"Mmm."

He could hear the smile in Mieka's voice as he said, "Dream sweet, Cade."

{It was perfect.

Lights blazed onto the stage, blinding him, dazzling the tiny shards of broken glass that lingered in the air like stars. He knew there were thousands of people out there, clapping their hands raw, screaming, chanting "*Touch*stone! *Touch*stone!" He blinked at the glare, and turned in time to see Mieka soar lightly over his glisker's bench and land with an exuberant bounce. Cade seized his wrist, pulling him in, and they collided: laughing, triumphant. Mieka tossed his head back and shook his long wild hair, yelling, "And *you* thought they wouldn't like it!"

Jeska arrived, grinning wide enough to split his gorgeous face, and rumpled Mieka's hair fondly. Rafe joined them, slinging an arm across Jeska's shoulders, and they all stood there arm-in-arm, drinking in the adulation that never got old.

And then he and Mieka were in the carriage, Cade

stretching out across one whole seat with his boots propped against the closed window and his head on a velvet cushion. Pleasantly tired, still thrumming inside with the triumph of their show, he gazed over at Mieka, noting how the skin around his eyes crinkled when he smiled. Despite the lines crossing his forehead and framing his mouth, and even despite the silver in his hair, he looked at least fifteen years younger than his age.

"You were brilliant tonight," Mieka told him. "On the tricky bits of *Window-wall*, especially." He paused. "But you're always brilliant. Why do I bother saying it?"

"Dunno. P'rhaps because you're crazy?"

"P'rhaps," he allowed.

A few miles later, Cade pushed himself upright and peered out at the night. "We're not goin' to the Downstreet for a drink? And now that I think on it, why aren't you out with that little Elfengirl? Oh, don't pretend you didn't notice her fluttering about backstage in the tiring room," he scoffed when Mieka made innocent eyes.

"Not in the mood. C'mon, off your lazy bum, we're home."

The carriage came to a halt, and they climbed the front steps of a riverside town house built from mellow old brick. Glimpses of drawing room, terrace, garden, the doors leading to the kitchen where Mistress Mirdley concocted her daily wonders. Upstairs were four bedrooms, his library, Mieka's studio. They went into the front room, designed to look like a very exclusive tavern. But instead of their usual after-performance snack of tea and muffins and whatever fruit was in season, arrayed on the bar were bowls of berries dipped in mocah powder, and a silver ice bucket with a bottle of sparkling wine, and a pair of crystal glasses that didn't match the rest of the barware.

"You didn't remember, did you?" Mieka challenged.

"Remember? What's all this, then? Remember what?"

Excited as a child, he gave a little bounce of delight that his surprise had turned out a surprise after all. "Happy Namingday, Cayden!"

He was right; it was past midnight, and it was his Namingday. "Forty-five!" Cade groaned. "Holy Gods, Mieka, I'm too old to still be playin' a show five nights out of every nine!"

"Oh, *I* know that," Mieka said with his most impudent grin. "But try telling it to the two thousand people out there tonight who kept screaming for more!"

"You *are* crazy, Sir Mieka."

"I am that, Sir Cayden." He unhooked the little wire cage from the bottle and carefully popped the cork. "Pity His Gratuitous Majesty can't see us now—we'd be Knights of the Bar instead of—oh, whatever it is we're Knights of."

"The Most Noble Order of the Silver Feather of Albeyn. Why can't you ever remember that?"

"Doesn't get us good seats at Royal weddings or the racing meet, now, does it? Nor even a proper sword. So what's the bleedin' use of the silly things, that's what I'd like to know."

Mieka's idea of a proper sword was in all probability a double-edged Huszar's weapon taller than he was; Cade had never dared ask. "We'd only be Knights of the Bar if we were justiciars. And somehow, don't ask me how, it's just instinctive, but I can't see you in a black cassock waving a gavel—" Then he broke off, correcting himself with a grin. "I take it back— you *talk* enough for twenty lawyers!"

"I s'pose I have to be nice to you, as it's your Namingday, but don't push your luck."

He was suddenly alerted to trouble when Mieka flinched while reaching for a cloth to wrap the bottle. "Shoulder again, eh? Overdid the Mad Glisker act again tonight."

"Hark who's complaining!" He tapped lightly at the scrapes and cuts on Cade's fingers, tsking his disapproval. "Why do you *do* that? Rafe and me have it all planned and disciplined, but then you have to do your little stunt— stupidest thing I ever heard of, juggling exploding withies. Someday, you silly git, you're gonna slice off a finger!"

"Why should you two have all the fun? And what about you, you maniac? Someday you'll land wrong off your bench and break an ankle!"

Mieka poured wine. "Two choices. Argue or drink. Which?"

"Don't ask foolish questions."

The crystal sang with their silent toast. Blye's work was more exquisite every year.

"Forty-five." Cade sighed. "There's times, lookin' at you, when I feel a hundred. You don't get older," he accused. "It's disgusting."

Mieka snorted. "With all this gray in me hair?"

"You *don't* get older. It's un-fuckin'-natural, even for an Elf." His gaze went to the framed imagings behind the bar. "There's the proof."

"All I see is proof that you keep opening the best door."

Laughing, he toasted Mieka again. "Every single morning."

"This life?" His head tilted to one side, shaggy hair shifting to reveal the tip of one pointed ear where a tiny diamond gleamed.

"And none other."

The front door slammed open and Rafe roared, "You started without us!" and a minute later they were in the middle of a party that Cade knew full well would last until dawn.}

"Quill? Quill, wake up."

His eyelids drifted languorously open, and through his lashes he saw Mieka's face. He was almost disappointed that there were no lines framing his mouth, that his hair was coal-black without a trace of silver.

"We'd got old," he heard himself say, and smiled. "I liked your diamond earring."

Mieka sat back on his heels by the sofa, head tilting to one side exactly as in the dream. "*How* old?"

He heard something suspiciously like a giggle, realized the sound came from his own throat. "Your hair'd gone gray."

"Oh Gods," he moaned. "I was old and gray and fat and wrinkly, wasn't I? That's right cruel of you, Quill! What else?"

"Bubbledy wine." He stretched his arms wide and snuggled back into the cushions. "And mocah-dust berries." He ran his tongue around his molars, searching for stray seeds. "D'you know I can explode a withie in mid-air, just like you and Rafe?" Honesty made him confess, "Only sometimes I get a few cuts on my hands."

"So I'm guessing you liked this sort of thorn?"

"Oh, yeh. Let's do more."

"After Trials, I think."

Suddenly he grasped Mieka's arm. "You'll be there? You'll be with me?" He'd felt so safe in that dream, so happy. "Say you'll be there."

Mieka smiled. "Of course."

Cade turned onto his side, purring low in his throat. "This life," he murmured, and fell asleep thinking he'd heard Mieka whisper, "And none other."

3

Whatever Mieka had told Cade that night, he'd been very careful not to lie, especially after the thorn faded and Cade seemed so fretted about having Mieka there with him the next time he tried that particular mix.

But he hadn't joined Cade in pricking thorn. He'd wanted too much to know the truth. Finally, at least some of the truth about an Elsewhen dreaming.

What he'd learned had been amusing and, oddly enough, a comfort. Infinitely better than *"I think I hated you."* Cade had seen them old! For himself, he couldn't imagine it. But he rather fancied picturing Cade with gray hair, or receding hair... or no hair. This made him snigger, earning an annoyed glance from his mother at the interruption in her lecture about behaving himself at Trials, and especially at High Chapel. She knew very well that Mieka behaved badly when he bothered to behave at all. It was touching, really, that she might actually think his plans for marriage and a family and a home of his own would suddenly turn him into a fine upstanding subject of His Gracious Majesty the King.

"I'll be good, Mum, I promise," he said.

She looked him in the eyes and sighed a *Why do I bother?*

sigh, then gave him a fierce hug. "And no running off to Frimham all in a flutter," she whispered in his ear. "She's yours, no matter what her mother hints about other boys. You'll both just have to wait a bit, and it'll be all the sweeter for the waiting." Standing back, she looked him over, and he was afraid she'd cry and say humiliating things about her baby being all grown up and other suchlike motherish drivel. But then her gaze flickered over his shoulder and she let out a shriek. "Tavier! Come down this instant! Hadden, he's packed himself onto the roof!"

Mieka fell over laughing. His littlest brother had swarmed up the side of the hire-hack and found a perch amid the crates of glass baskets and withies, and the half-barrel of whiskey Auntie Brishen had sent for luck. They would have found him, of course, once they got to the Palace and unloaded everything to be transferred to the King's coach for Seekhaven. But if they couldn't coax him down soon, they'd be dreadfully late. There were threats ("None of Mistress Threadchaser's pies again, ever, not one, for the rest of your life!") and promises ("Be a good boy and come down, and we'll take you to see Blye's kiln—it's just like a dragon's mouth!"), but the only thing that impressed the child was Rafe's solemn vow to find him a dragon egg.

"It'll take a bit of a while," Rafe cautioned, "because the only dragons in the Kingdom live up in the far reaches of the Pennynine Mountains."

"I *know* that," Tavier said, peering down from the roof railings. "Will you really? A dragon egg?"

"I shall."

Mieka steadied his frantic mother as Tavier very calmly stood up and leaped down into Rafe's waiting arms, as casually as if at any moment he could spread wings and fly if the mood took him.

It was at this exact moment that the huge colorful wagon belonging to the Shadowshapers pulled up on the opposite side of the street, pulled by two of the biggest horses anyone had ever seen. Mieka admired the timing, and hoped Tavier did, too: the surprise arrival spared him the scolding that seethed in Mum's eyes.

"Oy!" shouted Rauel Kevelock from his perch next to the driver. "Excellent, we got here in time!"

"Look at that," drawled Mieka. "It's the famous Shadowshapers."

"In their famous wagon," contributed Jedris.

"So it famous is!" Vered Goldbraider grinned from a window. "What're all you lot waitin' for? Pile in and let's be off!"

Chattim Czillag's voice yelled from within: "And don't forget the whiskey barrel!"

The mostly familial commotion of loading the hire-hack for Touchstone became a mayhem that involved most of the neighborhood as people spilled out of homes all along Waterknot Street to witness the actual presence of the Shadowshapers. The lower servants stood and gaped, the implements of their early-morning duties dangling from their hands; the upper servants forgot to chide their underlings and indeed didn't notice that their own livery had been buttoned askew; their employers appeared in windows and doorways with dressing gowns hastily wrapped and hair left undone, not even bothering to call out to their children running wild across the cobbles. Fortunately, the horses were stoical creatures, inured to the noise of Gallantrybanks; Jorie, Tavier's twin sister, walked right up to the huge animals drawing the Shadowshapers' wagon and petted each velvety white nose in turn. The wagon had acquired a little parade of drays and carts selling everything from bread to milk to fresh flowers, and the local dogs raced madly amid it all while the local cats played sneak-feast on the fishmonger's cart.

Rauel, Vered, Chattim, and their fettler, Sakary Grainer, descended from their wagon into this uproar to greet the Windthistles, whom they'd met at Rafe and Crisiant's marriage celebrations last month here at Wistly Hall. When a trio of giggly maidservants from a house up the street approached with a placard, they smiled and obligingly signed their names. This seemed to be the signal for everyone to find any scrap of paper or parchment they could lay hands on.

Mieka strolled over to Cade. "Well, this is fun," he remarked.

"That's us, next year," Cade predicted resolutely.

Mieka's attention was caught by a tall, graying personage whose dignity as a gentleman's gentleman was in no wise diminished by the fact that his immaculate white silk gloves were stuffed untidily into a pocket and his immaculate white silk stockings ended in one polished black leather shoe and one dark green velvet slipper. The man approached with that consciousness of his employer's rank that always paralyzed Mieka between the urge to snap a salute and the urge to snap the man's braces.

"Oh Gods, he's coming to complain," Cade whispered.

"No, he's not."

"Next somebody will send for the constables."

"No, they won't."

The man paused in front of them with a bow almost as low as the one given Royalty. "If the young Masters would be so kind, the household which I have the honor to serve would be greatly beholden should the young Masters consent to bestow upon them their signatures." From the breast pocket of his blue-and-black livery he produced an immaculate white sheet of paper and one of the innovative new silver-nibbed pens, plus a tiny bottle of ink.

After they had scrawled their names, the manservant gravely inclined his head and departed to find Jeska and Rafe. Mieka looked up at Cade, who was still rather stunned, and crowed with laughter. "That's us, *this* year!"

It was another half hour before the hire-hack driver had been paid off and everyone and everything had been loaded into and onto the Shadowshapers' wagon. Jeska sat up top with Rauel and the driver—two beauteous masquers with a part-Giant alternately grinning and grumbling between them. Though Rist had inherited a Giant's ancestral aversion to horses, none but a Giant was in possession of muscle enough to control the two great beasts.

"When we get one of these," Mieka said, settling back with his boots propped on a bunk, "I'll ask Yazz to come work for us, shall I?"

"Your friend up in Gowerion? The one you had to beg not to damage me?" Cade laughed. "I'd like to set Yazz loose on that innkeeper up north—you remember, Prickspur."

"Prick-licker," Vered snarled.

"We heard about that," Sakary said, frowning. "The one who took the contract for the Winterly but won't allow Elfenbloods under his roof."

"Innocents, that's what you are," Chat observed calmly. "Never run across that sort of thing before, any of you. Wait till the artist exchange scheme with the Continent. You'll find out."

"What's the latest on that, anyway?" Rafe asked.

"It seems," said Vered, "that we're all waiting for a princess, two grand duchesses, and a few noble heiresses to make up their silly little minds about Ashgar."

Mieka glanced over at Cade, whose father was First Gentleman of the Bedchamber to the Prince. Cade nodded. "Once some poor girl finally accepts him, they'll send a few of us over there with the ambassadors to escort her to Gallantrybanks. A few shows for whichever court in whichever city, then back home. Depending on how well the players are received, a bigger tour will be organized."

Vered's brows arched. "And you know this because why?"

"Lady Jaspiela," Rafe said, then explained, "his mother, with Court connections of her own. She's in a bit of a quandary, she is," he went on with a smirk. "Can't decide if the horror and humiliation of a son playing the Circuit is worth Royal recognition of worthiness to represent Albeyn."

"Which isn't to mention the possible international contacts of a son who's been abroad at other courts," Cade put in. "She has it in mind for my little brother to become an ambassador or some suchlike."

Mieka snorted. "Oh, I can just see Dery making a knee and kissing wrists for a living."

As they all relaxed into the comforts of the wagon for the journey to Seekhaven, Mieka reflected that whatever was in that thorn last night had produced a happy, mellow, smiling Cayden Silversun this morning, and was definitely to be encouraged. He'd saved the twist of paper with its identifying marks on the inside, and would send to Auntie Brishen as soon as may be for more.

A little past noon, the eight young players reenacted the same scene from the previous year—a lavish lunching from baskets provided by Mistress Mirdley—under the same tree beside the same inn where other groups stuffed down whatever food they could in the minutes it took to change horses. Touchstone and the Shadowshapers greeted the arriving players with lazy smiles, idling on the lush spring grass, enjoying with indecent glee the envious glares of those who dared to think they might be competition.

The two shaggy-hoofed horses that had drawn the coach thus far would be waiting here for the last bit of the journey back to Gallantrybanks. Two fresh animals had replaced them, and with the other horses drawing the King's coaches to compare them to, Mieka saw how really massive those white beasts were.

"Rommy took himself a holiday on the Continent last summer, and came back with eight of these monsters," Chat explained as they strolled round the wagon, admiring the painted swirls and patterns. "We only need two between the traces for this trip, as we're not full-loaded—even with all your gear added on. But on the Circuit, four of them can take us almost twice as fast between stops, and we don't have to change, because there's all that time for them to rest while we spend five or six days performing, y'see."

Mieka didn't, quite, and said so.

"Four of the usual horses, drawing the usual coach, have to be switched off at intervals. Our wagon is bigger, but these horses are half again the size of usual horses. Given a breather every so often, they'll go all day and half the night." He walked around, patting flanks and smoothing manes. "Rommy's plan is to send the other four up to Scatterseed, to be fresh and rested and get us over the Pennynines two days quicker than usual." He chuckled. "More time, more shows, and especially more private bookings, which is where the real money is."

"Nice to be you, and rich," Mieka observed, sidling away from a huge, sceptical brown eye set in a massive white head. "How'd they ever get these beasts across the Flood?"

"You'd think they'd kick a ship to splinters, wouldn't you? But they're really very sweet-natured."

"I'll trust your word on that, and won't be testing it out."

"Rommy's of a mind to start a breeding scheme, once he finds a stud that suits. An investment, he says."

"Turning all pastoral, are you? Interesting plan for a bunch of city gits."

"Speaking of studs and breeding," Chat said with a sidelong glitter of blue eyes, "how do Rafe and the fair Crisiant like marriage so far?"

"They never left their bedchamber at Fairwalk Manor. Cade's of the opinion that they never left their bed, though he can't actually prove it." Knowing his friend was about to tease him regarding things Mieka didn't want to discuss, he waved merrily to the last of the King's coaches, just arriving in the yard. As the vehicle decanted eight tetchy young players, Mieka chortled. "Crystal Sparks and Black Lightning. If they manage to stagger into High Chapel tomorrow evening, I'll stand you a drink at the best tavern in Seekhaven Town."

"No bet. And I thought Pirro was a friend of yours."

"Not since he took up with that lot."

"Chat!" bellowed Vered. "We're off, with you or without you!"

Aided by Auntie Brishen's whiskey, they passed the daylight hours pleasantly enough. Mieka rode up top with Rist for a time, enjoying the pale yellow flowers that were the Tincted Downs' spring raiment, promising himself to bring her here when the blue and purple flowers bloomed later in the summer, and bed down with her in a meadow the color of her eyes.

Away from the others, with only the silent Rist for company, he could let himself think about her. She was his, he knew she was his, but with part of him he simply couldn't believe that anything that exquisite could belong to him. Somehow, talking about her with anyone else was impossible. He'd never even told anyone exactly how he met her. She was no longer a secret— he'd brought her and her mother to Gallantrybanks for Rafe's wedding, and they stayed at Wistly for three days thereafter. But he never discussed her with his friends, not even with Cade. To think of her was to feel things he'd never felt before in his life, things he couldn't identify with words. He had a fanciful notion that once he knew her name, all those emotions would settle quite happily on her like a silken cloak he'd made with his own magic. In her, he'd discovered that there was an eighth category of woman. All the plays and poems asserted that there could be only one Beloved for any man, and she was his. He'd known it the instant he caught sight of her, tending her mother's cramped little booth at the Castle Biding Fair. She was the most beautiful thing he'd ever seen.

But he couldn't talk about her. Not to his parents, nor to his sister Jinsie, nor to his older brothers, nor even to Cade. It occurred to him as the wagon rattled down the road between rolling golden fields that he might be able to talk about her with Blye. Perhaps when they got back home, before departing on the Royal Circuit. He was as sure of Touchstone's advancement from the Winterly as he was that Blye wouldn't tease him or mock his feelings.

At nightfall they took a break for dinner at a very nice inn. Rist predicted that they would be in Seekhaven well before morning, so they arranged themselves in the four bunks and two soft chairs, with Rafe choosing to join the coachman for a while and Jeska curling in a blanket and some pillows on the floor.

Everyone slept but the three tregetours and Mieka—who was beginning to think that the only way he ever learned anything real and true about Cade was by pretending to have taken thorn when he hadn't, or pretending to be sleeping when he wasn't. He found this deeply annoying.

The three of them traded compliments and analysis about past performances, commiserated over the relative recalcitrance of words, fettlers, and gliskers (though not of masquers; Vered and Rauel traded off that function, and avoided criticizing each other, at least in front of other people). Mieka bit back protests as Cade complained about how difficult he was sometimes to control before Vered goaded him into admitting that he wouldn't trade his "mad little glisker" for any other. Mollified, Mieka rolled over onto his back and grunted as a sleeping man might, and set himself to listening even more closely as they began to talk about ideas.

It started out with general chagrin that there just wasn't enough time in the average performance to do a really deep piece, something that touched the audience more powerfully with each moment. Vered made an acid reference to being bludgeoned for a quarter of an hour by Black Lightning and wanting never to repeat the experience. This set off a round of denigration that might have irked Mieka on his friend Pirro's behalf, except that

Pirro had given him some unknown and scary type of thorn this spring, for which Mieka intended never to forgive him. He was looking forward to blowing Black Lightning off the Trials stage.

Then the three tregetours got round to what they'd be doing for private performances while at Trials. There were the official invitations from the lords and gentlemen, and the unofficial invitations from the ladies, and it was Cade's opinion that one didn't have to modify a piece one little bit to suit an all-female audience. Rauel worried about women's emotions being more delicate; Vered told Cade he was an idiot if he thought the little shit-witted birdies at Court were capable of understanding more complex pieces.

"The one we're working on now, for instance," he said. "We've got it two ways, one mine and one Rauel's, and the one we'll do for the men and the other for the ladies."

Rauel laughed softly. "It's his way of being invited back to do mine for the gentlemen, or his for the ladies, I can't figure out which!"

"Why not do both in the same night?" Cade asked.

Mieka could almost feel them staring at him, and then at each other.

"You're the only group as ever works trading off tregetour and masquer. Do one version, then fill up the space with shadows the way you always do, and go right into the second version. I'd imagine," he added dryly, "they're different enough so nobody will think you're repeating yourselves."

More silence.

"Or combine them, p'rhaps," Cade went on. "Chat and Sakary would have to keep the magic separated, but—"

Vered interrupted, "So what've you been plotting out lately?"

"Nothing so complicated," Cade admitted, sounding slightly abashed now. "There's a dream I had once, about a hallway of doors—"

Mieka couldn't help it: he snorted and sat up in his bunk and hit his head on the ceiling. "Damn!" The three of them exclaimed in surprise, and he belatedly recalled he was supposed to have been asleep, and mumbled, "Are we there?"

Cade chuckled indulgently. "Not yet. Roll over and go back to sleep."

"'M thirsty."

Bracing himself against the gentle swaying of the wagon, Cade unfolded himself from the deep chair and gave Mieka his own glass of whiskey. "Don't worry," he said over his shoulder to Vered and Rauel, "his mother vows it's been years since he pissed the bedclothes."

"Quill!" Mieka spluttered on his swallow of liquor, and Cade laughed at him, patting his head.

"Back to sleep with you, there's a good little Elf."

What he wanted to do was demand why Cade had even considered telling rivals about so important an idea as the doorways. But what truly hurt was that Cade had mentioned his dream to Vered and Rauel, when it had taken Mieka months to coax even a portion of the truth out of him. He lay down, turned his back, and chewed on his annoyance, deliberately not listening now. Not that there was much to hear; they'd evidently decided that sleep was necessary sometime before arriving at Seekhaven, and the wagon soon grew quiet. For a little while Mieka tried to distract himself with thinking about her, but he was still too irked with Cade—and thinking about her always caused a physical reaction that in his present circumstances he could do nothing to soothe. This irritated him even more. Scowling he went to sleep, and woke scowling the next morning.

Touchstone had drawn the same inn as last year, a little away from the river. They had ample time to settle in before heading off to High Chapel, where Mieka noted that Chat should have taken the bet. Black Lightning were all present and correct, even elegant, in clothes from an exclusive Narbacy Street tailor. One good look at Pirro Spangler told Mieka why: bluethorn. Useful stuff. But if they were pricking thorn as often as Pirro's pinpoint pupils seemed to indicate, it was no wonder Black Lightning had a reputation for magic barely controlled.

Mieka used, too, when he felt it necessary. But it was just plain unprofessional to rely too heavily on thorn for the energy needed in a performance. Worse, it was potentially dangerous to an audience. What if the magic got loose in ways a glisker was too thorn-lost to keep in check?

He didn't mention it, though. Cade would only arch his brows and remind him of a time or two when Mieka had made mistakes that Rafe had had to correct. Mieka didn't feel like explaining that it was different. He couldn't articulate just *how* it was different, but he knew it was.

After a good night's sleep they headed off for their scheduled time at the rehearsal hall. It had been a wet spring in the south this year, and Seekhaven had been washed pristine by torrents of rain. The castle fairly glowed in the sunlight. The whole world was wondrous this morning, and Mieka couldn't help but dance a few steps along the river bank, planning how he'd present his Royal Circuit medal to her with flowers and flourishes and a proposal of marriage, and finally she'd whisper her name and he'd whisper it back in the darkness and—

"Oy!" Rafe shouted. "Mind how you go, you maniac!"

He turned just in time to see the stack of white bricks where boats tied up, and leaped awkwardly over it. *Must stop thinking about her during working hours*, he told himself sternly. There was his life with Touchstone, and there was the life he would make with her, and the two shouldn't intrude on each other.

So it was with his entire attention that he settled in a chair on the rehearsal hall stage and listened to Cade's harangue about the Thirteen Perils, and how they knew all of them backwards and forwards, so unless anybody wanted a brief run-through of any of them, he had some more thoughts on how to stage "Doorways."

"You're assuming we'll get the invitation to perform for the gentlemen of the Court," Rafe said.

"Or the ladies," Jeska put in.

"And why shouldn't we?" Mieka demanded. "I've been thinking about those doorways meself, Quill, and it seems to me there's two ways to block it out. One long hallway, stage right to stage left, so Jeska walks along it to open the doors, or—"

"Or maybe tilt it a little, have it at an angle so it's not so squared off, and there's a depth to the scene," Rafe suggested. "And then Jeska walks either upstage or downstage, depending on how you want to work it—"

"Or not have him do much walking at all!" Mieka exclaimed. "Move the *hallway* instead of him!"

"I like that," Jeska said. "Each door is different, yeh? If you use colors to set them apart from each other, or make some of wood and others of iron—the doorknobs and handles and things have to be really distinct, really noticeable, otherwise people might get confused—"

"Once again," Rafe chuckled, "it comes down to deciding just how stupid any given audience might be."

"Now you sound like Vered," Mieka accused with a grimace. "I can give you as many different sorts of doors as you like, that's no problem. But what I'm wondering is whether Jeska walks into the scene inside, or if it comes out to him, y'know?"

"Hmm. Interesting point."

Cade stuck two fingers between his teeth and blew an ear-stinging whistle. "Who the fuck wrote this thing, anyway?"

"Who the fuck will be playing it?" Rafe countered. "If you've something to say, say it."

They went on arguing it out, pacing the stage, throwing ideas at one another, finally deciding that there would indeed be an angled hallway and that Jeska would both walk through it and have it slide forwards to meet him.

"It might work," Cade allowed.

"Don't overwhelm us with your enthusiasm," Rafe muttered.

"Are you sure," Jeska asked, "that you want to present it here for the first time? We could work on it some more, open it sometime during the Circuit."

"We need to make at least as big an impression this time as we did last time." Cade walked slowly from one side of the stage to the other, arms folded around himself. "I'd like to have Jeska walk *inside* each of the doors, and as he does, the scene within expands to cover most of the stage—"

"He can do both." Mieka felt his hands clench into fists with the sudden excitement of the idea. "The audience won't know which is coming. One door, he'll open and they'll see inside, feel what's there, hear it—but the next, or maybe the next after that, it'll come swirling out to grab at them."

"And maybe leave some doorways kind of blank," said Jeska. "I don't mean empty, exactly, just—something's there that I don't like, or that scares me, it doesn't have to be specific, and I slam the door shut before anybody has a look inside—"

"Like the way the Shadowshapers did 'Dancing Ground' that time, remember, Cade?" Mieka leaned forwards in his chair, hands wrapped together now. "They did this thing at the end—everybody felt he actually *had* what he most wanted in the world—nothing specific, like you said, Jeska, but the magic fitting their own desires like a bespoke suit of clothes. It was brilliant!"

"No specifics?" Cade was frowning.

Rafe eyed him sidelong. "Aren't you the one talks about the communal experience of theater?"

"But this would be the opposite. Not one experience shared by everyone, the sort of thing that gives the feeling of cohesiveness—"

"It'd set them talking, though," Mieka told him. "How good are we, that everyone had a *unique* experience while sitting through the very same show?"

Jeska sank gracefully onto the stage, wrapping his arms around his drawn-up knees. "It would pull them in, like," he ventured. "Make a space for them to be inside the character."

"Have their own fears or delights seep out at them—or catch them by the heart." Rafe stroked his beard thoughtfully. "I rather like this."

Cade was pacing again. "But it's not what I've written. It's not—"

"It's not imposing your vision on the audience?" Rafe suggested with a wry smile. "They've got used to sitting there and soaking up feeling and sensation—like Vampires, just as you said. But what if we make them participate? Leave room, like Jeska says, for them to inhabit portions of the character?"

"What if they don't experience what we want them to experience?" he challenged.

Quill really was a stickler for control, though Mieka supposed he'd call it *precision*. He knew he mustn't laugh. He wanted to, very much, but if he did, it would take another half hour to haul Cade out of whatever sulk he'd plunge himself into, and they had work to do before vacating the rehearsal hall by noon. So he said, mildly enough, "That's just it, though, innit? We're not dictating everything to them. We're letting them do some of the work interpreting what they see."

"More work for them," Jeska grinned, "and less for us!"

"For you, mayhap," Rafe growled, but he looked intrigued.

"They won't just be part of the audience," Mieka went on. "They'll sort of be part of the performance itself, won't they?"

Cade's frown deepened, and for a moment Mieka thought he would be even more stubborn than usual. Then he said, "Reaching them in ways other groups aren't smart enough or subtle enough to accomplish." He squinted at Mieka. "*Are* we smart enough and subtle enough?"

"Only one way to find out!"

Late that night, as the two of them sat in the moonlit garden over a last pint of ale, Cade ran a long finger round the rim of his glass. "You really think I want to have total control over everything an audience experiences?"

"I think it might be something you can't help yourself about. I understand, Quill. There's so much you can't influence at all, leave alone make it come out the way you'd like it to. So you do what you can, where and as you can. The stage is easy, that way. It's what we're there for."

"But aren't we stealing the idea from the Shadowshapers?"

"You heard what Vered said that night at the Kiral Kellari. You told me later, remember?"

"He was furious," Cade mused, "that Rauel had worked it so everyone *felt* things. Whatever a man's heart's desire, that's what Rauel gave him."

"Without regret and without a sense of loss afterwards—and that was the real skill of it, y'know, what Sakary did in controlling the magic."

"But what Vered wanted was for them to be… I don't know, *tempted*, I guess, pushed into thinking about what it was they wanted most in the world. He wanted to engage their minds, not their emotions."

With an innocent flash of his eyelashes, Mieka asked, "If that's not manipulation and control, what is?"

Cade snorted. "Do they still work the piece that way? I might like to go see it again, if we've a chance."

"To find out who won, Vered or Rauel?" Mieka laughed. "That one night I did their glisking, I heard them backstage before the show. Arguing, as usual. Rauel yelled, 'When does this end?' and Vered yelled back, 'It ends when I win!' But with those two, it'll end only when one of them is dead!"

"Still, I'd like to see it again."

"Would you let yourself really feel it this time?"

When Cade said nothing for a long while, Mieka was afraid he'd gone too far.

"No," Cade said at last. "I don't want to know how it feels to have what I most desire."

"The struggle, not the prize? Like Tobalt wrote about you."

"I never asked what *you* experienced that night."

"Whatever it was, it'd be different now." For a few heartbeats he seriously considered telling Cade everything about her, from how they'd met to how it felt to kiss her, what it was like simply to be in her company with those incredible eyes watching him and wanting him—

"You're a year older," Cade said suddenly, "and I hope your desires have matured beyond a bottomless barrel of whiskey!"

Mieka cuffed him genially on the arm. "Snarge!"

"C'mon, up to bed. We've the draw tomorrow, and I want to be sure Jeska's locked in for the night."

They shared a laugh as they walked towards the back porch, remembering last year's horrifying shock of Jeska's bruises, souvenirs of an encounter with a pretty girl's jealous lover. Tomorrow would be very different, Mieka knew. Not only did Jeska have strict orders to keep it in his trousers until after they'd won their place on the Royal Circuit, but this year they were Touchstone, known and admired, and people would be frantic to see their show. They wouldn't be getting *looks* from the Stewards; they would be *watched*.

Halfway up the stairs, Cade murmured, "What Jeska said, about leaving space for the audience to inhabit the character—"

"Every so often he pops up with a good one, don't he? He knows his work, Jeska does."

"I always thought it was my job—*our* job—to make as

complete a picture as possible. Not some undeveloped mess that any amateur could put together, but all the sensations, all the emotions, all the words—a *precise* experience."

Mieka hid a smirk. "I think mayhap Black Lightning has changed the way we all think about things. Getting bludgeoned about the head is rather a total kind of experience."

"That's what Vered said last night—'bludgeoned.' Mieka…"

"Hmm?"

"D'you think it might be time we stopped shattering glass?"

4

Having heard it all before, Mieka didn't pay much attention as the Master of His Majesty's Revelries explained how Trials and the three Circuits worked. His gaze wandered about the hall, noting statuary and paintings (good but not the best, here in a reception room where the common folk assembled for tours of the castle grounds), clothes (vile sea-green tunics on officials, and too many of those fussy pie-frill wrappings knotted around players' necks), and especially attitudes.

The groups who didn't matter he passed over swiftly. The Nightrunners, still looking as disgruntled as they had on last year's placard. Some new quartet called the Smokecatchers (why couldn't anyone think up any original names?), who'd connected up on the strength of an advertisement in *The Nayword*. The Enticements were still around, though for players their age, a glass basket was useful only for planting kitchen herbs. Same for the Cobbald Close Players. Kelife and the Candlelights were as usual guaranteed a spot on a Circuit no matter how awful and old-fashioned they were; their tregetour was married to a lord's sister's cousin or somesuch. Then there were the Wishcallers, who had so mysteriously dropped out of third flight on the last Winterly. Black Lightning had replaced them.

Black Lightning were present in all their snooty arrogance. Mieka behaved as if he hadn't noticed them. Nearby were the duo of Redprong and Trinder, a tregetour and glisker who would yet again audition for a masquer and a fettler, and yet again drive either or both quite mad. As for the Spintales—Mieka repressed a snigger as they drew the most dreaded of all the Thirteen, a numbing story about how treaties had averted a war. Not even Cade was able to make that one interesting, and Mieka nearly fell asleep every time they rehearsed it.

Next to draw were the Shorelines. Mieka had a soft spot for the Shorelines, for they were the first group he had ever seen perform. He'd been seven; he was now nearing nineteen; everybody knew it was long past time the group got out of the way for younger and better players, but people still enjoyed seeing them work.

And that left the three best groups in the Kingdom: the Shadowshapers, Touchstone, and Crystal Sparks. If the Stewards hadn't been bought off—which was unlikely but not unheard of—that would be the line-up for the Royal this year.

Most people would not have included the Sparks in the top three. Mieka knew his preference for their work was more than personal taste; he'd discussed them with Quill. What the Sparks did was innovative in ways different from the Shadowshapers' intensely original pieces, from Touchstone's daring rewrites. The Sparks played only the traditional, the same scripts that everybody had used for ages, but in ways that never failed to surprise. Mieka had seen them a few times this spring in Gallantrybanks, and what they had done with "Piksey Led A-Straying" had left him blinking. As usual, young lordling got lost on a moor, lured by Pikseys, and eventually turned his cloak inside out to break the spell. But in between, the Sparks toyed with the theme of invertedness: clouds and sky underfoot, hillsides overhead, rain that fell upwards, trees with leaves that shrank back into the branches as the trunk dwindled into the ground and became nothing more than a seed. For a little while during the performance, Mieka feared that the thorn he'd pricked beforehand contained some of what Pirro had given him this spring, stuff that had befuddled his mind and sent him running through Castle Eyot to find safety with Cade. The creativity of Crystal Sparks' performance, the gleeful warping of perception, had impressed Mieka, as did the strict control exerted by the fettler, Brennert Copperboggin. To modulate safely such confusion without sending the audience reeling and yarking to the nearest garderobe was much more difficult than the pummeling that seemed to be Black Lightning's only real knack. Once the Sparks began doing original work, they'd turn out almost as good as Touchstone.

Thirteen aspiring groups at Trials meant that all the Perils would be performed. Mieka felt sorry for anybody who got the one about the Dragon. Last year Touchstone had made it so spectacular a piece that nobody would ever be able to perform it again without someone muttering, "Not a patch on *them*!" The points awarded for some of the Thirteen were always greater than for others, and Mieka frankly suspected that this contributed to the continued presence on the Circuits of dilapidated groups like the Spintales. Luck in the draw had much to do with it—

Jeska elbowed him, and he walked forwards with his friends so Cade could accept the token of their draw. He could see the long, nervous fingers exploring the face of the token, trying to discern which it was. Mieka wasn't worried. He knew they'd be on the Royal this year. It was only a question of second or third flight—the Shadowshapers would of course take first. *For now, anyways*, he told himself as everyone bowed and left the hall for the walk back to their various lodgings.

Cade said nothing, and showed the token to no one, until they were well into Seekhaven Town. At last he stopped, looked at his glisker, masquer, and fettler. He grinned.

"The Treasure," he announced happily.

Mieka wrapped his arms around his head and moaned. "Nobody ever gets important points with that one!"

"*We* will." Cade was actually smiling. Excited. Looking forward to performing the second-dullest of all the Thirteen.

Someone laughed behind them, and Mieka whirled round to find Black Lightning sauntering up the street.

"We drew the Dragon," said Thierin Knottinger, with a sneering smile that almost disfigured his darkly beautiful face. "Can't think how we'll find the courage, can you, lads?"

Mieka caught a little shrug of apology from Pirro. He ignored it.

"Oh, I think we'll manage," Thierin was assured by his masquer, Kaj Seamark. "Once they get a look at what the battle wins."

"Not just a 'shadow' or 'insubstantial,'" taunted their fettler, Herris Crowkeeper.

"Substance, that's the ticket," said Knottinger. "Lots of substance."

Mieka interpreted this to mean that they would go for the sexiest, most gorgeous Fair Lady ever seen onstage, wearing as few wisps of clothing as permitted, a vision calculated to appeal to an audience in a whorehouse. There'd be no thought to the piece at all, none of Cade's introspection or reasoning, not a hint of perspective beyond the best look at the girl's gargantuan tits.

"Here's luck to it," Cade said amiably, and walked on.

As much as he wanted to fling a *Gods know you'll need it!* at Black Lightning, Mieka took his cue and smiled sweetly before running to catch up. Jeska was seething, Rafe was coldly amused, and Mieka furiously demanded, "How can you not want to take that arrogant pillock apart?"

Cade laughed. "He's still stuffing his trousers, didn't you notice? He can't get beyond 'See how big mine is.' He's still thinking with his cock. And while he does, we've nothing to worry about."

During the rest of the walk back to their lodgings, Mieka considered this. They'd made the turn from the river up the two blocks to the inn when he asked, "What happens if he ever discovers he's got a brain?"

Cade replied with a quote. "'Open things, and things will be open to you.' Do you honestly think the man who wrote that *has* a brain?"

Mieka joined in the laughter, and even bought the first round at the bar. But he kept fretting over the question of arrogance.

It was an hour after dinner, and they were up in Cade and Mieka's room going over the Tenth Peril, before he decided that Cade had *earned* his arrogance, and went on earning it every day of his life. He was the smartest man Mieka had ever met, and the most creative. Those things clasped hands more or less constantly with a tendency to anguish himself about matters Mieka found supremely silly, but maybe that was what having a brilliant mind meant. And if that were true, he was very glad he hadn't got one. As he listened to Cade outline his new plans for making "Treasure" an experience such as no audience had ever known before, Mieka knew that as irksome as he might find it to deal with, the anguishing uncertainty was necessary to Cade's art.

He doubted that Thierin had ever concerned himself with anything more consequential than which stockings to use in stuffing his crotch.

"The rhyme that's been used for fifty years or more," Cade told them, "it's not the original. Somebody rewrote it to make it scan better."

"Not exactly great poetry now, is it?" Jeska said, then recited the verse that had been the stock bit of this playlet for more than half a century.

> *As soon as fell the night*
> *Along the crumbling walls*
> *The stone a-tumbling falls*
> *To hide the golden light*
> *Ere morning touched the field*
> *Regal bells had pealed*
> *To doom the wretched thief*
> *Condemned and hanged aright*
> *Long years bring no relief*
> *Of poverty and blight*
> *Scepter, ring, and crown*
> *Ever lost and never found.*

"It's putrid," Cade agreed. "But it does what it's supposed to, which is condemn an innocent man, destroy his family, and conceal the real Treasure. We're going to change all that."

"Why didn't you tell us this when we were rehearsing back in town?" Jeska complained.

"Because there was only a one-in-thirteen chance we'd draw the thing."

The gleam in his eyes was positively fiendish. Mieka jumped to his feet and grabbed the pitcher. "Back in a tick-tock," he said, and went downstairs for more beer. He had a feeling they were going to need it.

The invitations came as Touchstone had expected: one to perform for the ladies in the Pavilion with its great copper roof, and one to Fliting Hall. Lord Kearney Fairwalk brought the elegant rolls of parchment, waxed and sealed and beribboned, when he arrived on the third morning of their stay at Seekhaven.

"Looked in at the Castle, don't you see," he explained over a late breakfast. Touchstone had been up half the night revising

"Treasure" and could work up very little enthusiasm for the coveted invitations. "How is everything so far?"

"Well," Rafe said in his laconic way, "Cade's the only one getting any sleep. I miss my wife, Jeska hasn't put a polish on his blade since we left Gallytown, and Mieka's worried that Cade wants us to quit breaking glass."

Fairwalk's pale, watery eyes suddenly took up half his face, and his already limp sandy hair seemed to wilt further. "Oh, no! You simply can't do that! I mean, it's what you're known for!"

"And if that's *all* we're known for—" Cade began.

"Ignore him," Mieka advised His Lordship. "The rest of us do. Did we say we drew the one about the Treasure? Cade wants to rewrite the whole bleedin' thing."

"He's been busy thinking again." Jeska shrugged. "It's a right bother, it is."

For a moment His Lordship was torn between the glass and the Treasure. It was odd, Mieka told himself, that sometimes he could watch the thoughts forming in the man's eyes: as if an idea was like a nutmeat to be examined for quality, put back into its shell, and replaced on the tree, and only then could he back away and understand it. There was an old saying about being unable to see the water for the waves, but that wasn't how Fairwalk's mind worked. Individual things made sense to him only as part of a larger whole.

"Curious," he said at last, and Mieka had the impression he was looking at a whole grove of walnut trees, or the entire Ocean Sea. "No one drew it last year, or the year before…"

How this mattered was of course about to be explained to them. Mieka poured more tea.

It so happened that the last descendant of the family held responsible for losing the Treasure had discovered on the last of his ancestral lands a nice seam of coal. The proceeds these five years enabled him to slink his way back to Court, though not in

Gallantrybanks where he had no place to stay, the family mansion having been sold long since. Half the nobles at Seekhaven hired rooms for the duration of Trials, invitations to guest at the Castle being rare, and thus Lord Oakapple could blend in with the crowd. And thus here he was in Seekhaven, renting rooms along with everyone else.

"But here's the interesting thing," Fairwalk concluded. "This is the first time he'll see 'Treasure' performed. The first time anyone will see it with an Oakapple in attendance. I mean to say, there hasn't been anyone of that name anywhere near the Court in longer than anyone can remember. Will he be just frightfully humiliated at the reminder, or—"

"—or pathetically grateful that somebody's finally doing the *real* version?" Cade gave Fairwalk's shoulder a gentle shake. "We're going to be in trouble, aren't we?"

He didn't sound vexed by the prospect. Mieka didn't waste mental energy trying to figure out why. Cade could never resist sharing when he'd been especially clever.

Sure enough, his next words were, "If we do the old version, Lord Oakapple is humiliated anew and probably never sets foot off his lands again—and hates us forever. Depending on how rich he is, he might be able to annoy us one way or another. If we do the new version, *my* version, he's thrilled, he's grateful, he can't do enough for us—which might be interesting, depending on how rich he is! But there are factions at Court who won't like us mucking about with one of the sacred Thirteen."

"Had you considered," Fairwalk said diffidently, "that whereas the traditional playlet isn't what one would call… erm… vigorous, don't you see—"

Mieka interrupted with a snort. "People talk, there's thunder, they talk, a flash or three of lightning, more talk, it rains, and some yobbo runs in blithering about a rockslide. Fair tingles the hairs on me neck, it does, every time!"

"Yes, of course, but you're very good at thunder and lightning, Mieka. Unbeatable, really." If that had been meant to soothe and flatter, His Lordship was much mistook. "My point is," he went on, once Mieka had given another snort, "don't you see, that Touchstone can work the piece with your flourishes, and startle everyone at the most unexpected moments—"

"Nobody ever earns enough points with 'Treasure' to make the Royal," Jeska stated.

"You could." Fairwalk took a dainty bite of toast. Mostly Gnomish though he looked, he had the small, square white teeth of a full-blood Human. Mieka wondered suddenly if those teeth were really his—and just how much Gnome he really might be. He certainly dressed with an un-Gnomish flamboyance, and spent money like a drunken Elf.

"How long since it all happened, anyway?" Jeska asked. "I mean, everybody seems to behave as if it was last fortnight."

"Hundred and fifty years, give or take," Rafe said at the same time Cade announced, "Two hundred and eighty-one years ago." When they all stared at him, he added, "It's a simple calculation, really, even though everything's been confused a-purpose. It all has to do with how King Meredan's family got and kept the throne in the first place."

"Oh Gods," Mieka whined, "spare us, won't you?"

"But it's important!"

"So was the Archduke's War," Rafe reminded him, "and look who's going to be at every performance at Trials: his very own son and heir."

"Well, that's not long enough past that they can muddle things up, now, is it?" Cade retorted. "Wait another century or so, and there'll be a Fourteenth Peril."

"Beholden unto all the Gods that we won't be around to perform it!"

"Speak for your ownself," Mieka told Rafe. "Me great-great-granny's still making everyone's life a misery, and looks to be doing so for *another* hundred and five years." Abruptly he realized that if his plans went aright, one day he would have grandchildren, and even great grandchildren, which would make him old. Gods, what a thought.

Jeska turned intense blue eyes on him. "But it's a young man's game, innit? Bein' a player. And glisking the way you do—"

"Everything still works," Mieka snapped. "Now, if nothing's been decided, and isn't likely to be in the next hour or six, I'm off."

"Stop a while, please," begged Fairwalk. "Cade's right, this is important."

"Just tell me what to do and give me the magic to do it with. See you at rehearsal."

"Mieka—"

The kitchen door to the back garden was closest. He used it.

Cade wasn't the only one who'd been doing a lot of thinking lately. This new idea, the one about grandchildren, needed contemplation. But despite himself, and despite Cade's Elsewhen where he'd seen them both old, he just couldn't picture it. More to the point, he couldn't picture *her* as anything but sixteen years old and achingly lovely, a girl to steal a man's breath and heart every time he looked at her.

Old? Never.

But that was what inevitably happened if one lived long enough, even those substantially Elfenblood, who kept their youthful looks well past the time when other races turned gray and wrinkly. Hells, his own mother still looked barely thirty. Mieka would look young, feel young, for a very long time—and Jeska was a right fool to worry about theater being a young man's game. What did a masquer have to anguish himself about? Any glisker worth his withies could make Jeska look like anybody in the world even if he could barely totter across a stage.

No, it wasn't youth that mattered. It was—he struggled with

the words, and a passing Trollwife grunted at him when he nearly bumped into her. Sidestepping, he sought out a nice little patch of grass by the river and sat down, scowling at the water.

Inspiration? Was that it? The older groups—the Enticements, Kelife and the Candlelights, even his well-loved Shorelines—they were all doing the same things they'd always done. They were still good enough for the Circuits (well, mostly), and audiences came to see them because they were comfortable, reliable, always good value. They were *safe*. But when was the last time any of them had done something new? Something original, shocking, thought-provoking, amazing?

Cade was all those things and more besides. Cade was inspired, and caught up Jeska and Rafe and Mieka in his visions. They refined Cade's insights, flashed new ideas off one another. Touchstone would never be safe and stale any more than *she* would ever be old.

No thinking about her during working hours, he reminded himself, and jumped to his feet, and ran back to the inn to share the planning of how they'd astonish the judges this time. *Mad and clever*, he reminded himself, grinning. It was all part of his job.

The last needle-fine shards of glass glittered to the stage. Mieka stalked out from behind the glisker's bench, stood between Cade and Jeska, waited for Rafe to join them, bowed, and wrenched his arm from Cade's sudden, warning grasp. He kept a wide smile on his face as Touchstone took another bow, snapping at Cade, "Leave me the fuck alone!"

The curtains drew shut. Servants, warned in advance to be armed with brooms, scurried out to sweep up the glass. In the wings, he saw Black Lightning congratulating themselves. Rather than exit stage left as all the other groups had done, Mieka spun on a heel and strode off stage right, where the remaining three groups waited in varying states of nervousness to perform their Perils.

If Cade didn't stop grabbing at his arm, he'd be experiencing *peril* in ways he'd never imagined.

"Mieka—"

"Let go of me!" he snarled.

"We had to do it the old way, we couldn't take the risk!"

He found a staircase and climbed it, two and three steps at a time, infuriated anew to find his eyes stinging. He knew Cade and the others were following him; he could hear their boots on the well-worn stone. Up the narrow spiral he ran, until at last there was nowhere to go but outside onto the crenellated walls. Excellent view of the sunset across the river, he supposed, had he been able to see through the wash of angry tears.

"Mieka."

Knuckling his eyes, he whirled round and shouted, "I couldn't *believe* it when I felt what you put into those withies— what you left out of them—*why*?"

Cade approached warily. Jeska and Rafe hovered in the doorway behind him, looking at each other and then at Mieka and then back to each other again. He wanted to chuck all three of them off the battlements. But he'd settle for breaking Cade's nose. A nice, big target. Not that anybody would notice. Might even be an improvement.

"We had to. We need the goodwill of the Court, we couldn't overset everything we've worked so hard for—"

"So you did what was *safe*!"

"I did what was necessary to win us a place on the Circuit." He paused, his long face flinching a little. "Please, Mieka. Try to understand. I can't bear to have you disappointed in me."

"Should've thought of that before you forced us to do that useless piece of shit!"

Jeska spoke up from the doorway. "It wasn't just him. It was me as well. And Rafe. And Kearney."

"And *he's* a player now, is he? Part of Touchstone?" *Something worth being part of* rang mockingly in his mind. "What the fuck does *he* know about—"

"He knows the Court," Rafe said.

Cade took a half-step forwards, one hand reaching, pleading. "Mieka, I'm sorry I didn't tell you beforehand, but I knew this would happen, I knew you wouldn't—"

"You spineless, gutless—"

Temper flashed in the gray eyes. "You want to spend the next year playing for trimmings in taverns? If you ever paid attention to anything beyond your next drink, you'd know that Jeska's mother hasn't been well for months—he needs the money! So does Rafe. He's married now. He—"

"And what of you? What is it *you* want, O Great Tregetour? Think they'll pat us on the head for being good little boys and send us off on the Ducal or Royal? *They were bored!* What they expect from us is something brilliant, something amazing—and we gave them safe and traditional and—and—" Tears threatened again and he turned to stare out at the town and the river beyond.

"Mieka…"

"You saw them," he said thickly. "You saw their faces. We could've been *anybody* up there, anybody except Touchstone. We were safe and comfortable and ordinary. Did Kearney Fairwalk take that into consideration when he told you what to do?"

"It wasn't just him. Jeska and I agreed with him. So did Rafe."

"Everybody but me. All of Touchstone except me. You let me rehearse something that *meant* something, and then for the real performance you—"

"I'm sorry," Cade repeated. "We were wrong not to tell you."

"Yeh, you were. But I'm beholden to you. For showing me what I'm worth. Find another glisker. I'm through."

"You don't mean that."

"Don't I?"

"We need you."

"I don't care. I'll stay through the invited shows, but then I'm off."

Thin, powerful fingers dug into his shoulders. "Mine you are, and mine you stay."

"Are you going to hit me now?" Mieka sneered, and Cade let him go as if scalded. "Beat me bloody to prove that you own me?" Turning, he saw anger in Cade's tightened lips and fear in Cade's pallor, but what made him want to laugh was the stricken hurt in Cade's eyes. "Go ahead!" he taunted. "C'mon, it's what you want, why not do it? Only have a care to those precious fingers, won't you—don't bruise them too bad, might interfere with writing your next piece of nice, safe, comfortable crap!"

"Mieka!"

He ignored Rafe's warning growl. "Me, I can't wait to read it! Can't wait to put it out in front of an audience and watch their eyes fog over like windowpanes!" And that reminded him of another way to hurt Cade. "What d'you think Blye will say when she finds out about this? That you listened to that mincing fribbler Fairwalk—"

Cade was no longer listening.

By now Mieka knew what an Elsewhen looked like in Cade's eyes. "Don't you fucking *dare*!" he shouted. "No escaping for you, no running off to hide in one of your dreamings! Come back here and take it, Cade!"

Rafe pushed him away and put an arm around Cade's shoulders. "Leave him be. He can't help it." His voice was soft, his blue-gray eyes intent on Cade's empty gaze. "He'll come back when he can." Then, angrily: "And you're not going anyplace. Have your tantrum as you like, you're impressing nobody—"

All at once Cade sobbed aloud, and slumped against Rafe for a moment before shoving free. He staggered towards the walls and Mieka cried out, grabbed for his arm before he could lose his balance and tumble over the side onto the courtyard cobblestones far below.

"Quill!"

Sense returned to the gray eyes. Mieka was aghast to see tears in them, and dampening his thin cheeks. "So... so I'm Quill again, am I?"

"What did you see? And don't say 'nothing' or I really will leave," he threatened.

"It's that dream I kept having... the same one, over and over..."

"The one where you hated me."

He nodded.

"Why? You have to tell me why, Quill—"

"Don't make me tell you, Mieka, I can't, I just can't—" He almost touched Mieka's face but then jerked his hand back, as if touching would hurt—or as if he feared that Mieka might not be real. "Don't leave," he whispered. "Please."

"Rafe!" Jeska called from the doorway. "They're finished, they want us downstairs! Now!"

Cade seemed not to have heard. "Please." Fresh tears smeared his face.

Mieka threw his arms around him, and felt him trembling. "I won't, you know I won't. You just make me so damn *furious* sometimes, Quill—c'mon, it's all right, we're fine—what you saw, that's never going to happen. I'm still here, and we're still us."

"Y-you promise?"

"I promise." Remembering what Blye had said last year— *clever and mad*—he gave Cayden his most impudent grin. "No yellow shirts, not ever!"

Back in Fliting Hall they learned that safe, comfortable, and traditional had scraped enough points for first flight. On the Winterly.

Black Lightning, with their garish and vulgar "Dragon," had won third flight on the Ducal.

There was a reception in the torch-lit courtyard from which it took half an hour to disentangle themselves. Eventually they made it to the gates, and across the moat, and back into town. Elf-light glowed golden from each corner streetlamp; Mieka made it his mission to kick the metal base of every single one.

"Two points," Rafe kept muttering. "Two lousy, gods-damned, stupid, miserable, miscreated, fucking points—"

"And I know exactly how they got those points," Mieka fumed as he assaulted another lamppost. "One for each breast."

"Stop that," Cade said absently. "You'll break a toe."

"I don't think it was just the tits, Mieka," Jeska said. "One for them, but one for that glimpse of her—" He broke off and mimed sudden extravagant enlightenment. "Good Lord and Lady and all the Angels! Do you think it wasn't hers at all?"

Mieka caught on at once. "Gods, Jeska, you're right! It wasn't hers, it was Kaj Seamark's!"

"Loose, I'd wager," Rafe contributed.

Cade nodded wisely. "Poxed, too."

It set them to laughing—not that any of them felt like laughing, but it was better than screaming, at least until they got back to their inn's taproom and into several bottles of brandy.

"You down there!" someone yelled from an upper window. "There's decent folk what's tryin' to sleep!"

A voice from the end of the street shouted back, "And we're *indecent* folk what's tryin' to find a drink!"

Vered's long white-gold hair was unmistakable by lamplight. The other Shadowshapers were with him.

"Oy, Miek! We're buying!" Chat called out.

Mieka glanced quickly at Cade, saw him nod, then called back, "Beholden, Chat! Our digs, then! Best brandy in Seekhaven!"

They spent the rest of the night getting as roundly drunk as if they'd *all* won first flight on the Royal. Their innkeeper and his wife and their Trollwife were horrified that "their boys" had been cheated, so along with the free brandy came dinner for eight, and to hells with the vouchers. They ate, drank, and sang—and complained—long into the night, and to hells with protests from the neighbors, as well.

The next morning, Mieka came to in the back garden, curled on a blanket on the grass, sun dappling down through a beech tree overhead. Nearby was the sound of someone being very sick into the bushes. Mieka sat up, and regretted it.

"Absolutely *no* head for liquor," said Chat as he levered Vered upright and gave him a glass of water. Catching sight of Mieka, he asked, "Alive, then, are you?"

"Matter of opinion."

Vered groaned and bent over the bushes again.

Chat left him to it, ambling over to where Mieka sat holding his head between his hands. "Twenty-four years old, he is, you'd think the idea might've got through by now. You'll come to our show tomorrow night? We'll leave word at the door. No other group but Touchstone gets in, and the best seats. You have to be there, Miek."

"Beholden. Why?"

"We're all agreed. We—" Hearing another moan, he hurried back to Vered, who had swayed to his feet. There was a delicate greenish cast to his dark skin as he half-fell into Chat's arms, and his long, pale hair was matted around his face. "Steady on, mate. A prickling of Master Bellgloss's best, and you'll be fit again. Sorry, Mieka, must get something into him or he'll be neither use nor ornament for days."

Mieka waved them away. Once the gate latch snicked behind them, he indulged himself with a low whimper. A bit of bluethorn and he'd be lively enough by the time of their show for the ladies tonight, but this headache was like to a wyvern clawing its way out his eye sockets.

"For such a scrawny little thing," said a voice high above him, "you can guzzle more brandy than anyone I've ever known." A hand appeared in front of his face. He grasped it and was hauled to his feet. The change in altitude was sick-making. "Can you walk, or do you want Rafe to carry you the way he just did Jeska?"

It was tempting, but—"Point me to the stairs."

Cade chuckled and slung a supporting arm around his back. "You really oughtn't to get quite so paved, y'know. You miss quite a bit. Like Kearney coming by earlier—"

Surely it couldn't be more than slightly past dawn. The angle of the sunlight said otherwise. He felt as if he hadn't slept more than a few minutes. "There was an 'earlier'?"

"Several hours of it. Anyway, a certain man had a word with a Crown servant who talked to a Steward who sent another servant to speak to one of Kearney's new footmen, who—"

"Out with it!" he snapped.

"We have a commission."

"A what?"

"In the arts—painting, sculpture, poetry, and the like—when someone pays for a particular work in advance, it's called a 'commission.' And we have one, from Lord Oakapple his very own self. We're to write and perform the real version of the Treasure. And be paid for it!"

Mieka squinted upwards just as they were coming out from the shadow of a tree. The sunlight stabbed right into his brain. "Tell me this again when I can care."

5

Opportunity, Cayden called it. No greater compliment, no better indication of Touchstone's growing importance than this commission from Lord Oakapple.

However Mieka might try to look at it from different angles—and admittedly he didn't try very hard—he could see it only one way: Lord Kearney Fairwalk was attempting to become the fifth member of Touchstone.

What he did for them as their manager ought to have made Mieka feel grateful, he knew. But the man was being paid, wasn't he? Tenpence of every hundred Touchstone earned, that was Fairwalk's share. He saw to the private bookings on the Circuit and the contracts with venues in Gallantrybanks, took care of transporting them and their equipment, made sure they had decent lodgings and food, doled out regular portions of their money to their families, arranged for publicity, and—this was the thing Mieka truly was beholden for, though it had nothing to do with earning money—arranged for the Crown to cancel the contract held by that Prickspur snarge up near Dolven Wold, the man who had refused to allow Mieka under his roof. There had been legal terms for it, and a mortifying afternoon this spring when Mieka had had to give evidence to a Crown attorney, but

King Meredan took the comfort of his players personally. Not only had the contract been canceled, but Prickspur had also been ordered to return all the money. The route had been changed, other accommodations had been found, and the upshot was that Prickspur now had another reason to hate Elves. Without His Lordship's Court connections, Prickspur would still be counting up coin while forbidding anyone of Elfenblood inside his doors. And for Fairwalk's intervention, Mieka truly was grateful.

But Fairwalk had begun insinuating himself into the group's performances. It had been his suggestion that they do the traditional version of "Treasure" rather than the one Cade had been working on. Their reputation as innovators had suffered. Mieka stubbornly believed that Cade's version, with the text altered to fit the oldest form of the poem, would have put them onto the Ducal, perhaps even the Royal. Now Lord Oakapple had commissioned them to write and perform the work Cade's way. Fairwalk's involvement in this handsome offer was a bit murky, and Mieka suspected there were things he wasn't saying, and that it hadn't been so indirectly accomplished as he made it out to be. Mieka knew he oughtn't to complain, or even think about complaining, but this was another example of Fairwalk's well-kept fingers twitching strings he had no business even touching.

The long and the short of it was that he was beginning to tell them what to do and how to do it. Worse, Cayden was heeding him.

Mieka approved of the way His Lordship encouraged Cade, who for all his arrogance could be so appallingly insecure about his work. The opinion of an educated, cultured, titled gentleman was precisely what he needed to buck him up when he began to fret. Telling him that his work was good, however, was vastly different from telling him what that work ought to be.

And why, Mieka grumbled to himself as they walked to Seekhaven Castle to perform for the ladies of the Court, couldn't

Cade find support enough within Touchstone itself? They didn't jeer at his sometimes peculiar schemes—well, mayhap they did, a little, but it was all in service of making the work the best it could be. It wasn't as if the rest of them had ever flat-out refused to play a piece the way he wanted it done—well, Jeska sometimes rejected the interpretation of a line or two, and on that very first night in Gowerion, Mieka had turned the stale old "Sailor's Sweetheart" into a rollicking comedy (which they still performed, Mieka's way, to thunderous applause). Still, that was how it should be: contributing, participating, not standing humbly about waiting for Cade to pull strings and make them dance the way he wanted.

Now it looked as if Fairwalk was busy tying strings onto Cade. Mieka didn't like it, not one bit.

Tonight's performance was a chance to soothe their bruises. The ladies of the Court had invited them to the Pavilion, a huge open-air structure of thirteen columns holding up a vast copper cone of a roof. Over supper in the back garden of the inn, Jeska had argued that they could use the show to redeem their reputation as original and daring performers. Mieka had said simply that if Cade gave him the magic to do it with, he'd blow the roof off the columns. Rafe had agreed, with one of those steady, piercing stares that usually ignited defiance in Cade's eyes before he relented with a nod.

There had been plenty of defiance this time, but no nod. They wouldn't be doing "Doorways," because it wasn't yet perfect.

"Perfect in whose opinion?" Mieka had snarled. "Fairwalk's?"

Mieka had once observed that he and Cade had a talent for saying exactly the wrong thing to each other at the worst possible time. Cade threw a plate of sausages across the yard and stormed upstairs. As quickly as if conjured, a pounce of cats appeared to devour the sausages.

"That's us later, then, innit?" Jeska muttered, nodding to the feast. "And in case anybody was wondering, I don't mean the cats."

Rafe turned to Mieka. "What's left in the withies? Anything you and I can use tonight?"

He considered. "I've two from the 'Doorways' rehearsal. A bit lingering from 'Treasure.'"

"Thunder and lightning?" Jeska snorted. "Fine, if all the doors lead into rainstorms."

"Yet only think about what he primed into them this afternoon for 'Hidden Cottage,'" Rafe suggested. "Jeska's fool of a lordling goes a-wandering, doesn't he?"

Mieka felt a smile tug the corners of his mouth. He knew, and Rafe knew, and Jeska knew—and Cade should have learned by now—that Mieka had enough magic of his own to do more than tweak a withie. Suddenly they were all grinning at one another. Jeska went back to the kitchen for more beer, and over new pints they planned the further education of Cayden Silversun.

They had done "Hidden Cottage" last year as a straightforward piece for the lords and gentlemen of the Court (boring Mieka witless in the process: not a laugh, leave alone an idea, in the whole agonizingly sincere production). This time Cade had planned to make it their more accustomed interpretation. The basics of the plot remained: arranged marriage, kidnapped girl, fleeing young lord, long journey, forest cottage, love at first sight, triumphant return. The emphasis, however, would be on the comedy. The journey portion always let Mieka indulge himself with creating fanciful landscapes while Jeska tripped over everything in sight, including, eventually, the pig that Rafe had suggested could be the poor kidnapped girl's company in her captivity. Sometimes Jeska played the young man as so nearsighted that he addressed half his lovelorn lines to the pig. Mieka had grown quite fond of that pig. Whatever they decided to do with the playlet on any given night, audiences roared.

That wouldn't be happening tonight. "Hidden Cottage" was

what Cade thought they would do. He'd primed the withies to provide appropriate scenery, sensation, emotion. But by using the magic within these, and leftovers from others, Touchstone would be giving the ladies something entirely different.

Many things were the same as last year. Footmen showed up to carry their glass baskets and escort them to the "secret" performance. (Everyone knew what was going on, but everyone pretended it was rash and daring for women to view theater, so there were masks and other silly disguises.) Little redheaded Lady Torren was again their guide, though the golden bracelet on one wrist proclaimed that she was now bespoken; Mieka eyed Cade to see how he felt about this, for last year Her Ladyship had been warmly disposed to the tall, lanky tregetour. Cade didn't even seem to notice her beyond a smile of greeting. He wouldn't come back to the lodgings reeking of her lavender scent again; that was for certain sure. Mieka wondered if Princess Iamina would disrupt things the way she had last year, but one glance from the stage as he set up the glass baskets showed him the famous yellow pearl-and-diamond flower prominently displayed on an intoxicated-looking hat that sported a veil across her face. She was seated fifth-row center with her ladies, and seemed disposed to behave herself. He rather hoped she'd give him an excuse to terrify her the way he'd done last year with the dragon—and then he decided he didn't need any excuses, and he'd play it full out no matter who was in the audience. He and Rafe and Jeska were about to be wading through shit so deep with Cayden that even Royal outrage would be like unto skipping across a meadow of sweet clover.

The three of them traded one last confirming glance as the crowd settled. *Yes.* Nobody announced them; everybody knew they were here to see Touchstone. Before Cade could draw breath to announce the piece, Rafe sent a quiver of magic swirling round the Pavilion. Startled, but only a little, Cade flattened his palms to the inlaid wood of his lectern, smiled slightly at Mieka, and readied himself to watch.

If Mieka had had any lingering doubts, the reminder that Cade would only ever *watch* drowned them like gnats in a rain shower. One day, Mieka vowed as he selected his withies, one day the man would experience the whole of something. Mieka didn't know how he'd accomplish it, but if necessary, he'd use Cade's own magic to force him into it.

But that night Cade's magic, primed for "Hidden Cottage," was in Mieka's clever hands modified to the service of "Doorways." The creation of assorted environments for the young lord to lose himself in was not so very different from crafting worlds behind doors. He had enough from the rehearsal to make those doors, and the slanting hallway that moved forwards on the stage as Jeska moved into it—a tricky little bit of skewing the perspective that he didn't get quite right, though nobody but the four of them would know the difference. That Jeska wore his own face, body, and simple clothes meant there was just that much more for Mieka to work with in fashioning the visions that spun out from those doors as Jeska opened them, one by one.

A beautiful wife, a family, a home, a life no man in his right thoughts would turn from. Yet he did turn from it, unsatisfied. Scholarly solitude high in a castle tower, surrounded by books; dragging himself, drunk and filthy, through a city street; striding through richly golden fields he'd ploughed and planted; lazing on pillows aboard a pleasure barge, nibbling berries and sipping wine, surrounded by beautiful girls; white-robed in the paneled severity of a law court, eloquent in defense of the innocent; wearing red robes as he pointed a stern finger at the guilty; stalking about a gigantic stage shouting *This is a* comedy, *you talentless snarge, so why am I not laughing*—

Love and disillusion and loneliness and disgust, glutted sensuality and utter boredom, fury, delight—and flickering around and through them the scents of grass in the sunshine, of parchment and book-binding leather, cheap alcohol and vomit, the sounds of the river and the laughter of children, the feel of silk and flowers, of sickness, of a sheaf of folio pages clenched in one hand. The doors kept opening and the visions kept coming, each of them possible, and with them the tastes of pleasure and failure and satisfaction and despair.

And then the final door, the one they had argued about. Make it happy and lovely with lots of bright colors and pretty scents and bells tinkling in the distance—or leave it blurry, misted with shadows that drew the minds and imaginations of the audience right into the play? This door was the one that accompanied the lines about choosing *this* life, every morning before he woke from his dream of doorways: this life, and none other. But should they give a specific vision, or allow each woman to fill in the empty places for herself?

Vered Goldbraider had wanted his audience to think about what they most desired; Rauel Kevelock had given them fleeting moments of emotional fulfilment. Without Cade to contend that the more detailed the experience, the more satisfying it would be, Mieka, Rafe, and Jeska had decided to make the audience create its own experience: *This life, and none other*.

As Jeska walked through the magic-hazed doorway and vanished, every woman in the Pavilion gave voice to a cry or a shout or a sob or a laugh, and Mieka knew he and Rafe had crafted it perfectly. They had seen, felt, heard, sensed—for a few instants *lived*—whichever life their instincts yearned towards. They would remember it.

Mieka heard the applause as if from a great distance. He was exhausted. He hadn't danced his way through this one—too risky. He'd had to reach for and explore instantly withies that hadn't been distinctively primed for this piece, and if necessary choose another without faltering. The intensity of concentration and caution left him drenched in sweat even in the cool midnight air. He didn't have the energy to leap over the glisker's bench and the glass baskets when Touchstone gathered onstage to bow.

Cade wore the kind of smile a mountain cat might smile while choosing especially succulent chunks of raw meat. Mieka could already feel the bite marks.

Offstage, someone came up to him with a large goblet of wine. He drained it down his throat. Then he smiled, handed the cup back to the serving girl, stripped off his shirt, twisted it, and wrung the sweat into the glass. He saw in her eyes—and the eyes of every woman within twenty feet of him—that bedding down alone was his only choice tonight. It wasn't only that selecting any of these ladies—or any two, or three—would mortally offend the rest. He knew himself to be so tired that he'd never be able to do justice to even one. So he distributed a flourishy bow amongst them, slung his shirt over his shoulder, and started across the grass towards the Castle.

"Hold up," Rafe called softly.

Jeska was nowhere to be seen. Well, he hadn't worked as hard as Mieka or Rafe tonight, either. The fettler was looking a bit frayed around the edges, but satisfied. Cade, striding along beside him, still wore the smile.

Mieka sighed.

"I'd kill you right now," Cade said in surprisingly mild tones, "but you're too knackered to appreciate it." And with that he took off his own jacket and draped it around Mieka's bare shoulders. "No sense getting a start on a cold when we've the whole Winterly ahead of us for you to get sick in."

He could almost interpret that as forgiveness. He might have asked, but the boys carrying their crated glass baskets had caught them up, and all was silence amongst the three of them on the way back to their lodgings. It wasn't until Rafe had gone to bed and they were in their own room that Cade spoke.

"I have a few memories of having said this before, but it's worth repeating. Don't ever do that again."

Mieka shrugged off the jacket. "Don't make us do it again, and we won't."

The candle Cade had lit with a glimmer of blue Wizardfire flared, then died out. Mieka snorted at the betraying reaction, then rolled himself into a light blanket before collapsing onto his bed.

A long while later, Cade murmured, "I *would* kill you, but it was brilliant."

"Still don't understand yet, do you?" Mieka asked. "Understand what?"

"It *was* brilliant, yeh. It was *yours*. Dream sweet, Quill."

Even after their triumph of the night before—and they knew by the looks they were given that word had flashed through the whole of Seekhaven Castle—it was humiliating to walk into Fliting Hall, scene of their defeat by Black Lightning. Specifically invited by the Shadowshapers to the performance, Touchstone frustled up in their best clothes and walked up to the gates as if they and not Black Lightning had won third flight on the Ducal Circuit. No other group was present. The Shadowshapers were letting it be known that they considered Touchstone to be the only other players whose opinions were worth anything.

As they approached Fliting Hall, shoulder-to-shoulder, off to one side Kaj Seamark and Thierin Knottinger were oozing through the crowd. Mieka nudged Cade in the ribs and pointed. The briefest suggestion of a smile twitched the long mouth before he widened his gray eyes to anxious innocence and plucked timidly at the sleeve of a nearby footman.

"Dreadfully sorry, but—I think I recognize those men over there, the dark one in green and the fair one with the curling hair."

"I don't think they've been invited," Mieka contributed.

But not even he would have dared what Cade said next, in a low, worried voice that brought a terrible frown to the footman's young face.

"Efters," Cade whispered.

"Muchly beholden," said the footman, and hurried off.

Mieka bent his head to keep his face hidden, and shook with silent laughter. "Gods, Quill, you are just wicked cruel," he said at last.

"Did I lie?" Cade challenged grimly. "All a matter of interpretation, innit?"

Efters were thieves who robbed theater patrons before and after a performance—and sometimes during. Mieka tiptoed to see over the crowd, and nearly choked on giggles as Thierin and Kaj were marched crisply down the cobbles to the front gates.

Touchstone's seats were sixth row, just left of center, three rows back from the King Himself. The theater settled quickly. Glass globes of light over each door dimmed, the sea-green and brown curtains parted, and the Shadowshapers walked onstage. The lords and gentlemen of the Court were too sophisticated to greet them with applause, but the excited murmurs that rippled through the crowd were as good as a standing ovation. Sakary and Chat took their places, Vered and Rauel stayed where they were at center stage, and the variance from the usual configuration caused renewed whispers. Vered's blazing eyes searched the theater, found Touchstone, and a brief, broad grin decorated his face.

"'A Life in a Day,'" he announced.

For the first time ever while he watched a performance, Mieka tried to do what Cade did, to keep a portion of himself apart and figure out what they were doing, how it all worked. He couldn't. The Shadowshapers were that good. He knew them all, had shared his whiskey and their wagon; Chat was a good friend, Vered and Rauel were becoming so, and Sakary was even talking to him these days (as much as Sakary ever talked to anybody—and what was it about fettlers, he wondered, that made them so reticent?). But when they were onstage, they became Players: the Shadowshapers, the best in the Kingdom, and he defied even Cade Silversun to resist them.

He thought all this in the few seconds of his struggle to stay at least partially removed, a struggle he didn't mind losing. The Shadowshapers were that good.

Afterwards, he could understand why they'd used a configuration nobody had ever used before: both tregetour/masquers onstage, Chat's withies becasting each of them according to their roles in the piece. As the signature shadows wafted through Fliting Hall, Mieka saw Rauel quietly move upstage a few paces and bite his lip. They were all nervous. Chat especially was concentrating on the glass baskets of withies, arranged tonight with a visible space between one grouping and the other, keeping the two separate according to which of the tregetours had primed them. And he was using both hands, the way Mieka always did but few others could. Mieka reminded himself to congratulate his friend on this new dexterity. And then he forgot everything else as the play surrounded him.

An ordinary day. Vered wore a middle-class merchant's plain, neat clothing and a nondescript face to match, hiding his fierce black eyes and dark skin and white-gold hair. Walking into a cozy little kitchen, stretching, peering out the window to judge the weather. Sitting down to tea and toast, a broadsheet before him on the table. Shouldering into his coat. Pulling on his gloves. Walking out his front door. All of it perfectly commonplace, the sort of thing thousands of men did every day.

He never saw the carriage that ran him down and left him broken and bloodied in the street.

It was done in perfect silence. It was done without any emotion at all.

There were scents of cinnamon tea and toasted bread. There was warmth on shoulders and back as he donned his coat. There was a slight breeze touching skin as the door opened, and then a few droplets of rain that brought a vague wish for a cap. But there were no sounds of knife scraping butter and jam onto the toast (though there was a faint flavor of raspberries), no click of a closing door, no street noises, not so much as a footstep. The horse trampled him in silence. Bright yellow wheels crushed his bones without sound. The garish crimson carriage bumped over his body onto the cobbles and lurched away into deathly quiet shadows.

The pain was real, and piercing. Back, legs, arms, belly, one cheek where a hoof slashed his flesh—but there was no emotion.

The shadows shifted, the flashing agony was gone, and Rauel, wearing the same nondescript face and plain, neat clothes, was seated at the breakfast table.

"I never thought. I never think. And today I'm going to die. I didn't know. Does anyone?"

This time there was emotion—great searing spasms of regret, fear, fury, denial. He mourned what he had done and what he had left undone. He pounded his fists on the table and set the plates and cup rattling right onto the floor to shatter with a sound like branches cracking in a windstorm. He raged at everyone and everything and cursed the Lord and Lady and Angels and all the Old Gods for doing this to him. When the shadows melted from the other side of the stage, and he saw his own ruined and dying body in the street, he covered his face with his hands and wept.

The pain was twofold now—physical and emotional, joined inextricably as the two voices joined, one from each side of the stage.

"I didn't know. I never thought. All the things I ever did, all the things I could have done, should have done—"

Then a gasp of a death rattle, and an abrupt blackness.

The withdrawal of the magic was so wrenching that Mieka

trembled. The audience, shocked and horrified, was a rustling and muttering thing that seethed softly at first and then more and more loudly as the shadows dissipated to reveal the four players standing together onstage: proud, defiant, knowing they had done something catastrophic to every man there.

It was Cade who pushed himself to his feet and began to applaud. Mieka swayed upright to stand beside him, arms above his head as he clapped. Others joined them, and it wasn't long before every one of the four hundred men present were giving the Shadowshapers an ovation that rattled the glass globes above the doorways.

All at once, Chattim flung a withie into the air. It twirled upwards, arcing high above the stage, and abruptly shattered. The Shadowshapers bowed as motes of bright glass drifted down onto their shoulders, and when they straightened up they were grinning.

The reference and the tribute were unmistakable. Mieka felt his jaw drop a little, felt Cade give a violent start of surprise beside him. Nobody else understood why Touchstone had been singled out this way, but Mieka and Cade did—and Mieka had to remind himself to remember that he was supposed to have been asleep at the time, he wasn't supposed to know that it was Cade who had provided the spark of an idea that had resulted in this performance.

It was quite a while before they could extricate themselves from the tumult. Buffeted about, with many mumbled apologies, they finally stumbled out a door, down some steps, and within a few strides there was relative quiet, and soft grass beneath their boots. They walked on for a ways, with no idea where they were inside Seekhaven Castle, until the noise had faded behind them.

Mieka looked up at Cade, then at Rafe and Jeska. They were all shaken.

"I've never seen anyone do anything that dangerous," Jeska murmured. "I think they might just owe you their skins, Cade."

"If you hadn't stood up—" Rafe shook his head.

"Sakary had a little left in reserve," Cade told them. "Didn't you feel it? He was still holding on to the magic through the shadows. It was incredible."

Mieka caught his breath. "You mean if the crowd had come at them, he could have stopped them?"

"That's exactly what I mean."

"I couldn't have done it," Rafe said. "No disrespecting meant to your magic, Cade, or your use of it, Mieka, but that's beyond what any fettler should ever be called on to do."

"They planned it that way." Cade paced ahead of them into the tree-strewn grounds. Then he spun, arms outstretched. "Couldn't you *feel* it? It was Rauel's magic Sakary saved to use if he had to. From the right-hand baskets. Rauel's withies, not Vered's." He gave a harsh laugh. "Knowing Vered, he would've welcomed a riot! But Rauel gave Chattim what might be needed. It was there for Sakary to use, just in case. Gorgeous!"

"Insane," Rafe stated.

"You really sensed all that?" Jeska asked.

Cade nodded. "They almost got me, I'll admit that. It's a powerful piece of work."

But he never let anything touch him. Mieka folded his arms around himself, shivering in the night chill. Nothing touched Cade: not even the greatest group in the Kingdom, and certainly not Touchstone. Never allowing himself to be caught up in the magic, his brain always bubbling away until steam came out his ears, forever picking things apart to find out how they worked. One day, Mieka swore to himself, one day—

Cade was still talking. "—set every other group to wondering if two masquers isn't the way to go in future? I mean, it wasn't just a stunt. It could've been that they were flaunting the fact that they can do it, but—"

"Recall, please," Jeska said in the accent he reserved for

portraying the haughtiest of stick-up-his-bum lords, "that both of them are also tregetours. They made their own magic to be used on themselves."

"In case you were thinking of hiring another masquer," Rafe added maliciously.

Cade threw back his head and laughed. "Or another tregetour? Or maybe learn how to do the masquery myself? Oh, yeh, that's what'll happen!"

"Imagine our delight," Jeska said, still a bit coldly.

"Oy! Miek! Why are we forever runnin' after you, eh?" Chattim panted to a stop beside them and cuffed Mieka genially on one arm. "You'll miss the party!"

"Not in this lifetime," he declared, knowing Cade would catch the reference. "Where to?"

"Our lodgings," said Rauel, who had one arm slung across Vered's shoulders as if they had never exchanged a belligerent word in their lives.

"Not the same as last year," Chat hastened to add. "Much better drinks!"

"We owe you," Vered said. "'Twas the two of us at each other's throats over this one, y'know, until you set us right."

"Not two pieces, but one," Rauel affirmed. "Woven together, like."

"And never mind the trouble it caused," Sakary muttered, but only for form's sake. He knew as well as everyone else what the Shadowshapers had accomplished tonight.

"C'mon," Vered urged. "Took half an age to find you— shouldn't've run off like that, should you?—and I'm all the thirstier for it."

"Everybody will be there," Chat told Mieka. "And two or three drinks ahead of us by now."

"Not everybody," Mieka confided. "Unless you want to stop in at the local quod and pick up half of Black fucking Lightning."

6

"Quill?"

"Go 'way."

"No, really, you have to get up. We're off to High Chapel in half an hour."

Cade buried his face in his pillow. "Have fun."

"We missed it last year. We have to go."

Was he expected to bow his gratitude to Whomever or Whatever for giving them first flight on the Winterly instead of the Ducal or Royal they deserved? Not bleedin' likely.

"Quill."

"No," he mumbled, and turned onto his side with the covers over his head.

"Lady Torren will be there."

"She's bespoken now."

"Ha! So you *did* notice!"

Of course he'd noticed. Who could forget that red hair and silky skin? Who could forget making love to her? Who could forget hearing her say afterwards, *"You're nothing like your father"*?

Thinking of whom—Zekien Silversun had once more managed to avoid his elder son completely. Cade had glimpsed him last night at Fliting Hall before the Shadowshapers' performance, attending upon Prince Ashgar. There'd been no words exchanged, not even a nod of greeting. What did Cade have to do before his father acknowledged his existence someplace other than the privacy of Number Eight, Redpebble Square?

He looked up, squinted round the room, and saw Mieka seated on the other bed. Bright-eyed, smoothly shaven, none the worse for last night's party, the sight of him was a profound annoyance.

"We've two choices, y'know," Mieka told him. "We can get there a-times, and everybody'll be looking at us, and we can brazen it out. Or we can get there late, and sit in the back where nobody will notice us, and sneak out as soon as the clasp-hands and chanting's done."

Cade grunted.

Mieka said casually, "Or, you're right, we could not go at all."

He knew precisely what sort of smirks and falsely pitying glances would be targeted at them. The notion of smiling back, shrugging, saying *Much beholden* to those who commiserated, as if losing to Black fucking Lightning didn't hurt like six different hells—it was unspeakable. But if no one saw them, everyone would think they'd stopped away out of shame.

Cade wasn't ashamed. He agreed with Kearney that the traditional version of "Treasure" had been the wiser move, and he regretted not having informed Mieka beforehand, and if he blamed anyone, it wasn't himself for not having given Mieka more work with. He blamed the Stewards and their incomprehensible favoring of Black Lightning. No, it wasn't his fault and he wasn't ashamed. He was furious.

Mieka, watching him carefully, nodded. "That's the way," he encouraged. "Wear the blue-gray jacket, won't you? There's a good lad." He bounded off the bed and was out the door before Cade could snarl that he wasn't a five-year-old to be congratulated as if he'd just learned to tie his bootlaces all by himself.

He washed, shaved, slid into last year's jacket, and went with his partners to High Chapel. Or, rather, he went with them as far as the courtyard of High Chapel.

Mieka spent the whole walk bemoaning that he'd had no breakfast. Jeska kept reassuring him that right after services, they'd buy some ale and find a congenial spot on the river and dig in to the bread, cheese, sausages, and fruit packed for them by the inn's Trollwife. Rafe kept swinging the wicker basket of food in front of Mieka to coax him along the streets, like a chew-toy tempting a puppy. They were in the crowd moving slowly towards the huge carved doors when Mieka suddenly lurched against Cade, making him stumble into an overdressed matron and her three unlovely daughters. While Cade was apologizing, Mieka snatched the basket from Rafe, stuck his face inside it, and proceeded very noisily to yark.

The immediate vicinity became abruptly uncrowded. Mieka sank pitiably to his knees, still retching into the basket.

"Are you all right?" Jeska was all sweet solicitude, a hand patting Mieka's shoulder.

"Oh, the poor lad!" someone said.

Rafe crouched beside the suffering Elf. "Bit too much to drink last night, eh?"

The boy raised his head, tears streaming from those big, soft, innocent eyes, and whimpered, "I think I'm better now."

"Should we go?" Cade asked, concern and suspicion knotting his brows.

All at once Mieka bounced to his feet, shook back his hair, and distributed a dazzling smile all round. "No, I'm fine. Still hungry, though."

And with that he reached into the basket and withdrew a gnaw of bread soaked with something brown, liquid, and lumpy.

Which he happily stuffed into his mouth.

The immediate vicinity became abruptly vacant. Jeska looked

round the empty courtyard and grinned at Mieka. Rafe stifled laughter behind one hand.

Cade *knew* it was sausage gravy. He'd seen it in a cauldron on the kitchen stove not twenty minutes ago. He'd watched the Trollwife seal up a jar of it and put it in the basket. He *knew* what it was. What it *looked* like, however…

"That is without question the most revolting thing I've ever seen," he announced. But he heard the tremor in his voice that meant his mad little glisker had done it to him again.

"Worked, dinnit?" Mieka asked indistinctly, then swallowed, giggled, and dangled the basket in front of Cade's face. "C'mon, let's go eat!"

That night Touchstone performed "Doorways" in Fliting Hall for the gentlemen of the Court—with Cade's full knowledge and cooperation this time. Touchstone's was, in fact, the honor of giving the final performance at Seekhaven that year.

"It ought to have been the Enticements," Cade heard one of the Stewards say backstage after the show. "A farewell performance."

His companion gave a bark of laughter as they approached the drinks table. "Eh, who wants to see those tired old crambazzles?"

Cade kept his back carefully turned, and took a long time to decide which of the eight different fruit brandies he wanted the serving girl to pour.

"Their masquer wanted one more go at Trials, though, didn't he? Said they could be great again."

"They should've gone out on top, or near it—and that was at least two Trials ago. Their Second Peril this year was just embarrassing."

"People still want to see them. People will still pay for a ticket—"

"Apricot, p'rhaps, sir?" asked the girl, holding up yet another bottle, her professional smile growing a trifle strained. Cade nodded mindlessly and accepted the glass she poured out.

"So why didn't you and the others give them the necessary points?"

"Because there would've been a bloody riot if they'd taken a spot better taken by someone else. Still, we couldn't let them come in dead last. They've friends at Court. This way, they're just barely out of the Winterly, so they've salvaged a bit of dignity."

"But they're through. Everybody knows it now."

The Steward gave a reminiscent sigh. "They were great, in their day."

Beaten, broken, but not knowing it was time to hang it up... Cade repressed a shiver. The Shorelines, Redprong and Trinder, Kelife, Cobbald Close Players—all veterans like the Enticements, none of them aware (or admitting) that their day was past. Still, if all of them left the Circuits, who would take their places? The Nightrunners, who'd garnered even fewer points than the Enticements? Cade's lip curled. At least the older groups were professionals who, though past their prime, could yet provide a decent show. They weren't what they had been, and never would be again, but there was talent remaining in them. If they quit the Circuits, stopped coming to Trials, who would there be for Touchstone to beat?

He knew the answer to that one.

He'd heard that someone at the Castle gates had recognized Thierin Knottinger and Kaj Seamark, so they hadn't spent the night in quod after all. Pity. They'd be leaving on the Ducal Circuit soon, so at least Cade wouldn't be running into them in Gallantrybanks... while Touchstone waited through the long summer months and half the autumn for the Winterly to commence.

He didn't need anyone to tell him that it wouldn't stop

hurting until next year at Trials, when Touchstone blasted Black fucking Lightning off the Fliting Hall stage.

The next morning he waved farewell to Rafe and Jeska as they set off for home with the Shadowshapers. Cade would be returning to Fairwalk Manor, the better to scour Kearney's library for references he could use while rewriting "Treasure"—and this time there'd be no thorn to distract him.

"When's His Lordship collecting you?"

He glanced down at Mieka, who would be leaving at noon on the public coach for Frimham. "An hour or so."

"You won't have *Lost Withies* to hand at Fairwalk Manor," Mieka fretted. "D'you really think you'll find enough to work with?"

Cade shrugged and led the way back inside. The Trollwife was just waddling into the taproom, carrying a tray laden with huge pot of tea and two cups plus a plate of various herb breads, on the chance that they'd grown peckish in the hour since breakfast. They took stools at the bar and expressed their gratitude, but the moment she was back in the kitchen, Mieka made a face at the steaming cup of tea Cade poured out for him.

"Not a drop left of Auntie Brishen's whiskey these three days gone," he mourned, "or I'd be finishing it off. If we're to make a practice of sharing with Chat and all that lot, next year it'll have to be half a barrel for the ride here and another half for the ride back." Raising his cup in morose salute, he said, "You should've asked Rafe to tell Dery to send you your book."

"Trust my copy of *Lost Withies* to the Royal Post? Not bleedin' likely! I'll be all right without it. I think I've memorized half of it by now, anyway."

"Someday, y'know, you'll wear out your brain with thinking all the time." Mieka chuckled as he slathered butter on a slice of bread. "You're already planning the piece in your head, aren't you?"

"I've an idea or three. The difference is that before, I worked on it for my own curiosity. Now that there's a commission, I have to consider Lord Oakapple, and—"

"Quill!" Mieka looked horrified and set down the bread untasted. "Don't write it because you think it's what somebody else wants! Write it because you've no choice *but* to write it—and write it the way you have to write it or you'll end up hating it and eventually yourself."

The vehemence startled him. "When did you start pondering the way I write?"

"Since before that night in Gowerion," he stated. "I know what's real. I know what's honest. Look at Blye with her glasswork. Does she love the stuff she does for money?"

"Hells, no."

"All right, then. Those little boxes she made for our first Trials medals—she loved making them and it shows in how beautiful they are. They each have a bit of her in them—and that's what you're afraid of."

Mystification was a condition familiar to him by now in Mieka's presence. This time, though, he sensed a certain danger. He couldn't have said why.

"You behave as if putting too much of yourself into your work whittles away at your soul," Mieka went on. "Like with 'Doorways' and how you said you didn't want to perform it until it was perfect—whatever *that* means! You still don't think it's perfect, I'm dead certain you don't. But that piece is more *you* than anything else we've ever done onstage. I tried to tell you, that night we did it for the ladies, but you didn't listen, did you? You said it was brilliant, and I said it was *yours*."

"But it wasn't 'Doorways,' it was cobbled together from—"

"That's the whole point!" Mieka exclaimed. "The magic you put into those withies is *you*."

As if that explained everything.

Exasperated, Mieka rapped his knuckles on Cade's forehead.

"Solid granite! There was enough in the withies we used at rehearsal to shape the whole piece. Did you think *I* was the one providing all that? And when we did it last night there was so much more of you to work with—but do you feel less than you were? Like something's been yanked out of you?"

"No," he admitted, dimly seeing where this might be going.

"Just like Blye. Each of those boxes has something of her, something she made within herself and put into her glass. It's her magic, yeh, but it's also her mind, all her experience at her craft, and it's part of her heart as well. She loves us, and she put that into the work. It's real and it's honest. The boxes were inside her head, she'd made them in her thoughts before she ever went to the kiln, and then she made them real. That's what you do, as well. There's something as gets created inside you, and when you put it into the withies for me and Jeska and Rafe to use, it's not like it's part of you that's been taken away or—or stolen, or something. You're not the less for what you give us."

"I s'pose not," Cade mused.

"What *would* make you less than you are is things you do because you think they'd be popular, or please somebody else. If you work like that, without putting yourself into it, then you may think you're keeping your heart whole but you're really crippling yourself. 'Doorways' is brilliant because it's *you*!"

"All right, I understand." Suddenly he laughed. "If anybody'd told me, that night in Gowerion, that you'd be the one to aggravate me into being better than I ever thought I could be—"

Those bright, changeable eyes went wider than ever, genuinely astonished. "Me? I do that?"

"You do that. Didn't you know?"

"You're not gammoning me?" he asked suspiciously. "You're not laughing at me?"

Cade set down his teacup and made the hands-open gesture that meant *You may trust what I say.* "It's true that you can make me laugh when no one else can, but it's never *at* you, Mieka." He left his palms open, and Mieka matched his small hands to Cade's long ones, laced their fingers together, and smiled. After a moment, Cade drew away, oddly humbled, and picked up his tea for something else to do with his hands. With a sidewise glance at the Elf, he said, "I can tell you for certain sure, though, I'll never see sausage gravy the same."

"I been thinkin' about that," Mieka replied earnestly. "More colorful next time, I fancy. What d'you think of carrot-and-lentil soup?"

The laughter was still tugging at his lips when he waved at Mieka from the window of Kearney's carriage. It had to be imagination that the Elf looked a bit forlorn, standing there all alone with his satchel over his shoulder. What did he have to be glum about? He was about to walk over to the Seekhaven Coaching Inn on his way to see the girl, wasn't he?

Strange, Cade thought as he lounged back in cushioned elegance, how they never spoke about her. Hells, he'd barely heard *her* speak—just a few words when they were introduced—without her first name, of course—at Rafe and Crisiant's wedding. He'd known what her voice sounded like long before that day. He'd heard her, and her laughter, as she and her mother agreed on the taming and the breaking of Mieka Windthistle.

Pushing the Elsewhen out of his conscious mind, he watched as Kearney arranged his cunning little traveling desk on his lap, attending to letters, giving Cade a running commentary.

"You've plenty of bookings coming up. The Kiral Kellari, of course—once each week until autumn. There's a nice new place out by the Plume that wants you for ten nights, scattered through the summer. Here's one from the Jubbe and Jar—no, that's not your sort of place at all, very working-class, and we want only the upmarket venues from now on. I've seven requests for private performances in town, and two more at country homes."

"So we won't be destitute, even though we're still on the Winterly? We won't get the fee we could've got if we'd made Ducal, though."

"Not a thing to worry on, Cayden, not a thing," Kearney assured him. "We were right, you and I, to do 'Treasure' the usual way. Touchstone is safe on the Winterly Circuit, and you've the commission to do the piece your way."

"Yeh, all I have to do now is write the damn thing." *Safe*—that was the word Mieka had flung at him in a rage. Innovative, glass-shattering Touchstone, playing safe. They'd got back at him, though, hadn't they? "I still have to polish up 'Doorways' as well, y'know."

His Lordship folded away the desk, set it on the floor of the carriage, and composed himself to listen. When Cade couldn't find a way to begin, Kearney suggested, "You're still angry. While 'tis true they defied you, by doing 'Doorways' when you said not to, they do trust your judgment. They thought you were wrong this time, but that doesn't mean they don't trust—"

"They'll do it again," he blurted. "The questions, the doubts, arguing about interpretations—defying me even as far as doing a play when I told them not to—they'll do it again because they got away with it this time."

"It'll come clearer to them as Touchstone goes along," His Lordship soothed. "You're the brain, Cayden, the visionary. They know it. They're just not ready to admit it and give themselves over to your guidance. They will, eventually. But for now… let them win."

"What the fuck d'you mean, 'let them win'?"

"If they're wrong, they'll find it out, and learn that much faster to trust your direction. If they're right—as I'm compelled to say they were about 'Doorways'—then what do you lose? Nothing. It doesn't really count yet. It's a year from now, two years at the most, when it will really matter. Touchstone is making a name, but it's not yet *the* name. By the time it truly counts, you'll be in charge. They'll turn to you for every decision. And that's when the strength of your vision will make Touchstone *the* name in theater."

"Let them win," he repeated sullenly.

"For now." Kearney smiled brightly and clasped his hands together with a *Well, that's settled it!* air. "When we get to the Manor tomorrow night, all you'll have to do is work on 'Treasure' for the next bit of a while."

"I already have some ideas," Cade said.

"Excellent! Tell me all about them!"

B ut for the first two days at Fairwalk Manor, Cade worked on "Doorways." It wasn't perfect, no matter how enthusiastic its reception at both performances. Even the version done with his full knowledge and cooperation hadn't been what it ought to be. Perhaps he was being overly meticulous, fussing with it like this. Something else goaded him on, though, and eventually he understood that it was Mieka's voice in his head, urging him to make it better, make it even more *his*. "Doorways" had so much of Cade in it—rather more than he felt comfortable with, but there it was—and "Treasure" would have to as well if it was to be any good. That was what Mieka had been telling him: Putting his heart as well as his mind into a piece was his only choice. Otherwise—He didn't like to think about *otherwise*. Although an echoing voice saying, *"His mind's cold, but his heart's colder"* could still frighten him, he saw that to avoid it he must do the work with joy, not fear.

Kearney provided an airy little office for him just down a hall from the library. He worked from just after breakfast until tea, then went for a ride or a walk to clear his head, then returned to bathe and dress for supper. He imagined that this must have been the sort of life some of his ancestors had lived, the Highcollars and the Blackswans, before choosing the wrong side in the Archduke's War had ruined them. Gazing out on one's hereditary acres; strolling paths one's forebears had strolled; swinging up into a saddle used for three generations on a horse with registered bloodlines going back as far as one's own; dining off porcelain plates ordered by one's great-great-grandmother. Cade could enjoy the life of a country gentleman because he knew he would always go back to town. Though his ancestors had owned places like this, he was a Gallybanker down to his bones.

He missed the turbulence of the city, the noise and crowds and smells and being careful where you put your feet. He'd never seen a day-old pile of horseshit at Fairwalk Manor—he'd never seen any horseshit at all, not even in the stable yard, not even in any of the two dozen stalls. He began to doubt that Kearney's horses were allowed to shit, any more than raised voices or snapping logs in the fire or the slightest speck of dust were allowed. One afternoon Cade forgot to leave his muddy boots at the garden door, and tracked footprints all the way to the back stairs before realizing his rudeness. Turning, he saw a manservant down on his knees, already wiping up the mess. An attempt at an apology was met with "Oh no, sir, not at all! My pleasure!" and a further kneeling to remove his boots for him. Moreover, instead of having to pad upstairs in his stockings, he was given a pair of black velvet slippers conjured from the servant's pockets.

Mistress Mirdley would have made him clean it all up himself, and assigned him to scrape clean every pair of boots in the house for a week.

When he thought of home, that was what he missed: the Trollwife, dictating, scolding, dispensing buttered muffins and hangover remedies and excellent advice that he rarely had the brains to follow. He missed his little brother, too, especially when on horseback, thinking how Derien would adore a long gallop across flower-strewn meadows. He missed Blye, who listened to him when no one else would. He even—and this was a shock—missed his mother. Not often, and with a wry twist to his lips, but he did miss her.

Delving into his own feelings for the purpose of writing "Doorways" compelled him to admit that one reason he was here at Fairwalk Manor rather than at Redpebble Square was that he simply couldn't face having to tell his family that Touchstone was once again on the Winterly Circuit. He could endure the quickly masked dismay of Lady Jaspiela—though she deplored his profession, she had at last recognized there was a certain distinction to having so many important men admire her son's talents. But Dery's furious protests of injustice—Cade writhed inside at the thought of how disappointed the boy must be. Blye wouldn't say much, but he wasn't sure that wouldn't be even worse. What he dreaded most was a long, assessing look from Mistress Mirdley, a look that understood him perfectly. He didn't want to be understood. He wanted everyone to leave him alone so he could work and make "Doorways" and "Treasure" into plays that would have the whole Kingdom talking for the next ten years. And on the *Royal* Circuit, not the Winterly.

Ten years on the Royal Circuit…

Back in this place where he'd dreamed that horrific Elsewhen over and over and over, it was too easy to catch the echoes. As he struggled day after day with the scripting of the two plays, alternating between them, dissatisfied with both, he gradually realized that he couldn't work in this house where he'd known such fear. The enjoyment he needed, the delight in his craft, the opening of his heart as well as his mind to shaping the words and visualizing the ideas—none of it could be found at Fairwalk Manor.

He suspected it was in Frimham. But there was nothing he could do about that.

He would have to go back to town. He was getting nothing substantial done, he missed home, the quiet unnerved him, and Mieka had been right: He needed *Lost Withies*.

Besides, he'd had another dream.

In it, the tavern was just a nondescript taproom, no better and no worse than a hundred others like it up and down the Kingdom. This version of Tobalt Fluter was older but not yet gray, his broad, genial face a pattern of regret and perhaps some anger. The man interviewing him was different, though: young, fair-haired, his thin features intense as he scribbled his notes. Nothing too frightening, really, until Tobalt began to speak.

{"I've talked with Cayden at least a dozen times over the years, and he's always full of the meaning of this and the significance of that, how Art reveals Truth—" The sardonic tone gave the words capital letters. "—but he's a cold-hearted bastard and I don't wonder his wife finally left him."

"Cold?" The young man stopped writing. "But—the plays—they're—"

"Yeh, I know—emotes all over everything in his work, doesn't he? But the only feelings that matter are his, and a feeling's important only if he can use it. Oh, he *feels*, that's not in question—he'd never be able to prime a withie if he didn't. But an emotion is no more than a bit of scenery to him, a bell chiming in the distance." He smiled without humor. "Just part of the illusion."

The young man wasn't ready to concede the point. "Touchstone gives a great show."

"Not up to their earlier work. Cade's impulses were always dark, but in the last few years they've gone frightening."

"Well, consider what he's been through."

"What he's put himself through." Tobalt paused for a

sip from his glass. "About a year or so after it happened, I saw him in a tavern one night, hunched in a corner. Empty bottles on the table and a pouch of dragon tears half-falling out of his pocket—oh, don't look shocked, son, the rumors were everywhere."

The young man had dropped his pen. He picked it up and started writing again. "Are you confirming them?"

"Let's just say there was no mistaking one of those little gold velvet bags old Lullfinch used for his best customers. Of course, this was before the Crown sent him to Culch Minster for murdering a couple of his girls at the Finchery. Anyway, there sat Cayden Silversun, Master Tregetour, stinking drunk and three thorns lost. I called a hire-hack, got him into it, and told the driver to take us to Criddow Close. That's where his glasscrafter lives. There'd been some bitterness between them, but I was sure she'd take care of him."

"Bitterness?"

"None of your affair, son." Another swig, deeper this time, from the glass. "Cade sprawled across the seat for about half the drive, then woke up, looking sober as a High Justiciar, and stared at me for a moment. Then—and he was dead serious—he asked, 'Why should that fucking little Elf have all the glory?'"

"'Glory'?" The pen slipped from his fingers again, leaving a splotch of dark blue ink on the paper. "He *died*!"

"I might have mentioned something of the sort. But the dragon tears had taken him back by then, and he was unconscious when we got to the glassworks. I took the liberty of relieving him of that gold velvet pouch before he woke up and started for the stairs." Tobalt shrugged. "I was trying to explain it all to the glasscrafter—she wasn't half pleased to see him, I can tell you that—when he came tumbling back down the stairs, landing in a heap at our feet. He'd had a bit more thorn tucked into his boot, and he'd used it. He was damn near dead. I think he wanted to be dead."

"But he survived."

"Yes, he's still here. For all the joy it gives him." Tobalt stared into his glass, then said, "His life's a horror and there's naught he can do to change it. His tragedy is that he could have chosen to do so a hundred different times, and didn't. When Touchstone lost their Elf, they lost their soul."}

Cade had discussed various emotions with Vered Goldbraider the night of the Shadowshapers' party at Seekhaven, and how to evoke them in an audience rather than simply provide them with magic. As he lay awake in the early morning hours after rousing from that dream, he blinked the sweat from his eyes and recalled what his fellow tregetour had told him.

"True horror comes from inside, and it won't be the same for any two men in the theater. Real horror, it ain't just fear, it's shock. Mindless. Like joy, or love—you're helpless. The trick is to choose enough specifics without sacrificing the subtleties."

It was akin to what Jeska had said about leaving space enough for the audience to inhabit the character. And it had surprised him to hear Vered, so much the advocate for thought over emotion, discuss feelings so perceptively. He'd thought he knew all there was to know about structuring a play, but he'd learned from Jeska, and from Mieka, and from Vered, and was humbled. It seemed to be his season for humility, he reflected, and, remembering Black fucking Lightning, outright humiliation.

He didn't like it much.

He left for Gallantrybanks the next noon, unaccompanied by His Lordship, to whom he offered an apology and no explanation beyond a letter that had arrived that morning. Two laconic sentences from Blye: *Jedris and I are getting married next week. I thought you might like to be there, if you're done sulking.*

"Well, of course you must go! I can't accompany you—so much to be done here, don't you see, I really can't leave just yet—only wait while I scribble a note to the Brother Superior—"

"If I know Blye, she won't want High Chapel. She's a good bit Goblin, y'know."

"She—well—oh, that's fine, then," Kearney stammered, as if he'd said something embarrassing. "But at the very least I must send along a present. Now, what would be beautiful and appropriate?"

As he bustled off, Cade remembered his manners and called after him, "It's very kind of you to offer, Kearney—I'm sure she'll be grateful—"

A languid hand waved in the air above his head. "Not at all, dear boy, not at all! And I think I know just the thing to send her!"

Kearney's idea of *just the thing* turned out to be a matched set of twenty silver serving dishes. They certainly were beautiful, all scrollwork and curlicues, but Cade wondered (silently) how appropriate they might be to the home of a builder and a glasscrafter.

"You'll note the monogram in the center," Kearney said as the plates, bowls, salvers, and platters were lovingly packed into a huge crate that Cade was certain would end up weighing more than he did. "*W*, for my grandmother, who was a Winterwold." Then, anxiously, he added, "Will she like these, do you think?"

Cade smiled. "*W* for Windthistle. I'm sure she'll love them."

As the carriage clattered down the graveled drive, Cade folded himself into a corner and stared sightlessly out at the countryside. He'd have to find a wedding present, himself—*two* wedding presents that were appropriate to Windthistle.

What was it Vered had said about horror, and joy, and love? That they were shocks that left a man bereft of reason. That they were different for everyone. And that to evoke them, Cade had to choose specifics, but be subtle.

Would it be unsubtle to give Mieka a yellow shirt?

Just to remind him. Just to warn him.

Just to be snide and superior and let him know that Cade could run his life better than he could.

7

Unexpected arrivals, even at unsightly hours of the morning, had no power to startle Mistress Mirdley. When Cayden dragged himself through the kitchen door she looked up from pounding bread dough into submission, arched a brow, and said, "Your bed's fresh made, and you'd best use it, by the looks of you."

Cade was so glad to see her that he paused long enough for a hug, which she returned, and a kiss on her cheek, which she did not. Then he trudged up the wrought iron stairs to the fifth floor, stripped off, and fell into bed.

He was brusquely awakened that afternoon by a voice demanding, "What's that bloody huge wooden crate with my name on it, then?"

Blinking himself to consciousness, he shrank back in bed with the covers clutched to his chin. "Mistress Cindercliff! What are you doing in a man's bedchamber? And you so soon to be wedded! The scandal and the shame of it!"

Blye gave him a poisonously sweet smile as she set a large tea tray on his desk. "Who's going to tell? Not you! Jed's just as tall as you are, and half again your heft. They'd be carrying you out in more pieces than your glass baskets could hold." She pulled the chair out and sat herself down. "Now. That crate downstairs in the kitchen."

"Wedding present from His Lordship."

"Good Gods." She sat back, a bit stunned. Then, with brisk suddenness, "You already know everything I could say about what happened at Trials, so I won't say it. I'll not be discussing the wedding, neither, not yet, except to say that if you think you'll not be the one putting my hand into Jed's, think again. Dery will be up soon with the teapot, so tell me quick—how did Lord Fairwalk know to book Touchstone everywhere from Kiral Kellari to the Keymarker before the ink on the Winterly list was dry?"

"Did he?" Cade parried.

"Chivvy-chavvy all over town has you playing four nights a week the whole summer! Tobalt Fluter came by the shop for a gossip. Not that I could tell him anything, or would. At least he bought a candleflat for his mother's Namingday—while he was looking at the last windowpanes for the Keymarker. He wants to talk to you, by the bye."

"Another interview!" He gave an elaborate shudder. "I'd rather talk about your wedding."

"Open the door!" yelled Derien, and with a scowl Blye jumped up to oblige. "Mistress Mirdley said I wasn't to bother you and I didn't, not all morning long—beholden, Blye," the boy said as she took the teapot, then rushed on, "and she also said I wasn't to say anything about Trials and how unfair it was and how they could *ever* pick Black Lightning over Touchstone—so I won't," he finished, and threw his arms around Cade. "But it *was* unfair," he muttered as Cade hugged him tight.

And suspect, said Blye's expression.

Cade didn't want to discuss it. So, as his little brother—who'd grown at least an inch in the weeks Cade had been away at Trials and Fairwalk Manor—settled at the foot of his bed and accepted the cup and laden plate Blye handed him, he regaled them with the story of Mieka, the High Chapel courtyard, and the yarking that really wasn't.

Mayhap not the best tale while they were eating. But even when he wasn't physically present, the mad little glisker could make anyone laugh. And that got him to thinking, after Derien and Blye had taken the tea things back downstairs and he was getting dressed, about something Kearney had said.

They had been talking over a selection of wines. Kearney was teaching Cade how to drink. Not that he didn't know the theory, and had become quite adept at the practice. His months of working in Master Honeycoil's wine shop had taught him the names of all the best vintages and vintners, but he'd been only twelve at the time and had rarely tasted any of them. Until Touchstone started making good money, all Cade really knew were the names, years, and makers of fine wines and brandies. His experience of beers and ales had taught him that the difference between tolerable and awful was the vehemence of his hangover the next morning. And having once tasted Brishen Staindrop's whiskey, he scorned all others. Kearney had been willing to concede the point about the whiskey, but Cade's total lack of discernment about other liquors appalled him.

"*That is a glass of twenty-year-old wine! Do* not *throw it down your throat! You're tasting a vintage, not filling a bucket!*"

Cade had laughed, and mocked Kearney for trying to give a yobbo like him lessons in Snob. His Lordship had taken a moment or three to smile, and that had led to why certain people thought certain things were funny and others didn't.

"*Humor, don't you see, is something extremely personal and frightfully manipulative. To share with someone what you think is funny, or to laugh at someone else's joke, is a surprisingly intimate thing.*"

Cade had remarked that there'd been a boy at littleschool with him and Rafe who found it riotously funny to pluck the wings off flies. Since the age of seventeen, the boy had been an involuntary guest of His Most Gracious Majesty, and was said to be very good at breaking rocks at the quarry attached to the prison.

"Well," Kearney had said, "*that was rather predictable, don't you see? What someone finds ridiculous, hilarious, witty, or ironic says much about the sort of person he is. Once you know how to make someone laugh, you can manipulate him so he has no choice but to laugh. He'll think of you with pleasure. And then you can get away with just about anything.*"

Nobody else in that courtyard would recall Mieka Windthistle with pleasure. But it was true that he did get away with just about anything. Cade was looking at his own face in the mirror while shaving when it occurred to him that whereas there was much more to Mieka than the laughter, the laughter was all he allowed most people to see. With it, he manipulated; behind it, he hid. And to think he had the bollocks to goad Cade into putting more of himself into the magic.

Their first booking after Cade's return was at the Keymarker, a new tavern at a prime corner location in a district the other side of the Gally River. The area had undergone extensive renovations in the last few years, turning abandoned warehouses into flats for the families of merchants who oversaw the Kingdom's ever-growing trade. There were a few blocks of swank dwellings with views of the river, places where the rent stayed the same no matter how many flights one had to climb; fresher air and wider skies were considered ample compensation for more stairs and smaller rooms.

Along with the residences came shops, tea-rooms, and several taverns, and the newest of these was the Keymarker. Its ambitious owner had ordered reconstruction that almost made it into a real theater. There were two tiers of seating, each with its own bar. Necessity dictated that the renovations include replacing ancient worm-eaten rafters with steel girders—an expense indicating how serious the owner was about competing with the Kiral Kellari. That Touchstone was engaged to play on opening night, at what Kearney Fairwalk made sure was a considerable fee, was another sign of the owner's determination to succeed.

It was rumored that Black Lightning's new manager had promoted the group as ideal for the purpose. Had they not just bested Touchstone at Trials? But the Keymarker's owner had heard about Black Lightning's propensity for magic so wild as to be almost uncontrolled. Because nobody had ever played there before, nobody knew what effect steel in the ceiling might have— and Touchstone had a reputation for discipline strict enough to select precisely which glasses would shatter along the bar.

And besides all that, Jedris and Jezael Windthistle had done some of the renovation work, and Blye Cindercliff had made every pane of the front windows. Colored dark blue, with an iron key embedded in each ten-inch square—it was no wonder she and Jed could afford to get married, Cade told himself with a grin as he walked past the place an hour before the scheduled rehearsal. She had worked all that winter and spring to pay off her debt to Touchstone with a bank draft presented to Kearney shortly after Rafe and Crisiant got married. Although Touchstone retained a substantial interest in the glassworks, Cade reasoned that soon enough she and Jed would want to buy them out. Making withies for Touchstone and the Shadowshapers, and windows for Windthistle Brothers, had compelled her to hire an assistant to keep up with the work. Not an apprentice; just someone to do the tedious jobs of polishing, cleaning up around the glassworks, minding the shop, and so forth. The person Blye hired could never become an apprentice. Not that Rikka Ashbottle particularly wanted that distinction. She was quite frank about it. All she really desired was to earn enough money to pay a chirurgeon to straighten her almost cripplingly crooked Goblin teeth.

It was Rikka who had sent him on today's errand before

rehearsal. Her great-uncle was the crafter from whom the Keymarker's owner had purchased all those spare iron keys that had gone into the windows, and his workshop was about eight blocks from the tavern. Cade needed something for Derien's Namingday present. He already knew what Touchstone would be giving Blye and Jed as a wedding gift. As for that other wedding gift—he'd think about it when it happened.

No one entered a Goblin's workshop without multiple references. Cade hoped two would suffice: the Keymarker and Rikka. But it was a good five minutes after telling the old man— through a very low peek-door in a side wall—his name and his connections before a section of brick wall vanished just like the artists' entry to the Kiral Kellari. This opening was too short for Cade to enter in any fashion other than a low crouch. It might have been Goblin spitefulness or simple mischief, but Cade certainly felt the unflattering absurdity and straightened to his full Wizardly height as soon as he could.

He found Master Ashbottle staring up at him with magnificently large eyes almost the cloud-gray color of Cade's own. Above those eyes spread a single silvery eyebrow that went straight across his forehead. Rikka's great-uncle certainly couldn't have had more than a few drops of anything but Goblin in his veins. From the rather lumpy nose to the mismatched yellow teeth to the bandy-legged belligerence of the stunted frame, this man was as classically Goblin as Mieka was classically Elfen. The pale skin of Master Ashbottle's face and hands was blotched here and there, the way Blye's sometimes became when she'd been working too long at her kiln, but on him the smudging looked permanent. His Human traits included a receding hairline and the shoulders of a longshoreman.

"Master Ashbottle," Cade said with a polite nod.

"Master Silversun," the Goblin acknowledged in a voice soft and musical.

Cayden waited, and said nothing more. If anything proved Blye's shortfall of Goblin blood, it was her verbal agility. For those of primarily Goblin ancestry, one or two choice, terse words sufficed to communicate. After another minute or so, Master Ashbottle evidently decided that Cade was no idle chatterer come to waste his time, and pointed to the shelves lining the brick walls.

"Fancy aught?"

The selection of wares was far vaster than keys and locks. These there were, and in every size and elaboration imaginable. There was also an extensive selection of hinges, dead-bolts, door knockers and doorknobs, drawer pulls, and other small hardware. Cade considered his next remark carefully, editing out three-quarters of the words he would ordinarily have spoken. "Namingday gift."

This received due contemplation. Finally: "Whose?"

"Brother." He waited a few moments, then added, "Eight."

Master Ashbottle pondered this for a time, then went round the counter and hefted up a large wooden box. A gesture invited Cade to have a look as, one after another, a selection of painted toys appeared for his inspection.

Pretending a sudden worriment, Cade dug into a pocket for his purse and dumped some of the contents into his hand. "Enough?" he muttered as if to himself, sneaking a glance at the Goblin. *"Don't try to pay in regular royals,"* Rikka had advised. *"They're a mix of metals and Uncle can smell that a mile off. He's of a generation that scorns aught but pure silver or gold."* The coins Cade poked through were solid silver crowns. Master Ashbottle squinted slightly, and his bumpy nose seemed to twitch at the tip before he relaxed and nodded his approval of Cade's manners.

Leaving coins and purse on the counter, Cade happily inspected the offerings. There were boats ranging from sculls to three-masted ships with bright-colored sails, all sorts of animals and birds with movable limbs and heads and wings, castles, puppets, and a wonderfully gaudy green snake that coiled and uncoiled just like a real one. But what caught Cade's attention, and made him forget his manners, was a four-inch-tall knight on horseback.

"This is perfect! Could you paint the knight's shield with a silver sunburst?"

This unprovoked verbosity caused the Goblin to contort his single silvery eyebrow into what Cade assumed, mortified, was a scowl. Then he vanished through a door, apparently to his workshop, and returned a moment later with a jar of paint and a brush. The sunburst was limned in absolute silence while Cade occupied himself with sorting coins on the counter.

A sudden flash of green-white fire made him leap back with a cry of alarm. Master Ashbottle was looking exceedingly pleased with himself, and there was a sardonic glint to his pale eyes as he pointed to the knight's shield. "Dry."

Cade nodded feebly. He gestured to the coins. The Goblin selected the appropriate number—rather fewer than Cade had anticipated, but perhaps he'd received part of his fee in amusement by startling Cade half out of his wits. The knight was transferred to a blue box padded with curled wood-shavings tinted purple, and tied shut with white cording. Cade accepted the box, bowed, and turned to leave.

And stared stupidly at the solid brick wall.

A noise like creaking iron chains came from the Goblin—laughter, presumably—as he meandered over, placed his spread fingers to a bit of wall that looked like every other bit, and the short door once again opened. Cade gulped, bowed once more, and said, "Beholden."

"Touchstone," said Master Ashbottle, pensively. "Clever, agreeable work."

Cade was so astonished by this outpouring that he bumped his forehead on the lintel.

He hurried through a ginnel towards Sumpters Wend, knowing he was late for rehearsal at the Keymarker. Whatever complaints the others might have would vanish once he told them the why of his errand. He'd be forgiven. Everyone adored Dery. Of course, Mieka was perpetually late, rarely said why, and was always forgiven. Everyone adored Mieka, too.

It was dark in the tunnel between buildings, and scarcely any brighter when he emerged into an alley. A sultry rain had been threatening all day, though without enough cloud cover to ignite the softly golden Elf-light in the streetlamps. Turning a corner into another alley that ran behind the tavern, he dropped the package from suddenly strengthless fingers when he saw them. Even in the dimness he knew instantly it was them: her bronze-and-golden hair was as unmistakable as the cant of his ears. He was wrapped around her, and her arms were twined around his neck, and they were kissing each other wildly, obsessively.

Cade shrank against a brick wall, trembling, his stomach clenching against sudden sickness, his brain whining with shock. He shouldn't be watching them. This was wrong. He was disgusting.

He couldn't look away.

Her fingers were deep in his hair; his hands were all over her. She was moaning, high-pitched and needy. He was growling, low in his throat. They were both gasping in between kisses, each brief separation of their lips a wet, sucking sound that lasted only as long as it took to drag enough air into their lungs before their mouths fused again. Even from thirty feet away Cade could smell perfume, liquor, and lust.

"Mieka? Where the hells are you?" Rafe's voice, brisk with impatience, from the tavern's back door.

They broke apart, but just barely. "Gods, Rafe! You got the worst timing in theater!" There was breathless laughter in his voice.

"Sorry," Rafe said, not sounding it. "Cade get here yet?"

"How should I know? Got better things to do than keep track of him, don't I?"

"Obviously. But we need to get started, with him or without him."

"Right." He tightened his arms around her and kissed her again, long and deep. "That do you for a while, girl?"

"Mm… one more?"

He laughed and obliged. "You all right to find Jinsie and Jez out front and get home?"

"I don't see why I have to—"

"Don't pout, there's a good girl. If you could hide this figger in boy's clothes, it'd be one thing. But that can't be done, and beholden to all the Gods for it!" he added, a hand seeking her breast.

"But I want to see you onstage, and not just at rehearsal—"

"I know, I know. One day soon, I promise. You and Crisiant and all the ladies who care to see a show, nobody'll have to hide—"

"And who's Cade hiding these days?"

"Oh, there's dozens of 'em," Mieka replied airily. "Quite the lad, he is. I s'pose there's something about a tregetour." He laughed. "And nobody oozes 'moody' like Cade."

"Is that what it is? I would've called it his 'tormented artist' act."

"The 'artist' part ain't an act. As for 'tormented'—" His voice roughened. "He does that to himself, y'know."

"Mieka, why are we talking about Cade when you're supposed to be kissing me?"

Rafe shouted from the half-open door again. "Mieka!"

"Coming!" he yelled. "Go on now, girl, and I'll be back soon as I can tonight."

"All right. I love you."

"You'd be a fool not to!" Another kiss, laughing again, and he let her go. He turned and leaped lightly up the steps to the door.

It was only as she rummaged in her reticule that Cade realized he was still standing there, frozen, his back to the brick wall.

Before she was finished fixing her face, he had slipped round the corner and hauled in a deep breath. Then he walked into the alley as if just arriving.

"Oh! Cade!" She nearly dropped a little silvery tub of lip rouge. "You startled me!"

"Sorry." He paused as he came even with her. "Are you staying to watch?"

"No, heading back with Jinsie and Jezael. Mum thinks it scandal enough, coming anywhere near a tavern, even a lovely new one like this. I promised we'd only have a look, and then go home to Wistly."

Home now, was it? He made himself smile.

"Make sure Mieka doesn't stay too late after the show tonight, won't you?" She simpered, and he wanted to slap her.

"I've met nobody yet who can tell him what to do that he doesn't do the exact opposite, but I'll give it a try. I'd best get along," he said.

He was on the top step when she called his name. Turning, he saw her walking towards him, all silk skirts and full breasts and glossy waves of hair, her exquisite face still smug with Mieka's kisses. She had a mouth like a soft, ripe peach, the lower lip plump and pouty, the upper lip not quite covering front teeth that were slightly too large—a flaw in any other girl, but that gave her a look of breath-just-caught, of eager and childlike surprise. Her eyes added to this impression: huge, long-lashed, a startling shade of blue-violet, with delicate arching brows. Objectively, she was possibly the most beautiful girl he'd ever seen, and he hated her more than he'd ever hated anyone in his life.

She was holding the wooden box. "Is this yours?"

"Oh. I–I musta dropped it. My little brother's Namingday present—took me half the afternoon to find it—" Aware that he was babbling, he leaned over the railing, not meeting her gaze as she handed him the package. "Beholden."

"No trouble." She kept her grip on the box, though, until he looked her in the eyes. She was smiling. She knew he'd seen them. She wanted him to know it. She wanted him to acknowledge that she was winning, and that eventually she'd win. She stood back, let him look if he'd a mind to it, let him see what Mieka would be going home to: the lush figure, the perfect face. Then she tossed her long bronze-gold hair over her shoulder and walked out of the alley.

The artists' tiring room had a sink and garderobe stall, and a shelf of towels that smelled of citrusy soap. There was a mirror over the sink, rattling with the volume of frantic shouted orders on the other side of the thin wall as tables and chairs were arranged and everything made ready for opening night. Cade had just raised his head from splashing water on his face and was looking into his own bleak gray eyes when he heard it: short gasps that quickly became a long groan of release. He froze, staring in the mirror at the closed stall. He made himself straighten his spine, and kept his back to the opening door.

"Cade!" A hip bumped his, nudging him aside so he could wash his hands.

"You should've saved it," he heard himself say.

"Huh?" Those big, startled eyes met his in the mirror. "Saved what?"

"That." He pointed to Mieka's crotch. "Gets every barmaid in the place wet when you stroll about with a cock-lift. And that's free drinks the rest of the night, every time."

"Oh. You heard." He smirked. "I had to, Quill! These trousers are too tight. I'd be whimperin' behind me bench all through rehearsal!" He raked his wet hands back through his hair and turned to face Cade, grinning. "Maybe I oughta work up another one? Free drinks, after all!"

He looked down into that arrogantly beautiful face, wishing that just once he could forget his self-imposed restraint and use his fists until that face was a bloody, broken ruin. Would the girl still want him then?

Mieka's impudent grin faltered, and Cade knew what must be in his eyes. With a colossal effort he shrugged, and bent to splash more water onto his face.

"What's this, then?" Mieka plucked the box from the shelf above the sink. It had found a puddle somewhere in the alley, and the white cord was soiled.

"For Dery. His Namingday's coming up."

"A party? Can I help? Why don't I go back with you to Redpebble tonight and we can scheme up something for—"

His lip curled and he hid it behind one of the towels. "Shoulda asked earlier," he said, his tone easy, casual. "Got plans for afterwards, don't I?"

"The tall blonde?"

There was fierce pleasure in seeing Mieka frown. So he'd noticed the barmaid, seen her looking—

"It's the blonde, isn't it, Cade?" he insisted. "The one with no tits."

"All a man needs is enough to fill his hands, Mieka. And as for what a woman needs filled…"

"Oh, and it's a right rare stud you are," Mieka taunted. "The wonder of Gallybanks. Virgins whimper at the very sight of you. Ever had one, by the way?"

Cade tossed the towel into the sink. What he was about to say was as wrong and disgusting as watching them had been. It would be worse. It would be unforgivable. He said it anyway, with mocking innocence to rival Mieka's own. "Why? Haven't you? Wasn't *she*?"

Knuckles slammed into his jaw and his cheek slammed into the mirror. He staggered against the sink, gasping, seeing in the cracked glass the blood smearing his nose and lips.

"She's not to be talked of by you," Mieka hissed. "Never!

She's mine, and I won't have you talking of her!"

The trickle of blood from his nostrils and his cut cheekbone fascinated him. It wasn't even painful. He thought it ought to be painful.

"Cade? Cayden!"

The towel was still in his hands. The glass was whole. He looked at his own face in the mirror: pallid, with startled gray eyes.

"It just happened again, didn't it?" Mieka asked softly.

Fingers touched his arm. He jerked back, stumbling into the wall.

"You don't have to be scared. Not of me."

"No," he said, feeling hollow. "It—it wasn't—I mean, it was here and gone so fast, I don't even really know what I saw." But he kept his gaze averted. *"I've told you and told you, Quill, your eyes will always give you away."* With a massive effort, he let go of the towel and turned to look down into the worried Elfen face. "I'm all right. Truly. What were we just talking about?"

Disappointment flickered and was gone. "Nothing." Shouldering open the door into the hall, he said, "Have to go set up the baskets. A bit of 'Purloin,' just to see how the magic bounces?"

When Cade nodded, Mieka let the door swing closed behind him. Then he met his own empty gray eyes in the mirror one last time.

He could have said yes, could have taken Mieka back to Redpebble Square to plot Dery's Namingday party. He could have kept him out of her bed that night, changed just this one thing, and maybe from it more changes would come, and she wouldn't be able to tame him and break him and that little boy with the sad eyes would never be born, and—

Turned out he was wrong: there was one person he hated more than he hated her.

Jeska laughed later that night, watching Mieka gulp down

a post-show beer and then hurtle for the door. "Those two little beauties," he said, shaking his head. "Can't keep their hands off each other!"

Curfew hadn't yet rung—they'd done a short show tonight—and the tall blonde was waiting for him. He took his time looking her up and down, then gave her a smile and held out a hand.

"Fancy a drink, darlin'?" he asked when she joined him.

"Ooh, yes!" she breathed, gazing up at him as if he were all the Angels wrapped up in one man. She was perhaps eighteen, perhaps not. Her eyes by the lamplight were a dark, sultry brown. "I want to hear all about the theater, and what you're writing next, and—"

He tucked her hand in the crook of his elbow. "All about it," he promised. A lie, of course. He didn't discuss his work with silly little girls who couldn't possibly understand. Mieka had been right about him: There were only two sorts of women as far as Cade was concerned—people, and not.

No, not entirely right. There were women who were women, there were women who were people, and there was *her*.

8

After receiving no satisfaction from Cade on the question of Lord Fairwalk's seeming prescience about the Winterly, Blye applied to Mieka.

"How did he know to put together all those bookings?" she demanded on the morning before her wedding. They were seated on the floor of the small dining room at Wistly Hall, every other available surface—chairs, table, sideboard—and much of the floor itself covered in decorations, stacked plates, crated glassware, unopened gifts, and baskets of clean table linens. "It's as if he knew you were going to fail—"

Mieka arched a brow. She blushed.

"—not *fail*, I didn't mean that," she continued hurriedly. "That you wouldn't make the Ducal Circuit, that's what I meant."

He smiled and went on tying white and purple ribbons round the stems of twenty little glass nosegays, one for each female guest. Blye hadn't made them; they were the work of one of her late father's friends. Delicate rosebuds of white and various shades of purple nestled in real ferns, and after the ribbons were on, he'd be taking them to his mother so she could becast the flower petals to open when Jed and Blye were pronounced husband and wife. Mieka had to make sure the ferns fanned artistically around the roses, then tie them off, clip the uneven ends, and set them upright in a tray of water so the real greenery would stay fresh. After the tenth nosegay, he was grateful that this was a very small wedding.

"The weather looks nice for tomorrow morning," he said, looking out the wide windows at the river. "Mum's been dithering for a week that it might rain—"

"Mieka! I don't care about the weather!"

"You will if your gown gets sopped," he predicted, then gave in as he finished yet another bow. "Oh, all right, then. Yeh, I admit it smells a bit, His Lordship grabbing up all those bookings. But Cade says, and I agree with him, that he was just bein' safe. If we'd got the Ducal, we just would've shifted the Gallytown dates to this winter." He frowned as he clipped the tag ends of the ferns. "Cade also says we got more money this way, too—if they'd known we *wouldn't* move up, the way everybody expected we'd do, they would've offered less."

"But that doesn't make any sense! They booked you for the summer at a rate the Ducal or Royal groups get on the strength of an expectation that you wouldn't be available this summer?"

"I'm not understanding it much, meself," he admitted. "But the fact is we're here, and we need to work, and work is on offer." He measured out another length of white ribbon and another length of plum, snipped them even, and poked through the basket of ferns. "I must really, really like you," he said darkly, "to be doin' all this lot."

"It's not so much that you like me," she scoffed, "it's that you're scared of your mother!"

"So is three-fourths of Wistly Hall, else everybody'd be coming to this wedding and I'd be tying bows all night!" He eyed the glasscrafter sidelong. "It's quite the tribe you're marrying into, y'know. Might be a good notion to search Jed's luggage when he moves into Criddow Close—you never know, there might be a cousin or three stowed away."

Most of the relations living under Wistly's capacious roof had been strongly encouraged by Mishia Windthistle to give polite regrets when invited to the wedding. Blye had insisted on the inviting; Jedris had pointed out that she hadn't even met most of them; she retorted that they were his family; he rolled his eyes and replied, "Only at dinnertime."

So it was to be a small wedding in the garden, and Mieka was making copious mental notes.

Not that he'd asked her yet. He'd come very near it, when time came to put her and her mother onto the public coach for Frimham.

He'd wanted her to stay for the wedding, but her mother had insisted that they must return home. They still had work to do, finishing up garments for sale to the throngs who descended on the resort town during the summer. Mieka had come very, very close to saying chuck all of it and start on a wedding gown, but something had held him back. Only later did he understand that their absence was not just mannerly, it was kindly—for who would look at any other girl, even the bride, when *she* was around to look at? Much as he loved Blye, and as pretty as he knew she'd be tomorrow, no girl wanted to be outshone on her wedding day.

"Mieka! Aren't you finished *yet*?" His mother strode in, trailing white and purple streamers from the overflowing box in her arms. "Cade's here, and with him His Lordship, and you're already late."

He reached for the scissors. "I'm almost done, Mum, honest."

"A likely tale," Cade remarked from the doorway. "Come on, we're off to get a polish on."

"Lord Fairwalk is here?" Blye jumped up from the floor and smoothed her tunic. "I didn't know he'd be coming—I must tell him how beholden we are—"

Cade grinned and pretended to cower to one side as she

hurtled past. "Not *fluttery*, exactly, d'you think?"

"More a *flurry*," Mieka replied. "You know, like snow going everywhere at once." To his mother, frowning over him: "I'm nearly through, Mum, really!"

"Oh, go on with you," she said. "I can get it done faster meself. And if you see Jinsie on your way out," she called after him as he sprinted gratefully for the door, "tell her I'm wanting those stickpins for the gentlemen polished up *now!*"

"Stickpins?" Cade asked as he and Mieka headed for the front hall.

"Rikka Ashbottle's great-uncle gave us a bargain—well, he would, wouldn't he, considering the business Jed gives him, and Rikka working for Blye now. Little pewter thistles for a neckband or lapel," he explained. "And you don't want to hear the tale of whether the paint on the flower ought to be plum, grape, violet, wine, amethyst, or just plain ordinary serviceable *purple*. Gods, I thought Jinsie would never shut up. Then Fa wandered in and said, 'A thistle's the color of a thistle, innit?' They rounded on him like starving sparrows on stray bread.

What do people do, I wonder, when they haven't anything in their names to use as a theme for wedding keepsakes?"

"Clan, I s'pose," Cade mused. "Though I could have done without the spiderweb tea-tray mat. But with Rafe's sense of humor, I'm surprised it wasn't actual spiders."

So Quill was back in a good mood, Mieka told himself. Looking forwards to the wedding tomorrow, he decided, slanting an upward glance at him. But an instant later he revised his opinion. Cade wasn't just in a fine humor; he was practically quivering with excitement.

"—don't know how I'll ever bring myself to use them, they're so beautiful—"

"—instant I learned of the marriage, don't you see, I thought you might like them—"

"I *love* them—"

Blye was still trying to express her gratitude for the silver plate, and His Lordship was still stammering that it was nothing, really, nothing at all, when Mieka and Cade arrived in the front hallway.

"—never even use them, really truly—"

"—to think you'd give up a family heirloom, it's so kind of Your Lordship—"

"—ought to go to someone who'll enjoy them, and the initial was the same, and all that sort of thing, so—"

Cade grinned down at Mieka, then stuck his fingers between his teeth and gave a shrill whistle. The pair spun round, startled. "Blye, you're beholden to Kearney. Kearney, your gift is a grand success. Agreed? All right, then." He bent to kiss Blye's cheek. "Go worry about stickpins and streamers, won't you? There's a good girl."

She smacked him a good one on the shoulder.

He was still pretending to rub the soreness away as they rode in His Lordship's sprightly little rig towards the center of town. "I hope Jed's a fast runner. She's got a good reach and one hell of a clout on her, for a little slip of a thing."

Mieka surveyed him sidelong, then said, "Tell me what's got you grinning like a giddiot or I'll give you a matching one on the other shoulder."

"Not the writing arm, not the writing arm!" he pleaded, laughing. "Kearney, why don't you do the honors?"

"Well." His Lordship folded his well-tended hands on his precisely placed silk-clad knees. "You'll know, of course, that Prince Ashgar has been waiting for a lady to accept him. Inquiries went out across the Continent last year—and oh, the delicacy of the negotiations, the subtleties involved—"

"Somebody finally accepted," Cade cut in.

"Poor girl," Mieka sighed. "Who is she?"

Fairwalk intoned, "Her Serenity Tregrefina Miriuzca of—"

He broke off, clucking his tongue. "Lord and Lady witness it, I can't pronounce the name of her homeland, no matter how I try or who gives me lessons. But she's to become Ashgar's Princess, don't you see, and eventually our Queen, and—"

"And we're to go over and help escort her home!" Cade blurted. "Us! Touchstone!"

Mieka could do nothing but stare.

"It's the first time any theater group from the Kingdom has played on the Continent since the Firemongers—"

"The who?"

"About a century ago. But nobody's been over since then, and it's gonna be *us*, Mieka! Oh, and Kearney doesn't think he can arrange it but what I'm thinking is that Alaen would be a good person to bring along as well, because they're all mad for music in Gref Jyziero—"

"Is that how it's pronounced?" Fairwalk asked earnestly. "Say it again, please, Cade?"

He obliged, then took another deep breath and rushed on, "If the idea is to show everybody how cultured and civilized we really are, and promote goodwill and all that sort of thing, then Alaen is essential, don't you see? I'm already working on a list of which of our pieces would play well over there—considering the language differences and so forth—but *we're* the ones who'll change the whole way they look at theater, Mieka. They'll find out that magical folk are worth having around after all, and there won't be any more Escapings necessary, and—"

"He's going to change the world," Fairwalk said with an indulgent smile.

"And all that sort of thing," Mieka heard himself say.

"I'll have a good go at it!" Cade retorted. "It means a lot of work, of course, but we can use the shows we've already booked to refine things—" He turned to Fairwalk, frowning. "Have you seen to that? Cancelling the summer shows with our apologies?"

"I only found out two days ago, Cayden," he protested. "Hurried at once back to Gallantrybanks, don't you see, to tell you and start planning. It's not only clothes you'll be needing, it's new imagings, which remembers me you've an appointment next week with one of the Court imagers. And—"

"We should go round to all the taverns and say sorry in person," Mieka interrupted.

"There's hardly time for that," Fairwalk said. "There'll be letters from the Master of His Majesty's Revelries, and the Prince's Private Secretary as well, I shouldn't wonder—"

"In person," Mieka insisted. "And promise a return engagement when we get back, to make it up to them."

Cade patted him on the head. "How very courteous and respectful of you, Mieka."

"I can do it if I try very, very hard," he replied with judicious use of The Eyes. Then all at once it really hit him: Touchstone had been chosen for this, not the Shorelines nor Black fucking Lightning nor even the Shadowshapers. *Touchstone.*

Cade laughed again, knowing what he was thinking. "Yeh—us!"

"And here we are," said Fairwalk as the rig clattered to a decorous halt outside a small arcade of shops. "We shan't be above four hours or so," he added to the driver as he stepped round to pat the horse's neck. "Take the old girl back home."

"Very good, Y'r Lordship."

Shopping with Kearney Fairwalk was quite the experience. They weren't just picking up Cade's and Mieka's new jackets for the wedding tomorrow. They were also being kitted out for the trip to the Continent. The names discreetly painted on the shop windows were always followed by someone's coat of arms to indicate the patronage of one noble house or another, and once or twice were accompanied by the simple RW that meant *Royal Warrant.* Mieka had never been in such expensive establishments in his life. The finest stock was brought out for their perusal and the service was so unctuous that for the first four shops, Mieka was sure they were all being mocked. This was not the case, as he discovered as they exited the hattery, where the owner held the door open, one clerk bowed as if to the King, and a second committed an appalling breach of manners by saying, "So grateful that Your Lordship thought of us, much beholden for your custom."

Kearney Fairwalk fixed him with a look to freeze molten glass. The other clerk gulped audibly. The owner, one hand full of doorknob and the other holding a large beribboned box with their choices inside, looked for a moment as if he'd rather have his fingers around the clerk's throat before a sort of frantic professionalism took over.

"Craving Your Lordship's pardon," he begged, flinging a glance of pure rage at the poor clerk, who had turned a remarkable shade of red. "And hoping Your Lordship can forgive my sister's lackwit son for addressing Your Lordship."

Mieka was fascinated to watch as Fairwalk unfroze and waved a careless hand. "No harm done, not a bit of it. Wouldn't dream of setting foot anyplace else, don't you see. Good day to you."

They proceeded grandly outside into the arcade, and Mieka asked, "What was all that, then?"

"First," Cade explained, "he actually spoke. Second, he expressed gratitude to a titled nobleman—which implies that now he owes that nobleman a favor, which is of course absurd and even insulting, because what service could a miserable lowly clerk in a hat shop possibly do for a lordship? Third—"

"There's a 'third'?"

"Certainly there is! It's the further implication that there might be another hattery with goods either as fine or—horror of horrors—even finer, which suggests that His Lordship doesn't know the best place to buy a hat."

"Or that I didn't know my own mind when it comes to choosing which shop to buy from," Kearney put in. "Where did you learn all that?"

"Kearney," he said patiently, "you've met my mother."

"Rot, ain't it, though?" Mieka asked. "I mean, implications of this and suggestions of that—fine for a farce onstage, but I never knew people really behaved that way."

"Take notes," Cade encouraged, smiling again. "You'll have to be on your snootiest best behavior when we're representing the Kingdom."

"Do I *have* to?" he whined, just to make Cade laugh.

Fairwalk wasn't laughing. "Yes, Mieka, you really truly do. Not behave snootily, I mean to say, but all your larking about, it won't do. *Please* pay attention when the Court Protocol Officer lessons you while we're on board ship. You understand, don't you?"

"Oh, he understands right enough," Cade said. "He's not quite as thick as he looks. You mustn't worry, Kearney. All we need do is threaten him with his mum."

Shop after shop after shop received them with honors. There were places with sample garments on display, where one pointed to one's preferences and clerks swarmed like ferrets over shelves that went to the ceiling. There were places with no windows, just an unobtrusive sign on the door, where one entered a room closely resembling a gentleman's private library but without the books, all brown leather chairs and dark wood, and while sipping freshly brewed tea perused sketchbooks and swatches. Not one of the shops was remotely like the warehouses Mieka was used to, where clerks bellowed to one another across bolts of cloth strewn everywhere and piled to the rafters, and there were boxes and boxes of shiny buttons and bright ribbons and rainbow spools of thread to rummage through. One establishment in the arcade sold *only* buttons, in fact, each sample had its own little compartment in wide glass cases.

Mieka had assumed that Rafe and Jeska would be joining them at some point; that this was a mistaken impression became clear when Fairwalk pronounced himself satisfied with the cut of a longvest.

"We'll want four, all in this material," he told the proprietor, "but of different colors. The wine-red, that sand shade over there, the sea-blue, and the pearl-gray. We'll send round the measurements. And for the shirts and trousers as well."

"Ready in a se'ennight, Your Lordship."

The most interesting thing about shopping with Fairwalk was that there were no bills to settle. During all the time they spent in the arcade, Mieka saw not a single price ticket on anything and not a glimmer of a coin sliding into a cashbox. All of it was on tick. In one shop specializing in leather goods, while Fairwalk probed through a selection of hides to be made into boots at a shop down the road, Mieka helped Cade choose a pair of bright blue cheverel gloves for Derien. When Cade reached for his purse, the clerk flung his hands in the air, dismayed and embarrassed.

"Oh no, young Master, certainly not!"

"But they're not for me, or on Lord Fairwalk's charge, they're for my brother."

"And I'm sure he'll like them—you've taste, young Master, no doubting of it. It's an honor to be of service to a refined gentleman." The clerk glanced round and lowered his voice to a furtive murmur. "If you've a mind to it, you might mention where they came from—nothing more pleasing than a referral from anyone connected with His Lordship."

"Does anybody ever pay for anything in these shops?" Mieka asked, also very softly so the owner wouldn't overhear.

The clerk shrugged and rolled his eyes—gestures that would have cost him his place had his employer seen, Mieka was sure. "There's them as do when the goods are sent round, and them as waits for a bill, and them as don't never pay up. But there you are, that's the nobility for you."

The glance was so swift, Mieka almost didn't catch it. Yet a glance there was, and at Kearney Fairwalk, with the words *them as don't never pay up*. Surely not, Mieka told himself. His Lordship was rich, and when the bills came in surely he must settle them. The alternative was a visit by one of the unpleasant men who on occasion used to come round to Wistly Hall, in the bad old days before Jedris and Jezael and now Mieka himself started earning decent money.

That set him to wondering how much Touchstone would be paid for the honor of representing the Kingdom—or whether the honor would be considered payment enough. He'd counted on making enough this summer to contribute to the rest of the roof repairs, and make sure his father got the best of the new exotic woods for his lutes, and—and get married before the Winterly Circuit began.

Rummaging through his rather sketchy education, he recalled that the journey across the Flood to the Continent lasted between three and five days, depending on the weather and the destination port. And here his memory failed him—or, more to the point, he succeeded admirably in being unable to remember things he'd never bothered to learn. He had no idea where Gref Jyziero was. How long it would take to get there, how long back. How many places they would stop along the way, how many performances—how many weeks or even months it might be before he'd see her again.

Back in the little carriage, he turned to Fairwalk and demanded, "This journey to collect the new Princess—how long will it take?"

"You leave in eight days," said Fairwalk.

"And we'll be back about a month before the Winterly," said Cade.

Mieka opened his mouth, but before the instinctive wail could come out, His Lordship added, "And if we're lucky, when the public celebrations occur next spring, you'll be asked to perform at Court."

Appalled, he scrunched into a corner of the seat and said not a word as they started back to Wistly Hall. Cade and Fairwalk went on discussing the journey and the pieces that would translate well—or at least not suffer too much from a lack of translation. Mieka wanted to yell at them to shut up, didn't they understand that this thing they were so excited about meant he wouldn't see her again for *months*? Gods, he should've asked her to marry him before she went back to Frimham, he should've married her while she was still here—*months* he'd be gone, who knew but that some other man would come along and be able to offer her so much more than he ever could—of course there'd be another man, a dozen other men, she was so perfectly beautiful, the most beautiful thing he'd ever seen in his life—

"I rather had it in mind," said Fairwalk, "that you'd do well with a few of the Thirteen. 'Dragon,' of course, it's still your signature piece, but Jeschenar works a frightfully good comic ambassador in the Fourth. And of course 'Treasure.' Yes, that one ought to play quite nicely."

Mieka glanced up. "You knew," he blurted. "You knew this was coming up, and that's why you had us do the old version at Trials."

Cayden stared at him. "What're you on about?"

"He *knew*. So that we wouldn't make enough points for the Ducal, and we'd be the only really good group available." He bounced upright in the seat, fists clenching. "Think on it, Quill! Who else were they going to send? Somebody who didn't even make Winterly? Not bleedin' likely! They can't take anybody off the Ducal or Royal, there'd be all those bookings scrapped—both Circuits would be in an uproar."

"They could have done," Cade argued. "They could've chosen the Shadowshapers or Kelife—"

"And sent us out in their place?" He snorted. "*That'd* play well with customers who paid to see them and got us instead! D'you know how much harder we'd have to work to win them over?"

"Actually," murmured Lord Fairwalk, "I'm told the Tregrefina herself asked specifically for Touchstone."

For an instant Mieka was confused—he'd thought Tregrefina was her first name. Cade settled back against the upholstery, a triumphant smirk all over his face. The grin vanished with Fairwalk's next words.

"Though in a roundabout way, you're right, Mieka. I was hoping Touchstone would be selected, and it did occur to me that your availability without oversetting any Circuit arrangements might be an advantage, don't you see."

"Just like I said," Mieka flung at Cade. "He *knew.*"

"So what if he did?" Cade challenged. "It works out, doesn't it? She wants us, we're available, it can't do us anything but good!"

"It's *months* away from home, Quill!"

"You mean 'away from *her.*'" In a lethally quiet voice he asked, "Which takes precedence with you, Mieka? Your work, or your cock?"

"Boys, boys!" Fairwalk pleaded. "It's perfectly understandable that Mieka will miss his lady—and nobody's accusing you of neglecting Touchstone's career, Mieka, not in the least little bit!"

"*He* just did." Mieka sat back, fists tucked tight beneath his elbows so he wouldn't use them to make a few necessary adjustments to Cade's face.

"It won't be for that long," Fairwalk went on, alarmed when they continued to glower at each other. "It's such a tremendous opportunity, once-in-a-lifetime—"

"So is she!"

Cade laughed nastily. "And now you're about to tell me I'm

just envious because *you* have someone to come home to."

"Please," Fairwalk begged again, hands fluttering helplessly. "This isn't necessary—"

"Maybe it is," Cade said in that velvet-over-a-vial-of-acid voice. "Your choice, Mieka."

"You got that right! *My* choice!"

There was a certain satisfaction in seeing all the color drain from Cade's face. There was a definite shame in hearing him say softly, "Yes. Always."

He couldn't ask, not in front of Fairwalk. His Lordship didn't know about the Elsewhens. Mieka couldn't ask if Cade had seen some grim and desolate future—maybe the one where he hated Mieka.

"Quill—"

He shook his head. "No, it's all right. I'm sorry. I shouldn't have said that, not any of it."

"Nor me," he replied. It was as close as he could get to an apology. After all, the whole conversation had been Cade's fault. The instant he thought this, he wanted to squirm. Cade had been generous, so why couldn't he? Then he remembered that *"Your work, or your cock?"* question, and what it implied, and wanted to snarl all over again.

A fundamental and inconvenient honesty demanded that he admit, if only to himself, that smashing Cade's face apart for the insult to her reputation would make him a hypocrite. That she had been a virgin when he'd first had her was undeniable—but it was equally undeniable that he'd had her. And with that thought, he ached anew at how long it would be before he could have her again.

The rig pulled up in front of Wistly Hall and Mieka jumped out before the horse had come to a stop, bypassing two startled sisters and his parents on his headlong flight up the stairs. He paused only long enough to fumble through the desk in Jedris and Jezael's office. Armed with pen and ink and paper, he went straight to his secret little turret room and then sat there, staring at the blank page, without an idea in the world what to write.

How did Cade do it? How did he organize his thoughts into words and sentences? How did he fill great gaping empty page after page after page with words that *meant* something?

It wasn't as if Mieka hadn't written to her before. After Castle Biding, he'd worked hard to compose letters that would amuse, endear, coax, entreat, or all of these and more besides. Difficult as those words had been to find, even after he'd got started, now he couldn't even work out how to begin.

Minster chimes up and down the river had rung five before he was able even to write *Mistress Caitiffer*. The rest of the page, white and pristine, mocked him. He wasn't giving up, he told himself as he climbed back up through the trapdoor and trudged downstairs for dinner. He was just taking a bit of a break. Get his thoughts in order, arrange what he wanted to say in a fashion that made sense—that would make her fingers tremble and her heart race and—and—

"Not nervous about the trip, are you?"

His father's low, worried voice. Mieka looked up from his almost untouched plate and smiled. "Me?"

"Quite the adventure," he mused. "Seems my boys are growing up. It's an interesting thing, it is, watching my sons spread their wings and fly." A grin that Mieka knew was the model for his own suddenly decorated his face. "And then there's Tavier, of course."

"I'll bring him back a collection of Continental worms, shall I, to grow into dragons?"

"That would make him very happy," his father said, nodding. "Though how you'd keep them alive and wriggling is something I'm quite sure I don't want to know."

Jeska and Rafe had come to dinner, because Touchstone had

a gift to bestow on the happy couple before the wedding on the morrow. Once dessert had been passed round, Cade unfolded his long body from his chair and cleared his throat portentously.

"After due consideration," he declared, towering over them all, "which lasted about as long as it took this pair to fall in love—oh, shush up, Blye, you know it happened the instant you clapped eyes on him—and a discussion that took about as much time as it took Jed to forget everything and everybody in the world except Blye, which was by my precise calculations about an eyeblink—we concluded—"

"Get on with it!" Rafe shouted.

"I'm working my way there!" Cade grinned. "Where was I?"

"Consideration, discussion, conclusion," Jeska summarized.

"Of course. Beholden. The conclusion was that the four of us really have no idea how to run a business."

"Being *Artists*," Mieka contributed, just a bit spitefully, "we've no time to spare for anything other than being brilliant."

"Thinking great thoughts," Rafe added.

"Planning how next to startle the world," said Jeska.

"Unquestionably," Cade agreed affably. "So, except for a paltry two percent each—just to give us an excuse to make nuisances of ourselves—"

"When did you ever need an excuse?" Rafe wanted to know.

"—we hereby bestow upon Mistress Blye Cindercliff, soon to be Windthistle, all of Touchstone's share in the glassworks at Criddow Close." When Blye gasped and started to her feet, he pointed a long finger at her. "It's already done and dusted, nice and legal, so don't even think about objecting." Raising his glass, he proclaimed, "To Blye and Jed!"

As Mieka shouted an echo of the toast along with everyone else, he happened to glance at Lord Fairwalk—who looked even more stunned than Blye and Jedris, and not with the same delighted gratitude. Mieka had no idea what Touchstone's percentage of the glassworks was worth in terms of profit, leave alone the value of what they'd just given as a wedding present. But he was certain sure that His Lordship knew down to the last penny.

Mieka escaped the evening's chatter about tomorrow's wedding and slipped off to his turret. The words still wouldn't sort themselves, no matter how he tried. Cayden would know how to phrase things, but asking for his help was so impossible that he physically flinched. When he heard curfew bells ring, he very nearly gave up.

Then he remembered the little collection of thorn.

Not half an hour later he was finished. The letter wasn't entirely coherent, but he couldn't help that. The basics were there: the journey, the longing, the need, the fear. The plea to wait for him. The love.

Back downstairs in his brothers' office, he folded, addressed, and sealed the letter with the purple wax used by the Windthistle family forever, then left it on the desk atop a small pile of other post. The thorn was fading as he trudged up to his bedchamber. Cade was already asleep on the rickety old couch, curled on his side, looking perhaps fourteen of his twenty years. Their clothes for tomorrow hung neatly in the closet, and on the windowsill rested the small white velvet bag containing the necklet Blye would give Jed. It would be fastened with magic, just as Rafe's and Crisiant's had been, and only magic would ever unfasten it. Some couples chose bracelets or earrings to show they were bespoken or married. Mieka's parents wore rings. But whatever kind of circle signified the vows, those circles were always sealed with magic for magical folk.

As he settled into bed, and the thorn withered and left him exhausted, he wondered sleepily what she would want him to give her when she became his wife. He ought to have asked, in his letter. He really ought to have asked.

9

"**D**amn it to all hells!"

The stack of letters on the office desk was gone. The post had a ready gone out—some younger cousin whose duty it was to see to it every day had been too efficient this morning. Mieka ground his teeth and resisted the urge to skive off the wedding and write another letter this very instant. He'd woken with the thought in his head that he hadn't asked what marriage token she'd like, and that on the Continent he might find something truly spectacular by way of rings, bracelets, necklets, or earrings. Stupid, stupid.

Cade was already dressed and gone when Mieka got up. Good; Mieka's pride was still smarting from their exchange of words yesterday, and he wanted to give it a bit of time. The wedding would be the perfect distraction. By day's end, their scrap could be conveniently forgotten.

But by day's end, he would have only six days until Touchstone and who knew how large a parade of nobles and functionaries would sail for the Continent, and that was barely enough time for a return letter from Frimham. If he bought bracelets, she might want rings or necklets instead. If he didn't hear from her before they left, to be safe he'd have to buy sets of each and let her choose. And he still didn't know what, or indeed if, they'd be paid.

Rafe, he thought suddenly. He'd take Rafe shopping with him. Rafe could bargain down the price of anything even better than Mieka could. Between them, they could haggle until Mieka had a set of everything. Imagining the exquisite wonderment on her face when he kept pulling jewelry out of his pockets, he grinned to himself and went downstairs whistling.

Blye looked as close to perfect as a girl who hated wearing a skirt would ever look. The gown was simple: three layers of misty white silk, close-fitting sleeves, cuffs of wide purple ribbon matching the sash around her tiny waist. She seemed to float across the lawn, one lace-gloved hand resting lightly on Cade's wrist, the other clutching the nosegay of white and purple flowers. Her silver-blonde hair was loose around her face, a soft breeze off the river catching it now and then to reveal amethyst earrings set in silver that had belonged to her mother. She had found them in her father's things after he died, safe inside a tiny glass box.

Standing with Jezael as their brother's patrons, Mieka heard Jedris catch his breath when Blye came into view. Mieka grinned and caught Cade's gray eyes, and Cade winked at him. They were all right again, Mieka thought with relief. Neither of them could hold on to a begrudgement very long—and all at once it struck him that with whatever terrible things Cade must have seen in the Elsewhens, he didn't bear any grudges about those, either. How could one resent things that hadn't even happened yet? Mieka didn't resent Cade for having seen them, did he?

Well, mayhap he did. Just a little. Life had been a lot simpler before he'd acquired a friend who could see the future. Mieka did as impulse took him, without worrying much about consequences and without ever thinking that there might be other choices to be made. He wondered idly if Cade had foreseen this wedding or the trip to the Continent, then remembered something about if the choices weren't his to make, he wouldn't glimpse any futures that might come of them. So, because the decision to fall in love had been Jed and Blye's—

He stifled a snort. Who ever *decided* to fall in love?

Cade was fulfilling a paternal role today, escorting Blye across the lawn while Alaen Blackpath and his cousin Briuly traded delicate phrases on lutes made by Hadden Windthistle. Cade would present her to Jedris—but not "bestow" her as her father would have done. She had chosen as her patron none other than Derien Silversun: wearing his first grown-up suit of clothes that matched Cade's elegant gray and white (with purple neckbands), and terribly serious as only an eight-year-old could be as he stood with Mieka and Jez as guarantors of each partner's good behavior towards the other through the course of their lives.

As Cade tucked Blye's gloved hand in Jed's and the couple faced the Good Brother and Good Sister, Mieka watched his tall, broad-shouldered, redheaded brother smile down at tiny, silvery Blye, and all at once they were the most perfectly matched pair in the world. The quirks of heredity—Elf, Goblin, Wizard, Sprite, Piksey, Human, and who-knew-what-else—in the Windthistle and Cindercliff bloodlines had somehow created these two people who were right for each other. And who'd found each other, Mieka told himself gleefully, all because of him. If ever he needed proof that one decision—*his*, to travel to Gowerion on the chance that he might sit in with Cade, Rafe, and Jeska as their glisker—could change lives, the sight of Jed and Blye claiming each other convinced him beyond all doubting.

Chat and Sakary parted from the other guests, Chat holding a withie in one hand. White latticework sprang up from the grass to arch over the couple's heads, and vines began to swirl up each side, covered in white rosebuds and purple thistles. It was a lovely illusion, and Mieka was irked that he hadn't thought of it himself.

A Good Brother and a Good Sister officiated, but as usual Mieka wasn't listening. When he wasn't busy imagining the lawn crowded with friends and family for another wedding, he was scanning the gathering. Chat was here with his wife, Deshenanda, who was hugely pregnant. Next to her was Sakary's new wife, the poutingly lovely Chirene, who had pinned half a garden of daisies in her black hair to highlight her gown, a vast billowing of yellow so ruched and frilled and gathered that she looked rather like a walking plate of scuffled eggs. Vered and Rauel had sent regrets, and gifts, from their holiday cottages in, respectively, a village on the eastern coast and Romuald Needler's new horse farm.

As for the other guests—there were Rafe and Crisiant, Rafe's parents, Jeska (though not his mother, still seaside), those amongst the uncles and aunts and cousins that Jed actually liked, and some of Windthistle Brothers' favorite clients. (These included a wine merchant whose rotted roof had been sussed out in Jed and Jez's instinctive fashion; he'd paid for the repairs with three cases of the finest Frennitch Colvado brandy, and Mieka had endured a blistering lecture from his mother when he'd tried to swipe a bottle in advance of the wedding.) A few of Master Cindercliff's old friends were here as well. The Threadchaser–Bramblecotte wedding had been a business occasion as much as a family celebration; Jed and Blye were doing much the same thing on a smaller scale; Mieka was glad that his own wedding would be reserved for those he loved.

Lady Jaspiela Silversun had also received an invitation. Mieka had bluntly inquired of Cade whether he wanted Mieka to charm her into accepting or rejecting it; he was capable, of course, of either. Cade had only laughed. "Can you seriously imagine my mother gracing the nuptials of someone barely a cut above a servant? She's already declined."

Blye was removing her white lace gloves with the grace of an accomplished glasscrafter. She gave them to the Good Sister.

Jed was having trouble peeling off the plain white silk gloves Jinsie had sewn for him, and cursed under his breath as a stitch ripped. At last he gave them to the Good Brother, who placed them in the little brass bowl on the grass between himself and the Good Sister. He struck flint, and when the flames had steadied and burned low, she poured water from a little silver pitcher. Thus the pair came to the marriage with clean hands, all their past graspings burned away. Blye and Jedris then clasped hands, fingers intertwined, and smiled at each other. Mieka heard a sob and knew it was his mother. She'd wept buckets when Rafe married Crisiant; with eight children of her own to marry off, there was a real danger that her tears would get tired.

Cade reached into a pocket, which was Jezael's signal to do the same, and the silver necklets were handed over. Blye stood on tiptoe to drape the plain silver links around Jed's neck, and Cade moved to take each end in his fingertips. There were Good Brothers and Good Sisters who officiated at weddings and sealed bracelets or rings or necklets so often that their fingers showed the scars of even these tiny bursts of magical fire. But Blye had wanted Cade to do this, and he did—quickly, gently, first Jed's and then Blye's.

And that was when all the glass flowers in the keepsake nosegays and all the real flowers on the trellis unfolded into full bloom. Mishia Windthistle had done the first, but the second was the work of Chat and Sakary, with a wafting scent of roses in the sunshine and a delicate pealing of silvery bells.

The gasps of surprise, the scattered applause—the delight on Blye's and Jed's faces—these things were almost as good as and in some ways better than the accolades of an audience of four hundred. Mieka decided that in the unlikely event that he ever tired of life on the Circuit, he and Rafe could hire themselves out for weddings. For although it was Chat's magic in that single withie that had produced the effects, it was Sakary's graceful handling of that magic that spread joy and laughter through the air.

Mieka suddenly realized that Cayden was wrong about the true significance of theater and magic. It wasn't the example a play could provide that the striving was the important thing, or the communal experience that let each man in the audience become a part of the same connecting event. It was the emotion. To make fifty or five hundred people laugh, weep, flinch in terror, cry out with joy—the plot wasn't the impetus for the feelings, it was the other way round. The emotions had to be real for the story to work. Otherwise it was all illusion forced on people who knew what they were feeling but didn't know why they were feeling it. Mieka and Rafe could make an audience experience anything they chose; but if Cade's words from Jeska's lips didn't serve those emotions, it was all empty.

This was Black Lightning's mistake. What had Thierin Knottinger said about their very name? Rafe had coolly observed that a flash of black in a night sky made them rather invisible, and Thierin had replied, *"You'll never see us coming."* Their audiences never saw the connections. You didn't pummel audiences with feeling just because you *could.* They had to understand why and how the story led to specific emotions. Otherwise it was like conjuring up a bell that rang with the sound of a dozen barking dogs, or roses that smelled like burnt toast. Interesting, mayhap, but ultimately a journey through a bewilderland that only rankled an audience and left them, in the end, unsatisfied.

A bright flash in the summer sun brought him back to the wedding. The Good Brother and Good Sister were holding aloft the loving cups to be admired by the guests before they were filled with consecrated Chapel wine. It was the first time Mieka had seen them, and he stifled a giggle, telling himself that his much-loved but generally unimaginative brother Jedris must have some creativity rattling round his brain after all. The cups weren't the fine cut crystal one might have expected of a glasscrafter. Each was one half of a thistle, the bases and stems made of stone and the flower-cups of silver. The joke usually was that the more breakable the loving cups, the less likely they were to be used as emphasis in a marital spat, but that wood or metal was just begging to be flung at an offending spouse. Mayhap it was noting more than a pun: the *thistle* of Jed's name, the *cliff* of Blye's. He reminded himself to ask later on—and whether Jed intended the loving cups to survive their arguments even if he didn't.

The couple drank, received the blessings, and exchanged their first kiss as husband and wife. Jed hoisted Blye up into his arms and she wrapped one leg around his waist. They were both laughing. The Good Brother and Good Sister looked slightly scandalized.

"All right, all right!" Mieka yelled. "That's enough! You're wed, it's legal, so let's get this party started!"

Ten minutes of laughter and hugs later, Mieka was applying a large flagon of ale as a cure for his thirst. One more, mayhap two, and then he could get down to the delightful business of getting drunk on that superb Colvado brandy. Then he caught sight of two new arrivals and knew that all five barrels of ale plus every bottle of brandy would be insufficient to remedy what had just intruded on the wedding.

"Great-grandmother!" Hadden Windthistle exclaimed, striding to the top of the lawn where an inconceivably ancient, wizened, twisted specter had appeared, escorted by the preposterously Elfen-garbed Uncle Barsabian. Not that Sharadel Windthistle, born Snowminder, was any the less "classically" attired, for an Elf; a vivid green gown, heavily embroidered about the hem with gold and silver squiggles presumably mysterious and arcane, was topped with a bright yellow jacket sporting a diamond-studded silver snowflake pin the size of a dinner plate that looked to overbalance the old ghoul at any instant. Atop thinning yellow-white hair, scraped back to show off emphatically pointed ears, was the sort of spry little red cap that Mieka conjured for Jeska when they did one of the "Elfen Mischief" farces. Below the velvet cap was a face so warped with age and spite that to look at it was to grimace. She stumped angrily from the terrace, leaning on Barsabian and a gnarled walking stick that dug deliberate chunks out of the velvet-smooth lawn. Cilka, who was clever with plants in the way of the Greenseed side of the family, had worked very hard to make the river garden perfect. Mieka caught a glimpse of her in the crowd; the poor darling was near tears.

Alaen and Briuly Blackpath had been wandering the outskirts of the garden together, playing for the guests. Their complicated duet faded into a few startled, forlorn plucked strings. And the silence was complete as Sharadel Windthistle screeched, "Where's the ghastly Goblin girl?"

Jedris turned slowly from receiving the Threadchasers' congratulations. Mieka decided his elder brother must possess a truly vivid imagination after all, for in those sky-blue eyes were promises of permanent and painful injury, inventively inflicted.

"I hope, Great-great-grandmother," he said, "that you are not making a reference to my wife."

She wheezed in an outraged breath. *"Wife?"* Then, craning her neck to squint up at Barsabian, she demanded, "You said we'd be in time to stop it!"

"Did you honestly think you could?" Jed asked.

"The money's mine, boy!"

"I've my own," he snapped, then added with scrupulous politeness that was like a slap in the face, "beholden all the same."

Barsabian was practically hugging himself with glee. "Did I tell you? Did I? I knew she'd find some way to claum on to one of us! Good thing it's only one of the *Human* ones—but still, a Windthistle mating with a *Goblin*! It's beyond belief!"

Cade moved closer to Blye, who had turned as white as her dress. Mieka was torn between protecting her and joining Jed and Jez in what he knew would be satisfying violence. The conflict rendered him effectively paralyzed for a crucial few moments.

"Here's an ending to it!" shouted the old woman, waving a rolled-up piece of parchment with a large purple wax seal and many ribbons depending from it. "Not a clipped penny to any of you! This tumbledown pile may be yours, Hadden, but the money goes to the only truly Elfen Windthistle left!" She gestured with the other claw at Barsabian.

Hadden laughed in her face. "At last!" he cried. "It took him long enough! This house, as you say, *is* mine—" His face hardened like cooling glass. "—and you are about to leave it. Permanently."

Jed turned slightly, bowed to Blye, and said, "Pray excuse me a moment, love, there's some rubbish as needs to be removed before it causes any greater stink."

"Jed," she whispered. "Please—don't—"

He gave her a tight little smile and started forwards. So did Jezael. So did Mieka. But Jeska, consummate street fighter and collector of vanquished opponents' teeth, was closer and quicker. He grasped Barsabian by one pointed ear and marched him down the grass to the river. The old man's squeals were literally drowned when Jeska shoved him into the water. He emerged, drenched and incoherent, fists flailing impotently against a foe no longer there: Jeska had started back up the slope for the house. Barsabian staggered from the shallows, spitting—and then screaming, for Chat had a bit of magic left in the withie. He and Sakary sent it in the form of a swirling of wasps that appeared out of nowhere to swarm around Barsabian's head. The stings might be illusory, but the pain was real. They were half of the Shadowshapers, and very, very good at their work.

Jeska joined the three eldest Windthistle sons and their

father in a grim advance on the shrieking crone. But they weren't fast enough. Jinsie had snatched up a chair. She set it behind the old woman just in time for it to catch her as Mishia gave her an unambiguous shove. There was nothing left for the men to do but hoist the chair and carry her, kicking and howling, back into the house—after Mieka had relieved her of her dangerously flailing stick.

When they had set her outside in the street near her boxy antique of a coach and slammed the front door on her, Mieka grinned. "That was fun!"

"Wasn't it?" his father laughed. Then he glanced towards the stairs, and farther up at the gallery above. Dozens of relations— curious, horrified, scared, approving, confused—looked down on them. "Well?" Hadden snapped. "You heard her! There's no Windthistle money and never will be! So any of you not liking the looks of the future at Wistly Hall can clear out and go beg house room of Barsabian and that pustulant old horror! *Now!*" he bellowed, and flung the front door open.

Mieka supposed he really shouldn't have been surprised by the sudden scurrying. He lingered in the entryway with his father and Jez—Jed and Jeska had vanished, probably to collect Uncle Barsabian for ejection. Within minutes, a ragabash of Windthistle relations was trudging down the stairs carrying bags and boxes, and armfuls of clothes.

"Fa," Mieka whispered, "they might be taking—"

"I don't care," he snarled. "As long as they're finally out of my house, I don't give two shits! As for which of them is responsible for her coming uninvited—" To a middle-aged cousin trying to sneak past: "Was it you, Mander? Or mayhap your bitch of a wife? You'll not get *her* past the front doors of Clinquant House unless you lie and say her ears were kagged when she was born!"

Mieka traded amazed glances with Jez. Neither of them had ever seen their father more than mildly annoyed; this level of rage, and so cold a rage at that, was unprecedented. They stood together and watched as twenty and then thirty people of all ages slunk past, some of them shamefaced, others defiant, a few openly scornful and muttering about sordid alliances with Goblins. Granted, Mieka had never kept track of who lived here as long as they left him alone, but he could have sworn he'd never seen some of these people before in his life. Wistly wouldn't exactly echo with their absence—there would be at least forty or so assorted relatives remaining. But good riddance to these. Blye's cat Bompstable evidently thought so, too: he had stationed himself beside the front door, hissing.

"Gracious me," drawled Jinsie as the last stragglers went out the door into the street. "I *knew* we should've let them come to the wedding."

Mieka nodded solemnly. "Dangerous, these social snubbings." He glanced over at Derien, who had been guarding a table of gifts not yet unwrapped. "Remember that, when you're a Lord High Ambassador."

The boy wrinkled his nose. "I'll remember it when I want to get rid of somebody!"

"When I'm grown up," announced Tavier, who had hitched a ride on Rafe's broad shoulders, "I'll send me dragons after them all, I will, for being so mean to Blye."

"Aroint!" shouted Uncle Barsabian. "Unhand me, you clumpertons!"

Jed and Jeska were hauling the sopped and furious old Elf by the elbows. When he saw through the open door that outside was a substantial collection of persons who might or might not be related to him milling about the hideous old-fashioned coach, he turned an even deeper shade of crimson.

"You won't be lonely, Uncle Breedbate," Mieka assured him.

Jinsie nodded. "Though how he'll stuff them all into that rig back to the Clink might make for an entertainment."

"Ah, but he has the *money* now, doesn't he?" Jez murmured, poisonously sweet. "He can hire a whole convoy of hacks to carry them."

"Gleets, every one of you!" shouted Barsabian.

Mieka frowned. "Does he mean us or his new houseguests?"

"Oh, take that old pillock out of here," said their mother. "He's dripping on my carpets."

Hadden had called it aright: Great-great-grandmother, still in the chair, was inspecting each refugee for acceptable Elfenness. Mander had somehow talked his wife into her favor, and they stood with the more obviously eared. As the rest of them shuffled forwards in a line to be judged, Mieka heard someone say, "I may not have the ears, but look at these hands and feet! Look at my teeth! I'm Elfen, no denying it!"

He looked at Jinsie. "Nice that there's a few independent witnesses. Nobody would ever believe this."

"Not off a stage," she agreed. "It's disgusting. C'mon, let's get the taste out of our mouths."

"What a scathingly brilliant idea."

He slammed the door shut and looked round. His mother was arm-in-arm with his father, looking more in love with him than ever. Mieka wondered why his father hadn't done this years ago.

Cade had joined them, and in his hand was the gnarled walking stick. "Anybody have any use for this?" When no one said anything, he nodded. "Excellent." And with that he flung the thing into the air as if it were a withie to be shattered, and halfway to the rafters it caught fire. There were gasps of surprise, and then laughter and cheering.

Mieka exchanged grins with Cade as naught but ash drifted to the floor. "That's me Quill," he announced happily. "*Now* it's a party!"

* * *

"Sjus' like th'old Winnerting song," said Briuly Blackpath to his cousin. His tongue might be slurring and his eyes might be blurring, but his fingers were flawlessly steady on his lute strings. Mieka, sprawled in a drawing-room chair with a bottle of brandy cradled to his chest, knew a kindred spirit when he saw one: a man who could get drunk everywhere but his hands.

Alaen was considerably more sober than his cousin, whom he resembled not at all. Alaen was brown and golden, long-mouthed and sharp-chinned; Briuly had black hair, dusky skin, a high-arched nose, pointed Elfen ears, and a certain spidery fragility about his thin limbs. They had the same hands, though, Mieka noted idly: too big for a glisker's quickness, but they made up for it in the nimbleness of the fingers. Briuly struck an introductory chord. His singing voice wasn't drunk, either.

> *I beheld me at a wedding such wondrous sights to see:*
> *Ten flasks of ale a-quaffing—nine down my throat by sunset,*
> *Eight twin Windthistles—seven not yet wedded,*
> *Six famous players—five of them drunk a-reeling*
> *Four lissome ladies dancing, three old glasscrafters snoring,*
> *Two Elfen dreadfuls banished, one swarm of magic waspies,*
> *And a wedding to remember, it was!*

Mieka would have applauded, but that would have meant relinquishing the bottle—and Cade, lounging nearby on the rug and too lazy to get up and fetch his own, had been casting covetous eyes at it for the last half hour. The food had been eaten, the toasts had been raised and drunk, the dances had been danced, and Jed and Blye had been waved joyously off to their wedding trip—a week on a river barge floating through the countryside towards Seekhaven, where they'd catch the public coach back to Gallantrybanks. Many of the guests had departed, and those who remained had got down to the business of serious drinking.

"In my professional opinion," Cade mused, "the lack of rhyming is a drawback." He sank his chin into his purple neckband and belched daintily. "But it sows promish."

Chat wandered in with Deshenanda, who was leaning heavily on her husband's arm, to say their farewells. "Mistress Mirdley vows that if I don't take Desha home," he said, "she'll deprive me of the means to father any more children after this one. And I believe her."

"You better!" Cade laughed, rising to give the girl a slightly unsteady bow, take her hand, and brush his lips gently across her wrist. "It was good to see you again. We'll bring back shomething—some*thing*—lovely for the baby's Namingday present."

"Pale and tired as she is," came Mistress Mirdley's sharp voice from the doorway, "that might be sooner than anyone thinks if you don't get her tucked up in bed! Cayden, make yourself useful and help her to their carriage!"

Cade rolled his eyes and did as told. Mieka had yet to meet anyone who didn't do as told when Mistress Mirdley was doing the telling. Cade returned with a fresh bottle of brandy, and when Mieka sat up and looked hopeful, he received only a broad grin in return.

"But mine's nearly empty!" he whined.

"Poor you." He sank to the floor, folding his long legs, and uncorked the bottle. After a long swallow, he sighed and announced, "I do love a wedding. Let's have another when we get back, eh?"

Mieka fluttered his eyelashes and in a perfect imitation of Jeska's simpering maidens, exclaimed, "Why, Master Silversun! Was that a proposal?"

Cade pretended to consider, then shook his head. "You'd look dreadful in a white gown and lace gloves."

"So would you," Mieka retorted.

Alaen began a melodramatic version of "Wilt Thou Favor Me,

Heart's Darling, with Thy Pretty Glovèd Hand?" Mieka threw a pillow at him. A small snowfall of feathers escaped a ragged seam; Cade waved a lazy finger and the feathers drifted back to the pillow.

"Flaunter," Mieka muttered. "Went to a Wizardly academy, he did, with all sorts of silly tricks up his sleeves. Never anything useful, though, not him!"

Alaen wasn't listening. Neither was he playing his lute. Mieka glanced around and immediately knew why.

Sakary and Chirene had come in. The fettler was saying something-or-other to Cayden while his wife drifted elegantly through the drawing room with that instinct all supremely beautiful women had of finding the exact place in any setting where the light (in this case, sunset) and the backdrop (the only reasonably intact tapestry left at Wistly) showed her to perfect advantage. She glowed against the rich colors behind her, the daisies in her black hair like tiny sunbursts, the crumples and ruffles of her yellow skirts swirling with dark golden shadows. She was, Mieka supposed, a prize beyond anything most men ever dreamed on. Yet his own instinct told him that she was the type of woman who expected admiration from every man who set eyes on her. It wasn't that she silently demanded to be stared at; she didn't have to. Men did that all on their own. She adorned any scene she condescended to inhabit, but the air around her seemed oddly empty, as if all words and thoughts had fled, afraid of trying to compete. How she had ended up with dour, glowering Sakary Grainer was a total mystery. Something about his adoration must be different from the rest, more satisfying in some way Mieka couldn't even begin to guess.

Even with his heart bespoken, Mieka was not immune to the allure of a fabulously beautiful girl, but not only did she fall into the category of *Another Man's Possession*, he frankly found very little about Chirene that was truly alluring. There was a remoteness to her beauty, like a statue in High Chapel: not cold, but oddly distant. Instinct told him that although a man could look—he'd have to be three days' dead *not* to look—she'd rarely if ever welcome touch. It might disorder her hair or smudge her lip rouge.

Alaen was looking at Chirene as if he would be content to touch the sole of her slipper with a single fingertip. There was a stunned helplessness in the musician's blue eyes, much the same look most men wore around her—at least until they remembered their manners, as one of the glasscrafters had not this afternoon until his wife trod deliberately on his foot. But there was something else about Alaen's eyes, too, something vulnerable and yearning. Something hopeless.

As Sakary held out a hand to his wife and she glided back across the room to him, Mieka glanced at Cade. He was frowning slightly, his gaze darting from Alaen to Chirene and back again. So he saw it, too, Mieka thought. It was an excellent thing that they'd be inviting Alaen along to—oh, wherever it was they were picking up the new Princess. A couple of months away, and the spell would fade. There would be other women, and she would be forgotten.

That was how it was, he reminded himself wisely, when the attraction was nothing but physical. A month or two, and—

Months away. *Months.*

He swore on his next swallow of brandy that tomorrow he'd write to her again, and the day after, and the day after that, so she would know this long separation wasn't of his choosing.

Well, not exactly, anyway.

10

Riotous as Wistly Hall could be on any given day, the morning of Touchstone's departure for the Continent was pure pandemonium.

"Rafcadion Threadchaser, don't you *dare* tell me you left your good cloak at home!"

"Just as you like, sweet love. I won't tell you."

"Has anybody seen Mieka?"

"Not recently, Mistress Windthistle. The cloak's right here, Crisiant," soothed Jeska. "He was using it to play dragons last night with Tavier."

"Tavier? Oh Gods, he's not in Mieka's trunk again, is he?"

"No, Mum," came Petrinka's assurance, "he's helping Cilka put Bompstable into his carry-basket so he won't get outside again. I do wish they'd taken the cat with them. The poor thing cries for them every night."

"He'd cry louder if he fell off the barge into the river," Rafe pointed out.

"Where's His Lordship got to?"

"Jinsie! Damn it, she was here just a second ago—Trinka, if you don't get your thieving little fingers out of that food basket, I'll tell Mistress Mirdley!"

"Mum! I didn't, I swear—"

"Has anybody seen Cade?"

"Did that Blackpath boy get here yet? I've another set of strings for him. Just in case."

"Crisiant, what happened to that little polishing kit Blye sent over?"

"Jinsie! Where *are* you!"

"Cade had it last—it must be in with the glass baskets and already in the carriage. Which remembers me, which of you has that little box Blye made for the new Princess?"

"Cade has that, too. I think."

"You *think*—? Oh, Gods! Where is he? Jeska, have you seen him?"

"When did she have time to make it?"

"*Jinsie!*"

"The night before the wedding, I'm told. She said she'd not be sleeping anyway, what with the fidgets, so—"

"Too much to hope that Mieka's shown his ears down here yet, eh?"

"Haven't seen him, sorry, Master Windthistle."

"Hadden, give those strings to Rafe. Is anybody interested in the fact that if you don't get out of here right now, the ship sails without you?"

"And where's Cayden?"

"Haven't seen him. Now, Rafe, you be sure to mention that these are for the rosewood lute, not the spruce—"

Mishia had had enough. She climbed nimbly atop the hall table and shouted, "Outside! Everybody! *Now!*"

There was a scuffle and a scrum at the door, and a slamming, and then a silence.

"Cade! Over here! No, you idiot, *here!*"

"Jinsie? What are you doing lurking under the stairs?"

"Shushup! I have to talk to you."

"If you're about to tell me to keep an eye on that brother of yours—"

"Not on him. On his letters. Like this one."

"Jinsie—!"

"I took it off the pile on the desk yesterday morning, just like I took all the other letters he's written to her since we found out about this journey."

Another silence.

"And you want me to do the same, while we're away."

"Yes."

"You don't like her."

"I pretend, for Mieka's sake. I keep thinking it will burn out. But she's—there's something about her, Cade, it's not just me, Cilka feels it, too! And that mother of hers, I *know* she's becasting him, or her, or maybe both. Mum says we're imagining things, but—you have to make sure he thinks his letters were lost—"

"No."

"You *have* to! It's months you'll be gone, and if she doesn't know why and doesn't hear from him, then she'll think he's forgotten about her, and then she'll set her sights on someone else—"

"Don't you care how much it would hurt him?"

"Not if it saves him making the worst mistake of his life!"

"If it's a mistake, it's his to make."

"I know my own brother! It isn't just that she's not right for him. She's so completely wrong that it scares me. You have to help, Cade. You have to do this for me. For him."

"The only thing I'll do for either of you is never say a word about this to Mieka. Not what you did, nor what you asked me to do."

"Haven't you seen the way she looks at him? Like he's a prize to be won at a village fair! She's winning, Cade, and she can't, and you have to help me stop it."

"I said *no!*"

Mieka peeked again through the crack between the hinges of the partly open dining room door, and saw Cade stride angrily out into the street. A moment later Jinsie followed, scrubbing furious tears from her cheeks. When he could think again, breathe again, Mieka got a better grip on the half-barrel of Auntie Brishen's whiskey that he'd stashed in the dining room cupboard and went outside. Jinsie was lucky his hands were otherwise occupied; he didn't trust himself not to slap her. As for Cayden—he couldn't even meet the man's eyes. All the farewells had been said and all the last-minute advice had been given and all the baggage had been checked one more time and they were all in Fairwalk's carriage rattling down the cobbles before he could even begin to think about what Cade had said.

Mieka was scrunched in between Jeska and Rafe, his feet propped on the half-barrel and his knees in his face, opposite Fairwalk, Cade, and Briuly Blackpath, who had accepted the invitation that Alaen had refused. If Mieka had his suspicions about precisely why Alaen had refused, he kept them to himself. He didn't like riding with his back to the horses, and he was nervous anyway with the excitement of the voyage, and to put the crowning touch to his discomfort, his unsettled stomach was knotting around itself with rage. The drive was nearly over before he'd managed to argue his breakfast into staying where he'd put it, and then they were loading themselves and everything else onto a tall-masted ship, and he still hadn't begun to work out what he thought and felt.

Briuly turned out to be even more obsessed with the safety of his lutes than Cade was about the glass baskets and withies. It did no good to soothe him with reminders that Mieka's mother had becast the cases with the same cushioning spell Mieka had long since used on the basket crates, and that the cases themselves had been constructed by Jezael to each instrument's exact dimensions. When the two polished, big-bellied wooden boxes were taken down from the carriage, Briuly had to check to make sure the lutes were all right. He carried them himself up the gangplank to be inspected by the Crown Port Officer for whatever such persons inspected for (a right nuisance, and one would think that players in the Royal employ sailing on a Royal ship on a Royal diplomatic mission would be exempt, but there it was). Then he had to check them again. It wasn't until they were securely stowed in a cupboard of the stateroom he would share with Kearney Fairwalk (now, *there* was a pairing, Mieka thought, briefly amused) that Briuly breathed freely again. And headed for the nearest bottle of wine.

Mieka was sorely tempted to do likewise. He felt every tiny movement of the deck beneath his feet, and the ship hadn't even left the dock. This didn't bode well for what might happen when they actually set sail. He had a sketchy idea that there were spells that could move things and even people great distances in an eyeblink, but the Fae Folk had jealously guarded those as well as so much else. Now such spells were lost. There were stories of Wizards and Elves who had tried to replicate these spells based on what little information lingered. These stories always ended messily.

It remained, however, that at some point instantaneous transfer had been done, and he wished the shifty Fae to whichever hell least suited them for keeping the secret to themselves. He was *not* looking forward to the next few days. Cooped up with Touchstone, Lord Fairwalk, Briuly Blackpath, assorted Court functionaries of the lesser sort, servants, and a collection of sailors who ranged from twelve-year-old cabin boys to leather-faced veterans of a hundred voyages—no, he was not looking forward to it at all. Auntie Brishen had sent along the essentials, both for seasickness and otherwise, but even if he made use of them and stayed the whole time in the cabin he'd be sharing with Cade—still, it was a cabin he'd be sharing with Cade.

Which meant he'd best sort himself out, or a few days would seem like many, many years.

He stood at the ship's railing, holding on tight, looking out at the south shore. Of the six bridges connecting the north and south banks of the Gally River, there was only one below the Plume—only about a half mile from Wistly Hall, in fact, but no ship this size with masts this tall could fit under it. The docks for vessels plying the Ocean Sea were downriver, and the banks were lined with warehouses, chaundlers, taverns, and brothels, and the dwellings of those who serviced the Kingdom's trade. A rough district, for certes. It was just past dawn and already he could pick out four fistfights and a brace of trulls arguing with their customer. A warehouse door slammed open and two boys pelted out, arms full of burlap bags, and an instant later a hugely muscular man, at least half Giant, came running after them, knives in both hands. A Crown Constable was marching along behind a well-dressed and protesting gentleman, encouraging him to step lively at the point of the gentleman's own sword—all a constable was allowed to carry was a truncheon, though most of them secreted other weapons about their mud-brown uniforms. Everybody shouted and nobody listened.

Cade strolled past Mieka, talking with Fairwalk. He nodded and smiled as he went by, nothing self-conscious or wary in his eyes, no hint of worry over what Jinsie had told him. Mieka frowned after him, noting that as the ship left the dock and was caught with a little jolt by the river's current, Cade stayed sure-footed as a cat. Good image for him, Mieka told himself sourly: make sure he was fed and petted and praised, and had a nice warm place to sleep and his own way, and he was purringly content. Otherwise…

Mieka didn't like being at odds with Quill. It always showed up in the magic. Those six illicit withies he'd made last year, for instance—Mieka had sensed the fear inside them, and had eventually found out why. Knowing what to feel for after working with the man this long (was it only a year and a half?), he could tell by the taste of the magic in the withies whether Cade had been annoyed, amused, tired, bored, unhappy, excited, or just doing his job when he primed them. The importance of their upcoming shows meant that Cade had to be cosseted into a good mood, a productive mood. To accomplish it, Mieka had to be, as usual, both clever and mad.

Just coming into view were the Royal Standards flying atop the Keeps, twin fortresses that faced each other across the river, protecting the approach to the city. Mieka had always wondered why anyone bothered to build anything that ugly even once, leave alone twice. The new Princess would be spending her time in the north tower until the official marriage, which he supposed was a good thing: after a month or so in that grim, gray place, even the grimiest Gallantry-banks street would seem a paradise. Not that she would ever be allowed to see any grime, of course.

Cade strolled by again, talking with Briuly this time as they shared swigs from a wine bottle. Mieka's hands clenched around the wooden railing. Had Jinsie thought she was being clever when she tried to enlist Cade in her plot? How dare anyone not understand that all his happiness for the rest of his life was bound up in *her*?

Well, he'd deal with his twin sister another time. What was important now was Cade's refusal to enter into Jinsie's scheme. Cade wouldn't make choices for Mieka. He'd said so before, of course, but Mieka hadn't really believed him. And that shamed him. He was awestruck now by Cade's faith in him. It was a degree of trust he knew he'd done little to deserve. Never consciously analytical, especially about his own soul, Mieka nonetheless knew himself to be capricious, impulsive, and thoughtless. He wasn't the sort of person anybody ought to trust.

Cade trusted him.

He suspected Cade was an idiot.

What had Mieka ever done to demonstrate that he'd think a decision through instead of simply plowing on ahead as pleased him, and be damned to the consequences? Consequences were for charming himself out of. Was *that* what Cade trusted in him? That whatever happened, Mieka could—

"I think I hated you."

He stared unseeing at the passing view of the wharves. It was his life, not Cade's. He had to please himself. He had to do what was right for him. But how was he supposed to know which was the right choice—the one that wouldn't lead to *"I hated you"*? It wasn't as if he was the sort of person who sat down to analyze alternatives, to pick and choose the way one would ponder the bill of fare at an inn. It wasn't as if he had Cade's education or intellect, or inclination to pick his own emotions to bits just so he could examine the component parts.

It was those damned Elsewhens, Mieka decided. They'd taught Cade to see everything in terms of which decision might lead to what future. Look at that "Doorways" piece, with its score of options. Touchstone only ever presented five or six of them during a performance, but Cade had cooked up plenty more in that overactive brain of his, and suddenly Mieka wondered which of them he'd actually dreamed, and which were the products of his imagination. But maybe for Cade, *dream* and *imagine* were the same thing.

"You said you opened the right door. How do you know there were wrong ones?" Mieka had asked him once. *"Or—no, not wrong, just different."*

Was there just one right door, one right decision? Or was each merely different from the others, variations that led to lives that weren't necessarily inferior, just not what he'd originally had in mind? *Dream* or *imagine* could turn to *nightmare* as far as Cade was concerned, but—how was Mieka supposed to decide?

Gods, this was giving him a headache. The morning sun was too bright on the water, and the shouts of the sailors were too loud as they made ready the sails. He squeezed his eyes shut but it didn't help.

It was his life to be lived. Cade couldn't and wouldn't live it for him. Cade had faith in him.

Cade was a fool.

"I think I hated you."

Suddenly he felt sick, and told himself it was the uncertainty of the wooden deck beneath his feet. Shivering, he turned from the railing, leaning back against it, wrapping his arms around himself. Somebody placed a bucket at his feet. He could hear laughter as he fell to his knees and vomited until his stomach was empty—"Still in sight of the docks, and he's already seasick?"—but he didn't care. An arm wrapped about his ribs and long fingers supported his forehead, and a light voice spoke into his ear.

"This isn't another High Chapel prank, is it? No, I didn't think so. You about done? Come on, then."

Cade helped him stand, guided him down some steps and along a passage that smelled of wood and citrus wax. A little while later he was huddled in the lower of two bunks, a blanket round his shoulders and a cup of water in his hands.

"I hope Auntie Brishen sent along something to the purpose," Cade remarked. "Or was this just your delightfully subtle way of claiming the lower berth? You're sure to have a laugh every night, watching me clamber about, and every morning, watching me tumble to the floor."

He looked up, and all amusement fled those clear gray eyes. "Quill—" But he couldn't say it. He couldn't ask why Cade trusted him. Instead: "I'm fine now. Just nerves, I s'pose. I'll take the upper."

"We'll see. And there's no need to fret, Mieka. It's Touchstone they want. Not the Sparks or the Shadowshapers. *Us.*"

Us—such a little word, surely too small to contain so much meaning. Their lives were their own to live, but hadn't their lives become intertwined the instant Mieka set up the glass baskets that very first night in Gowerion?

And then he remembered what he'd realized the day Jed and Blye got married: that the decision to follow Cade and Rafe and Jeska to Gowerion had turned out just fine. Instinct: the motive behind almost all his choices. Without it, there'd be no Touchstone. No *us*.

That had to be what Cade trusted about him, the trait in Mieka's character, the quality in his heart that Cade believed in. It had served them very well so far.

Cade had crouched down in front of him, rocking lightly to keep his balance as the ship moved out into the river. "Mieka?"

He smiled, pleased that he'd solved the puzzle and even happier that the solution meant he didn't have to think about any of it anymore, and tossed back the rest of the water. "You can't sleep in the top bunk, Quill, don't be so bleedin' silly. That's where the window is, and the way you jostle about in your sleep, you'd put a knee right through the glass."

"I think they call it a 'porthole.' But you're right, you should take the top." He grinned. "That way, you can yark right out the side of the ship."

He chewed his lip, then slowly made the face he'd used in Seekhaven to such brilliant effect, and whimpered, "Quill—I think I need the piss pot—"

It worked. Cade looked around frantically, scrabbling under the bed with both hands. Mieka made dreadful noises and clapped a hand over his mouth, hunching his shoulders convulsively. Cade overbalanced and landed on his bum, scuttling back like an upside-down crab to get out of range. He looked so ridiculous that Mieka fell back onto the bed and howled with laughter.

"This is a *Royal* ship, Cade! You don't think they use anything so vulgar as a piss pot, do you? There's a garderobe at the end of the hall!"

"Why, you little snarge!" Clambering to his feet, he loomed over Mieka with an awful frown. "How did you know there's a garderobe?"

"Mum packed nightshirts and told me to wear 'em on board ship no matter how hot and stuffy it gets. So I asked, and she said about the garderobe, and no traipsing about starkers, she'd die of the shame."

Cade chuckled, then scowled again. He snagged his satchel from the shelf and poked through it, eventually extracting a long linen nightshirt. "Touch this while we're on board this ship, and you're dead," he told Mieka.

He pouted because he was expected to, but what he was thinking was that Cade had made a dreadful mistake. He hadn't said anything about when they *weren't* on the ship, now, had he?

By evening he was convinced they'd be on this poxy ship forever.

Once they left the river and were sailing across the Flood, Mieka found his sea-knees and Rafe took to his bunk. Auntie Brishen's certain-sure seasickness remedy had no effect, other than making him moan more softly. The son of a baker, he could well afford to go a few days without eating. But Jeska flatly refused to sleep in their cabin—it being impossible to get any sleep in their cabin—and so arrived at Cade and Mieka's door, vaulted up into the top berth without a by-your-leave, and opened the porthole to the fresh salt air.

"Where am *I* s'posed to sleep, then?" Mieka wailed.

"There's a bed in my cabin."

"Listen to Rafe yark and whine all night? I don't bloody think so!" Back on the Winterly, whenever they had to share beds, the rule had become one tall and one short occupant. But those had been beds, actual beds—not shelving with mattresses and sheets.

Mieka and Cade looked at the lower bunk, then at each other, and Mieka waited for him to offer to sleep elsewhere.

He didn't.

"Fine, then!" Mieka snarled, and slammed the door shut behind him.

There was a room on the next deck down where the junior officers had their meals: a trestle table, two benches, and a soft chair over in a corner. To Mieka's astonishment, Briuly was there with a lute, and the off-duty crowd included a few men with significant gold braid decorating their sleeves. Once the musician began to play, he understood why they'd ventured into their subordinates' domain—and couldn't imagine how anyone could stay at his post when Briuly Blackpath had a lute on his knee.

Mieka knew enough from hearing his father test the instruments that Hadden Windthistle made the best in the Kingdom. His father was no musician, but even he could bring wonderful sounds from strings and wood. Briuly was a master, and barely twenty years old. Individual notes caught at the heart; lush chords enwrapped the senses. The strings and wood seemed connected directly to his hands, his body, mayhap his soul. Mieka understood for the first time why Fa refused to sell his instruments to amateurs. It would be a crime to put a lute like this into the arms of anyone but a master.

Mieka had no idea how long he simply stood there, swaying lightly to the rocking of the ship. Then he swung round and ran back up the stairs, not bothering to knock before shouldering the door open and exclaiming into the darkness, "Quill! You have to come listen to this!"

"Who is that? How dare you!"

He'd got turned the wrong way round. By the meager light from a hallway lantern, he saw something that brought a hot flush to his cheeks. He had always known Lord Fairwalk's inclinations; seeing them in practice was another thing entirely.

"Sorry," he stammered, "d-didn't mean—I'll just go now, shall I? Yeh, I better—sorry—"

He pulled the door shut and leaned back against it, biting both lips between his teeth. The scuffling sounds and a muffled snigger from within the cabin sent him fleeing down the hall, up the stairs, and out onto the windswept deck.

He'd always known about Kearney Fairwalk. This wasn't the first time he'd ever seen two men together. He knew enough about these things that he shouldn't have made such a fool of himself, blithering like a fourteen-year-old girl.

The night air cooled his face, and as he considered more calmly what he'd seen, he was glad it hadn't been some little cabin boy or one of the servants, who had no choice when a great lord beckoned. The clothing strewn about the floor had been fine and silken, rich with embroidery. One of the Court officials, he supposed, a man grown, who could please himself as he liked.

If only he hadn't seemed, for just an instant, so much like Cayden.

The same long, lean, lanky body. The same slightly curling brown hair. Not the same face; there could never be two faces like that in the world, with those gray eyes and that nose. It hadn't been Cade, of course, but for just an instant—

He'd always known what Fairwalk really wanted from his association with Touchstone, too.

"Where'd you end up sleeping?"

He gave Cayden a dull-eyed glare over breakfast. "Junior officers' mess, in a chair, under somebody's cloak. It stank of fish and rumbling. Pass the butter."

They were up on deck, seated on benches at a trestle table hauled outside to take advantage of the gorgeous day. The second ship, larger and more luxurious because that was the one that the new Princess and her attendants would sail in, bobbed in and out of view over the railing. Sunshine gleamed off polished brass and the wind filled the sails so that the ships skimmed at exciting speed across the ocean. Mieka was not at the moment disposed to enjoy life at sea; he had a crick in his neck, he wanted a wash, and he hated mornings anyway.

"D'you think you might recover from your sulk by lunching?" Cade asked. "I don't know what your plans are, but—"

"Plans?" He used the nasty-innocent version of The Eyes. "You mean there's actually something to do on this scow other than make faces at the other one?"

Jeska looked up from shoveling in eggs. "I didn't know a person could get up on the wrong side of a *chair* in the morning."

Mieka pointed his fork at him. "Find out tomorrow, after *you've* slept in it."

With a long-suffering sigh that made Mieka want to kick him, Cade said, "I'm working on 'Treasure' this morning, but Kearney wants to discuss finalizing our folio for the performances. The captain's cook has promised to give Rafe something to settle his stomach, so I thought we could all meet in Kearney's cabin after lunching."

"Spectacular. Can't wait."

They left him alone after that, which was fine with him. There was nothing to do but walk from the front of the ship to the back again, nobody he wanted to talk to, nothing to distract him from his own thoughts. If he wasn't careful, he told himself morosely, he'd spend the whole bloody voyage with only himself for company, trying to work out what he felt and thought so he could face the people those feelings and thoughts were about. He couldn't even return to the cabin and seek refuge in a judicious application of thorn; Cade was in there, doubtless adrift in his own little sea of books and papers, muttering and scribbling.

"What's chasin' you, Elferboy?"

He nearly tripped over his own feet. The sailor was about fifty years older than Great-great-grandmother, and if the last of them hadn't died out long ago, Mieka would've sworn this man was pureblood Gnome. He was chewing on a smelly stick that looked like bark-wrapped cow cud, regarding Mieka with amusement.

"Fourth time you been stridin' past," he went on. "But that's the thing 'bout a ship, ain't it? Can't outrun nothin'. Nowheres to go." He paused, removed the stick from between his teeth, spit over the side, and grinned. "'Ceptin' down there, o' course."

"I hate boats," Mieka heard himself say.

"Now, y'see? We've that in common, we two. Forty year I been hopin' pirates'd get me, but no luck yet."

"Pirates?" he echoed, wide-eyed.

"Aye—but that's more to the south. No cause to worry, boy. Escortin' a Princess, we'll be, and safe as safe ever was. There's talk she's full young, but eesome and then some."

It was an invitation to gossip. Mieka might have succumbed to the inherent flattery—he was part of the delegation, after all, and thus assumed to be privileged to the choicest rumors—but he wasn't in the mood. So all he did was smile and shrug, and say, "We'll all soon see, won't we?" and continued on his walk.

It lasted another two rounds of the deck. Then he went downstairs to his cabin, flung open the door, and announced, "Quill, I'm *bored!*"

Cade was seated on the lower bunk, talking earnestly with Briuly Blackpath. He paused in speaking long enough to reach into his satchel. Mieka caught the book he tossed over and stared at it, outraged.

"I'm *bored*," he repeated, and threw the book back.

It missed Cade's head by about an inch. Briuly looked startled. Cade merely looked annoyed. Mieka slumped onto the floor and folded his arms across his chest, fixing Cade with an affronted glare.

"How old did you say you were? Twelve?" Cade stashed the book in his satchel and brought out a corked bottle. "Here. Make a start on lunching, why don't you?"

"Then I'd be half-drunk and bored."

Turning to Briuly, he said, "Not much sleep last night. He gets cranky. And then he gets into trouble."

"Not a worry about it," Briuly replied, a grin teasing his lips. "We can talk more later, yeh?"

"I'd like that."

The musician unfolded his thin limbs, tucked a few locks of wildly curly hair behind one pointed ear, and picked a path to the door, pausing along the way to pat Mieka on the head. "Only another couple of days."

"Lovely—then I can be bored in a foreign country."

"You're a right little stab of sunshine today, aren't you?" Cade remarked when the door had closed. "C'mon, let's go stretch our legs."

"I did that already. I wore a trench in the deck."

"Poor you! No shops to visit, no girls to chat up, no rehearsals to get through, no sisters or brothers to plague, and no mum to tell you to settle down or she'll tie you to a chair and put a gag in your mouth." Cade laughed at him. "Tell you what. After our meeting with Kearney, why don't you bring out Auntie Brishen's finest, we'll lock ourselves in—and lock the porthole!—and see what there might be to see?"

Torn betwixt the mockery and the offer, Mieka scowled. Then he understood. "Having trouble with 'Treasure,' are you?"

"How did you know that? Never mind," Cade said, waving it away. "I should know by now. My eyes, right?"

"They always give you away," Mieka confirmed. "All right, then, let's. But there's still at least an hour before lunching."

"And you're *bored*, I know."

There was a short silence. Then Mieka blurted, "Kearney was with somebody last night. In his cabin."

"Was he?" Cade shrugged.

"I mean he was *with* somebody." When Cade still failed to react, Mieka said, "They were—you know. In bed."

Cade appeared to consider this. "Did you learn anything?"

"Did I *what*?" Then he saw the wicked gleam in Cade's eyes.

Everything within reach was either lashed down or too heavy. So Mieka hauled off a boot and threw it at Cade, who ducked, laughing. At that precise moment the door opened inward, hitting Mieka on the shoulder. He yelped and scrambled out of the way. His Lordship apologized profusely, and finally got round to stammering that the cook had been kind enough to arrange a private meal for them.

"It might be a bit crowded in my cabin, don't you see, but—"

"Sounds fine. In an hour or so?" Cade started gathering up sheets of paper, all of them closely filled with his quick, upright script, liberally spattered with cross-outs.

"Is that 'Treasure'?" Fairwalk asked.

"It will be, eventually."

"Excellent! Lord Oakapple will be thrilled."

When he was gone, Mieka searched Cade's face. "Why were you talking about 'Treasure' with Briuly?"

"There, you've done it again," he sighed. "How do you guess these things? It happens that Briuly and Alaen are not just each other's cousin, they've connections to Lord Oakapple as well."

"So if you end up vindicating the family—"

"—they're all restored to grace and favor, yeh. But I don't want just a good story that includes more of the truth than usual. I want this to *be* the truth. Briuly remembers a few family stories, things they whisper amongst themselves when nobody's looking. Interesting, of course, and I'd like to use them if I can, but what I'm after is what really happened."

"Hence the thorn. Can you direct your dreaming like that? I mean, you're talking about the past now, right? Can you see backwards like that?"

"I have absolutely no idea." Stashing the pages in his leather folio—each member of Touchstone had been gifted by His Majesty with a new folio in the Royal colors of brown and sea-green—he propped his elbows on his knees and his chin in his hands. "Briuly was talking about something else, too. Incorporating music into plays. Alaen's notion, really, and Briuly doesn't think much of it." He smiled. "*His* music isn't there just to adorn somebody else's words and scenery. *His* songs aren't mere embellishments for some wretched little play!"

"Music specific to the piece?" Mieka asked. "Not just using a snatch of a tune like we do sometimes, but something composed just for—" His imagination leaped ahead. "Jeska can sing, y'know. If a song fit into a play, he could—"

"I admit it's intriguing. It would add a dimension to the work I've never thought about before."

"Another Touchstone innovation?" Mieka grinned up at him.

"Well, it's been more than seventy years, anyway, since anybody did it. There was a masquer named Falvieno Kilatas—"

"Huh?"

"I read about him in your book. *Lost Withies*. He came from Chat's part of the Continent. He had a spectacular voice, and hired himself out to various groups, never really had one of his own. His last show was about ten years before my grandsire started performing. It's said he was so good that nobody dared try the same thing after he retired."

"It's been so long that everybody's forgotten him, then."

Cade regarded him curiously. "You want to try it?"

"We can talk to Alaen when we get home. But I think we ought to save it for when we need it. You know, something to get people talking about us all anew."

"You *mean*, of course," Cade said stiffly, "that we ought to use it when the piece demands it."

Mieka arched his brows. "Did you just call *Briuly* arrogant?"

"Not in so many words," he admitted, smiling again.

"Well, he has reason for it," Mieka said frankly. "I heard him play last night. What him and Alaen did at Blye's wedding was beautiful, but—he's a real artist, Quill. Fa would never have sold him a lute if he wasn't, of course. It's not just that he can play. You have to hear it to believe it."

"You wouldn't have heard him last night if you hadn't taken yourself off in a temper," Cade said innocently. "So don't you owe Jeska a debt of gratitude for thieving your bed?"

Mieka made as if to haul off the other boot and throw it at him, and they ended, as usual, by laughing. But Mieka took it as one more example of how his instincts were the right ones. Just now, talking about Briuly and music and "Treasure," Cade's twisty-turny head worked compatibly with his own in some uncanny fashion. Cade would always want to figure out the how and why of whatever happened; it would always be enough for Mieka that things did happen. He had every confidence that Cade would be forever explaining it all to him later.

11

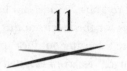

"Oh, and just by the way," said Kearney as he dipped his fingers into a bowl of scented water—an elegance unexpected on board ship, even a Royal one, "Master Blackpath says he'll be performing tonight for the crew down in their quarters. So if you've a mind to discuss what you're doing with 'Treasure,' Cayden, I'll be available all evening."

Firmly banishing from his thoughts what Mieka had said about Kearney's doings of last evening, Cade nodded. "Beholden. There was something else I wanted to ask about," he went on as the cabin boy collected empty plates. It had been a cramped meal, but an excellent one, with four of them at a tiny table and Rafe over on Kearney's bunk, restricting himself to dry toast and tea but looking much better. They had settled on which plays would be done for which audiences, ranging from their old rollicking "Sailor's Sweetheart" to "Doorways" and "Dragon," things that wouldn't require people to understand every word. This pained him, because he'd worked hard on those words.

Mieka was constructing little barricades out of chicken bones. The cabin boy was hovering, his dilemma clear in his face: He had orders to clear the table, but one of the guests hadn't finished with his food. Cade ended the boy's agony by handing over Mieka's plate.

"Oy!"

"Shut it," Rafe advised. "Or I'll throw you overboard."

Smirking, the Elf asked, "You and which regiment of the Guard?"

"What I wanted to know," Cade said hastily, "is if we might be doing a few shows for the locals. Something for people who aren't the nobility. Are there any outdoor spaces we might—"

"Have you run mad?" Kearney laughed shrilly. "We've talked about this before! Of course you can't do that!"

"Why not?" Mieka demanded.

Spoiling for a fight, Cade thought—or the diversion from boredom offered by thorn. Mieka had gone through three cups of wine with the meal and was working on a fourth. Cade had seen this before—they all had, on the Winterly—but being stuck in a coach all day, at least there was always something to look at out the windows, and the stop each night at an inn. There was distraction to be had even in finding that their beds were a half-step above lice-ridden, or that the ale was blashed, or that the food was awful. On board ship there was nothing to see but the ocean and nothing to do but pace the deck. Cade counted himself lucky that the book he'd been fool enough to suggest earlier today hadn't been flung directly at his head.

"It's just not possible, Mieka, don't you see," Kearney was saying, a bit more calmly now. "Recall where we're going, and what these people are like."

"They're people, ain't they?"

"They look upon magic as manipulative—"

"It is."

"—and sometimes evil."

"Not in the right hands."

"And who's to assure them that your hands are the right

ones? The few magical folk who are tolerated tread a very thin line, very thin indeed. The skills they learn are of use to the whole community, and those skills are the only ones they're taught. Whatever else they might dare to learn on their own, they keep it to themselves."

Cade sat up straighter. "And theater, performance, entertainment by means of magic—all that's useless?"

"That's not what I meant at all," Kearney assured him. "It's only that they're not accustomed to—"

"If we were Black fucking Lightning," Mieka interrupted, "I could see where there'd be a worry. But it's *us*, innit?"

Cade nodded. "Just as powerful—"

"*More* powerful," growled Rafe.

"—but not reckless."

"Unless you count the broken glassware," Jeska murmured to his winecup.

"Kearney," said Cade, "I think that showing them theater magic, how it can bring people together in a shared experience—"

"Oh Gods!" Mieka groaned. "Not that again!"

"I'm right, though," he retorted. "And you know I'm right. We can show them we're not wicked or anything to be frightened of. We're just people, like them."

"What you'd show them," Kearney said, sounding desperate now, "is that you're not like them at all! Think what happens onstage, Cayden. You can make them see and hear and feel whatever you like, whether they will or no. Don't you see how frightfully dangerous that is to people who don't understand?"

"Then why are we going at all?" Cade demanded. "The audiences at the courts, they won't have seen theater the full-out way we do it any more than the rest of the citizenry ever has. Won't that be dangerous as well? Won't we be threatened by a mob?" he finished derisively.

"Courts have rulers, and rulers have guards," Rafe said

quietly. They all turned to stare at him. "You plan as you like, Cade, but don't include me. I don't fancy leaving my wife a widow and my child fatherless."

Jeska turned all the way round in his chair. "Crisiant's pregnant?"

Mieka crowed, "Gods witness that she has every reason to be!"

The fettler's fragile state precluded the heartier sort of congratulations, and the ribald toasts that went with them. Especially the toasts. After agreeing to celebrate in earnest once they were on dry land, they also agreed that Rafe was looking a bit greenish again and needed to rest.

"A baby!" Mieka exclaimed as he and Cade strolled the deck, soaring up summer sunshine. "They kept *that* quiet!"

Cade smiled, but he was thinking that Crisiant was a woman in a million: she understood that Rafe had to go on this trip. Any other pregnant wife would have sulked or pleaded, demanded or wept. True, she'd reconciled herself long ago to the life that Rafe intended to lead. But she'd probably assumed with all the rest of them that Touchstone would make the Ducal and be gone during summer and autumn, back in time for the birth. He didn't like to think what her disappointment had been when it turned out to be the Winterly again. And now, instead of having Rafe with her at least for the first few months of her first pregnancy, he would be gone most of the summer as well.

But he knew she'd never spoken a syllable of complaint. And if she blamed Cade, as she very well might, he knew he'd never hear a word about that, either.

"We've got the crib quilt, of course," Mieka said suddenly. "The one we bought at the Castle Biding Fair, Cade, you remember. But we'll have to find something pretty just for Crisiant. They're s'posed to do wonderful woodwork in the new Princess's country. Fa told me there's a kind of wood comes from their forests, very fine-grained. Perfect for making lutes."

Cade put a frown on his face. "Interesting—but I don't think there's room in your bags, is there?"

Mieka's turn to be confused. "For what?"

"Aren't you planning to bring him back a tree?"

They spent the next few minutes trying to trip each other, Mieka's quickness matched evenly by Cade's long legs. At length they fetched up, laughing, against the railing, aware of the disdainful sniffs and arched brows of their fellow passengers and not caring in the least.

"Are we *ever* going to get there?" Mieka sighed.

"We just started!" Then, with Jinsie in mind and what her cruel trickery had made him realize, he ventured softly, "You miss her."

A slow flush spread up the boy's cheeks. "She—she has really beautiful hands, you know? Narrow, with long fingers… the nails are like pearl, almost, pink and white pearl…" He paused, looking anywhere but at Cade. "I don't want—I mean, a ring would be—I don't think it would look right. I've been thinking a lot about it, and her hands are so perfect, any sort of ring would—you know?"

Amused in spite of himself, Cade said, "I think I might understand the essence of your incoherence, yeh. Damned good thing *you're* not the one who has to write the plays. And talking of that, don't we have an appointment?"

Mieka brightened at once. "That we do. And I've an idea or three about it."

In their cabin—scrupulously tidy now, their usual morning clutter stowed, the water jug replenished—Cade got out his folio while Mieka dragged his satchel out of the closet and sat down on the floor.

"What sort of ideas?" Cade asked. "About what thorn to use?"

"That, and how to coax your head into going where you want it to. Simple, really, if it works." He looked up. "Sometimes

I have dreams about whatever I fell asleep thinking about. Why wouldn't that work with you?"

"I never tried it."

"If we talk about 'Treasure' and what you've already found out, that might carry over into what you see on thorn. Auntie Brishen says this is much the same sort we used at my house that time, and that's kind of what gave me the idea. I mean, you were with me, and you had an Elsewhen about me, didn't you?" He made a face. "The one where I was old and wrinkly."

Cade laughed. "I was old, too," he reminded the Elf. "It was my forty-fifth Namingday!"

"Forty-five?" He gave an elaborate shudder. "That means I'd be comin' up on forty-four, and no self-respecting Elf gets wrinkles or gray hair that early."

"Don't tell me you're about to turn all More Elfen Than The First Elf, like Uncle Breedbate! And I never said you were wrinkly." He paused as if remembering. "Some lines, and an extra chin, I think."

"I hope you'd gone bald or something equally appalling." He selected a little paper twist and took one of the glass thorns from their padded box. "Warts," he decided. "Hairy ones."

"No warts," Cade told him. "Not even for you. Do you want to hear about what I've learned?"

"Say on."

"I've been doing research—"

"I know. I foresaw it," Mieka teased as he prepared the thorn. "I had a vision of you in the Royal Archives, dropping dead of sheer boredom!"

"You're funny, aren't you? Just hilarious. Why is it I'm doing all the work on this commission, and the rest of you just loll about—"

"—waiting for you to be brilliant?" He flung Cade a grin. "We worship at your feet, O Great Tregetour, we grovel in gratitude, we breathlessly await your next spate of golden speech, we—"

"Oh, shut up." Cade laughed. "Do you want to hear this or not?"

"Talk."

Cade looked over his notes. Working on "Treasure," he'd found that the intellectual challenge of sifting through all the sources for the truth, or as near as he could judge to be the truth, had often made him restless—not at being unable to reconcile various versions, but at being unable to comprehend the underlying reasons for the events. All that the standard script provided was conversation, some thunder and lightning, more conversation, a lot of rain, and the breathless arrival of a messenger who reported that there had been a mudslide and the Treasure had vanished. Then everybody ranted and moaned for a while, news came that the culprit had been caught, we'll hang him on the morrow, Royal Justice triumphs, The End. Well, except for the very bad poetry that Cade had discovered wasn't in the original at all. Someone was hanged, but the culprit was never named. Although for years it had been assumed that it was the contemporaneous Lord Oakapple, he was never actually identified as the thief. Neither was the reason for the theft, if theft it had even been. In one commentary on the tale, it was speculated that the culprit-without-a-name and the theft-without-a-motive were symbolic only, that none of it had ever happened at all and the whole story was meant to show that justice had been established in Albeyn with the accession of the Royal Family. Put a name to the thief, and he became a real person, an individual; keep him nameless, and he was a proxy for anyone who broke the law. Cade thought this an interesting interpretation, but the fact remained that the Oakapples had been destitute and despised ever since. Until the coal had been discovered, anyway.

"That poem at the end, it's been nagging at me. I won't

burden you with the tale of exactly where I found it all, but some of it was in your book." He paused, smiling inside that the copy of *Lost Withies* Mieka had snupped for him had become in his mind *Mieka's Book*. "I cobbled together what I'm pretty sure is the oldest version, though I'm not all that confident about the spelling."

"What's the spelling got to do with anything?"

"Probably nothing, but I do like to be thorough."

"Forgive me. I ought to've known."

"The rendering we did at Trials, it's only about eighty years old. And it's been diddled—you can trace the changes back through the old manuscripts at Fairwalk Manor and the Archives—"

"I thought you said you wouldn't be burdening me poor little brain with all your scholarly gibberish."

"I was only trying to say that I'm not making this up, it's all there for anybody who cares to look."

Mieka sighed. "You looked. I believe you. Get on with it!"

"From the oldest version of the poem, then." He found it in his notes. "'No night bedarked as soonly'—I think that means the shortest day of the year, don't you? The day it gets dark earliest."

"But that would be Wintering Night. Didn't you say once that the Treasure was stolen in the summer?"

"You were listening to me?"

"I always listen to you, Quill."

"Let's say it's Wintering Night that's meant. 'As athwart the crumbling wall' means that night fell first on that wall. So this wall has to be in the shadow of a hill, and the sun goes down directly behind it—"

"Why?"

Impatient, he conjured up a bit of Wizardfire. "You won't be able to see it clearly, there's too much light in here. But watch." He brought one hand in front of the blue glow balanced on one fingertip, then lowered the fire behind his palm. "Look at the shadow on the wall. It moves upward as the sun goes down."

Mieka squinted, then shook his head. "Can't quite see it, but I'll take your word on it. What's next?"

Cade banished the Wizardfire and consulted his notes. "Then comes 'Cold stone a-tumbling fell,' and the 'cold' ties in with its being winter. If it was in summer, the rock would be warm with the sun, wouldn't it? Even at twilight."

"Not if it was raining that day. And there'd go your sunset and shadows, as well. Cloud cover."

"Damn."

Mieka patted his knee consolingly. "Never mind. Keep on with it."

"There's thunder and lightning, and then the rain starts up, and the mudslide. The next line is 'Klunshing and climping all'—"

"Wait, that's one of Uncle Breedbate's words! 'Climp' means to put your dirty hands all over something shiny, smudge it all up. He used to yell at Fa for associating with Wizards and Humans and other riff-raff who'd climp his Elfen heritage."

"Is that what it means? I've been looking all over for a definition." He scribbled it down as he went on, "Jez told me what 'klunsh' is—a mixture of mud and dung used for building about three hundred years ago. Though it's usually spelled with a *c.*"

"My brother knows how to spell? And they don't use it anymore, do they?"

"He said not. Somebody discovered how to make good, reliable bricks at an affordable price, and—"

"All right, all right," Mieka said hastily. "Enough. But how does that get us forrarder?"

"It's a starting," Cade defended. "The wall tumbles down, making a mess of whatever shiny things it's falling onto. And that's the mud-slide, right?"

"If you say so." Mieka shrugged. "Next line?"

"'Ere morning brighted the field,' which is obviously dawn, but what field?"

"The sun's up, anyway, and the rain seems to have stopped."

"It goes on, 'Regal bells had pealed' and that's always been taken to mean the bells in a Royal castle, which is where it really gets confusing. The specific castle is never named. It's s'posed to have been someplace around Sidlowe, but I talked with some people there last year on the Winterly and the only place belonging to the Royals is a hunting lodge. All the Royal castles of the time have been considered as the location. Nothing was ever found. But the thing of it is, the Oakapple family didn't hand over Feazings Keep until later—"

"They gave away their castle?"

"To the King, as reparation for the theft. Why do you think the family got so poor? A nobleman needs land to support him. Especially back then, when it was degrading and even shameful for a lord to be involved in trade. Even now people like my mother look down on people like Lord Piercehand for his fleet of ships—"

"They're all just annoyed that they didn't think of it first. But I know what you mean. Everybody knows Piercehand makes another new fortune whenever his ships dock, but he keeps saying they're only exploring, finding new lands and countries, and the goods they bring back are secondary."

"Naught like a nobleman for glossing over the truth with a fresh coat of varnish. Anyway, I was about to say that all versions of the poem agree on 'Regal bells,' but what if they were the bells from a Minster established by royalty?"

Mieka gave him a look that was amused and admiring all at once.

"My Gods, Quill, how do you keep your head from exploding? If I had all those brains inside me poor little skull—"

Eyeing him narrowly, Cade said, "I'm going to buy a really, really stout pair of boots, and then I'm going to throw them at you."

"Shush that talk, or you'll have an Elsewhen about shopping on Narbacy Street. What's the rest of the poem?"

"It goes, ''Ere morning brightened the field / Regal bells had pealed / To wrongly doom the thief.' *Wrongly!* I got that out of your book, and I nearly fell over when I read it!"

"Somebody innocent was executed for the theft?" Mieka whistled softly between his teeth. "His Gracious Majesty won't like that."

"He didn't do it, he wasn't personally responsible, so what does he care? It's the truth that matters."

"If it was all a mistake, then he might have to give the castle back. Is that what Lord Oakapple is after? Feazings Keep?"

This gave Cade pause. "That would be part of it, I suppose. That and the family honor. But only if I could prove it. Anyway, the poem finishes up, 'Condolement there be none / Long shadows scrape the throne / O'erset and e'er cast down / Spun carkanet and crown / Ever hidden, never found.' So there's no consolation, that appears in all the variants in one form or another, but what throne?"

"Whatever it is, it's overturned and likely destroyed, right?"

"That's how I read it, but whose throne are they talking about? Not the King at the time—he'd been robed and crowned. So whose throne does it mean?"

Mieka shrugged. "You're the one with the brains and the books. What's a *carkanet*?"

"A necklet. As for spinning—you can spin anything from glass to thread, no help there. And the last line is the same in all the poems, with the necklet and crown forever hidden and never found."

Mieka scooted across the polished wooden deck, the glass thorn ready in his fingertips. "Hold those thoughts," he murmured, and Cade settled back into the bunk, extending an arm. He felt the tiny piercing at his wrist, watching the excitement in Mieka's opalescent eyes. It would work, he was sure it would work. He'd sink into the thorn—he could already feel the flush of heat spreading up his arm—and he'd see what he needed to see. He heard the rustle of paper, and then Mieka's soft voice reciting the poem.

> *No night bedarked as soonly*
> *As athwart the crumbling wall—*

Dream, imagination, Elsewhen—it didn't matter, so long as it led him to the truth, a truth he could use the way he used everything else, picking it apart, analyzing it, discovering how it worked, putting it back together the right way round, the way only he could envision.

But it felt so different. A chill replaced the heat in his veins. He could feel it swirling through his chest, down his body, up into his brain—no Elsewhen had ever felt like this, no dreaming while he slept or sudden turn while his eyes were wide open. Not even his purposeful imaginings had ever felt like this.

… *as athwart the crumbling wall—*

{And there it was, backshadowed by the setting sun that slid down to a notch in the farther hills beyond the lake and rested there for a small fraction of eternity. He ran through the snow, competing with the shadows in a race he had to win. Skidding to a stop, gasping for every breath that laced his lungs with ice, he wanted so badly to touch the wall, find out where the throne had been—he could see how stone had once mated with stone, strong and solid, but there was nothing resembling a throne here amid the ragged tumble of rock and mud and snow.

It was so cold that the tips of his ears had gone numb. All at once the sunshaft from the Westercountry pierced his eyes and he stumbled to his knees. When he could see again, it was summer. And before him the brilliant shine of gold and silver threaded through spun glass: a chain of a hundred perfect links and a crown that was a circle of sunbursts and crescent moons and diamond-studded stars. The Rights rested on a flat rock that formed the seat of the throne, its back the stone wall. Whole, immaculate, glowing like rough-carved chunks of moonlight sparkling in the new morning sunshine at his back.

Triumph sang in him. He would take up the carkanet and crown, and sit upon the throne, and the suns and moons and stars would ignite to proclaim a True King. How dazzling bright it would be, no paltry yellowish Elf-light nor sickly blue Wizardfire nor red-gold glower of a Caitiff's spell-casting, but the pure silver and gold radiance of the Rights—

—but they were coming now, he could hear them, they had followed him despite all his caution, and they were hunting him down. He could hear the hoof-beats of their horses and the belling cries of their dogs and if he didn't hurry himself gone, they would find the Rights and the throne, and they must not, they must not—}

"Cade? Cayden, come back!"

He blinked up at a white, frightened face. And smiled. "It's still there," he whispered. "Mieka, it's still there!"

"Gods, Quill, you looked—" But then he turned away, scrabbling for pen and paper. "Tell me, quick, while you remember it clear—let me write it down—"

He laughed softly. Silly little Elf! The images were there in his mind, waiting to be locked away until he needed them. He didn't have to write them down; how foolish. He watched Mieka's slender, swift fingers nervously smooth a fresh sheet of paper onto the floor, dip the silver-nibbed pen into the ink bottle—

{They were not Mieka's hands. He knew them all the same. Narrow, long-fingered, but not the smooth young hands that had sewn the iris-blue neckband Mieka so often wore. These hands were older, with knotted veins, the nails ridged and brittle. Not her hands; her mother's hands.

—a secret knowledge about Master Silversun, was all he could read before a final word was scrawled at the bottom, and a flourish added; sand from a pottery shaker strewn and blown free; fingers trembling slightly as they folded the paper in on itself. Purple wax, heated with an oddly red bit of fire, the color of a fox's tail; no seal. Direction printed carefully on the other side, and this he could read, the large firm letters spelling out *His Grace the Archduke—URGENT.*}

"Quill!"

He opened his eyes and immediately turned his head away. "It's all right," he said mindlessly. "I'm all right."

"Are you sure?"

Nodding, he propped himself on his elbows and forced a smile. He called up the images of snow and stone and abrupt summer, thinking about them and nothing else. "Didn't expect to fall back into it, that's all. D'you want to hear?"

Still looking worried, Mieka said, "You told me 'It's still there.' What's still where?"

"The Treasure, of course."

12

Pacing the deck was Mieka's solution for the next days of boredom. Unsatisfactory as it was for Mieka, Cade was grateful. He was left alone in their cabin. He most certainly was not bored.

Mistress Mirdley had told him several times that any sort of disruption in his life seemed to bring on more Elsewhens. She hadn't used that term, of course; that was Mieka's word for what happened to him. In the main, she was right, and an orderly routine with few surprises usually caused his own mind to let him live and work in peace. But the life he'd chosen—couldn't help but choose—was one of necessary commotion, and he was aching for some quiet. Two weddings, two visits to Fairwalk Manor, Trials, the commission from Lord Oakapple, preparing for this journey—all had produced not just Elsewhens but an intense need to sort them. Yet now the journey itself was most unexpectedly giving him time to breathe.

The problem was that it was also time in which to think.

He was starting to understand Mieka's frustration with shipboard life: There was nowhere to go, and precious little to distract him from his thoughts. Their lessons in protocol had been mercifully brief, as they were not expected to mingle much with the highborns. Play when and where they were told, and otherwise disappear and cause no trouble; if he had his doubts about that last bit, he kept them to himself. He could have spent more hours working on "Treasure," of course, but there was something bothering him about what he'd seen, something he didn't want to confront just yet.

That night had provided diversion in the form of Briuly Blackpath, who had taken his lute down to the common sailors' quarters. Cade was no musician, as Hadden Windthistle had confirmed, but he knew brilliance when he heard it. From just after dinner until well after midnight, Briuly had played everything from the tenderest of ballads to the lewdest of tavern songs. Jeska and the sailors had roared along with the lyrics, and in Jeska's case contributed a few songs to everyone's acclaim. Except Briuly's, Cade noted with interest; the lutenist didn't half enjoy not being the absolute center of attention. He could almost see the calculation in the man's eyes: Jeska had looks and the talents of a masquer, so why did he need to upstage someone whose only gift was his music? Cade had the impression that Briuly often considered life to be grotesquely unfair.

Rafe was feeling much better, so Jeska slept in their cabin that night. Cade had forgotten that Mieka snored. Whenever the strangling-a-goose noises woke him, all he had to do was reach up and push at one of the slats supporting the bunk above, jostling it enough to make the Elf roll over. Nevertheless, he did spend a lot of that night gazing at those slats by the faint glow of an oil lamp by the door.

He could barely admit it, even to himself, but for a second or three he'd been tempted to go along with Jinsie's demand. Destroy any letters Mieka might write to the girl… it would certainly put a crimp in any plans she might have. Surely she'd heard about the journey. Everyone in the Kingdom must know by now. There'd been no letters about it from Mieka, of course. Jinsie had seen to that. But what if there were no letters from the Continent, either? Would she give up?

It had been hideously tempting.

But then he'd had a brief, instants-long turn, there and gone so quickly that he might have lied to himself, might have convinced himself he'd imagined it. He'd seen Mieka, crimson with fury, heard him scream, *"You bloody bastard! I'll fucking kill you!"* And he knew that as afeared as he was of the girl and what she might mean to the futures, he was even more frightened that Mieka would come to hate him.

Letters. He'd seen a letter, and he knew whose hand had written it. He knew to whom it had been—would be—addressed. But had he seen it because a part of his mind had been thinking about those letters Jinsie stole, or because he'd seen Mieka with pen and paper and ink? Had his brain imaged him a thorn portrait that wasn't real?

It hadn't felt like other Elsewhens, but it hadn't felt like a dream, either. Auntie Brishen's thorn made it feel different somehow.

And that meant he couldn't entirely trust it.

And *that* meant that he couldn't entirely trust that other thorn vision, the one where Mieka had surprised him on his forty-fifth Namingday.

So what about the things he'd seen pertaining to the Treasure? He remembered being so cold that he couldn't feel the tips of his ears, and his hearing had seemed abnormally acute, and surely that meant he'd had the pointed ears of an Elf. In the thorn dream, he'd been someone else. That had never happened to him before. It had to have been his imagination showing him the result of all his researches, giving him the scene as it had to have been, shaped by hearing, in some portion of his mind, Mieka's voice reading the poem. His mind had gathered and stored information, working on it with logic and instinct, and the thorn had released it all as a narrative he could use. The sudden slip into summer dawn from winter sunset convinced him that his imagination had been the source of that dream, for surely such a shift was impossible.

And mayhap that the other dream, the one that had tormented him with its visions of Mieka's decline into thornthrall and death, had been imagination, too.

He wanted to be home. He wanted to commandeer Kearney's carriage and spend the summer searching out every Minster that dated to that time period and had been established by a member of the Royal family. Near one of them was a lake, and a ruined wall that caught the last rays of sunlight on the evening of Wintering. And somewhere beneath that tumble of stone and mud and cow-shit glowed a necklet and a crown.

But whose?

Shortly before noon the next day, Mieka rousted him out of bed for lunching. He got dressed, rubbed his stubbly cheeks and chin, and decided that shaving with a straight razor was not something he wanted to try on board ship. He envied Rafe his beard, and envied even more the Elfen blood that gave Mieka and Jeska thick but slow-growing hair. And that reminded him.

"Mieka, how cold does it have to be before the tips of your ears go numb?"

After a momentary blankness, the Elf hooted with laughter. "It *was* winter, wasn't it? When you saw the Treasure, it was winter! And you were an Elf!"

He was treated to a lecture about woolen caps versus fur hoods, and how much alcohol effectively countered frozen ears. Almost to the deck, Cade realized something. He stopped and put a hand on Mieka's arm.

"I wasn't an Elf. I had the ears, but I wasn't an Elf. I was too tall."

"So you could only have been Fae."

How stupid of him not to have guessed. "That's what's been

missing out of this whole story!" He bit back sudden excitement and lowered his voice. "The rendering everyone always does includes all the races except one. It talks about Goblins, Gnomes, Elfenfolk, Humans, Wizards, Trolls, Pikseys, Sprites, even Merfolk and Harpies and Vampires. But it never mentions the Fae."

"Was it their necklet and crown?"

"I don't know. We'll talk about it later." He pointed out to their left. "We seem to have arrived."

Not quite, but close enough to look at something other than the Ocean Sea. Fishing villages along rocky shorelines, green fields rolling into the distance, tidal inlets where tiny houses perched on stilts, and at last a spit of land with a thin stone lighthouse at its end.

"That'll be the Vathis Beam," said one of the other passengers, a young man dressed in Prince Ashgar's brown-and-buff livery. "Entrance to the river. Won't be long before we're off this tub. It can't happen too soon for me!"

Cade glanced over at him—lanky, brown-haired, as tall as Cade but Humanly so, with nothing of Wizard about him. All of Ashgar's servitors on this trip were fully Human to look at. Suddenly he wished there were a way to disguise Mieka's ears.

"Seasick?" Cade asked, just to make conversation.

"I'm one of those tiresome people who's only happy on horseback." With a respectful dip of the head, he added, "Drevan Wordturner—which would be more apt to you, wouldn't it, Master Silversun?"

Cade smiled. "Word*twister*, perhaps. Are you with His Highness's Master of Horse, then?"

"If only that were so!"

Drevan Wordturner was on loan from the Archduke. His ancestor had come to the Kingdom with the very first Archduke, and his name reflected five generations of the same occupation: translator. There was a whole library of books at His Grace's main residence that only the Wordturner family could read nowadays. They also kept the spoken language alive, which explained Drevan's presence on this journey.

"The farther eastwards one goes, the more these Continental languages have in common. The Tregrefina is said to speak our language quite well, so I'm not entirely sure why I'm here. I'd rather buy myself a place in the King's Cavalry, but…" He trailed off with a shrug.

Cade knew what it was like to aspire to a profession not approved by one's family. "Surely there must be brothers or cousins to take your place."

Whatever the young man might have replied was lost in an almighty blast. The deck shuddered again and again as the cannons fired. Cade managed not to stagger with the shock and the noise, but it was a good five minutes before he felt his heartbeats calm down again. Smoke drifted through the air, making him cough.

"I think they know we're here now," Rafe commented.

"What?" Mieka shouted.

Cade glanced at Jeska, who was shaking his head as if to clear it. "You, too?"

"What?"

"Elfen ears," Rafe said. "Poor delicate little creatures."

"You know, of course," Cade mused, "we could say absolutely anything to either of them right now, and get away with it."

"What could we say that we don't already say when they can hear us?"

"It's the concept that intrigues me." He grinned as Mieka patted his ears as if to comfort them, or to make sure they were still attached.

"Whatever you're saying," Mieka yelled, "I wasn't there, I didn't do it, and you can't prove anything!"

"Frightfully sloppy," was Kearney Fairwalk's verdict. "All the guns were supposed to fire in unison on both ships."

An hour's sail upriver, and the two ships docked in a bright and busy port that sprawled, like Gallantrybanks, on both sides of the river. The passengers were ushered into carriages for a drive through cobblestoned streets, out past the eastern edges of town, and deep into the countryside. The carriages moved swiftly, and the change from the rocking of the ship to the sharp juddering of wheels turned Rafe a bit green again. When Cade switched seats with him so he could have access to a window if necessary, the jostling nearly landed him atop one of Briuly's lute cases. Snarls ensued. Cade apologized. Briuly glared at him for the whole rest of the drive.

The cobbles ran out and the coaches bounced over the packed dirt of a country road. Eventually they emerged from behind a grove of laurel trees, and ahead was a castle.

"Good Lord and Lady," Jeska breathed in awe. "It looks made of whipped cream!"

Mieka regarded the view. "Laced with beet juice—and bits of shrimp for extra pink."

This proposed combination was, for Rafe the baker's son, too much. The window was desperately opened and immediately deployed.

"I thought it was Crisiant who's s'posed to get sick," Mieka remarked.

The coaches pulled up to an airy rose-colored confection of slender columns, and turrets topped with pointed puffs of pink tile, and more white-curtained windows than seemed architecturally or aesthetically appropriate. This, it was explained by a stout little man wearing a silver badge of office that covered half his chest, would be their home for the night while the luggage was offloaded onto barges for the journey upriver. After this, coaches would be waiting to take them the rest of the way to Gref Jyziero.

Cade wished Derien were with him; the child adored maps, and could have told him precisely where he was in relation to everything else, and how long all this traveling would take. Every sign he'd seen thus far had been in a script familiar to him but a language unknown. He made a mental note to tell Dery that if his ambition truly was to represent Albeyn in foreign lands, he'd have to learn a lot more languages a lot more earnestly than he had hitherto studied their own. Perhaps Drevan Wordturner could assist with a book or two.

Except for the fussing little official, the castle was empty. A cold though copious supper had been laid on in the main hall by servants who were nowhere in evidence. A plan of the castle had been drawn onto a board propped beside the stairs, with names or titles assigned to bedchambers on upper floors. TOUCHSTONE, for instance, was neatly lettered across a fair-sized room on the third floor, just above LORD FAIRWALK and just below OTHER STAFF. The only servants were those who had come over on the two ships, and several of them wearing orange-and-gray livery flustered about with much wringing of hands. These men belonged to the Archduke, who was to serve as Prince Ashgar's proxy.

"But—baths, and breakfast—"

"And what of the sheets? Are they clean? Properly scented?"

All at once a deep, powerful voice spoke into the confusion. "I am convinced that the bedding will be entirely satisfactory."

Thus Cade got his first close-up look at the Archduke. Not quite so tall as Cade, and proportioned more sturdily, he had a broad and high-boned face dominated by golden-brown eyes as luxuriantly lashed as Mieka's. Above them were straight dark brows and a wide forehead and thin chestnut hair with a slight wave. The smile he wore was patient, indulgent, as he addressed his anxious servants.

"As for bathing—I'm told we shan't be departing tomorrow until well into the morning, and there's a lovely lake behind the castle just begging to be splashed in on a warm summer day. Now, if you've no other worries, do go get some rest, won't you?"

He seemed pleasantly lenient with his servants, for a man who was as close to Royal as one could get without having to be addressed as *Your Highness*. Kearney had explained it all one evening at such length that after the third generation, Mieka simply put his hands over his ears and moaned. Unencumbered by Kearney's meanderings, the story was this: King Kearnian (Lord Fairwalk was named after him, because the queen's younger sister had married into the Fairwalk family) had a son to inherit, another son in case of accidents, and a daughter to marry off. Princess Veddie, showing perhaps the feistiness of an Elfen strain in her mother's bloodline, refused point-blank to wed any of the eminently suitable nobles her parents proposed. By twenty-two, she was almost of an age to be unmarriageable. Then a young man came traveling on behalf of his own father, a Prince of somewhere-or-other on the Continent; the Archduke and the Princess fell in love; the King gave them vast estates and allowed him to keep his title. The couple's granddaughter married the heir to the throne, and became the grandparents of King Meredan. As for the spare prince—his granddaughter had married the heir to the Archduchy. The end result after five generations was that the current Archduke was cousin twice over to Prince Ashgar, and as a senior Royal had been chosen to bring Ashgar's bride home to Albeyn.

Descended as he was from King Kearnian and Queen Saffa, the Archduke was known to have Wizard and Elf in his bloodlines. Nether could be seen in his solid build, his ruddy complexion, his small, lobeless, rounded ears. Neither had ever been evidenced in his character or talents. No rumors had ever been bruited about that he had even a dollop of magic in him. He was, to look at and to deal with, entirely Human.

And he was approaching the little knot of young men that was Touchstone, an affable smile on his face. "Forgive me for not introducing myself earlier—departure was rather chaotic, and shouting from ship to ship seemed even more impolite than not saying anything at all. Cyed Henick. I've had the great pleasure of seeing you perform several times."

Kearney greeted him as a kinsman, almost as an equal. Introductions were made, nods given on the one side and half-bows on the other, and they all moved towards the food spread out on tables in the great hall. Everyone ate while standing, or found a chair or stair to sit on. Kearney carried the conversation, with some assistance from Jeska. Cade didn't say much; more unusually, neither did Mieka. Wondering if, like him, the Elf was remembering the man in the Archduke's livery who'd come round asking about Blye's glassworks last year, Cade finally decided it was time to collect a few bottles and go upstairs.

"And I understand, Master Silversun," the Archduke suddenly said, "that Lord Oakapple has commissioned a play. Might one ask its subject?"

Mieka chose this moment to open his mouth for reasons other than shovelling food into it. "One might ask, Your Grace, but one wouldn't receive much of an answer!" The words were delivered in an accent quite as upper-upper as Kearney Fairwalk's. Moreover, the grin was his most innocently disarming, but there was something in those eyes that told Cade he'd been thinking exactly what Cade had suspected he was thinking. "The creative mind, and all that sort of thing, don't you see. Why, he doesn't even let his own partners know where his thoughts are taking him, not until he's quite finished being clever. Mere slaves to his artistic visions, that's all we are." A quick, teasing glance upwards at Cade. "Talking of that, you were busy being brilliant all day, even on the drive here, weren't you—there's a look he gets," he confided to the Archduke, "no mistaking it, all clouded and misty-eyed, hardly speaks a word, and wouldn't notice if I cracked a withie over his head! He's got a bit of that look right now, so mayhap it's time to toddle off to write it all down before he forgets. Your Grace's servant," he finished with a bow, and nudged Cade towards the stairs.

"What was all that, then?" Cade whispered when they had manoeuvred around those seated on the steps and reached the first landing.

"Couldn't bear another instant alongside him, could I?" He made a face. "Oily as a fish fry, that one."

"You could've waited until we'd snagged a few more drinks," he complained.

Mieka shook his head mournfully. "Still underestimating me, after all this time!" Whereupon he parted his jacket to show a bottle clutched to each side with his elbows.

The next morning, the sun through their chamber's east-facing windows was startlingly bright. And hot, especially lying next to another's body heat. When Cade woke, sweating, he flung off the sheets. Mieka rolled onto his other side, snarling in his sleep. Nothing in the world seemed lovelier to Cade than a plunge into that nice, cool lake he could glimpse from the windows. But as he turned to find something to wear downstairs, laughter drove everything else from his mind. He prodded Mieka in the shoulder.

"Wake up!" he whispered. "You have to see this!"

On the Winterly Circuit Cade had learned that the Elf was a matchless grouker. Unless startled from sleep by the abrupt removal of warm blankets or application of a pitcherful of water in the face, it took him upwards of ten minutes to rouse from slumber, longer if it had been a short night, longer still if he'd gone to bed drunk. Fuzzy-eyed, surly, he would turn onto one side, then the other, then bury his face in the pillows, and finally flop over onto his back and glare. After only one bottle of wine and a good ten hours of sleep, he had bypassed the turning and the pillows and was at the glaring stage.

"Look!" Cade pointed to the other bed.

Jeska was cuddled into Rafe's arms, both of them sleeping as serenely as Angels with folded wings. Mieka gave a snorting giggle. "Gods, they're adorable! D'you think Rafe thinks he's Crisiant?"

"I surely as all hells hope so!"

"I heard that," said Rafe, and pushed Jeska to the other side of the bed. A mumble and a snuggle closer made him shove the masquer against the wall.

"Wha–? What'd you do that for?"

"Maybe," Cade mused, "*he* thought *Rafe* was—no, not with that beard."

Bleary and disoriented, and slightly bruised, Jeska blinked a few times before catching on.

The pillow fight was still going strong when someone knocked on their door. Kearney walked in to find Touchstone, stark naked in a cloud of feathers, laughing themselves silly.

Cade found that he wasn't as instantly contrite as he might once have been at being caught in a rough-and-tumble by the grown-ups. He was having too much fun to be sorry—and there were servants to clean everything up, weren't there? Not that he'd seen any, but somebody must take care of this pile of pink pudding. Not his responsibility. So he grinned at Kearney and found a pillow not yet gutted of its feathers, and threw it at him.

His Lordship was not amused. Two hours later, he was still picking bits of white off his immaculate turquoise brocade jacket.

They were back in the coaches, but heading southeast away from the port town. It had been explained that they would reach the barges upriver by late afternoon. All their luggage and gear had been transferred while at the docks, and from here until they reached Gref Jyziero they would be spending each night sleeping on the barges and each day on land. Various excursions had been designed for their amusement: outdoor meals, scenic walks, and a shopping expedition in a locally famous market town with a thoroughly unpronounceable name.

During the long drive Mieka was, as expected, bored. Cade entertained himself by staring out the windows without taking in a single feature of the countryside; he was working on "Treasure" in his head.

And then he saw the river.

Into the sudden hush within their coach, Rafe murmured, "Makes the poor old Gally look like a downhill stream of horse piss."

Cade had seen one or two imagings of the Vathis River, but never any that looked directly across at the opposite bank the way he could now, at trees he knew had to be at least thirty feet tall but that seemed less than the height of his little finger. It hadn't looked this big back at the port, and when he asked Kearney about it he was told things about dams and diversions that he supposed explained it. All he knew for certes was that it had to be a mile across, and very likely more. When the coaches came to a halt, he jumped out and strode to the end of the wooden docks where a fleet of four barges awaited. As far as he could see, both down and up the river, the water was just as wide, just as intensely blue for what looked like a hundred miles.

"We could've sailed our own ships up this monster," Jeska said.

Kearney shook his head. "I was told that our sailors won't come near it. I mean to say, they know the Ocean Sea, and there's a certain amount of snobbery involved, I should think. A river as opposed to *real* sailing."

"A boat's a boat," Rafe observed. "And a sail's a sail."

"But that's no river," Mieka retorted. "It's a baby Flood."

"Probably has something to do with hidden shallows," said Cade. "You'd have to know the river to navigate safely."

Jeska snorted. "As if you have the least idea what you're talking of."

"Logically—"

"Your Lordship!" Drevan Wordturner was hurrying towards them. "You gentlemen are in the second barge—I checked to make sure all your things had been loaded into the proper rooms."

"Good of you," said Kearney. "Show us our cabins, won't you?"

They were sorted through a minor anarchy onto the barges. Nothing seemed out of the ordinary to Cade until Mieka, sprawled on the upper bunk in the cubbyhole they had been given, suddenly said, "Where are the horses?"

"Hmm?" He was sorting through his notes, trying to find the section recording his speculations on the location of the Regal bells.

"Big brutes. Tails, hooves—you know. Horses."

"I thought you didn't ride."

"I don't. But how are we to travel upriver if there's nothing to pull us there?"

Cade gave him a pitying look. "And here you just spent days on a ship with sails."

"There aren't any. This is a barge. Like ones on our rivers and canals. Going downriver with the current, that's one thing. You just float. But how do we go upriver without horses to haul us along?"

"Maybe they bring them out at night while we're asleep. We'll be traveling by coach during the day—"

"Then why's there no towing path 'longside the river?"

"You know all this because—?"

"I helped Jed plan where he's taking Blye."

"They ought to be back in Gallantrybanks by now," Cade mused. "Wish we could be there to sing them into their house."

Mieka shook his head emphatically. "Shout, yell, or shriek, Quill, but don't you *ever* sing!"

Dinner was served on the decks, and then everyone was invited to tuck themselves in for the night. Touchstone had two cabins. The servants were crammed six to a room. Cade had intended to get some work done, but found himself yawning by nightfall, and went to bed just as he felt the barge drift gently out into the river. He slept heavily.

The next morning the barges were tied up, and everyone disembarked for breakfast in a meadow. In the distance, people were working the land, riding or walking the roads, but nobody came near the visitors. Once again coaches showed up to carry them twenty or more miles inland, this time to a pretty hillside with a view of far-off mountains. The afternoon was spent strolling, talking, drinking, or lazing about in the sunshine. Cade joined Mieka in being bored.

Back to the barges—which were many miles upriver from where they'd left them. Cade began to understand Mieka's puzzlement about how they'd got there. Dinner was served on trestle tables dockside, and at sunset everyone once more returned to the cabins. Unlike on board ship, there was no evening social life, no drinking, no talking until all hours. Cade didn't mind; he intended to use the time working. But Mieka wasn't used to going to bed this early.

"Tried their best to wear us out today, didn't they?" the Elf observed irritably as he clambered up onto the top bunk. "Like mums making their children chase round the park."

"It's nice to stretch our legs," Cade replied idly. His new portfolio was open on the bed, and he was organizing pages according to subject.

"You didn't drink much wine tonight."

Another of Mieka's swervings. Not if he lived to be a thousand would he ever get used to them. "Too strong for the fish they served."

"Ooh! Ain't we got grand and all, lately!"

"Just because I don't guzzle down anything put in front of me—" He stopped and frowned. "You didn't drink much, either."

Mieka's upside-down face appeared over the side of the bunk. "I've had enough different sorts of thorn to know when I'm being coaxed to sleep."

"Are you serious?"

"And I can't get the porthole open. It's locked." He looked at the door. "So's that, I wager. Or will be."

"But why—?"

"Shushup!"

A few moments later he heard the footfalls outside in the narrow corridor. Steps; pause. Steps; pause. All at once Cade caught on—or caught Mieka's suspicions—and when the steps approached their door he yawned loudly and slurred, "Gods, can't keep m'eyes open—g'night," and closed the lamplight. Mieka responded with an equally sleepy "Dream sweet" in the darkness. They listened, and sure enough there was a soft click at the door.

Cade counted his own heartbeats for a while, then realized he was breathing too quickly and shallowly for an accurate guess at the elapsing time. Instead he recited "The Song of the Harpy's Lair" inside his head—a trick he'd learned back at Sagemaster Emmot's Academy during mathematics class, when at a certain speed it measured out fifteen minutes of frustrated boredom. He was halfway through it when he heard Mieka drop lightly to the floor.

"They're gone," the boy breathed. "What don't they want us to see?"

"Whatever it is, they *really* don't want us to see it," he whispered back. "Want some light?"

"Don't need any, beholden." By the sounds, Mieka was rummaging about in his satchel. "That little polishing kit Blye gave us—I need that thin metal file…"

Cade was about to ask a foolish question when he heard, in rapid succession, Mieka's bare footfalls on the deck, a fumbling, and another click at the door.

"Ha! Gods, I'm good!"

"Where'd you learn to do that?"

"Jez taught me. C'mon, there's some glowy sort of thing out there, up ahead. I want to find out what it is."

"Let's wait a bit more."

"But I want to know *now!*"

"I can't bloody wait for you to grow up and add the concept of *patience* to your collection. Just as an abstract idea, you understand."

But they did linger for caution's sake, and after a while Mieka inched the door open. A single lamp burned at the foot of the steps. All else was darkness. Barefoot, they crept along the passageway. Cade was edgily aware of the length of his own limbs, the size of his hands and feet, the scant distance between his head and the ceiling. They were in the second barge down the row, and as Mieka picked the locked overhead hatch at the top of the steps, Cade wondered if they'd have to sneak all the way up to the front to see whatever there might be to see.

At intervals of about six feet or so, all along the perimeter of the deck, were footlights—small lamps encased in glass. They would allow for safely negotiating the deck at night, but there were no lights above the railing, nothing to shine down onto the water. Cade thought that rather odd, but didn't have time to ponder it, because Mieka elbowed him in the ribs. They ducked back below the hatch. Footsteps approached, continued on towards the back of the barge. After an agony of waiting, Cade dared to peek his head out again.

Mieka tugged his arm and they went topside. The barges were moving now, picking up speed. Up at the prow was a catwalk connecting this barge to the one ahead, but Cade felt no temptation to cross. He had the blood of Wizards and Elves, Pikseys and Sprites, and even Fae in his veins; he had studied for several years with one of the most accomplished practitioners of magic in the Kingdom; he was a not inconsiderable Wizard himself. But it took a journey to a land where magical folk were shunned to show him the strangest thing he'd ever seen in his life.

Up ahead was the glow Mieka had glimpsed: a swirling cloud of purplish-gold, with sparks flitting amid it, hovering just above the black water and pulling the barges at a now remarkable speed. Limned against this light was a hunched figure seated on the prow of the lead barge. Hands lifted and fell, and to their rhythm the shining cloud pulsed. Below it, submerged in the water, were huge pale shapes that surged towards the glowing haze.

Mieka's fingers dug into his arm, yanking desperately. Cade wasn't entirely aware of scurrying back down to their cabin. Not until he stood with his back against the door did he hear the harshness of his own breathing. Mieka pushed him aside and he heard the sound of the door being locked again.

He stood there, shaking. The stark sound of a flint-rasp at a wick made him flinch. Mieka was shaking, too, as he set the candle on the floor and curled on the lower bunk, arms wreathing his knees. After a moment Cade took up a blanket and sat beside the Elf, draping the warmth around both of them. They huddled there together, silent and wide awake, until dawn.

13

He dared say nothing the next morning, nor at breakfast, nor on the drive to the distraction of the day. Neither did he dare to look for more than an instant at Mieka. Sometime before dawn they'd felt the barges slow down and slide towards shore, and heard their door being unlocked. A little while later, a bell sounded to wake everyone up. A quick wash with the warm water from the ewer left outside their cabin, a change of clothing, a few glances of worry and speculation, and then they were up on deck again, open carriages waiting for them this time. Cade didn't even dare look up at the prow of the lead barge.

He was surprised to learn that thus far they'd traveled through two Grand Duchies, a County, and three Marches, all independent of one another and of any larger kingdom. He learned this through the simple expedient of asking the little man with the big silver badge of office where they would go today. The name of the place was unintelligible to him, but when he made further polite inquiry about its location, he was told that the nobility had vied strenuously for the honor of hosting each day's excursions, but when it came to excellence of musicians, dancers, and acrobats, none of the three Markgrefins or the Count or even the two Grand Dukes through whose domains they had passed could compare with the Markgref of Kladivo, whose family was known across the Continent as highly cultured patrons of the arts.

Cade knew that name. He'd found it in *Lost Withies*, mentioned several times as one of the few places outside the Kingdom where players had been welcome in years long past.

A lingering malicious touch of Sprite in Cade's blood made him smile down at the official. "Then we ought to perform for him, shouldn't we? How about it, Lord Fairwalk?" he said as Kearney turned all the colors of the rainbow. "Why not grab a few withies and show everybody how it's done?"

Kearney looked stricken. "You—but you can't—you just simply—"

Jeska took pity on the stuttering nobleman. "If His local Lordship's as expert as all that, he'll prob'ly be invited to the castle or the palace or wherever it is we collect the Tregrefina from, eh?"

"Quite right, Your Honor, quite right indeed," the official blurted, "so wise of you to understand—must see to the horses now, pray do excuse me—"

"Whatever possessed you to say that?" Kearney hissed at Cade. "You were there when protocol was discussed, you know you're not supposed to mix with—"

"We're guests, it's only polite to offer."

"Do us all a service, Cade, and shut it." Rafe paused, eyeing him sidelong. "And don't sulk."

He did, though, all during the drive and until the carriages pulled up in an excruciatingly picturesque town. Every wooden shutter and awning had been carved and painted to within an inch of its life. Garlands of flowers and ribbons stretched from one side of the main street to the other. A minor fair had been laid on for their benefit—and that of the local merchants—with colorful booths of wares on the streets outside the shops. Lunching would be provided at the central square, and afterwards a performance of music and dancing. Cayden, still feeling contrary, found himself a stone bench and sat on it, watching the display of good cheer with a scowl on his face.

It seemed to him sheer folly, this deception of days on land and nights on the river. Surely someone else would realize what Mieka had realized last night—that the dinner wine was laced with a sleeping draught. But why should anyone suspect anything? After a pair of long drives, and an active afternoon between, with a heavy dinner and lots to drink, why shouldn't everyone be too tired to stay up late?

Granted, the river was the quickest way to travel. If he recalled correctly, Kladivo was more than halfway to Gref Jyziero. Had they been loaded into coaches for the duration—

"What else don't they want us to see, I wonder?"

He glanced up, startled. Mieka was juggling three green apples.

"I mean, obviously the way they move those barges up the river is meant to be secret, but what happens during the day?"

"What do you mean?"

"It's all been very pretty so far, hasn't it? Castle, meadows, fields, trees, charming little villages—"

Cade reached out and snagged one of the apples. "Stop that and sit down and tell me what in all hells you're talking about."

Shrugging, Mieka sat and bit into one of the apples. After munching and swallowing, he went on, "We must be making at least a hundred miles each night, prob'ly more. I don't like to think how long it would take in coaches. But why risk anybody seeing those *things* in the water? Why not just let us bounce and bruise our bums for a fortnight or so through the countryside?"

"Mayhap they want us in a good mood when we arrive."

"Who cares what mood we're in? Except for the Archduke and Fairwalk, we're all common folk and servants. And you're avoiding the issue. Why get us away from the river during the day?"

"You're imagining things." But he couldn't put much assurance into the statement.

"Did we each of us have the same hallucination last night, then?"

Cade turned the apple over and over in his hands. "We're off the river every day from halfway through the morning until just before sunset. We have dinner, and the drinks are dosed to send us to sleep. Once everything's quiet, we're locked in. Then the barges start moving."

"And there's somebody up front who makes a light appear, and somehow that controls those *things* in the water, and they're what's pulling the barges."

"I wish I had a library to hand."

Mieka chortled. "Only you, Quill! D'you think there's any book could tell us what happens during the day that we're not supposed to see? We already know what they're hiding by night."

Cade lifted the apple to his lips, then looked at it. An awful idea had occurred to him. "Feeding time," he blurted. "Those things must be hungry after swimming upriver all those hours."

Mieka blinked several times, then whispered, "What d'you think they eat?"

"Oy, Mieka!" Rafe called from across the street. "Jewelry shop!"

He looked blank for a moment. Then, with a muttered apology, he scampered between horses and carts. It took Cade a while to figure it out. When he did, he swore under his breath and told himself to ignore it, and go look for gifts for Mistress Mirdley and Derien.

He found Jeska outside a woodworker's establishment. Spread on the counter and hanging all around the booth was a selection of intricately carved toys, brilliantly painted. Cade was reminded of Master Ashbottle's ironworks, though he knew that there would be no magic in these toys—except for what a child's imagination brought to them, of course—and he had the thought that for a child at play, imagination was more than enough.

"I thought I'd find something for me girlie," Jeska said,

holding up a doll with articulated joints for Cade's inspection. Big blue eyes in a smiling little face were framed by golden curls, delicately carved. She came with two dresses, one green and one pink, and a white apron tied with blue ribbons.

"Beautiful. Rather looks like her, too."

"D'you have any coin on you?"

"Skint already?" Kearney had distributed spending money the day before the trip.

"Had to send most of it to her mother." He gave the crafter his most ravishing smile, then tilted his head in a silent question. The man held up three fingers. "Three of what, though?" Jeska muttered, frustrated.

Cade dug into a pocket and picked out four different sizes of coins. The first and second made the crafter shake his head, but when he held up the third, there was a vigorous nodding. Cade was fairly sure the price was moderately outrageous, and held a brief debate with himself, then decided that in the interests of international harmony he'd pay up without haggling. The doll was wrapped in clean burlap dyed blue, tied with string, and after much bowing and more smiling Cade and Jeska moved on.

"Is she after you for more money?"

"She wrote to say she'd had nothing since before Trials. I talked to Kearney on it. His clerk forgot, or something." He pointed to a booth frothing with piles of lace. "I think I'll get her something of this, to apologize." Then, with a sidelong glance: "You might bring your mother a gift, too, y'know."

Cade shrugged.

"She's proud of you, though she'll never say it."

"She's reconciled to my superfluous existence."

They ambled on through the town. Every paving stone was spotless, all the faces were smiling, the scent of the flower garlands was overwhelming, and it all made Cayden extremely annoyed. The show being staged for them was every bit as elaborate as the most complex play. A good impression for visitors was desirable, of course, but this was doing it up a bit too brown.

"Are you sleeping all right?" he asked Jeska.

"What? Oh—yeh, out like a snuffed candle." He pulled a face. "No reason not to sleep, if you see what I mean."

Cade snorted. "When we finally get there, you can seduce every woman in sight. Just keep your pretty paws off the Tregrefina."

"When we finally get there, I'll have forgot how it works!"

An outdoor lunching was followed by the promised entertainment. By midafternoon they were all back in the carriages, waving farewell to the happy populace—who grinned and simpered as if they'd all done something quite cunning. Cade supposed they'd all made a lovely profit. Mieka was in a foul mood. Despite a dedicated search, he'd found nothing to his liking by way of wedding jewels. He hadn't been impressed by the glasswork, either.

"All crizzle and bubble," he was complaining as their carriage rounded a turn in the road. "Swirly colors like cat-yark on a really ugly rug. And—"

The carriage lurched and skittered. Cade knew what a popped wheel felt like; they'd experienced enough of them on the Winterly last year. To be inside a closed coach, rattling about like bees in a jar, was bad enough, but this was an open carriage. Rafe pitched sideways, half atop Kearney; Cade grabbed for Jeska with one hand and slammed Mieka back against the seat with the other arm as packages went flying. So did Briuly Blackpath, tumbling over the side of the carriage, landing on one shoulder in the dirt.

The horses stopped almost at once. The driver leaped down, Cade right behind him. Theirs was the next-to-last carriage in the procession—and the one behind them merely slowed to maneuver past, and did not stop to help. Their driver busied himself unbuckling the straps holding the boot compartment closed, muttering under his breath. Rafe ambled back down the road to collect the wheel.

Briuly sat up, cursing as Cade stripped off his neckband to use as a sling. "How in fucking hells am I s'posed to fucking play me fucking lute?"

"No worrying on it, mate," Mieka told him. "I've got a bit of something in me satchel back at the boat that'll do for the pain."

"Praise the Lord and Lady it wasn't a finger, don't you see," Kearney contributed helpfully. "Or your whole hand—"

Briuly looked ready to rip off the sling and throttle him with it.

"Wheel's intact," Rafe announced, rolling it up to lean against the listing carriage. Then the driver's string of curses—the words were unknown to them, but the tone was unmistakable—made all of them flinch. A moment later a box was flung into the road, scattering a collection of wooden pegs.

"Nothing that fits, I take it." Rafe shook his head. "Remind me, when we acquire our own nice, big, expensive wagon, to hire a coachman who understands that a repair kit is useless if he doesn't keep it stocked."

"Did you see the axle peg lying about anywhere?" Jeska asked.

A search yielded the splintered halves of the peg in the roadside grass. Examining the pieces, Cade saw it was a clean break, no bits missing. It had split right up the middle.

"I can mend it," he said.

"Don't!" Kearney exclaimed.

"Magic," Rafe muttered. "It's either that, or we walk."

His Lordship clutched at Cade's sleeve. "You don't understand—we're under the strictest orders, what you do in a theater is one thing but out in the open where people can see you—the common folk—"

"Briuly's hurt," Jeska said, eyes wide with amazement. "We

have to get back as soon as may be. And there's nobody about but the driver."

Cade looked at the two pieces of wood in his hand. An Affinity spell would take care of the break in a trice. "What d'you think they'd do to us? And who gave these orders?"

Mieka appeared at his side with the box and all the useless pegs. "Mend it," he said simply. "And pretend you found it in here, that he overlooked it."

The little farce was played out, and the wheel was secured, and they climbed back into the carriage with the driver none the wiser. Briuly was settled carefully against the cushions, and everyone sorted themselves—and Jeska found the doll he'd bought for his daughter crammed under the seat, one leg and both arms broken.

"Give it here," Cade commanded—though he did wait until the driver's back was safely turned before becasting the poor little wooden doll with the same magic he'd just used on the axle peg. Kearney stifled a whimper and turned his face away.

"If you could do that to roof timbers and such," Mieka remarked, "Jed and Jez would hire you in a flash."

"If I ever get sick of you lot," Cade retorted, "I'll consider it."

It was full dark before they reached the docks where the barges had tied up—a different location from the morning, of course. After shock and dismay were duly expressed, and gratitude that everyone was mostly all right, Briuly was looked after by the Archduke's own physicker. Cade took his dinner down to his cabin, and ate very little of it. And drank nothing.

"Sulking again."

He didn't look up as Mieka entered the cabin.

"Jeska was right. So was Fairwalk. And so was I." He paused. "And so were you."

"We had to get Briuly back here, I'll go along with that. And you can applaud yourself all night for being clever if you please, I don't give a damn. But how can you say that Kearney and I were *both* right? How can you knuckle under to orders that we don't even know who gave them, and—"

"Did you note how nervous the bargemen are tonight?" Mieka interrupted. "No, of course you didn't. You were too busy being self-righteous. They keep looking out at the water and muttering things. And there's not a sign of the old man with the magic." He searched through his satchel and came up with a wyvern-hide roll of thorn—a new one, Cade saw, dark purple and stamped along the edges with a repeating pattern of silver raindrops, seeds, candle flames, and at one corner *MW*.

He watched as a paper twist of powder was selected and one of five glass thorns was removed from its cushioning spell. Suddenly he wanted nothing so much in the world as to lose himself in dreams. Mieka was here, and wouldn't let him get too lost.

"So," the Elf said at last. "After I deliver this to poor Briuly, shall we go exploring again tonight, or do you want to sit here and cherish your huff?"

Knuckles tapped at their door, and a voice whispered, "Cayden?"

"Come in, Kearney," he said.

His Lordship was not alone. Drevan Wordturner was with him—or, rather, supporting him, for Kearney was as unsteady on his feet as if he'd plunged into a barrel of Brishen Staindrop's finest.

"Appalling imposition," he said in the forcibly clipped manner of the very drunk who knew it. "Dreadf'ly sorry."

"Master Blackpath," said Wordturner, who was looking a bit fuzzy around the edges himself, "isn't to be disturbed until morning."

"Have the lower bed," Mieka said at once. A little smile played about his lips as Kearney was maneuvered the three steps across the cabin and Cade got up to make way for him on the bunk.

"Fri'f'ly good of you," Kearney managed, then turned onto his side and began to snore.

"The physicker gave Briuly something for the pain?" Cade asked.

When, after a moment's thought, the young man nodded, Mieka sighed and replaced the packet and thorn. "Won't be needing these, then."

Belatedly recalling his manners, Cade said, "Mieka Windthistle, this is Drevan Wordturner—a librarian who'd rather be a cavalry officer."

Mieka shivered. "There's aught to choose betwixt the two?" Then, peering up at the young man's face, he went on kindly, "You're yawning like a mine cavern. D'you think you'd make it to His Grace's barge without falling overboard? Let's make sure he doesn't, eh, Quill?"

Drevan protested that it wasn't necessary. Mieka insisted. Cade went along with it, wondering what the Elf had in mind. They had just escorted Wordturner up onto the deck when a boatman caught sight of them in the gloom and gestured them back down.

"Just taking him to his bed," Mieka said cheerfully. "One of His Grace's men, and all that sort of thing—"

More gestures, and a lot of sharp words.

"What's he saying?" Cade asked, and Drevan shook his head as if to clear it. "Can you understand him?"

"He—he wants us gone," the young man slurred. Whatever had been in tonight's wine was catching him up fast.

Mieka was nudging them towards the front of the barge. Cade opened his mouth to say that the one up ahead was reserved for the Archduke himself and his personal retinue, and couldn't possibly be where Drevan belonged—and then realized what Mieka was doing.

They had reached the catwalk, which was barely wide enough

for two people. Cade looked at it doubtfully. Mieka flung him a wide and challenging grin, white teeth flashing in the footlights glinting beneath the railing.

"Your Honors, Your Honors! Please return to cabins that are yours! Please!" It was the little man with the big silver badge. "Soon departing—a threat to stay above—"

"Just helping this gentleman along," Cade said.

"Why is it a threat?" Mieka asked at the same time.

"I–I worded wrongly," he amended anxiously. "I meant not safe, Your Honors, please—"

Drevan was swaying against Cade now, well and truly paved. "'S all right," he muttered, "jus' lemme sleep—"

"Yes, yes!" The little man nodded. "Sleep for you all, the best thing—"

Cade exchanged a glance with Mieka. "Mayhap a little more light," he suggested, and balanced a flicker of blue Wizardfire on the tip of one finger.

Someone on the first barge bellowed words that made Drevan flinch violently against Cade's shoulder, nearly toppling them both.

"What did he say?" Mieka demanded.

"M-magic—"

"I beg Your Honor, please, stop!"

"—no magic, no light—"

The yelling grew louder.

"—'specially light *made* o' magic," Drevan mumbled. "Pretty sure tha's wha' he said. Lookit up t'morrow, promise. C'n sleep now, yeh, Uncle Teremun?"

The lead barge surged forward. The catwalk broke in two. Someone came running past them and leaped the railing. Cade lost the Wizardfire in his astonishment—and lost hold of Drevan, who sagged to the deck and passed out.

The odd misty glow appeared ahead, larger and more

intense, sparking with brighter lights. Once again Cade saw the outline of a man signaling with his arms, but frantically this time, desperately.

"Oh no, oh no," moaned the little man, "please to all the Powers, don't let them get loose—"

Between the glowing cloud and the man conjuring it erupted one and then three and then five or more gushes of water, spouting like fountains twenty feet into the night. The barges jerked forward again—like carriages, Cade suddenly thought, carriages collared to restive, bad-tempered horses. Yellow-pale, sleek-necked horses, with hawk's eyes and carnivore's teeth.

The river-horses screamed. Plunging towards the magical light up ahead, they surfaced and spewed water from red-rimmed nostrils and threw back their massive heads and screamed.

Into glass withies, Cayden had worked magic that made dragons roar. He had created the crack of lightning and the shrill cries of mythical birds and the deep solemn rumble of Minster bells. The screams were all these combined and a warning besides, and without conscious thought he hauled Drevan across the deck with one hand and grabbed Mieka's wrist with the other and fled.

He didn't even feel the bruises of their crazed tumble down steps, or the battering of his shoulders against passageway walls as the barge rocked and shuddered. Somehow they were back in their cabin, and Kearney lay sleeping on the lower bunk. He let Drevan lie where he and Mieka dropped him. All at once the Elf was tucked up against his side in the darkness, shivering. Cade put an arm around him: slight but solid, unseen but real.

They waited for the sound of doors closing, and the ebbing of worried, angry muttering. They waited in darkness for the snick of the lock on their door. Mostly they waited for the screaming to stop.

When it did, they crawled up to the top bed and huddled there for a long time. At last Cade whispered, "Are you all right?"

"No!" Mieka pulled away into a corner. "They'll kill us for seeing that."

"Don't be stupid." The barge was moving more smoothly now. Cade stretched out his cramped legs and said, "We didn't see anything."

"Didn't we?"

"No."

The sky outside the porthole was just beginning to pale and the barges had stopped moving when their door was unlocked and a small, wizened man entered, holding a lighted candle. He glanced round the cabin: Drevan Wordturner, still in a heap on the floor; Kearney Fairwalk, still soundly asleep. Looking up, he saw Cade and Mieka in the upper bunk.

"Was you, yes?" he asked in a thickly accented voice that seemed much too deep to come from so scrawny a chest. "Magic yesternight."

Cade nodded. He stumbled down from the bunk, joints stiff, head aching after two nights without sleep. Mieka slid down to stand beside him.

"Rule has reason," the old man said.

"We didn't see anything!" Mieka blurted.

A dry cackling chuckle. "Afeared? No need. *Vodabeiste* undanger—*not* danger," he corrected himself. "Control is mine—" He smiled up at Cade again. "—until other magics. Wizard, you?"

Cade nodded.

"*Vodabeiste* feel it."

"Rules have reasons," Cade ventured. "The light I made last night—"

"Light was, also, before?"

He didn't understand. Mieka did.

"No, that was a joining spell. The axle peg broke, and he mended it with magic. Did those—things—feel it?"

"Yes," said the old man. He hesitated, then reached out a

hand, almost touching Cade, head tilting to one side as if asking permission. Cade stood still. Thick, crooked fingers touched his arm, his shoulder, his cheek. "Wizard," the old man sighed. Turning to Mieka, he brushed back the concealing black hair. "Kin," he whispered.

Startled, Cade looked at the old man's ears. Not pointed. No sign of having been kagged. *Kin?*

"Water Elf?" Mieka ventured in a very small voice.

"*Voda*, yes. And other." The ringing of a bell up top seemed to be his signal to depart. He took his candle, blew it out, and put his fingers on the door handle. "Rule has reason," he said again, with a twinkle directed at Cade. Then he opened the door and was gone.

14

Even if Mieka had been able to phrase the questions, there was no one to ask about the happenings of the night. There was no sign of the old man the next day. ("*Kin*"?) Neither Fairwalk nor Wordturner remembered a thing. The little man with the silver badge scurried the other way when he saw Mieka coming. And the expression in Cade's gray eyes discouraged conversation. If not for his bumps and bruises from that wild retreat back down the steps, Mieka might have thought he'd dreamed the whole thing while under the influence of some especially cryptic variety of thorn concocted by Auntie Brishen.

But he hadn't dreamed it.

He would remember those screams until his dying day.

Whatever those water-things were, there was no suggestion that they even existed by daylight. They might have been taken someplace for a feed, or mayhap they were sleeping. And there would be no chance to investigate further tonight, even if he'd been able to gather the courage to do so, for the passengers and all their belongings were loaded into coaches for the last part of the journey to Gref Jyziero.

In a way, he was relieved. Thinking of those things plunging through the river current, dragging the barges behind them—it gave him the weirds. As much as he tried to tell himself it was no different, really, from horses hitched to a carriage, he knew it was very different. He didn't know quite how, but it was. Cayden would probably have been able to explain it. But Cayden wasn't talking. For the whole long, jostled, cramped, miserable journey, Cade didn't say much of anything to anybody.

During the next four days it was like being back on the Winterly.

They were rousted out of bed at dawn, chivvied into the coaches, allowed out at lunching, and repacked until dusk. Then they ate dinner, got sorted into beds at taverns or inns (in the Archduke's case, the nicest house in whatever town or village was privileged to host the delegation), and did it all again on the morrow. Through it all, Cade took refuge in books, thought, and gazing silently out the widow. Never much of a reader, Mieka had long since discovered that attempting it while in a moving coach made him sick to his stomach. All the things he could think of to think about were annoying, upsetting, or depressing. And once he'd seen one lakelet, manor house, grove of trees, or glimpse of distant mountains, he'd seen them all.

Besides, this place made him jittery. It was too big. The river was too wide. The fields were too vast and the trees were too tall. It was all familiar, even the mountains, but on a scale that unnerved him. The roads stretched out to infinity and the sky was just too damned blue. He reminded himself time and again that he ought to be collecting impressions to use as backdrops for future plays, but he couldn't keep his mind on his work, either. On the Winterly, one endured the tedium of travel for the excitement of a new town to explore, a new theater to analyze, a new audience to play for, a new girl to bed. A brief show for the locals would at least have kept him from feeling that rust was eating away at his magic, or maybe it was roof-rot in his brain. What he knew for certain, and with displeasure as well as discomfort, was that with all this sitting about with no exercise beyond climbing into and out of the coach, his belt was getting tight.

And Cayden wasn't talking.

Fairwalk filled in a lot of the silences, of course. He was good at that, Kearney Fairwalk was. And at reiterating what everybody already knew. They would be playing two outdoor and three indoor shows. The new Princess had specifically requested "Hidden Cottage." The primarily visual pieces would be received better than the talkier ones by people who didn't understand their language. Mieka was about ready to stuff Fairwalk's neckband down his throat to shut him up when he actually said something new: that they would not be returning to the port town on the barges.

Mieka perked up at that. "Crossland, then?" he asked, not sure whether the daunting length of such a journey would be worth it for not having to think about those water-things again.

"No, on the river, as before—but we'll be sailing on ships her father has hired. Something about the winds and the current, and all that sort of thing."

"None of that on-and-off nonsense? Good," Rafe said.

Mieka tried to catch Cade's attention, and couldn't. But he knew they must be thinking the same thing: *None of those water-things? Better than good!*

Their fourth night on the road, with dinner congealing like a lump of molten glass in his stomach, Mieka left the taproom after one glass of whiskey—very bad whiskey, though the wines were quite good here—and went up early to the room he would share with Cade, Jeska, Rafe, Briuly, and Fairwalk. Contemplation of his purple roll of thorn brought scant satisfaction. He didn't want to sleep, and he certainly didn't want to stay awake in this dismal place. He pondered blackthorn for a time. Yet when he recalled what had happened to Cade—that he'd dreamed about what he'd been thinking of just before the thornprick—he shuddered away from it. All he lacked were horrid dreams about those yellow monsters in the river. He could try, of course, to dream about *her* by fixing her image in his mind, but he didn't want to risk that his determination wouldn't be strong enough. Everything that meant *home* to him seemed so distant. Abruptly worried, he started to dig through his satchel for the neckband she'd made for him, then remembered with a curse that, not wanting to risk losing it, he'd left it carefully folded on a shelf in his aerie at Wistly.

The door was flung open and Cade appeared—genially squiffed, smiling for the first time in days. "Well? C'mon, then. Briuly says there's a tavern up the way with much better drinks, and music. And *girls.*"

A flick of his hand rolled up the collection of thorn. "Lead on!"

This was more like it, he told himself an hour later. He had a pretty girl on his knee and a pewter tankard of very good beer in his hand, and Jeska was leading the chorus of a children's song that seemed to be common to all countries—though Jeska's lyrics were definitely not suitable for children. When Mieka smiled, the girl giggled and snuggled closer. A charming little thing, she was, weighing no more than a feather, with big brown eyes and a dimple in one cheek. He dared a kiss to the dimple, and she blushed. But when he tossed his long, wild hair out of his eyes and joined Jeska in howling out the song's refrain, she was off his lap with a squeal like a scalded kitten.

"*Albeynvolker*—!"

The singing stopped. There was no shouting. No ugly words, no fists threatening a fight. Barmaids swooped in to seize the tankards. The barkeep didn't do anything so dramatic as vault over the bar; he simply walked around it, approached their table, and stood there, staring down at Mieka's pointed Elfen ears.

Briuly started to his feet. Rafe slammed him back down with a hand to his chest. Looking up at the barkeep, he drawled, "I hadn't finished my drink, friend."

No mistaking his tone, even if the words weren't understood. The man planted his hands on his hips and stood his ground. Staring.

"Let's—let's not make any trouble," Mieka whispered. It was the Prickspur incident all over again, only without any yelling, and somehow that made it worse. The silent menace of this tavern, the fear in the eyes of the girl who'd been giggling on his lap not two minutes ago—oh it was so much worse. "We'll just leave now, Rafe, please, it doesn't matter—"

"It matters to me." This from Cayden, who sat straight-spined and furious beside Mieka.

"I'm the one they're all lookin' at! And I say we're out of here!" He got to his feet. A murmur ran through the crowd. It took everything he had to summon up his usual beguiling smile. Jeska rose and came to his side. "No fists, eh?" Mieka whispered.

"No magic, neither," Jeska warned.

Chairs scraped the floor as first Briuly, then Rafe, and finally Cade stood up. With an ominous growl, Briuly raked back his long wild curls to reveal his own ears. Someone gasped. Mieka flung his best smile to the four corners of the room, then deliberately mimicked Briuly, tucking his hair back so everyone could get a good look. He hoped no one saw that his fingers were shaking. He bowed to the girl, then the barkeep, pivoted on one heel, and started for the door. Along the way, an elbow dug into his back. The toe of a boot caught his ankle, and he stumbled slightly. He heard Rafe snarl like a wolfhound. He lengthened his strides, gaze darting everywhere at once as he tried to anticipate where the next shove might come from—but none did. He was at the door and outside in the warm night and wanting so desperately to run that his whole body trembled.

Rafe slung a protective arm around his shoulders. They started up the dark street, not quite hurrying. Someone behind them called out *"Albeynvolker!"* again, and light spilled from opened windows.

"Down this way," Jeska said.

"No, the turning was two more lanes on," Cade argued.

There were footsteps behind them now, and angered mutterings, and the occasional shout of that odd word again that had sounded as if it meant more than *folk from the Kingdom of Albeyn*.

"Wasn't it a left-hand turn?" Jeska asked.

"Who the fuck cares?" Briuly gasped. "Run!"

"No," snapped Cayden. He pivoted and strode to the center of the street. Quite the little mob had gathered behind them, heads and shoulders dappled by the light pouring down from opened windows. Cade lifted both hands, and from his fingertips spread a curtain of blue-white Wizardfire.

It took only seconds. The street beyond emptied faster than a whorehouse after a rumor of pox. Cade staggered. Rafe abandoned Mieka and put both big hands around Cade's bony ribs to support him. The sheen of light flickered and died out, and Cade sagged back against Rafe.

"Idiot!" the fettler accused. "You *know* what that takes out of you! Well?" he flung over his shoulder at the gaping others. "Help me with him! Let's get out of here!"

How they found their way back to their assigned lodgings was something Mieka never knew and never troubled himself about. It was enough to be upstairs in their room and hear Jeska lock the door. Rafe hauled Cade over to a bed and dropped him onto it, then grabbed a blanket from another bed. Mieka tugged off Cade's boots. A blurry, surprisingly sweet smile touched the exhausted face before his cheeks suddenly glistened with sweat and he rolled onto his side and groaned. Mieka grabbed for the piss pot beneath the bed, and just in time, too. Whatever Cade had quaffed that night—and it seemed to be a lot—he parted company with it rather violently.

Rafe sat on the other side of the bed, ready with a wet cloth when Cade finally fell onto his back, breathing hard. "Nice show," Rafe remarked. "You done?"

A feeble nod, a little shrug of thin shoulders. He closed his eyes as the cloth was draped over his forehead.

"Rafe." Mieka blinked across at the fettler. "How come—?"

"Later. Let's put him to bed."

Fairwalk woke up then—and so did Drevan Wordturner, who was with him in the big bed over in the corner. Mieka smirked as the nobleman blithered witlessly with embarrassment; Rafe told him to go back to sleep, they'd explain it all in the morning.

Jeska doubled up with Briuly, and Mieka slid under the sheets of the other bed with Rafe so that Cade could rest undisturbed. In the darkness, after everyone had settled, Mieka whispered, "Why—?"

"Hits him hard. Always did."

"But—those torches that time—the inn yard up north, when that man wouldn't let me under his roof—" The first time Cade had summoned Wizardfire to Mieka's defense.

"That was different."

Mieka squirmed impatiently. Rafe sighed, and relented.

"Torches already know fire. And they're a *something* to attach it to.

Plain old air, it doesn't much want to burn, does it? And there's nothing to fasten onto, except what's nearby, and he didn't want to burn down the shop signs—or the shops. Takes a fettler's control, or damned near."

"I'm not understanding."

"Well, you stay awake thinking about it, then."

Sleeping very little, sleeping badly, and sleeping not at all— rotten nights were getting to be a tradition on this trip. Mieka wanted to go home. But he knew better than to say so out loud.

The next morning he pretended to be asleep as the others woke, got up, washed, dressed, mumbled—quietly, so as not to wake Cayden—and left the room. At last Mieka rose from the bed where Rafe had snored in his ear all night and crept over to Cade. He still looked knackered: pale, with dark circles under his eyes and a hollowness about him.

"Idiot," Mieka murmured, agreeing with Rafe's indictment of last night, now that he knew what it cost Cade to perform that sort of magic. "We could've outrun them, y'know."

"Not bleedin' likely," Cade whispered back, and opened his eyes. "It's sad, innit? That they're scared of the light."

Mieka didn't know what he meant, and for the moment didn't much care. "Why'd you do that, eh? You'll be neither use nor ornament all day long and probably into tomorrow." Sudden anger nipped at him. "And what if they'd braved all your flash and sparkle, what then?"

"They'd have strung me up right next to you, Elfling." He smiled and stretched. "I didn't much fancy either, now that you mention it. And it worked out. You're safe."

"For now." He could have bitten off his own tongue for the words. Cade's smile vanished. With an effort, he shrugged and said lightly, "I'll wear a cap from now on, that's what I'll do. But don't you ever again—"

"I'll do what I have to. No one touches you, Mieka. Not while I'm around."

He watched the fierce gray eyes for a time, then snorted as much of a laugh as he could manage. "My hero! C'mon, then, I can hear your stomach flapping against your spine, you're that empty. Let's get some food into you."

Mieka hadn't much hope that they'd come down late enough for breakfast to escape the *You did* what *last night?* and the *Oh good Lord and Lady preserve us!* and especially the *Didn't I tell you? Didn't I?* that he figured were inevitable from Kearney Fairwalk. So he was astounded when no such exclamations were forthcoming. No scolding. No demands to be told Fairwalk had been right about using magic outside a theater setting. Mieka let his eyebrows ask a silent question of Rafe, who shrugged innocently and passed the porridge.

Later, when they were dividing up into coaches one more time, he sidled up to Rafe and hissed, "What's with His Lordship?"

"He knows we went out drinking. He doesn't know about the other. Shall we keep it like that? Good."

Their route out of the town took them past the tavern. Mieka didn't really recognize the place, but he would never forget the face of the man who'd stared at him so ferociously last night. That face looked up from where the man was shaking out a small blue rug, and for just an instant Mieka cringed.

Even that one instant was too much.

"Stop! Stop the coach!" He grabbed for the door handle and jumped out before anyone could do more than speak his name. He stumbled a bit on landing, caught his balance, and stepped up from the cobbled street to the pavement. More rugs, none larger than a counterpane for a single bed, were draped over wooden hurdles; two barmaids, including the girl who'd sat on his lap last night, were slapping dust from them with woven cane beaters.

"Mieka! What in all hells—"

"Won't be a moment!" he called back over his shoulder as he sauntered towards the girl, who shrank back against the tavern windows. "G'mornin', darlin'!" He smiled at her as he unbuttoned his trousers.

"Mieka!" Cade yelled again.

He was pleased that the rug hadn't been washed; the dry wool, woven in an interlocking pattern of green ferns round a plain yellow field, soaked up moisture nicely. His aim was, moreover, excellent. He managed to monogram it with a large *MW* before he ran out of piss.

Behind him, he could hear cries of outrage—and howls of laughter. The barkeep finally found his voice as Mieka was stuffing himself back into his trousers, and Drevan Wordturner was kind enough to translate between guffaws.

"Mieka—he—he says you'll pay for that—"

"Delighted!" Digging into a pocket, he flung some coins onto the sidewalk. Then he grabbed the rug, admired his work, rolled it up, and heaved it atop the coach with the rest of their baggage. He gifted his audience with his most adorable smile before hopping back in, slamming the door, and calling out, "Oh, and by the bye—fuck you!"

He could hear the driver laughing as the horses were encouraged to step lively. Rafe and Jeska and Briuly were still chortling; Fairwalk looked ready to faint; Drevan seemed torn between admiration and disbelief.

Cade eyed Mieka sidelong, gray eyes glinting wickedly. "I'd been wondering what you'd bring home as a keepsake."

The next night they stayed strictly inside the immediate precincts of the inn they were assigned. Not that anybody suggested going anyplace else—they were too tired and too scared. Mieka went up to bed early, and this time went straight for the redthorn. He had just tucked it all away as Cayden trudged into the room.

"Want some?"

"Gods—please."

Mieka gestured to his satchel, turned onto his side, and went instantly to sleep.

The last night of the journey was spent beside the shore of a long, narrow lake. They'd been informed that now they were on the Tregrefin's land, and this was his family's favorite summer holiday spot. Not that they stayed in his lodge; that was reserved for the Archduke. The rest of the delegation was distributed amongst the inns on either side of the big timbered house. By night, sitting outside in the warm soft air, they could see the lamps of the other inns and a few cottages shining off the water. Pretty, Mieka thought, but nowhere near as lovely as a moonglade. The lights of a score of glass-shielded candles cast shadows on the benches and tables set out on the grass, and on the rug recently washed and left to dry on the pebbled shingle.

"Where'd you learn how to do that, anyway?" Cade asked.

"A fine, proud Windthistle family tradition, it is," he declaimed, "fabled in song and story—"

"Mieka."

"I think Jed managed his initials and Blye's in a snowbank last winter—"

"Mieka!"

"—but Jez always runs dry before he can finish the *W*. Bladder the size of a shrivelled almond, that one. Want lessons?"

"Lessons—?"

"Takes a bit of practice, o' course, to perfect one's style. And more than a bit of privacy. I mean, one doesn't just stand about waving it this way and that—"

Cade gave up and laughed.

Their lodgings were at the midpoint of the lake, with a view by day of hills ascending to distant peaks tipped even in summer with snow. They were relaxing after an excellent dinner of rabbit jugged in the local white wine, bread so feather-light it almost floated off the plates, and a pastry filled with five different sorts of berries. Cade looked happy, and not so hollow, and Mieka decided life was good after all.

"You could prob'ly take that cap off now, y'know," Cade said.

Mieka responded by pulling the thin knitted wool farther down over his ears. It was a ludicrous thing, concentric circles of green, blue, yellow, red, pink, purple, white, and black: the sort of item a girl undertook when she had yarn left over from a dozen other projects and couldn't think what else to do with it. Jeska had gone out to the shops for something to conceal Mieka's ears, and he was grateful. He didn't want to provoke those looks in anyone's eyes ever again.

"Actually, you might set a new fashion," Cade went on.

"In hiding what I am?" The flash of defiance after the memory of fear confused him. He stared down into his glass. "Quill... if it had been something I'd done—I mean, I'm used to that, gettin' meself into trouble, and I take the consequences I set meself up for—"

"No, you don't," Cade murmured. "When are there ever any consequences? You use those eyes of yours, and everybody forgives you."

"Not this time, though. If I'd done something, said something—but it was because of what I *am*. Why do I have to be forgiven for what I *am*?"

"And what are you, exactly?" Cade asked, even more softly. Mieka glanced over at him, not understanding. Cade smiled. "Mieka Windthistle. The best glisker in Albeyn—hells, the best in the world! An *artist*. A good son, a wonderful brother, a fine friend. Nothing that needs forgiving."

"Let's not forget Piksey, Sprite, Human, a bit of Wizard and a dash of Fae—and, oh yeh," he finished bitterly, "Elf. Windthistle, Cloudshaper, Staindrop, Moonbinder, Flickflame, Snowminder, Greenseed, Heartwood—every kind of Elf there is, Air and Water and Fire and Earth, with the ears to prove it. I can't help any of that, and I wouldn't if I could, no more than you can help having gray eyes or Kearney Fairwalk can help—" He broke off and glanced away.

"Ah, yes," Cade said. "Did you really think I didn't know?"

"But he acts like it's something he needs to be forgiven," Mieka argued. "Did you hear him, gibbering away, when we saw he was in bed with Drevan?"

"I didn't pay much mind."

"Is it something to be ashamed of?"

"I think it's complicated," he said slowly. "The Archduke can't help the father he was born to, but don't you think he'd rather not have that always in people's minds when they look at him or hear his name? I think Kearney's like that, in a way. He's not ashamed, exactly. But all that aristocratic arrogance, the way he talks when there's people about—"

"He talks like that all the time."

"Not really. He can be entirely sensible and direct. With me, anyway, when we talk about theater. Still, I agree that he tends to give people something to listen to and look at." Cade sipped wine and drummed his fingers on the table. "If you don't give people something they have to take note of, they won't. So it follows that if you shove it in their faces where they can't look away, they *have* to notice. And that's all they see. All they think about."

"But they *don't* think. All they do is react."

"You do the same thing as Kearney, in your own way. You give people plenty to see, you make them notice you, and you do it on purpose. So they won't see what's real about you."

Mieka sat back, stung. "I don't—"

"Yes, you do." He took the bottle from the table and shared it out between their glasses. "I'm not sure I have you worked out yet, not completely, but I do know that a lot of what you show the world is—it's like that cap. It's bright and noisy and makes people laugh. But it's hiding something you don't want people to see."

"Not because I'm ashamed!"

"Of course not. That's why this upsets you so much. Back on the Winterly, with that Prickspur snarge—you got a look in those eyes I never thought I'd see. I knew I didn't ever want to see it again. Yet there it was, the other night. Someone made you feel less than who you are because of what you are."

For a moment he considered saying something like, *Either I've had too much to drink or not enough, because I actually understand what you're saying!* But what came out of his mouth was, "It's how all people like us feel here, innit? Like they ought to be ashamed of what they are. That old man, hiding his magic, talking about rules. And what you said about them being afraid of the light."

"Exactly. Those people in that tavern—they saw your ears and knew you for different, for magic folk."

"They hated me."

"They were afraid of you."

"Me?"

Cade smiled at him. "If you were talking to anyone except me, you'd use another tone of voice. That *harmless little me?* tone, and a bit of what your mother calls The Eyes."

"But it's *you*, Quill." Suddenly Mieka remembered the Elsewhen, and *"I think I hated you."* He had to know. He had to ask. "Cayden—?"

But Jeska was coming towards them across the lawn with a fresh bottle in his hand, and the moment was gone.

15

Not knowing what to expect, for he'd not bothered to ask, Mieka was frankly astonished by how young their new Princess was. She couldn't have been more than seventeen. A tall girl, blond and long-limbed and with a neck like a swan, to his eye it would take another few years before she outgrew the gangly stage. From what he knew about Prince Ashgar, however, it would take much less time for her to outgrow her innocence. And that was a pity.

What surprised him even more was Cayden's reaction to their first sight of her. Arrival at her father's palace had involved a lot of trumpets and bowing, smiling and introductions, and when it came Touchstone's turn to be presented, and they got close enough for a good look at her, Mieka caught Cade's fleeting look of dismay.

"All right, then, what was that?" he demanded when they had been left alone in the banqueting hall that would serve as a theater. Huge, draughty old place, it was, with a low ceiling and worm-gnawed roof timbers ready to disintegrate if somebody looked at them wrong. Jedris and Jezael would have been horrified—and a lot richer, after they'd mended it all.

"What was what?" Cade asked warily. Jeska and Rafe were pacing out the dimensions, as usual during their first look at a new location. "I know you've never met the girl, but it was like you recognized her."

"I did." Giving up all pretense, Cade dug his hands into his jacket pockets and scowled. "You recall that time we did 'Hidden Cottage'? At Trials last year. For the Prince. I got a glimpse of her, running across a field—she looked so happy, so excited…"

"Elsewhen." Mieka thought about this, then bumped Cade with a shoulder. "You really do have to start mentioning these things, Quill."

"What I see—it's what *might* happen, Mieka, not necessarily what *will* happen."

"According to a decision you do or don't make, and you can't live other people's lives for them—yeh, yeh, heard it all before. And I'm not asking you to tell me the ones about me. Just a hint now and then, eh? We could talk it over, like." He paused, and added more softly, "You don't have to be completely alone with it, y'know."

He looked anywhere but at Mieka. "I'll think about it."

Aware that this was as good as he would get for now, Mieka ran the length of the hall and jumped up onto the platform where the high table traditionally stood. On the schedule of amusements were several musical performances and a masked ball before the marriage-by-proxy and celebration feast. Though the space was currently empty of everything but themselves and a lot of benches stacked round freshly whitewashed plaster walls, his imagination supplied it with all the flash and laughter of an authentic Royal banquet from the olden days. Jugglers roaming amidst crowded tables; musicians up in the minstrels' gallery behind the carved wooden screen; ladies in odd pointed headdresses, veils trailing in the soup; banners fluttering from the rafters; torches giving more smoke than light; cats and dogs scrounging for scraps; and in the center of it all a bonfire roasting a boar and a stag or two—

"Mieka!"

His envisionings vanished, and he was looking at his partners, who were looking at him with varying degrees of annoyance.

"What?" he demanded.

"Places, all!" sang out Fairwalk from the far end of the hall. "First performance is tonight!"

Following a dinner he couldn't eat, Mieka was disgusted to find that after so long offstage, he was jittering with nerves. Cade, standing nearby in a corridor as they waited for the audience to settle, gave him a long, level look.

"Kearney says *everybody's* in there." Jeska was bouncing up and down on the balls of his feet, fingers clenching and unclenching. "Not even room enough to stand."

"It'll be hot as a glass forge," Rafe agreed. "Too much to ask if they'd open those windows high on the outside wall, eh? Let some of the heat escape?"

"Maybe they're scared our magic will escape."

Mieka tried a smile in response to Cade's remark, but it was a very bad fit. He could feel the sting of sweat beginning in his armpits and across his brow.

"It was that third glass of ale what did it, right? And on an empty belly, too." Cade glanced about. A moment later some flowers had been evicted from a wide-mouthed ceramic vase, and Mieka was gratefully yarking into it.

"Your Highnesses, Your Grace, my lords and gentlemen— Touchstone!"

Rafe unwound the black neckband from Mieka's collar and wiped his face and mouth with it before tossing it aside. Jeska opened the door into the great hall. Cade tucked Mieka's hair behind his ears, grinned down at him, and said, "Remember, now—no pig!"

Rafe gave them both a push, and suddenly they were onstage, greeted by nothing more than indifferent applause. Mieka's lip curled. Didn't these people understand that they were here to see *Touchstone*? He jumped up onto the riser where the glass baskets waited, flexed his fingers, tossed a grin at Cade, and prepared to smack the audience into full awareness of what theater could be.

But gently, of course. Because of the language problems, they'd decided to play the piece more visually than usual. Because they had to play it straight, Mieka had to restrain his sense of humor. And because this audience had never experienced this kind of theater before, Mieka had to diminish, and Rafe had to keep tight hold on, the sensory effects. Which put much of the burden of the play on Jeska.

Mieka had always known their masquer was good. He'd never before realized just how good. The complications of the arranged marriage, the girl's kidnapping, the young man's flight, had to be expressed mostly with gestures and vocal inflections, for Mieka couldn't let loose the full power of emotions, could only hint and tickle, so as not to frighten the audience. The sisters' spite and the young man's rebelliousness could be only fleetingly conveyed. Once the youth was on his wandering way, Mieka could lark a bit as he usually did, giving Jeska peculiar backdrops to stumble through before he eventually came upon the cottage where the girl was concealed, but Cade had sternly warned against farce. Even though she wasn't officially watching, the Tregrefina had specifically requested this piece, and the Tregrefina had to be made happy. So Mieka didn't get to do the pig. The work became easier for Jeska once the cottage was discovered and the love-at-first-sight part was done, and as much as Mieka wanted to sneak a few laughs in, a single glance at Cayden's grim face kept him in line. By the end, with the lovers triumphant, he was bored out of his wits, and resentful, too. They were *Touchstone*, and they had their reputation to consider.

When the applause began, it sounded polite and reluctant, like the look on Mum's face when Tavier showed her yet another collection of worms he hoped would grow into dragons. Mieka had had enough. What these people had just seen was magic, and damned fine magic, no matter how much they might want to hide it away and pretend it didn't exist. So he tossed a spent withie high in the air towards the rafters and shattered it to splinters on its way down.

Through a million tiny grains of glittering glass he saw Rafe's sudden grin—and through the shocked gasps he heard sudden screams as the dozen small windows high in the side wall exploded outward into the night.

"Mieka was dead right, and so was I," Rafe said later on, after they had been hustled back upstairs to their room. Kearney Fairwalk was in agonies, actually wringing his hands. "It's us, and that's what we do, and if they don't like it, they shouldn't have asked us to come."

"We didn't do hardly any of it the way we could have," Mieka seconded. "They didn't get even a taste of what theater really is." And because the iron restraint still nettled: "I didn't even get to do the pig!"

"None of it matters," Cade said, lounging in a low chair, long legs stretched out to a footstool. "The girl is the only one we had to impress."

"But it was only men in the aud—" Jeska interrupted himself with, "The minstrels' gallery!"

"Yeh, she was watching." Cade nodded. "And a footman came up to me after with this." He held up a single little blue flower, five-petaled, with a yellow center.

"So it's a forget-me-never. So what?" Jeska asked.

"So it's her symbol, innit? Embroidered all over her gown when we met her. Same color as her eyes. I thought you noticed these things—and especially things about pretty girls!"

Fairwalk nodded slowly. "When Prince Ashgar saw her picture—just in watercolor, nothing grand—he said her eyes were the color of forget-me-nevers. Or so it's *said* that he said."

"Must've got back to her, eh?" Mieka shrugged. "She liked us, then."

"Even without the pig." Cade gave him a wink. "I know we were going to do one or two of the Thirteen, Kearney, but I think we can try something a little more interesting."

"What about 'Doorways'?" Mieka asked. "We don't need much dialogue for that—it's just Jeska getting out of bed, lots of swirlies to show he's dreaming, and then we can do as we like with every opening door."

Fairwalk's mood changed from dismayed to delighted in a heartbeat. "And the concluding one, that can be Prince Ashgar, don't you see, walking through the door to greet her—"

"No." Cade said it so grimly that they all turned to stare at him. He didn't elaborate on the stark negative.

Their large, airy bedchamber had a private garderobe adjacent. That night, as Mieka lolled in a warm bath before bed, Cade came in to give him a nightshirt and said, "I'll not be priming anything for you to do Prince Ashgar with, so don't even try."

"I hadn't planned on it. And I think I know why."

Cade stood there pleating the soft white linen. "Do you? Astonish me."

"Don't be a quat. When you reminded me that we did 'Cottage' at Trials, I remembered how Ashgar was sitting with all those ambassadors and suchlike, and had tears in his eyes."

"And?"

"And she heard about it. That's why she asked for us. So she could see what he saw."

"Yeh, but there's more. I talked with one of her ladies after the show tonight. She told me the girl was so moved that *he* was moved that it's a lot of why she decided to marry him."

"And now you feel guilty. You can't warn her what a shit-head he is—and even if you did, she wouldn't believe you, because she's already in love with him."

"She's in love with the *idea* of him," Cade corrected bleakly.

For an instant Mieka considered asking if Cade's father might look after the girl, guide her, help her in her new life. Then he recalled that First Gentleman of the Bedchamber Zekien Silversun was in essence the Prince's pimp, with cards from brothels like the Finchery in his coat pockets. So instead he tried to offer consolation. "You weren't to know what would happen when we did that play. I never realized how awful it must be for you, seeing things and not understanding. Feeling helpless."

"I'm used to it by now," he lied.

"Quill."

A shrug, and a smoothing of crumpled linen. "When Blye's mother was killed," he said in a low voice, "I didn't understand for a long time why I'd seen it. I didn't yet know that it was my choices that affected the futures I saw. I finally worked it out. The night before, Mistress Mirdley said something about fish for dinner the next day, and I whined and wheedled for bacon pie instead. Mistress Cindercliff called in that morning on her way to the fish market. Mistress Mirdley said no, His Lordship— meaning me—wants what he wants, and there's an end to it."

"So instead of both of them going—"

"It was just Blye's mother. That was the difference—the delay of a moment's conversation, or bartering with the fishmongers for two orders instead of just the one, or—"

"You said you can't live other people's lives for them, Quill. What I keep wondering is that with this thing happening inside your head, how you're sane enough to live your own."

"There's been times," he replied wryly.

"Seen much lately?"

"That's the odd part of it. Except for the thorn dreams, nothing."

Mieka clucked his tongue against his teeth. "Think it through! We're at other people's beck and call, and will be until we get home, most like."

"You mean that other people are living *my* life for me." A sudden broad grin decorated his face. "Can't say I'm enjoying it much!"

"That's the way," he teased, "leave all the decisions to the rest of us—like tonight with the glass!"

"But not Prince Ashgar, with 'Doorways.' Not that, Mieka."

Matching Cade serious for serious, he answered, "You saw her the first time because it was your choice to play 'Cottage' without the laughs. Well, partly your choice, anyway. But you've not seen any more Elsewhens about her, so there's no decision for you to make, right? It follows, then, that whatever we do, whether we show him in 'Doorways' or not, it won't matter." He stopped and shivered, though the night was summer-warm and the bathwater hadn't yet cooled. "Gods, and there's the other thing, innit? That whatever you try to do, *it won't matter.*"

Cade wore a small, sour smile. "At this point, Sagemaster Emmot would've sneered and said, 'Poor Wizardling, how horrid to be you!'"

"But he didn't understand, did he?"

The smile softened. "You *are* rather astonishing, y'know." Then he left the nightshirt on the little table next the tub and made his escape.

Though she had viewed the performance supposedly in secret from the minstrels' gallery, word of the Tregrefina's reaction to "Hidden Cottage" was common talk by the next morning and did indeed set the attitude for everyone else. Touchstone was celebrated, congratulated, and generally made much of whenever any of them cared to show his face around the palace or grounds. Even if they *had* broken most of the upper windows in the great hall. They mixed more with the nobles at court than expected, which had Fairwalk flitting from one to the other of them to make sure they didn't destroy diplomatic relations. More accurately, he kept watch on Cade and Mieka, for Rafe never said much and Jeska was every manner of charming there could possibly be. Their second show— "Sailor's Sweetheart"—was applauded to the rafters, and rather than sidewise glances during the daylight hours, they were greeted with smiling nods.

Mieka adored the attention, especially from the ladies. Someone, probably the Tregrefina again, had decided that his ears were, if not exactly normal, then at least socially acceptable. How much of this might be due to the performance and the power of the magic it implied, he couldn't have said. But he took to wearing his topaz earring instead of the knitted cap.

What he would wear to the masked ball was a poser, though, until a stroll through the palace gardens made the decision for him.

Palace was a bit of a courtesy title. The parts they had seen— great hall, grand staircase, their upstairs bedchamber—were trim and tidy for the most part, if a trifle frayed around the edges. But compared to the solid mass of stone that was the Palace in Gallantrybanks, this place was a joke. Constructed of everything from bricks to rounded river stones to timber-and-plaster to plain planks nailed together with nails growing rustier by the year, there was no discernible plan, not a hint of unifying style. A tower here, a turret there, a whole side wall of mismatched windows (facing west, terrible in summer), and a young forest of chimneys growing at random from the undulating roofs— it seemed to have been slapped together whenever need arose for more room, without the slightest regard for the look of the whole. It reminded Mieka a bit of Wistly Hall.

The gardens were beautiful. Usually Mieka found trees and flowers a bit dull, despite the Greenseed strain of Elf that made his sister Cilka such an avid gardener. But these gardens were marvelous, stretching from the back of the palace for at least a quarter mile to the lake-shore, laid out in a series of "rooms" separated by hedges of varying heights. Some had color themes—white, blue, yellow—and some were knot gardens, and there was a small orchard of stunted citrus trees in big earthenware pots. But what Mieka liked best was the graveled walk down to the lake, bordered by a dozen hedges sculpted into huge fantastical shapes. Ordinary bushes had been fashioned into a teacup (with saucer), a candle (with flame), a flight of steps (with banisters), a crown (with flowers blooming where jewels would be), a tilted pitcher (with real water flowing out its lip). There were two horse heads facing each other across the path, a cat, a dog, a squirrel, a fully antlered stag, and a gigantic urn with roses growing out of the top.

Mieka was enchanted. He spent a delightful two hours one afternoon inspecting the hedge sculptures from all sides. Gradually he realized that what these gardeners had done with wire frames and shears could be done even better by magic in the clever hands of an Elfen girl with Greenseed blood.

And there, he thought triumphantly, was another possible result of his decision to head for Gowerion that night last year: If his sister could figure out how to do these sculptures, and start a fashion for them, she'd get very, very rich.

Midafternoon heat sent him back up towards the palace, and along the way he glimpsed Drevan Wordturner in one of the smaller "rooms," seated on a bench in the shade, an open book in his lap. At Mieka's approach, he glanced up, turned pink, and fumbled to snap the volume closed. It slipped off his knees and fell to the gravel, open.

"Living up to your name, I see! Books, forever books!" Mieka teased, and bent to take a look. "As bad as Cade! What's this?"

"Nothing—it's just—no, don't—"

Mieka blinked. Several times. Drevan plucked up the book and clutched it to his chest. He wouldn't look at Mieka, and his cheeks were brick-red now. After a moment, Mieka asked carelessly, "Any girls in those drawings?"

A startled glance upwards, an embarrassed cough, and Drevan flipped through the book to the middle. Mieka frowned down at the pages. Not girls, but men dressed as girls, and obviously so.

"Th-they're called 'shims' back home," Drevan said with a failed attempt at casualness. "She-hims. Shims."

Mieka turned a few more pages, then gave a snort. "I can do better than this for Jeska onstage. Hells, I could do better than this meself, *offstage*!"

H ow did women endure such torture? For the twentieth time since he'd finished dressing, Mieka resisted the urge to rub where the corset pinched, reminding himself that ladies didn't do such vulgar things in public. At least there was no low-cut neckline to hike up in surreptitious haste, the way Jeska sometimes did with an onstage costume to get a laugh.

The shocked, giggling chambermaids who'd succumbed to his wheedling had been remarkably obliging, once they'd got into the spirit of the thing. All the frills and trappings had appeared by sundown in the lesser maidservants' tiring room—high up in a far tower, and it had been six kinds of hell coming back down all those stairs in high heels—and they'd helped him negotiate laces, buttons, clasps, hooks, and all the rest. His own experience was in taking women's clothes off women, not putting women's clothes on himself, but there he'd stood, regarding the vision in the brown-specked mirror: corseted and gowned, cheverel-gloved and silk-stockinged, and from whose wardrobe the clothes had come he hadn't a clue. Whoever it was, he was lucky that her feet were big and his were little. The girls had even provided jewelry suitable to a lady attending a Court entertainment. With a bit of furtive magic applied on his way down the stairs, the dangling necklace and armbands even looked real. Every time he tried to take a deep breath, he wished he'd dared do the whole thing with magic. Too late now.

As he wandered slowly about the great hall, he reflected that it was mildly intriguing, trying to form an opinion about a woman's beauty from a few hints. The shape and color of the eyes, the line of the throat, the angle of the jaw, the curve of the lips—one looked at the features one could see, or almost see, and judged accordingly. Of course, the skin beneath the mask might be pockmarked, the nose bumpy, the cheekbones wildly uneven, but as Mieka watched and speculated, he decided that to compensate for their hidden faces, the ladies were emphasizing their most striking physical features—and in some cases attempting to emphasize what wasn't really there. He had never in his life seen so many breasts so daringly displayed. Recent experience of padding a bodice allowed him to estimate quite accurately which of the ladies was as expert at illusion as the maids who had crammed enough silk between his chest and the velvet gown to give him a rather impressive bosom.

In the stifling crush of people, and under the blaze of a million candles, it was terribly hot in his stuffed and petticoated velvet. The windows Rafe demolished had not yet been replaced, but if a breeze strayed down to cool the crowd, he didn't feel it. Despite the discomforts of his disguise—hauling around half a mile of material that weighed half a ton was no thrill—Mieka was rather enjoying himself. A woman didn't have to be pretty to be bowed to or smiled at; all she had to do was wear a lot of glittery jewelry. This meant she was rich, and wealth always attracted notice. Besides, nobody could tell whether the lady in the high-necked dark blue gown with the long sleeves—and all those "diamonds" looping down to her waist and dripping from her wrists—was pretty or not. He'd debated about sneaking some of the leftover magic from a withie to rework his face, but not only would it require constant concentration, he'd also have to find a place to hide eight or ten inches of glass. So, knowing his eyes would give him away to anyone who knew him, no matter how much makeup was applied to alter the rest of his face, Mieka had donned a lacy black veil, draping it over his head to hide not just his face but his ears as well—and the fact that he'd flatly refused to have his hair crimped and curled. He wasn't the only one who'd chosen a method of concealment other than a mask; several ladies wore veils of varying thicknesses, and a few gentlemen had tied colorful kerchiefs over the lower halves of their faces so that only their eyes showed.

Cade had, of course, picked a full face-mask, forehead to chin, made of stiffened black silk and tied with silver ribbons behind his head. Some of the masks were painted, sequined, decorated with lace or beads, but Cade's was very plain and entirely mysterious, shadowing his gray eyes and concealing the long, curling mouth. Especially did it conceal his nose. Observing from a distance, Mieka had the distinct feeling that Cade was having a wonderful time hiding. He shook his head. All that nonsense about his looks again. And after their talk about concealing one's true self, too. Mieka toyed with the idea of using one of Cade's own withies sometime to becast him with a face as beautiful as an Angel's. What would he think, how would he react, when girls stared and stammered and simpered the way they did around Jeska? Was that what he truly wanted? As much as Cayden wanted to believe that his nose was the only thing people saw when they looked at him, having a face like Jeska's could be even more... distancing, that was the word.

Though *distance* was precisely what there wasn't between Cade and a tall, dark-haired lady in a shockingly narrow-skirted peach silk gown. Mieka grimaced beneath his concealing veil;

the only reason Quill was laughing and chatting with her so spiritedly was that his face was hidden. If she'd been able to see him, the conversation would never even have started.

Mieka decided he'd go have a listen, and concentrated on walking as naturally as he could in three-inch heels. There seemed to be a trick to the hips that ladies managed and men couldn't. The chambermaids had tried to teach him. Battling his sense of balance had at first produced a most unattractive—and inauthentic—mincing sort of walk. He called on memories of Jeska playing various women onstage, and how he'd moved, but Jeska was never actually wearing high heels, was he? He'd thought he had it mostly mastered by the time he entered the great hall, but then someone handed him a drink. For reasons that completely escaped him, the addition of a glass of cold white wine full of languid bubbles put him off-kilter again. Perhaps it was the action of lifting the veil a bit and raising the glass to his lips while still putting one foot in front of the other, but the warning was clear: He would not be getting drunk tonight.

Cade didn't seem much interested in liquor. He was giving his entire attention to the dark-haired lady. Mieka sidled closer, careful to keep behind Cade in the crowd, and nearly yelped his delight as he spied a chair not two feet from the pair. Just as he was about to claim it, a stout gentleman in a bright red mask sprouting fluffy white feathers sank down with a loud sigh. He looked like a prize rooster. Mieka snapped his gloved fingers, waved him imperiously out of the seat, rings and armbands glittering, and grinned to himself as the man lumbered to his feet and effaced himself. Mieka sat gratefully down—the shoes were murder on his feet, and giving him a backache—to listen.

"It says a great number of excellent things about Prince Ashgar, so kind he's being to my lady."

"Is he?"

"Oh yes." Her speech was fluent, with only a trace of an

accent, a slight slurring every so often; quite charming. "When her grandmother came from—I never recall the name of the place, but somewhere to the east edge of the map—she arrived in the dead of night, in secret, and was taken to the Court mediciners. Or do I mean physickers?"

"Physickers. And what in the world for?"

"They stripped her naked. Looking for flaws that might hinder childbearing, or so they said."

"I strongly suspect they were nothing more than nasty old men. What if they'd found something wrong with her? A freckle they didn't like the looks of, or a twisted toe?"

"Back to her own country with her, of course! We've advanced from such barbarianness, but not by much. Your Prince could have demanded the same."

"Good Lord and Lady! What happened next?"

"All her own clothes were taken out and burned, poor girl, as if she'd brought lice with her or something horrible. The next morning she came downstairs—"

"Not still naked, I hope."

"Dressed in our local peasant costume. Very pretty, but humiliating for her, in plain linen all a-lacking lace or a jewel, and with the whole Court in their finest. Then her new husband, though of course he wasn't being her husband yet, bowed so low to scrape the carpet with his head, and draped her in jewels." She shrugged pretty shoulders. "His way of apology for what she'd been through beforenight."

"I wonder how she felt," mused Cayden, "wearing a peasant's dress with a fortune around her neck."

"Ridiculous, of course! Bracelets, rings, pins, earrings, a belt, and of course a coronet. More pink diamonds than an apple tree has spring flowerings, it's said. All in gold, which was a great mistake since set right. Her daughter set them new in silver."

"Then that lady over there, the one in pale green—"

"—wearing the rope of pink diamonds and the white mask. Yes," she said fondly. "That's your new Princess."

Mieka leaned to the side, alarmed when the corset creaked, but couldn't catch sight of her. A servant approached with a tray of sweets. Mieka waved the girl away. He really had to stop stuffing his face or he wouldn't be able to get into his own clothes without a corset.

"…only child of her father's first marriage. Her mother died when she was very young. Now, of course, there are three boys and four more girls."

"So she's superfluous." An instant later Mieka saw his shoulders flinch beneath the pearl-gray jacket, as if he realized what he'd revealed.

The lady realized it, too. "Extra, not needed? You sound as if you are of the same experience." More lightly, teasing him: "And which heavy lordship inheritance have *you* escaped, then? Castles, villages, miles of wheat fields, a mansion in Gallantrybanks?"

Blithe as a breeze, Cade replied, "All that, plus two coal mines, a fleet of merchant ships, and a manor house overlooking the sea. Oh, and that's not to forget a perfectly obscene pile of money sitting safely in a bank. Tragic, but I bear up as best I may."

Mieka rolled his eyes.

"Ah! So you're a pauper, with nothing to recommend you but your good looks and charm?"

Her voice had shaded into mockery. Mieka was glad of his concealing veil. The voluminous blue velvet skirt helped, too; he could hide his clenched fists in its folds. But Cade was laughing softly, a note in his voice Mieka had never heard before as he parried, "I've always found those to be quite enough."

The mask was giving him the confidence to flirt as if he were the handsomest man in the room. Mieka felt like kicking him in the backside—if he could've found his own foot amid the billows and ruffles of the gown.

At that moment the worst happened: a gentleman approached, bowed, and pleaded to be allowed the inestimable favor of the next dance.

"I couldn't hardly *walk* in that damned dress and those heels—how was I s'posed to dance?"

Rafe and Jeska whooped with laughter. Mieka, who had spent the last hour maneuvering himself out of garments it had taken the maids less than half that time to get him into, sprawled on his bed to unroll the silk stockings off his legs and continued the tale.

"At first I didn't have a clue what he was saying. But it turns out the men have little cards to hand out to ladies they want to dance with, and he kept trying to give me one. He wouldn't go away! I growled at him, and shook my head, but he kept bowing and begging, it was *gruesome*! So then Cade turned around to see what the fuss was about, and—would you believe it, he started playing the gallant! 'You're annoying this lady,' says he, 'She obviously doesn't want to dance,' says he, 'Take yourself off elsewhere, my good man!' 'Twas all to impress that girl, of course, and the fool didn't understand a word. I fair choked, I did, and damned near bit my tongue clean through, trying not to laugh—"

"Serves you right," Jeska told him. "Did he recognize you?"

"With this thing over me face?" He waved the discarded lace like a battle flag. "It was hard enough to see *out* of it, nobody could've seen *in*! And don't let on it was me, right? Gods, that remembers me—I have to hide all this before he gets back." He leaped up and gathered clothing. "Help me find someplace to put it until I can return it to the girls."

They stashed various garments behind draperies and under beds while Mieka went on with his tale.

"So I'm trapped, with Cade fussing and the girl looking at me sidewise, because I didn't dare open me mouth to say a word. He snatches a glass of that bubbly stuff and hands it to me—oh, I had a time of it, getting it up under the veil to drink! One of the bracelets got stuck on the way back out and I couldn't get it loose, so it was all nearly up right there and then, only at that exact instant the silly man comes back with a couple of his friends! Don't wrinkle up that gown so much, Rafe, the girls will murder me. Anyway, I'm trying to unsnag meself before the veil comes off—*without* dropping the glass—and there's Cade still being all concerned and courteous, and the girl still staring at me, and that pillock still asking me to dance!"

Rafe was trying to fold petticoats into manageable size to fit into a drawer. "And so you did what?"

"I fainted. Well, *pretended* to faint. Like you do in 'Troll and Trull,' Jeska, and it's harder than you make it look! Down went the glass in shatters onto the floor. Down I went, a bit to the side, across another chair. Down Cayden went, onto one knee, grabbing me hand—thank all the Gods for those gloves!—while the girl's waving everyone off so I can get some air." He paused, holding up the corset. "There's iron bars in this thing, I swear— look, right along here—and when I went over to one side I got *stabbed*! Gods, like knives in the ribs! I jerked back upright again, lost me balance, and got Cade right in the stomach with a knee. So *he* falls over, and while the girl's helping him, I escaped."

"With your devoted admirers galloping after?" Rafe straightened up from tucking the last of the blue velvet under his bed.

"Took me another five minutes to lose them in the crowd. Twisted an ankle while I was at it, too."

"But you got out before the midnight unmasking."

He shivered. "Only just in time."

Jeska, on his way past with the high-heeled shoes, pinched

Mieka's chin. Mieka slapped his hand away. "I wager you were quite as pretty as half the ladies there. You should've stayed."

"Ah, but then we'd have to rescue him from the devoted attentions of his many admirers," Rafe drawled. "But I'm wondering why Cade didn't sense the magic on these glass trinkets."

Mieka shrugged and handed over a kerchief so Rafe could knot up the jewelry. "Didn't use much, really. And he was so caught up in the girl, he wouldn't have noticed if I'd used enough to turn meself into Queen Roshien with all her moonstones."

"Why'd you do it, anyway?" Jeska asked. "Why not just go as yourself, with a mask, like everyone else?"

"Why does he ever do anything?" Rafe countered, then shook a stern finger in Mieka's direction. "I won't mind Uncle Mieka stopping round to play, but you teach my son your style of pranking and I'll start my own collection of teeth—and all of them will be *yours*."

"Empty threats," Mieka scoffed. "And how d'you know it's to be a son? He'd only take after you in looks, and what a shame and a shuddering that would be! I'm hoping for a little girl who looks just like Crisiant."

Jeska sniggered. "So you can teach her how to dress? Lovely talking to you all, but I've an appointment." He paused to preen in front of the looking glass. "And she's *much* prettier than you, Mieka."

He pretended to consider. "But are you sure she's a girl?"

Jeska threw the shoes at him.

16

It had been Cayden's firm intent to vanish before the midnight umasking. He'd had much too good a time with his new friend to ruin it. He'd never met a woman like her, and he couldn't quite believe she was talking with *him*.

She danced lightly and gracefully. Her laughter could be softly teasing or low and throaty. Her conversation was quick, intelligent, discerning. The quirk of her smile beneath the delicate golden mask was appealingly wry, and her eyes were a lovely dark brown. He'd been startled when she approached him and asked in his own language how he was enjoying Gref Jyziero, then assured himself that although the cut of his jacket instantly identified him as being part of the foreign delegation, she could have no idea of his precise identity. A mask was truly a wondrous thing.

She hadn't told him her name, of course, but when he complimented her command of his language, she admitted to being the Princess's maid of honor. She was deeply fond of Miriuzca, looking on her as a little sister more than as someone who would one day be Queen of Albeyn. A little over a year ago she had been chosen to supplement the lessons of Miriuzca's tutors by attending classes with her; the two of them spoke nothing but Albeyni to each other in private and read aloud whatever books they could find.

"And your Master Blackpath has been singing to us, teaching such wonderful songs!"

"I'll bet he has. Just don't learn any from Master Bowbender or Master Windthistle—my masquer and glisker," he added.

"Oh, the beautiful ones? Why? They seem charming."

"They'd teach you songs with words your tutors can't possibly have mentioned in your presence—"

"Syllable by syllable, with no explanation!"

"Exactly!" He laughed. "You'd scandalize all Gallantrybanks."

"But it's likely we'll need words like that. Please to teach me some? After all," she reasoned, "if a thing isn't existing, there's no need to make a word for it, is there? So in logic we're like to encounter some of these things, and need their words." All at once she grinned. "And so lovely to scandalize someone!"

He pretended to be stern. "I refuse to contribute to the warping of your vocabulary!"

Thus he danced, and talked, and flirted, and enjoyed himself splendidly—at least, before he made a complete fool of himself trying to come to the rescue of the heavily veiled woman in the blue gown. Once he was on his feet again, more concerned with whether his mask had stayed in place than with the ache in his stomach from the silly woman's knee, his companion consoled him with a glass of bubbling white wine and a bracing laugh.

"Absurd creature, she was! And gone, praise to the Angels that watch over us. Don't concern yourself with apologizings, whoever she was. It's an advantage of masks that one can safely affront without consequences." She gestured at her own gown. "It's also why I can wear this tonight without scandalizing."

"But it's beautiful," he protested, and instantly blushed. Yes, a mask was truly a wondrous thing.

"Beholden to you," she said, dipping a brief curtsey. "A

fashion begun several years ago by a woman who was wishing implication of wealth without actual possession." To his look of incomprehension, she replied with a grin half-hidden by her mask. "What do most highborn ladies do all day? Nothing. They can wear layers of petticoats and frills and flounces—and a corset!—because they don't have to be moving."

"Because they *can't* move," he said, fascinated by this insight into women's garments. "The same with the style you wear."

"Yes. Fitted so close, I can manage a stately dance, but not a gallop-romp from one side of the room to the other." She leaned up closer and whispered, "It takes *much* less silk to hobble a woman than it does to be weighing her down with billows."

It also gave a man a much better idea of her figure. He didn't mention it. "If a lady doesn't have to move, it means she doesn't have to work."

"Just sit about and look elegantly," she agreed. "I'm sure you've seen women work in fields, or cottager wives tend homes and children. Full skirts, but nothing much beneath, and certainly not corseting!"

"I can't believe that you'd need one," he blurted. Oh Gods—and he was supposed to be good with words, was he? He blundered on, "Actually, I–I know a girl who wears trousers."

"I'd like very much to meet a lady daring enough to wear men's clothings!"

"She's not a lady—well, not exactly—I mean, she's so much nicer than most of the real ladies I've met, the ones with 'Lady' in front of their names—" A title that, as an intimate of the Tregrefina, she doubtless possessed. He cursed himself and hurried on, "Which isn't to say that everybody isn't nice in Gallantrybanks, and the ladies especially—" Worse and worse. Now she'd think he was a constant flirt. "But she's fun, and very smart, and she works very hard—not like a real lady, who doesn't have to work at all, but she's ladylike, and everything—"

Miserably, he remembered the first rule of holes: *Stop digging.*

"I'd like to meet her," she repeated. "Nobody here is much fun. They're all either terribly old, like the Tregrefin and his friends, or very young, like my lady's little brothers and sisters."

"I have a little brother," he said, groping desperately for a safer subject.

"Lucky! I have five sisters."

And abruptly he realized why she'd talked about gowns, and what she'd meant by her earlier teasing about his being a pauper. In the nicest possible way she was letting him know—if he had the wit to perceive it—that whatever her title might be, her family was not rich, and with six daughters to provide for there would be little or no dowry.

"They're all married," she went on, shattering his conclusions as neatly as a spent withie, "and that's why *I'm* extra. Superfluous. But it also means I can do as I like, and I can't wait to see your Kingdom."

"I—I'd be pleased to—" He bit back *personally show you round every inch of it.* "—tell you whatever you'd like to know."

"You are very gracious, Master Silversun."

Whatever confidence was remaining to him while the mask was on his face crumbled like stale pastry.

"My lady asked me to find you. 'The tall one with the gray eyes,' she said. She wishes for a nice long talking with you. Your work the other night was an amazement, and she'd love to know more—if you've time, of course."

"Glad she liked it," he mumbled.

She was silent a moment, and when he managed to meet her gaze she smiled. "Even if she hadn't told me to, I would have sought you out on my own."

He heard himself blurt, "Why?" and wanted to go drown himself in the lake.

"There couldn't be as many words in the piece as usual, most of us being ignorant of your language. But the words you did use—you made them a dancing."

All the instruments made a raucous noise, and then there was silence, and a bell rang. Everyone in the great hall laughingly snatched off masks and veils and kerchiefs, and there were squeals of mock outrage as ladies pretended to discover they'd been dancing or flirting with entirely unsuitable men. Cade's new friend kept her golden mask on and stepped lightly behind him to reach up and undo the ribbons securing his. It dropped into his hands and she returned to face him. Her mask was gone. The heart-shaped face presented for his inspection was appealing rather than beautiful, with strong cheekbones that weren't quite even and heavy straight brows. It was a face full of humor and just a touch of defiance, as if she knew she couldn't compete with the stunning beauties in the room and was daring him to make a false compliment.

It was a reassuring face. He liked it.

"Do you know what I want right now?" he asked with a smile. "Your name, and a dance."

The smile she gave him in return was everything a man could desire. "Vrennerie, and of course."

Cayden returned to Touchstone's upstairs chambers just shy of dawn. He spun the black mask around by its ribbons, humming tunelessly as he shut the door behind him, and started for his bed.

"And just where have *you* been, young fellow-me-lad?" Rafe demanded.

"Out carousing, I'll be bound," came Mieka's voice, "drinking too much expensive wine, breaking ladies' hearts left and right, dancing holes in his shoes—"

"—forgetting we've a performance tonight!"

"I wasn't *carousing*," Cade began.

"Frivoling, then, and frolicking. Shamelessly!" Mieka sat

up in bed with his arms wrapping his knees. Those wide, merry eyes inspected him head to heels in the daybreak dimness, and suddenly he let out a hoot of laughter. "In love, he's in love, just look at him!"

"Shut it," he growled.

"Is she pretty after all, beneath her golden mask?"

"How did you—?"

"I see all and know all—and what I see and know right now is that you're deep in it, you are, right up to your eyebrows!"

He sent a look of desperate appeal to Rafe, then realized he could expect no help there. Back when they were boys, and Crisiant had come along, Cade had been merciless in his teasing. But in his friend's blue-gray eyes was an indulgent kindness, and only a hint of amusement quirked the mouth half-hidden by his beard. Marriage must have a mellowing effect, Cade mused, and wondered if Mieka would undergo the same change.

"We have a show tonight," Rafe said. "Shut up or get out, Mieka, and let him sleep."

The Elf spluttered with outrage. "But—but—"

"You'd like a third choice? I could stuff a shirt down your throat."

He flung back the covers and reached for his trousers. "You are *no* fun!" he announced, and within moments was dressed and out the door.

Cade had meantime removed shoes, jacket, shirt, and trousers, and crawled into bed. Pulling the covers up to his nose, he turned his back and waited. When all was silent, he ventured, "Rafe?"

"I won't say *be careful*, because you already know you ought to be."

He thought that over. "I'm not in love with her."

No response.

"Truly. She's just—I had a good time tonight."

More quiet.

"I'm *not* in love with her."

"Get some sleep, old son."

"B ut there's too many words," Jeska said, bewildered. "Hasn't Kearney said all along we're not to use too many words?"

Cade ground his teeth.

"They don't understand more'n a few anyways," Rafe said with a shrug. "What's a few dozen more? As long as we get the feelings right, it won't matter."

"But—"

"Just put the damned words back in!" Cade snapped, and stalked off to keep his appointment with the Tregrefina. It might only have been his imagination, because it certainly wasn't an Elsewhen, that he heard Mieka laughing softly behind him.

He was escorted to a bower of woven branches down by the lake, where the Tregrefina sat in the shade, alone. Nearby were benches and chairs occupied by servants, not quite out of earshot. But that didn't much matter, because two of her brothers were playing tag with their servants all across the lawn, and the ruckus would be adequate cover for their conversation.

Miriuzca rose as he approached. He hadn't expected that— he was barely above the rank of servant, after all—nor the wide confiding smile she gave him along with her hand. He bent over but did not press his lips to her wrist.

"It's very kind of you to keeping me company, Master Silversun," she said, and her voice was light and soft, more delicate on the consonants of his language than they would have been on her own.

"An honor, my lady," he said. "Touchstone enjoyed performing for you the other night."

"Oh, it was wonderful! Even if I wasn't supposed to see!" She laughed and gestured to the chairs, and they sat, and a servant hurried up. When they had been provided with iced drinks, the man effaced himself and Cade found himself as alone as he would ever get with the girl who would one day be his Queen.

She plied him with eager questions about "Hidden Cottage," which he answered without a single hint of irony. She'd seen the sincere version, not the farcical one. As she praised Jeska's voice and Rafe's skills and Mieka's renderings of scenery and Cade's own flair for words, he dismissed all thought of Mieka's aggravation about the pig. She asked what play they would present that evening, hoped she wasn't keeping him from his work, simply couldn't imagine how much effort it must take to do what they did so effortlessly, and in general made him feel like a shit for what he had unwittingly done in performing "Cottage" last year for Prince Ashgar. For she admitted, eventually and blushingly, that it made her feel so close to her future husband, to have experienced the same play that had moved him to tears. *"Communal experience,"* mocked his own voice in his head.

Their drinks were refilled by a servant who cleared his throat in a meaningful way. She ignored the hint. When the ball her brothers were flinging about rolled over to the table, she hiked up her skirts enough to kick it back to them without blinking an eye or missing a syllable. She further charmed him by laughing at his jokes and listening wide-eyed to his every word.

Finally he remembered what was in his jacket pocket, and said, "If you'll permit, I have a gift for you from a friend."

She blushed, and he realized she thought he meant Prince Ashgar.

"A friend of mine, I mean," he added. "She makes glass."

"Oh." Recovering herself, she asked, "You mean like those baskets and the—what are you calling them?"

"Withies. Yes." Hearing what he'd just said, he hurried on in a minor panic, "She doesn't make those. She never makes those.

Nothing hollow, especially not withies. I'll explain it sometime."
He seemed destined to imbecility around pretty ladies, he told
himself, and shut his mouth. All this while he was digging into
his pocket, fingers fumbling with the little package, thumb
catching in the ribbon that tied one of Lady Jaspiela's best white
silk pocket-kerchiefs—stolen by Derien for the purpose. Blye
had been so careful about making it look nice, fashioning a bow
of many loops, and here he was about to ruin the whole thing. At
last he set it onto the table, the bow only slightly lopsided. "She
made this specially for you, and it's for keeping something in that
you don't ever want to take out."

With a child's smile of delight, she undid the sea-green
ribbon and unfolded the silk. Revealed were ten pieces of glass:
two of them square, eight rectangular, all crenellated along the
edges. She set them out one by one onto the table, then looked
up curiously. "I am not understanding, Master Silversun."

"You fit them together."

"But how will they stay put?"

He only smiled, and watched her work it out—each square
toothing four sides to make two equal-sized pieces that would
fit together as a box. When she had correctly assembled the
first half, a tiny flash of greenish light made her snatch her
fingers back and catch her breath. It was a lovely little display
of Goblin magic, something Blye had adapted from Cade's own
Affinity spell.

"Wh-what was that?" she whispered.

"Magic," he whispered back, smiling. "Now do the other one."

She did, cautiously, and when it was put together, the same
subtle glow sealed the crenellations. She looked up at him in
wonder.

"I've never seen magic doing."

"Of course you have—the other night, at our performance.
Even if you weren't supposed to be watching!"

"But not just for me."

"I'm honored—and so will Blye be. That's her name, the friend who made this. I know it's not very large, but one day when you find something you want to keep in it, send for me and—"

"And you'll seal it up with more magic?"

"Exactly."

She turned each half over and over in her fingers—long fingers, thin and delicate, but though the nails were neatly filed and buffed, she had bitten them almost to the quick. "It *isn't* evil, is it? All my life I am only hearing awful things about magic, how it can make you do what you don't want to do, and destroying things and people—and in your country—my country soon," she corrected herself, "the most terrible example of what magic can do was happening in the war."

He'd never heard it put so bluntly before. He'd never heard magic called *evil* like this. Carefully, he said, "A hammer can build a house or break someone's skull. Is it the hammer that's wicked, or the person using it?"

Her blue eyes blinked wide. "Oh! Then you've heard about the razers?"

"The what?"

"I don't know if you have a special word for it, but that's the meaning in our language. Magic leaving—*left*—from hundreds of years ago. Terrible magic." She leaned closer to him, her voice low. "A chip of wood or a stone once part of a building all at once is making the building all over again. There's no reason for happening that anyone knows, it just happens. And then you have to send one of the Guild for stopping it, and for destroying the magic once and for all."

It was his turn to be shocked. "But—if it's a building, and it rebuilds itself, why waste it by destroying it? Why not let the buildings stand? People could use them—"

"Oh no! Nobody knows what might be inside! They're magic!"

"And therefore evil?" He gestured to the two halves of the little glass box.

"Well... I am supposing this is different."

The servant was back with more cold juice and more harrumphing. Once more he was ignored. When he left, she touched the glass box and sighed.

"This is such lovely magic. I didn't know it could be lovely like this."

Cade heard himself say in a tone too curt for Royalty, "What's the Guild?"

Suddenly she looked worried—not frightened, he noted in puzzlement, just anxious. "You won't tell anyone I'm saying things? It's not talked about. It just... *is*," she finished helplessly.

"You mean like the *vodabeists* in the river?"

Now she did look scared. "You know about—but how could you know? They were told to be careful!"

"Careful to make sure all of us were dosed to sleep every night so we wouldn't notice?"

She pulled back from him, twisting her fingers together in her lap. "My father... the lord who owns the Guildman is owing him a favor, so instead of coming crossland—" She glanced up, pleading. "It was so much faster, and much more pleasant, yes?"

"Charming," he rasped, and set his glass on the table. "So someone owns those things, and the man who controls them with magic? Is this part of what this Guild does?"

She took refuge in something that sounded straight out of a book. "Magical folk are all having certain skills, and use them in service to—" She stopped, and gulped, and blushed again.

"They serve 'normal' people, you mean?" Cade was too disgusted to bother with manners. "They come round to destroy houses that build themselves, or they tease those water-things with light, or—what else do they do 'in service' that nobody talks about?"

And then he considered the weathering witches at home, and how they worked their feeble magic and were gone, and nobody thought about them at all unless they hadn't cleared the snow or dried up the puddles. And what about himself? Useful only as one of the King's curiosities, like the dancing, squawking birds in the Royal Aviary.

The Tregrefina looked so miserable that he was ashamed of himself. "Your Highness—"

But she was smiling at him, fingering the halves of the little box, and saying, "I'm being so grateful to your friend, Master Silversun. Perhaps if it's not much trouble, I might meet her one day?"

His glass was still in his hand. He hadn't really asked about this Guild. In some Elsewhen, though, he had. He needed to get away from here, sort this out. Was any of it true? He knew it hadn't been real. Not in this world he inhabited right now, with a pretty girl smiling at him.

He needed a drink.

"I'm sure she'd be honored," he managed to say. "And I've taken up far too much of Your Highness's time." Getting to his feet, locking his knees to keep himself from falling over, he bowed. She gave him her hand, he dredged up a smile from somewhere, and when he felt able started back up the lawn.

By the time he reached Touchstone's assigned chambers, his head was splitting. He was in no mood to encounter Mieka, pacing and fretful and waving a letter in his hand. Rafe lounged by an open widow, sipping wine, observing all with one eyebrow raised.

"—only knew to send her letter here because her mother heard it from a customer just arrived from Gallybanks—" He spied Cade and rounded on him with a ferocious challenge. "How could none of my letters reach her? Do you understand it? Do you?"

"Not now, Mieka," Rafe said. He poured another cup full

of wine and Cade took it gratefully, downing most of it in two swallows. "Bad one this time?"

"No. Just—unexpected."

"She thinks I've forgot her!" Mieka exclaimed. "She thinks—"

"Not *now*," Rafe repeated, helping Cade into a chair.

"I need paper and pen and ink," Mieka insisted. "I have to write to her—"

"We'll be home before the letter arrives," Rafe pointed out. "Hers was weeks behind us. The marriage is tomorrow, and we leave the day after."

"But I have to do something!"

"Go get drunk. Go prick some thorn. Whatever you do, do it someplace that isn't this room!"

"Fuck you, then!" Mieka snarled, and stormed out.

"What's he on about?" Cade asked, not really interested. His head hurt too much.

"She sent a letter—heartbroken, why doesn't he love her anymore, all that." Rafe refilled the winecups and hitched a hip onto the windowsill. "Reeking of her perfume, too—I'm surprised you didn't smell it halfway down the stairs."

"So he's wild to get home, and right now." And Mieka hadn't even noticed that Cade had experienced an Elsewhen.

"Mostly because he feels guilty. Been flirting, hasn't he, and quite a bit more than flirting in the maids' upstairs tiring room. The little redhead, I think. I've seen her looking at him all cow-eyed. I'm glad you came back—I've heard half an hour of he's a bastard, he's chankings, not worth the dirt that they'll bury his ashes in when he's dead, you know the sort of thing. He's a thoughtless, faithless, useless shit, and she'll find someone else and leave him." He gave a shrug that dismissed Mieka's panic. "What did you see, or don't you want to talk about it?"

"Later. It's just this damned headache—oh, Blye was right about the glass box." He made an effort. "Just the thing to introduce her to the kind of magic she'll be seeing at home. All she's ever heard is that magic is evil. And remind me to tell you about a Guild or something they have here—"

"All right, later. Get some rest. We're working tonight. Or did you want some bluethorn?"

"Maybe before the show. 'Doorways,' I think. And then 'Feather Beds' for the wedding feast. The *clean* version," he added.

"Sounds fine." Settling once more in a windowside chair as Cade stretched out on his bed, Rafe opened his discarded book. "I'll wake you at sunset so you can prime the withies."

He shifted restlessly for a few minutes, avoiding what he knew he ought to do—organize that flashing turn of foreseeing. "Rafe?"

"Mmm."

"D'you really think she'll chuck him?"

A brief, complex snort. "He ain't that lucky."

Shocked, Cade sat up in bed. Rafe sighed and put his book down once more.

"Remember what we used to say about the Ottercatch girls?"

"Wisteria," he replied, an image of the three sisters coming back to him from their days at littleschool. "Very pretty, highly scented—"

"—and will twist and twine and strangle in the end."

"You think she's like that?"

"I think her mother is." He scooted his chair around so his back was to Cade, and resolutely applied himself to the book.

17

All in all, Cade had much too much to think about without adding Mieka's frets and fumings to his worries. Fully aware that more than a few minutes in the glisker's company would have him shrieking or breaking things or both, he kept to his bed all afternoon and didn't go down for dinner. He selected a little packet of bluethorn instead, knowing it would give him the energy required to prime the withies and get through a performance.

He hadn't quite counted on how few of the paper twists of powder were left. Nor on Mieka's arrival just after dinner in search of the same boost.

"Will this last until we get home?" Cade asked as offhandedly as he could.

"It will if you don't nick it," snapped Mieka. "Who told you any of it was yours for the taking, eh?"

"I'm sorry. I ought to have asked." He kept his voice quiet and humble, hoping the volatile Elf wouldn't be too angry with him.

He ought to have known better.

Mieka snatched the thorn-roll from his hands. "Get your own!"

"I'm really sorry. It's just—tonight I need some, I really—"

"What d'you know about *needing* anything?" Clever little fingers busied themselves preparing a glass thorn. "I didn't want to go on this poxy trip anyway, and now look what happens! Jinsie's ruined everything!"

"Jinsie?" he echoed stupidly.

"Stealing my letters, trying to get you to do the same—"

"Wh-what are you talking about?"

Mieka froze, then slumped a bit at the table. "Oh, fuck," he said wearily. "I heard you. At Wistly, the morning we left. This is all her fault, I shouldn't be yelling at you, Cade, I'm sorry—but you don't understand! If I lose her, I'll die."

Cade considered his next words very, very carefully. It was difficult to do, with the thorn all ready and waiting in Mieka's fingers—guaranteed exuberance, surefire strength to put magic into the withies for the performance. At last he said, "I think Jinsie was wrong."

"I know. I heard."

"I also think if it's real and right between the two of you, she won't throw you over for someone else."

"Have to believe that, don't I?" he asked bitterly. Then, rising from the table, he asked, "Want to share? There's enough."

"Beholden. When have you had time to use all this, anyway?"

A shrug was the only reply. A few moments later Cade felt the tiny piercing of his skin, and looked up into Mieka's face. The misery was genuine. He did truly love the girl.

And then the warmth began to rush through him, and after a time he sat up, raked his fingers back through his hair, and said, "Right—where'd you stash the withies?"

What usually took him an hour to do required only minutes. Mieka always mucked about with "Doorways" anyhow, playing as pleased him, and poor Jeska had to react to whatever swirled through the doors. There was dialogue that went with each that Jeska could call up instantly, but the only words that really mattered were the ones at the end: the "This life, and none other" speech. If most of the audience didn't understand it tonight, that wasn't Cade's problem. He primed withies with quick assurance, tossing each to Mieka as he finished. On impulse he tucked an unused glass twig, the smallest one, into the breast pocket of his jacket. Mieka and Rafe weren't going to have all the fun tonight at the end of the show.

After he helped Mieka set up the glisker's bench, they still had an hour before the scheduled performance. Cade went in search of food. What he found, in addition to trays of breads and cheeses left out for anyone still peckish after dinner, was Lady Vrennerie, in pale rose tonight with lots of petticoats. Her dark hair curled about her face and neck in wild defiance of the elaborate arrangement of braids popular at this court. Naturally, the instant she walked up to him, his mouth was full.

"That was a lovely gift you gave my lady," she said. "Just a guessing, was it made by your friend wearing men's clothes and nicer than ladies with titles?"

He chewed, swallowed, gulped some wine, and replied, "Her name's Blye Cindercliff—no, that's not right, her name's Windthistle now. She got married this spring. To one of Mieka's brothers."

"How many does he have? And are they all doing theater?"

"Three. No, just Mieka."

"Then it isn't in families? Like the ears, I mean?"

"Not necessarily. Though my grandfather was a fettler. Like Rafe—the one with the beard."

"Ah." She frowned a little. "If it's not a family trade, why are you doing it?"

"Because we're good." An arrogant statement, but he knew Touchstone had earned that arrogance. Then he heard himself say, "If you want to know the truth… it has to do with power."

"Magical power?"

"That's a bit of it, but not all, not by any means. Jeska does it because he likes being other people. Oh, it's not because he doesn't like being himself—" He laughed suddenly, mayhap a bit too loudly. "In fact, I don't think I've ever known anyone who enjoys being himself more!"

Her brows arched. "So it's rumored amongst the maids."

"What I mean is that he's… secure, I guess the word would be. He knows who he is, and likes it, and that frees him up to become whatever the play calls for. It's not the way a little boy would pretend to be a knight or a sea captain or something, playing at being grown up. For Jeska, it's a craft. An Art."

"And your fettler?"

"Rafe likes to be in control. So do I—I'd never write a word if I didn't!—but for him it's like he can put this little portion of the world in order, and keep it there. He adjusts the magic, makes sure nobody gets hurt, keeps everything organized and disciplined."

"Could someone be hurt?"

"In the hands of a stupid or careless fettler, yes."

"Or a glisker?"

Cade shrugged it off. "Not if the fettler's strong enough."

"And Master Windthistle? Why does he—?"

"Because he likes—no, he *needs* to feel." His thoughts raced, and his words with them, and he listened to himself saying things it seemed he'd always known. "Elves are capricious, completely spontaneous. They let you know exactly what they're feeling exactly when they're feeling it. I don't think he feeds off the magic, the way a Vampire would feed—"

Her eyes widened, and he noted the little flecks of silver in their dark brown depths. "You are having those in your country?"

"Not many. I've never met one, if that's what you mean. Not that I know of, anyway. Why?"

"There's a country to the southeast full of them. Horridible place—*horrible*," she corrected herself. "Black stone mountains, black stone castles. But tell me more about your glisker."

"Mieka… he's more like a child playing with a shiny toy. Oh, he's as professional as the rest of us. We'd never have him in Touchstone otherwise. Still, it's more fun with him than with anybody else we ever worked with. He takes joy in what he does. Some of it's showing off—'Look what *I* can do!' But he's committed to the artistry of what he does. And he's always challenging me to give him more to work with."

"And that brings us to why *you* do what you do."

"It's more than the control. It's influencing what people think about. Giving them a good show, of course—Mieka's dead serious about that part of it, we all are. But—"

"You have things to say, and you want people to be hearing them."

"Conceited, innit?" He grinned and took a big swallow of wine. "To believe that what I think and how I feel about it would be of any interest to anybody else? But that's the real trick, y'see—to present it in a way that *does* interest other people."

"You want to make things," she mused.

He nodded, delighted that she understood. "Not just waft through the world and leave nothing behind."

"To create beautiful things—not just pretty pictures onstage, but things that are true."

His mood changed abruptly—the bluethorn, he told himself, and tried to stop his next words, and couldn't. "Truth can be ugly."

Vrennerie considered this, and shook her head. "Awkward, I think. Even if not comfortable to be looking at, doesn't beauty happen when we *do* look at a thing and see it for what it is? When truth is accepted, no matter how ugly or painful, I think there's a certain beauty in that, no?"

"I hadn't thought of it like that, but you're right. It's when we deflect and deny, and lie to ourselves and others, that we become ugly inside."

They looked at each other for a time, and Cade experienced something he'd never felt before in his life: a complete harmony of thought and feeling with a woman. It occurred to him that he might have been lying to Rafe early this morning.

She smiled then, and said something about how much the ladies were looking forward to the evening's performance. And that twisted his mood again, most unexpectedly.

"Even though it's magic?"

Vrennerie tilted her dark head, and her hair shifted like a silk curtain. "Someone is talking."

"Not enough. They didn't talk much when they chased us out of a tavern, once they got a look at Mieka's ears." He took a swallow of wine. "What's the Guild?"

Her generous mouth compressed into a thin, straight line. Then she shrugged. "If they have special skill, they're registered. When someone has a problem, they're sent for."

"And the rest of the time, everybody pretends they don't exist."

"Yes."

He wanted badly to ask, *What sort of problem, besides buildings that reconstruct themselves without warning?* But he didn't ask. Instead: "You don't seem worried by magic."

"Or your glisker's ears," she agreed wryly. "When I was little, there was an old serving woman who lit the fires on cold winter nights. After we sisters were tucked up in bed and it was all warm in our room, she'd come and tell stories before she banked the fire. Once, she did it with a flickering of her hand. My eldest sister wanted to run tell our parents that there was someone doing magic, but we others shouted her down." She gave another little shrug. "Oh, not because of worrying about the old woman and what might happen to her, but because we liked the stories. My sister tattled anyway, and it turned out that our parents knew, and we were to pay no attention. We had to work it out for ourselves, of course, that not all magic is evil. It took longer to realize what you told my lady: that it's not magic, but the person who uses it."

"I'm glad she has you to confide in." Thinking, *She's going to need you.*

"She's very sweet and—what's the word? Lacking in deceiving." All at once she frowned and glanced away, and muttered, "Better me than Lady Panshilara."

"Who's that?"

"She'll be representing my lady's stepmother in Gallantrybanks. And then, if the Lord and Lady are merciful, she'll be returning home. Never say I told you this, but she is not a very nice person."

"Amazing," came Mieka's voice behind them, and they both turned. "He's actually allowing you to talk. Cayden Silversun is the only man I know who can hold an entire conversation where only *he* speaks." He bowed to Vrennerie. "Mieka Windthistle, and eager to know how I may please you, Lady."

And now, Cade thought, they would be treated to a surfeit of charm, and those eyes. Lord and Lady, how he hated good-looking men. But no sooner had Mieka straightened up from his bow than Kearney Fairwalk was beside them, chattering about preparations for the performance and so exquisitely delightful to meet you, Lady Vrennerie, really truly must be getting along now, positive you comprehend.

Cade and Mieka were in the kitchen hall before they knew it. Rafe was already there. Jeska arrived moments later, escorted by Drevan Wordturner, and from the disgruntled look on the masquer's face, he'd been interrupted in pursuit of much the same thing as Cade.

But it wasn't like that at all, he told himself. He didn't want to bed Vrennerie—well, he did, but that was almost beside the point. What he did want was something he had no time to think about, because they had only minutes before the show.

"—do 'Doorways' just as you always do," Kearney was babbling, "only with *that special someone* at the ending," he smirked, "and be sure to project the finest and most tender feelings up to the minstrels' gallery, won't you, Rafe? Splendid!"

Mieka had taken Jeska aside and was whispering in his ear. The masquer looked shocked, limpid blue eyes bigger than ever, but as Mieka kept insisting, he gradually developed a look of little-boy cunning. Mieka stepped back and grinned.

They were up to something. Usually it was just Mieka who fooled about with a play—he had the magic inside the withies, after all—and left Jeska to revise and cope. This time they were in it together. Cade opened his mouth to demand a confession, but suddenly they were onstage. The applause was enthusiastic; evidently the Tregrefina had let it be known that she approved wholeheartedly of Touchstone. Cade had the sudden, awful thought that perhaps Mieka and Jeska would somehow put Prince Ashgar into this after all, and in ways no one else could possibly imagine. With a few of his many, many, mistresses, perhaps.

"Hells with it," he muttered as he took up position behind his lectern, stage right. The marriage-by-proxy wasn't until tomorrow; if Miriuzca saw something tonight that dissuaded her from it, more power to Mieka and Jeska.

Prince Ashgar did not make an appearance in the play.

Tregrefina Miriuzca did.

Mieka had taken careful note of her face, figure, coloring, clothing. There was no mistaking the person onstage for anyone else, especially not when Jeska flung back the concealing counterpane and rose from the bed and put on a dressing gown rife with big, bright forget-me-never flowers. The gasps and cries of astonished outrage assaulted Cade's ears and he gripped the lectern white-knuckled, suddenly terrified of what Mieka and Jeska were planning to do.

Apart from the initial shock, it was turning out rather harmless.

She walked in her dream along the angled hallway that receded into the far distance; she opened door after door, and there appeared scenes Cade had gathered up from their travels and primed into the withies. Green fields, distant mountains, lakes, the great river; her father, stepmother, all those brothers and sisters; the avenue of sculpted hedges leading down to the lake. Mieka had insisted on that. But there was a fiendish glitter in those eyes that caused Cade to clench the lectern even more tightly.

The effects were delicate: a breeze, the scents of growing things, laughter, warm sunshine on the skin. The emotions were not. Cade's original concept was for Jeska—as a man—to look upon these scenes with delight that transformed gently into poignant farewell as each door closed. There ought to have been gratitude for the beauty seen and the people loved, then anticipation of the possibilities to come. It was intended as a search for the doorway into the future rather than glimpses into likely lives. Instead, there was impatience, even rebellion, as doors opened and scenes were revealed and left behind. Restless need seethed through the great hall, flashes of anger—all of it Mieka's own. Cade knew very well who was provoking it. He'd seen the Elf tuck her letter into his breast pocket.

Rafe clamped iron control on the flow of magic, but Mieka was unstoppable. The final door opened onto an emptiness that swept the audience with anxiety for long moments. Nothing appeared. And then, once more of Mieka's own making, not Cayden's, there radiated hope and eager desire, a craving for love, a reckless certainty that *"This life, and none other"* would be the best of all possible lives. Jeska spoke the lines and vanished through that final doorway.

As always, Cade felt these things at a distance. The audience did not. The emotions came in torrents, though Rafe struggled to gentle the feelings, cushion them, make them bearable. As the magic faded and he used the last of it to cast soft shadows on the stage, there was a stunned silence. Cade's fingers nearly splintered the wood of his lectern when a moody murmuring began. Rafe looked across the stage at him, visibly exhausted, visibly furious. There would be no blithe shattering of glass tonight. Mieka didn't bother leaping over the glass baskets; he simply walked off. Jeska followed him. Unclenching his hands at last, Cade crossed the stage and grasped Rafe's arm.

"Gonna fuckin' *murder* that little snarge," the fettler muttered.

"Not if I get to him first."

Kearney waylaid them on the back stairs, quivering with a combination of fury and fear that effectively rendered him mute. For this, Cayden was profoundly grateful.

"You can start on us once we've finished with him," Rafe snarled, pushing past His Lordship and taking the steps two and three at a time.

"But that's—you don't—the problem—"

"The problem," Cade told him, "is Mieka. And we're about to mend it. Better call a physicker, though, because he'll soon be needing somebody to mend *him.*"

"You don't understand!"

"Don't I?" He turned, four steps above Kearney, towering even more than usual over the Gnomish little man. "He wears Rafe out trying to control him, changes up everything—takes my magic and does with it as he bloody well pleases! The only reason every person in that hall isn't blithering right now is that nothing gets past Rafe."

Kearney looked a beseeking up at him, then blurted, "The Archduke!"

Taken aback, Cade asked, "What about him?"

Wordless again, Kearney simply pointed up towards their

chambers. There was a footman stationed outside the door, not one of the Tregrefin's servants but one of the Archduke's, dressed in gray-and-orange livery. Cade shoved the door open before the man could do it for him, and strode into the room.

Jeska was posed by the empty hearth, leaning a casual elbow on the mantel. Rafe and a large glass of whiskey occupied a low chair. Mieka had perched on the windowsill, heels drumming lightly against the wall, a glass in one hand and a spent withie in the other; this he tapped at intervals against his thigh. This was unusual, for when he wasn't behind his glisker's bench he was rather muted, physically. It might have been the bluethorn making him restless; Cade hoped it was a justified fear of retaliation for what he'd done tonight.

"Ah, Master Silversun!" exclaimed the Archduke, who rose from his chair in welcome as if Cade were a fellow nobleman. "I see Fairwalk found you. Excellent. A brilliant performance tonight. Exceedingly powerful."

Mieka simpered.

"Most affecting," the Archduke continued. "And exceptionally skilled. We were just discussing—"

Mieka interrupted with a rudeness that would have made his mother faint. "We already have a manager."

"Beholden all the same," Jeska put in hastily.

For a split instant the Archduke's upper lip twisted with insult. A minor aristocrat such as Kearney Fairwalk, no matter his distant connections to the Royals, could amuse himself as he liked; Cyed Henick was *the* Archduke. He smoothed his expression swiftly and said, "What I propose is more on the order of a partnership." He looked down at his hands, hesitating, the very picture of diffidence, then glanced up with a half-smile. "What I had in mind is… well, I propose to build a theater."

A real theater, the Archduke went on, constructed specifically for the purpose, not just an overhauled tavern or a barn or warehouse or guild hall fitted out with a stage and seats. Not even like Fliting Hall at Seekhaven. A place of perfect proportions, with no odd bits of stone or steel to rebound the magic, no awkward roof timbers to muffle it. A real stage with real room to work in. Everything built to a player's most exacting specifications, so that all one need think about was the play itself. A theater designed by theater folk.

Designed by Touchstone.

"Under my sponsorship, and with my financial backing, we could build a theater in Gallantrybanks that would stun the entire Kingdom." Kearney finally found words sufficient, and sufficiently coherent, to make his point. "And Touchstone would be the featured players. *Your* theater, don't you see, *your* work—whatever you want to write, Cayden, whatever you want to present—"

"Complete artistic control," confirmed the Archduke. "My estimation is that it would take approximately two years to build—I already have my eye on a tract of land." He paused, looking directly at Mieka. "And Fairwalk tells me your brothers would be the perfect choice for the construction contract."

Cade asked, "And Blye Windthistle makes all the windows, I take it?"

"And lampshades. Don't forget the lampshades," Rafe drawled.

"Which you can shatter to your hearts' delight," said Kearney, smiling.

"Allow me to summarize." The Archduke gestured, and Kearney began pouring more of the whiskey into everyone's glasses, preparing to toast an agreement. "I provide the theater, you provide the performances."

"And the plans for the theater," Jeska said. "Anything we want?"

Kearney beamed at him. "Anything."

It was no oddity, Cade reflected, that he'd seen nothing of this particular future. He saw only things where a decision of his affected the outcome. Here, there was no decision to be made at all.

"Much beholden, Your Grace," he said. "But I'm afraid we'll have to decline your generous offer."

Kearney spluttered and nearly dropped the bottle. The Archduke's eyebrows elevated a trifle up his forehead; Cade noted that his hairline had receded quite a bit for a man of his years.

"Perhaps a more detailed proposal would—"

Again Rafe interrupted. "If the proposal took up more pages than all the scripts for all the Thirteen Perils, it'd make no difference."

"The answer's *no*," Mieka added helpfully.

"Beholden all the same," Jeska repeated, in an entirely different voice this time.

Cade watched him search their faces in turn. Mieka: a half-smile on his lips, heels and hands now still. Jeska, wearing the blandest of masks. Rafe, narrow-eyed and cynical. And finally Cade himself, who greeted the scrutiny with a tiny shrug of his shoulders.

"That is disappointing," said the Archduke, rising to his feet once more. "No need to see me out, Fairwalk, I can find my own way." He paused at the door, turned, and with a hard smile said, "Your performance tonight truly was inspiring. An education. Good night."

Kearney was almost in tears. Cade looked at him, not much liking what he saw, and said, "I think we'll get some sleep now."

The dismissal was delivered in Lady Jaspiela's frostiest accents. Kearney looked dazed, then furious, and finally despairing. Without a word he turned and left, closing the door behind him.

"You might've asked us first, y'know," Mieka said.

Cade spun round. "You disagree? You want to be owned by that man?"

"Hells, no! It just would've been nice if you'd asked."

Rafe said, "Makes us feel all warm and loved inside."

"Cherished," seconded Jeska, a grin beginning on his face.

"At least," Rafe went on, "we know now why Drevan Wordturner is here."

"What?" Cade said, at the same time Mieka started nodding. "What's *that* mean?"

The Elf hopped off the windowsill and headed for the garderobe. "Explain it to him, won't you? I'm for a bath."

"Explain what?"

Rafe sipped whiskey. "Why else would the Archduke bring him along?"

"To translate, of course," said Jeska, as bewildered as Cade.

"But why him in particular? If I remember correctly, you said he doesn't even like what he does. He'd rather be a cavalry trooper."

"So?"

With a look of vast patience, Rafe replied, "What better way to get Kearney to take his part than by providing a pleasant playmate?"

Cade laughed. "And that's why the Archduke brought Drevan instead of some other Wordturner from his collection? Don't be daft."

"You have a nice, long think on it, and let me know if it doesn't make sense." He finished his drink, stretched, and sighed. "I'm too tired right now to take that obnoxious little Elf apart. Remind me to do it tomorrow."

Cade turned to Jeska, who was still looking perplexed. "Do you understand what he's talking about?"

"Not all of it. But he may have a point. I mean, is it really coincidence that of all the people he could've brought along, he picked one who's... well... like that? Like Kearney?"

"You're as daft as Rafe," Cade announced, and went into the garderobe to make sure Mieka was informed of this fact, and that he was included in the analysis.

The garderobe was faced in brick—floor, walls, the long cabinet holding the sink, commode, and tub, though the last three were lined in plain green tile. The room smelled of sage, and Cade felt instantly calmer: it reminded him of Mistress Mirdley's soap. The Elf was lolling in a steaming tub full of milky white water. He was still working on his glass of whiskey, and his fingers had taken up their tapping again on the rim of the tub.

"You don't see it, do you?" he asked as Cade sat down in the chair before the shaving stand. "About Drevan."

"Nothing to see."

"He looks like you."

"No, he doesn't."

Mieka scowled at him. "Oh, it's that nobody could possibly be as ugly as you are, is that it? Let's save that bit of shit for another sweeping. He's about your height, he's built long and lanky like you, he has a—well, shall we call it a somewhat conspicuous nose? His hair's about the same color as yours, though lacking the curl, and I bet that if the light's low and Fairwalk squints a little, he can fool himself that Drevan *is* you."

"That's—that's—he's never—you're—"

Mieka let him splutter for a moment, then shook his head with mocking sorrow. "And to think you write for a living! He's never, you're right, but he'd like to. Rafe is right, too, but not right enough. How better for the Archduke to beguile His Lordship into favoring his cause than to provide not just someone who shares his habits, but who also looks like the man he *wishes* shared his habits?"

Cade could only stare stupidly at him, and watch him swallow whiskey.

"Oh, Quill! You don't see the way he looks at you when you're not looking. Like he's a drunkard and you're a bottle of brandy."

Gathering himself, Cade rose to his full height and looked down his nose at Mieka. "Perhaps *you* ought to do the writing," he said coldly. "With original images like that, you're a natural. And by the bye, when Rafe finishes killing you for what you did tonight, I intend to kill you all over again."

Mieka waved a lazy hand. "By appointment, I think. Shut the door on your way out, won't you?"

18

Whether it had been the shock of all those barely leashed emotions, or the impertinence of portraying the Tregrefina herself onstage, Touchstone was no longer the toast of Gref Jyziero. Cade had his suspicions that the Archduke had contributed to their disgrace, annoyed that his grand design hadn't been greeted with instant and effusive gratitude. Whatever the cause, Kearney Fairwalk, still mortified from the night before, arrived at dawn to inform Touchstone that they had been disinvited to play that final performance after the wedding feast. He delivered the information in a dull monotone, saying that the palace had decided everyone would be too intent on celebrating and wouldn't be disposed to appreciate their artistry. So the show was canceled.

Cade received this news through a throbbing headache, and really couldn't find it in himself to care that they'd been sacked. He hadn't slept much. Too many things whirred inside his head, and bluethorn wasn't the best soporific in the world.

The others simply grunted or growled, rolled over, and went back to sleep. This aggravated Kearney into a brief lecture on professional responsibilities and didn't they understand and they'd be lucky if they weren't thrown onto a milk wagon for the journey back home.

"Just like the old days," Rafe muttered.

"Nah, 'twas me Auntie Brishen's whiskey wagon," Mieka corrected drowsily. "An' we had lots more fun, too."

Jeska propped himself on an elbow, blinked slowly, and asked, "Can you get us a whiskey wagon, Kearney? Wine would do. That bubbly stuff, for choice."

His Lordship surrendered the field and departed, slamming the door. Cade almost felt sorry for him. He felt sorrier for himself, and curled up under the sheets to be miserable.

Mieka's usual grouk didn't last as long as it normally did. Five minutes after the bells chimed ten, he was dressed and out the door, presumably in search of food and drink. Cade mused that the palace really must not like them anymore; usually their breakfast arrived without their having to send for it. He dozed, and the pounding in his head receded.

"Cade! Cayden, wake up and listen to me! I've had the most scathingly brilliant idea!"

Mieka was back. Cade pulled the sheets over his head.

"Go away. I'm still angry at you."

"Oh, forget all that rot. Remember what Chat and Sakary did when Blye and Jed got married? Let's do the same for the Princess! C'mon, Quill, it'll be beautiful!"

"We're as good as under arrest," Rafe told him. "And not invited to the wedding itself, neither."

"Your Lady Vrennerie thinks it's a splendid idea," Mieka wheedled, and Cade flung back the covers to see him grinning. "She can get us in through a side door. And she says the Princess *loved* what we did last night!"

Cade regarded him sourly. "I hate your ideas. I always hate your ideas. Why is that?"

"Just a little magic in a withie, Quill, please?" he whined.

"And she's not *my* Lady Vrennerie."

"Could be if you worked at it a bit. You don't even have

to be there if you want to cower up here until it's time to leave tomorrow—"

"Go away!"

Still, he gave in eventually. He wondered sometimes why he bothered to resist. He was no more proof against The Eyes than anyone else, it seemed.

Lady Vrennerie showed up at their door, her hair dressed in ornate braids though her gown was only an everyday sort of linen. She led them through frantically crowded halls and up several flights of stairs to the Chapel. It wasn't called a Chapel here; it had some unpronounceable name that boiled down to *shrine*. The architecture was most curious. There was a long aisle, and at its head a half-circular projection off to each side, one for the Lord and one for the Lady. Vrennerie explained that the Archduke would stand in the former, the Tregrefina in the latter, they would be called forward to meet in the middle, and someone equivalent to a Good Brother would speak a blessing. There were no plinths for Flame and Fountain, no statues or paintings or much of anything but a pair of linked circles, one green and one blue, above a wide stone slab that looked like a merchant's counter. All it lacked was a cash drawer and a little sign warning that sneak thieves would be prosecuted to the fullest extent of the law. Not that there was anything to take, not in the whole shrine. No implements of religious service, no candles, no statues, no paintings, no stained-glass windows. There weren't even any chairs.

"I was thinking those flowers she likes," Mieka said, "and mayhap some bells."

"Silver or gold?" Cade asked, fingering the two withies he'd brought along. "A trellis, or clusters floating about?" He turned to their guide. "What's your opinion, my lady?"

"I think it's time you stopped calling me that," she said with a smile.

Cade ignored the snigger that Mieka didn't bother to swallow. "What will she be wearing, Vrennerie?"

"Green, of course."

"Green? For a bride?"

"She has white for the ceremony in Gallantrybanks," she assured him. "Here, the wedding color for women is green. For men, blue." She walked the length of the aisle, and Cade spent a few moments liking the way her skirts swayed gently with her strides. "Nothing during the actual rites, I think. But as they leave, and she shows herself outside on the balcony—" She pointed to the back of the shrine, where double doors were closed.

"Brilliant!" Mieka sang out. "A trellis, some bells—could you make them ring the way Chat did, Cade, or are you too completely tone-deaf?"

"I'm not tone-deaf."

"One would never know it, to hear him sing," Mieka confided to Lady Vrennerie. "Just give me a single nice note for all of them, won't you?"

So they left the shrine, and parted from Lady Vrennerie, and upstairs in their room he primed the withies to give Mieka and Rafe magic for a woven archway of blue forget-me-nevers and silver bells, though he knew he would be unable to supply the sort of delicate chiming Chat and Sakary had made.

As he worked, he heard Jeska's troubled questions about the shrine. "Did you note? Why are there no Angels? What exactly do they believe round here?"

"According to the books and the protocol flunky," Rafe said, "they venerate the Lord and the Lady, and that's as far as it goes."

"But what about the Angels?"

"They're sort of mascots—each town has one for luck."

"Nothing of the Old Gods at all," Mieka remarked.

"Well, you'd expect that, wouldn't you? In a land that chucks out magical folk from time to time."

"Here," Cayden said, tossing the withies to Mieka. "Enough to make your pretties. If you still want to, that is."

"Of course I want to!"

That was the showing-off Mieka, he thought, the one who shattered withies in mid-air and pissed his initials onto a rug. The one who got bored easily and rebelled just for the distraction of it. The one of whom a wagon driver had said, *"You'd do well to keep him, in spite of the trouble he'll be to you."* The one whose restlessness became recklessness in an eyeblink.

Touchstone was not invited to the marriage ceremony. With the other guests, plus the palace servants and the entire population of three nearby towns and representatives from everyplace else in Gref Jyziero, they crowded outside on the lawn and waited for the new Princess to show herself on the balcony. It was hot, and everyone sweated in their fine clothing, and there would be nothing to drink until the banquet began. Cade eyed Mieka, who had the two withies up his sleeves, and then glanced at the expanse of gardens leading down to the lake. What would it be, he mused, to have all that space to stretch in, to prime glass twig after glass twig with sounds and scents and scenery, to watch as some grand vision spread itself magnificently through the air?

The Archduke hadn't offered that, exactly. Cade knew what he'd offered, and what he'd left unsaid. He remembered what Derien had told him about the man in gray-and-orange livery outside Blye's glassworks, and he remembered the two Masters from the Glasscrafters Guild who'd tried to shut Blye down. He remembered what Mieka had told him about the Archduke's attempt to buy the Shadowshapers. Nobody owned Vered and Rauel and Chat and Sakary; nobody would ever own Touchstone, either.

Still… a theater built to their own designs and needs, where they could perform anything they pleased… the man knew how to tempt; that was for certain sure.

A startled cry went up from the crowd. Two stories up, a trellis of white and gold wove itself into an archway and burst into bloom. The girl stood there, astonished and then delighted, waving to the crowd, who cheered and applauded, proud of their young and pretty Tregrefina who had made such a splendid marriage. Cade held his breath until the bells appeared, and sighed relief when they all played the same high, sweet note.

He could see the Archduke hovering near the girl. It was to prove a theme of the afternoon and evening. Cyed Henick was her constant escort: from the balcony, into the great hall, around to the various tables to receive congratulations, up to the high table on what had been Touchstone's stage. He sat beside her and chose delicacies for her plate and filled her wineglass and Cade began to wonder whether he didn't want to own her, too.

Early on, Cade found a seat—and, more important, a tankard—and set himself to observing. The commonality were all still outside, feasting from trestle tables set up around the lake, entertained by jugglers, acrobats, and musicians. Briuly Blackpath was wandering the great hall, playing whatever he pleased, looking annoyed that the noise drowned out his efforts. After the food was devoured, the minstrels' gallery came to life. Tables were pushed to the walls and dancing began. Cade chose a convenient corner and stood watching, taking note of a face or a laugh, a ridiculous arrangement of braided and looped hair, a sophisticated seduction, a highborn who'd had too much to drink.

After a while, Lady Vrennerie approached, looking exhausted but happy. He smiled to see her, lovely in all her finery, and snagged a flagon for her from a passing servant with a huge tray of drinks so they could toast the marriage.

"Your trellis was perfection," she told him. "My lady—I should say the Princess—was thrilled."

"Once she got over the shock."

"Too strong a word! It was so beautiful, seeing her there in the sunlight with all the flowerings and bells." Something about her gaze hardened as she went on in a quieter voice, "And it was a perfect reminder that the land she will be ruling one day is a land of people who can work magic."

"Is that so important?" he asked, more for something to say than because he was interested.

"Oh, yes, Master Silversun."

{Into the terrible silence his own voice said, "But I'm still here."

He shut the door in the boy's face, went into the drawing room, found a chair. He sat, staring at Kearney's letter, at his own scarred fingers. Wondering why, on this night of all nights, the blood didn't show.

"Cayden? Cayden!"

The woman's voice—his wife's voice—calling from upstairs, irked and impatient. He wished he'd shut the drawing room door.

"Cayden!" }

"Master Silversun?"

He looked down at her. "Can't you say my name?" he asked irritably. "You never say my name."

"I will if you like, Cayden."

It wasn't the same voice at all. He saw the bewilderment in her eyes and hated himself. How stupid he was, to have ever thought that a *lady* could even think of being married to him. Whoever the woman was who called down to him in that Elsewhen, it wasn't Vrennerie.

He understood the turn instantly. What he decided to do about Vrennerie—whether or not he "worked at it a bit" as Mieka had recommended—could change things. If he did nothing...

if he didn't pursue her… if she didn't become his wife and the mother of his children—

—Mieka would die.

He knew he'd fallen as much in love with her as it was possible for him to do. He knew he would never see boredom or impatience in her eyes, that she would not end by despising him and the work that was his life. She understood and valued what he did. She admired it. He had felt things with her and for her that he'd never experienced before.

As he made himself smile down at her with what he hoped was reassurance, he reflected bitterly that this was the real horror of his so-called gift: that he could even for a few instants seriously contemplate using this girl he cared for in order to change a future he feared.

He hadn't lied to Rafe. He wasn't in love, not completely. There was more to giving his heart than mutual affinity and desire. He loved Blye, but without the wanting; he'd wanted Lady Torren, she of the red hair and lavender-scented pillows at Seekhaven Castle, but there'd been no love. He heard Mieka's voice saying *"If I lose her, I'll die!"* and knew there was no such need inside him for Vrennerie. There was nothing in him of that panic. And if that was what love was, if it came with dread and fear and anguish, then he could do without it.

Rafe and Crisiant were proof enough that it didn't have to be like that. Their loving was a sweetly comfortable thing, devoid of Mieka's wild desperation. And yet they needed each other. Rafe would not be the man he was without Crisiant; Cade could not say the same for himself regarding Vrennerie. If he never saw her again, it would hurt. But he would survive it. He could survive anything, it seemed—hadn't he heard his own voice saying, in response to the news that Mieka was dead, *"I'm still here"*? Hadn't Tobalt Fluter said in more than one Elsewhen, *"When Touchstone lost their Elf, they lost their soul"*?

He thought all this in the time it took to drain his tankard and look round for another. Rafe or Jeska or Mieka would have seen in his eyes that he'd had a turn, and taken him someplace quiet until he could recover. But he could see none of them in the swarm of dancers and drinkers, and told himself it was foolish to want so much the sight of Mieka's living, laughing face. Taking a sip from his fifth—or was it sixth?—drink of the evening, he shoved all else and Elsewhens aside, determined to enjoy what time he could get with Lady Vrennerie. Exerting himself to be polite, he found that she met him at least halfway, and soon they were discussing the woman she had mentioned earlier and pointed out to him in the throng.

"Lady Panshilara's pretty enough," Vrennerie said when Cade made some remark about the richness of her gown, "and knows it, too."

"The sort who uses that to get what she wants, and doesn't think she needs anything else?"

"The very same. Her family is very old and very poor— one of those extravagant ancestors, I'm sure you're hearing the same story a hundred times. She's the only child, so she inherits whatever's left to inherit. They scraped enough for some elegant school, but it doesn't seem to have worked. All the intellectual skills of a tree stump, that one."

He burst out laughing, and she blushed.

"Well, it's true! I know it's nasty of me, but she's so unkind to my lady. As unkind as decent behavior is allowing."

"Let me guess. She thinks *she* ought to have been the one to marry Prince Ashgar."

"It's not so much that as becoming Queen of Albeyn."

Cade tried to imagine her in Queen Roshien's moonstone crown, and couldn't. Not that it wouldn't look lovely in her high-piled dark braids. Her eyes were dark, as well, and the form in a much-embellished crimson gown was both lush and willowy.

"She's older than she looks," he said.

"And than she pretends to be. My hope is that a few months in Gallantrybanks will give her the set-down she needs."

"Ladies just as lovely, with brains and riches besides?" He snorted. "Don't count on it. But try to be there when she meets Princess Iamina, if you can. *That* would be a thing to see!"

She asked with arching eyebrows, and he told her as much about the King's sister as was appropriate. He left out his experience at Wintering when he was a young boy, and Iamina's battles with her husband, but told Vrennerie how she'd disrupted Touchstone's first performance in the Pavilion at Seekhaven Castle by arriving late and causing a fuss. When he finished the tale with Mieka sending the Dragon's fiery breath right at her, Vrennerie giggled.

"Please tell me you'll do something like to Panshilara!"

"We'll do our best."

A footman sidled up, all apologies, and whispered in Vrennerie's ear. She asked him something, looking apprehensive. When he nodded, she sighed. "So soon. Forgive me, Mast—I mean, Cayden—I have duties. Perhaps I'll be back later."

Yes, he liked this girl, he thought, liked her far too much to do to her what he had for a few moments thought about doing. Court her, marry her, have children with her—*use* her—all to keep Mieka alive. Do all of that without truly loving her, needing her, either in the uncomplicated way Rafe and Crisiant had or with Mieka's ferocity. Cade had more honor than that. It was a decision that left him sad but serene, which was a very odd sensation indeed.

He wandered about for a while, chuckling as he caught sight of Jeska dancing with two ladies at once. Quite the success here, was Jeschenar Bowbender. Both ladies looked as if they'd prefer to be doing their dancing with him while lying down.

"Master Silversun."

He turned, so quickly that he was light-headed. Too much wine. The Archduke stood beside him, with an expression in his eyes that sobered Cade at once. "Your Grace."

"I was under the impression that a performance was not required of you today. And yet—"

Cade shrugged. "Just a little gift for the Princess, Your Grace."

"I wonder if you've given any more thought to our discussion of last night."

"None at all," he lied.

"Pity. I feel we might do great things together."

"Touchstone is happy right like we are, beholden all the same."

"This will be your second year on the Winterly Circuit, will it not? I heard recently from a friend in Gallantrybanks that Black Lightning has become a great success on the Ducal."

Cade said nothing. The injustice would rankle until he took his last breath.

"They haven't your subtlety, of course."

"Rather like murder, innit?" said Mieka from out of nowhere, those eyes glittering with all their colors of green and blue and brown and gold. "What I mean to say is that there's the smotherment of a feather pillow, or a quick sword in the guts, or slitting a vein or two so the quarry bleeds to death. I'd say Black Lightning's more of the cudgel to the head and beating your brains out and then stomping on the corpse, wouldn't you, Your Grace?"

A thin smile twitched the man's lips. "You might very well think so. I couldn't possibly comment. And Touchstone? What for you, Master Windthistle?"

"Oh, slow poison, for certes," Mieka replied cheerily. "We get inside them, and before they know it they're thinking and feeling things they never thought or felt before."

"And survive it," Cade put in.

"An interesting symbolism. Perhaps we might discuss it

sometime. But if you'll excuse me, I believe I'm wanted up at the high table. I wish you a pleasant evening."

"And to Your Grace," Mieka said, all brightness and merriment. Once the Archduke was out of range, he dropped the pose and muttered, "Him, he's a knife in the back, he is."

"Beholden for the rescue, Sir Mieka," Cade responded. "But I don't need to be told to be wary of sharp shiny things around him."

"I'd like to shove something sharp and shiny up his—"

Someone bellowed a word, and then again, and the musicians stopped playing. The dancers stumbled midstep. The hall grew quiet. All eyes turned to the high table, where the Tregrefin had pushed himself to his feet and was holding aloft a bejeweled golden winecup.

"Gift from King Meredan," Mieka whispered at Cade's shoulder.

"How do you know?" Cade breathed back.

"One of the maids gave me a tour of the wedding presents, didn't she? The old man gets the gold, and we get the girl."

Cade considered theirs to be the better part of the bargain. But right now the new Princess was not looking as if she was enjoying the transaction. She had turned white as whipped cream. Her father proclaimed something or other, raised his cup once again, yelled a few more words, and the great hall erupted in cheers and laughter. Vrennerie appeared at the girl's side, gently coaxing her to rise. The Archduke was suddenly there, bowing over her wrist. She smiled tremulously, he said something, and her smile became grateful. Cade didn't trust the look on his face for an instant.

"Party's over, then?" Mieka yelled above the tumult. "Time and past time, if you ask me!" He held up an unopened bottle and two glasses. "I'm for the gardens. Come with me, Quill, I want to see the teacup hedge by moonlight."

But suddenly they were being swept along to the music of lutes and twittering fifes, out the great hall doors and up the grand staircase, along a corridor and finally to a set of gilded double doors carved with swirls of ivy and flowers. Unable to move any way but forward, crushed amid dozens of people, they could not escape. The doors were wide open, and beyond them was a bedchamber featuring a bed the size of a boat. And the new Princess stood beside it, wrapped in what looked like half a wall tapestry, the frills of a white lace nightdress peeking out just above her bare toes. Vrennerie hovered protectively nearby. Lady Panshilara also hovered, her face a pleasant mask from which envious brown eyes glittered maliciously.

The Archduke arrived and took up position on the other side of the bed. For show, he took off his jacket. His hairline might be receding at an early age, but so, too, was his waistline expanding, and for the first time Cade noticed the flush on his cheeks and across his nose. Signs of a dicky heart, according to Mistress Mirdley.

Vrennerie lifted the bedcovers so high that when the tapestry robe dropped to the floor, no one saw the girl below the neck. Miriuzca slipped quickly into bed and sat back against the pillows, sheets and counterpane clutched to her chin. With the curtains wide open, the Archduke sat beside her and they drank from the same glass of wine—not quite loving cups, but as close as one could get with a husband-by-proxy. He leaned over to kiss her cheek and she jerked back, crimson and stammering when people roared with laughter. Cade didn't understand the words being shouted all over the room, but he could guess their meaning from their tone: *I hope that's not how she'll receive Prince Ashgar's embraces!* and *Needs a real man, that one, to teach her what's what!* The Archduke set aside the wine, cupped her frightened face in his palms, and kissed her full on the lips.

"From your new husband," he told her. "Lucky man!"

"Take it all, Your Grace!" someone yelled. "Be first in, for the pride of Albeyn!"

Mieka snarled softly. Lady Panshilara was smiling.

The Archduke rose from the bed, bowed low, and departed with his manservant skittering along behind, holding his jacket. Nobody followed him; indeed, there was a nudging forward that pushed Cade and Mieka even farther into the room.

"Witnesses, witnesses!" cried one of the Albeyn delegation just behind Cade. Before he could turn to ask the man what this meant, Lady Panshilara elbowed her way round the bed, tapping this person and that on the shoulder or cheek, smirking. She chose several handsome gallants, three ladies, and a brace of elderly gentlemen who were eyeing the Princess with an eager interest Cade found obscene. Then it occurred to him that this might be a variation on the inspection Vrennerie had told him about, and when Lady Panshilara's sparkling fingers lifted once again, he shoved the chosen man aside and leaned forward so that her hand tapped his cheek instead. She looked startled, then annoyed; then smoothed her expression into a smile that said, *See this silly player-boy, wanting a peek at a pretty girl!* Cade looked her straight in the eyes and she didn't falter for an instant.

"Cade? What the—?"

He looked back at Mieka, who looked confused. Vrennerie made shooing motions, and the remaining crowd groaned disappointment. Cade stood his ground as everyone not chosen left. Miriuzca was fairly cowering in bed now, her eyes huge and very blue.

In two languages the witnesses were told to search every corner of the room for illicit persons. They were asked to testify one by one that only the maids of honor and servant girls were present, and no man lurked anywhere to soil the Princess's reputation.

Cade found it utterly barbaric. He stood guard on one side of the bed, catching Vrennerie's grateful glance from where she stood on the other, and watched in disgust as draperies and bedcurtains were pulled aside and shaken, chairs moved to look behind them, the lace swathing various tables flipped up to check for someone hiding underneath. All the while there was much rude and drunken hilarity, especially when one of the old men brandished a dagger like a sword, staggering about while thrusting it and his hips to the danger of everyone and everything in the room.

And then one man—Cade was astounded to see it was Drevan Wordturner—darted forward and playfully snatched the covers from the foot of the bed. The girl cried out in shocked dismay as she was revealed in her lace nightdress. Cade yanked down one of the bedcurtains, flung it across her, and moved to grab Wordturner by the scruff of the neck.

"Just a joke, Cayden—no harm meant—must be thorough, make sure there's no man lingering in the sheets!"

"Shut it!" Cade ordered. "You're making a fool of yourself."

Wordturner laughed in his face, his breath withering. "There must be no fucking tonight!" he announced, wagging a finger at Cade and then at the Princess. "You can make a playlet from this, right?" Wordturner continued, squinting at Cade. "Ripping good show, surefire laughs!"

With a look to strip the scales off a wyvern, Cayden said, "As one of the Archduke's attendants, perhaps you've never had the chance to meet my father. Zekien Silversun—First Gentleman to His Highness Prince Ashgar."

The implied threat was an empty one, but Wordturner couldn't know that. He blanched, and sweat broke out on his brow and upper lip. Cade knew well enough what that meant, and shoved him towards the door so someone could take care of him before he yarked all over the bed.

The shy gratitude in the blue eyes of Princess Miriuzca caught at his heart. She was so young, so gentle; should he warn her what sort of man Ashgar was, or let her find her own way?

"B-beholden," she whispered.

Vrennerie was righting the sheets and counterpane. "We'll look forward to meeting your father, Master Silversun."

He realized his mistake. All he'd meant was to sneer some sense into Wordturner. She had understood his mention of his father to mean that Zekien could be relied upon as someone to trust.

Lady Panshilara suddenly clapped her hands and announced that the Princess would now retire. Her accent was atrocious, but her words were perfectly comprehensible as she added, directly at Cayden, "Alone in her bed, proved and witnessed, also—or would you like another look?"

The words could have been sarcasm from a highborn lady to a commoner; the look in her eyes was pure malevolence. The Princess cringed back into the pillows again, and Vrennerie's fists clenched. Cade was no Jeska, able to swerve on a penny piece from one aspect to another. He could do nothing but shake his head and turn and leave the room.

Air. He needed air. The hallways were endless, the staircases packed with revelers, the noise deafening. Finally he got outside into the gardens through the simple method of climbing out a ground-floor window. He gulped in the cool breeze off the lake, walking aimlessly, staring up at the waxing moon. At length he found himself trudging along the path between looming hedge sculptures. When Mieka suddenly called his name, he nearly lost his footing.

"Have a drink, Quill."

Settling on a bench beside the Elf, he took a glass and watched the light of a thousand torches from the gardens glitter on the wine.

"Past midnight yet, is it?" Mieka asked.

"They've been ringing all their bells all evening—who can tell?"

"Hmm. Well, for the sake of convenience, let's say it is."

"Did you hear any of that? In the Princess's bedchamber, I mean."

"I heard enough. Never thought Drevan would turn out such a snarge." He emptied the bottle into his own glass. "Drunk, of course. And likely to have had quite a scold from His Grace, don't you think?" He wasn't looking at Cade, but back up towards the palace. At specific windows of the palace, Cade learned a few moments later when there was an awful *bang!* and a window shattered and smoke began to billow out. Mieka tilted back his head and roared with laughter.

"Gods Almighty!" Cade exclaimed. "What did you do?"

"It's me Namingday, Quill, I had to celebrate!" he said, not bothering to deny responsibility. "Everybody else forgot, so it was up to me, wasn't it?"

"I didn't forget," he protested, although he had. "But what did you *do*?"

"You 'member at the port, when all the ship cannons went off? Well, I sneaked meself down belowdecks later, with a flask or two of ale, y'unnerstand." He grinned. "Nice young sailors in His Gracious Majesty's service, that's thirsty work. They were glad to tell me all about how to fire off a cannon without a cannonball in it. It's the powder charge what makes it explode, so I palmed me one or three. Just for the pop."

"But—"

"There's a length of ropy stuff, and you light the end with a flint-rasp and wait for it to burn to the powder. They didn't measure right, and that's why the shots were off-timed in the harbor. I was worried I hadn't used enough—had to make me getaway nice and safe, y'see."

"But when did you do it? When did you have time to go back to our rooms and—"

He laughed and patted his pockets. "All the necessaries have been right here all night! Once Lady Vrennerie shooed everyone out, it was an easy run and nobody home. But I been waitin' out here for half of forever." He made a grand flourish of one arm and spilled half his drink. "Isn't it brilliant?"

"Mieka," he whispered, staring up at the smoke, "it's *on fire!*"

"No, it ain't. It's a garderobe, silly. All tile and stone. Well, and a bit o' glass."

"You—you *didn't*," Cade breathed, not knowing whether to be more awed or appalled. "Where in the garderobe did you put it?"

"Right next the shithole!" He chortled and bumped Cade with a shoulder. "Not where anybody could piss on it—up under the porcelain seat, like, and then I had to think where to trail the rope so the smolder wouldn't get wet either—"

A wonderful certainty came to Cade then, but to make absolutely sure he asked, "*Whose* garderobe?"

"The Archduke's, of course."

He had a sudden vision of the Archduke sliding through shit all over the floor. It was deeply satisfying.

He toasted the Elf with a heartfelt, "Happy Namingday, Mieka!"

19

"Hells!" Mieka cried. "And I went to all that trouble, too!"

They found out the next day that the Archduke had not been in his suite when the powder charge went off in his garderobe. No one had been there, and a fortunate thing that was, too, for the *pop!* Mieka had expected not only blasted the seat to splinters and blew out the window but totally obliterated the bathtub as well. He had to be content with knowing the Archduke would be compelled to use somebody else's facilities. It was that, or sit his noble posterior down on a piss pot, just like common folk.

Mieka found this to be scant reward for all his careful work.

Cade—who alone knew who was responsible—consoled him with, "Bear up, old son. Next time you'll get it right. Shall we arrange for an unarranged stop at Prickspur's this Winterly?"

That idea cheered him up considerably.

The morning after the wedding was the day of their departure, so there was no chance to celebrate Mieka's Namingday. The summer weather had broken with showers in the morning, followed by lowering gray clouds that obscured the mountains. The Archduke, in his farewell speech, made some pretty remarks about how the skies themselves over the country wept with the leaving of their dearest lady—an unfortunate reference, for with his words some sunlight poked through the clouds. Mieka grinned.

The change in weather demonstrated why they'd come to collect the Princess now. Another few weeks, and late-summer rains would mire the roads, and even Mieka knew that autumn sailing could be dodgy. But the poor girl would have to wait many weeks before officially wedding Ashgar. A decree of a century or so ago meant that no underage girl was allowed to marry a Prince. Miriuzca had not yet turned eighteen. This law had come from a heartbroken (and, Mieka suspected, guilt-ridden) king whose adored bride of barely fifteen had died in childbed. The time until the new Princess's Namingday this winter would be spent at the Keeps, where she would be further instructed in language, history, Court protocol, and religion. Then, because winter was a rotten time to hold public celebrations, the grand celebrations—including theater performances—would be held in the spring. Kearney Fairwalk was nervous that Touchstone would be disinvited to that, as well. Mieka didn't bother his head about it. The Princess liked them. Granted, she couldn't officially like them, because women weren't supposed to attend the theater, but still, she did like them.

Between those performances and the present were long days of travel in a coach and on the ship, and then rehearsals and some bookings in Gallantrybanks, and then the Winterly Circuit. Mieka shrugged off thinking about all that as well. His immediate concern was to be home as fast as possible. He had no idea how far it was back to the port city, but didn't really mind how many days in a coach were ahead of him. As long as he didn't have to think of those water-things dragging the barges, he was fine.

Then he found out that Touchstone's other performances had been canceled as well. They would be joining the selection of servants, travelling in coaches, who would arrive at the port before the new Princess to ready her shipboard quarters. She, the Archduke, and various representatives from Gallantrybanks, with their personal retinues, would be sailing the Vathis River, stopping at one minor and two major courts along the way. She was also keeping Briuly Blackpath with her.

"And the Lord and Lady alone know how long it will take us," sighed Kearney Fairwalk as he finally thought to mention this, right when they were about to get into the coach.

"Do you mean to say," Mieka asked in what he tried valiantly to make a normal tone of voice, "that we'll be rushing crossland, overnight, for a week—"

"Nearly a fortnight, actually."

"—then sit about with our thumbs up our noses while you dawdle?"

"Why aren't you coming with us?" Jeska wanted to know.

"Oh, distant cousin of the King, delegate, all that sort of thing, don't you see," he answered calmly. "I'd rather join you, of course I would, but—"

"I *don't* see," Mieka snapped.

"C'mon," Cade said, heading for the coach. "Let's get the fuck out of here."

Lady Vrennerie would naturally be sailing with the Princess, and Mieka thought this was the source of Cayden's foul mood. He was only partially correct.

It was just the four of them in the coach, so they had room to stretch out if they liked. But they would also be sleeping here at least three nights and possibly five, depending on whether they made good time. There were no fold-down seats, as there were in Fairwalk's personal carriage, only a pile of blankets. They had been relegated to their proper station in life. And Mieka knew who must be responsible.

In retrospect, he shouldn't have used the powder charge on the man's poor defenseless garderobe. He should've used it on *him*.

When, after the coach had been waved out of the palace

grounds, he said so, the whole of the tale had to be told. Jeska was torn between admiration and horror. Cade, grinning, congratulated him again on his success at not being caught.

Rafe, after a complex chuckle of a snort, said, "I heard one of the servants talk of a fault in the plumbing. Nasty vapors and such. But somebody else whispered of magic."

"But it wasn't magic at all!" Mieka exclaimed.

"And then," Rafe continued, "he said something about a Guild."

"So we've failed," Cade said slowly. "We were supposed to introduce these people to magic as used in theater, and instead it turned out a total cock-up and they're more suspicious than ever. We denied the Archduke the purchase of us. And thus we made an enemy."

"But friends in the Princess, and Lady Vrennerie," Mieka countered.

"That's as may be. Tell me, how much power will either of them ever possess at Court?"

Jeska gave him a shrewd smile. "Once the Princess has a son, quite a bit, don't you think?"

"That's at least a year away. And in the betweentimes we're off on another Winterly, and if we're not careful another after that."

Rafe glanced over from staring out the window. "Are you *trying* to hack me off?"

"I'm setting out the facts. We'll be paid well for this trip, but—"

"Not as much as if we'd played all the shows scheduled," Rafe countered.

Cade actually grinned. "Half of it was banked before we left. What we lost by not playing doesn't amount to the half we're still owed. And I've an idea or two for making up some of the difference."

"What's your plan for your share of the money?" Mieka asked. "Me, I'm buying a house."

Jeska's smile turned wry. "Once you get her, you don't want to lose her in that bloody great maze at Wistly?"

"*If* I get her," he sulked, but bluethorn wouldn't let him stay miserable for long. "Why can't we just steal one of the ships and sail home ahead of everyone else?"

Cade had stopped breathing when Mieka mentioned a house, but it wasn't the look of an Elsewhen. He was remembering one, Mieka knew it. But he didn't ask.

"I plan to sell the old house and buy a cottage seaside for Mum," Jeska said. "So she won't have to work ever again."

But why *shouldn't* he ask? It was about him, he knew it was about him, why in all hells shouldn't he—

"My parents wouldn't know where to put themselves if they didn't have to work the bakery anymore," Rafe was saying. "But I think Mum would like to join Fa on his trips now and again, and if they hire two more apprentices, she'll be able to travel with him."

"If his trips are anything like this one, she'd best stay home," Mieka told him. "I didn't want to come along, and I was right. It's been a fuckin' disaster."

"Not entirely—not for Cayden," Rafe reminded him. "What news of the lovely Lady Vrennerie?"

Cade replied with a shrug, and stared out the window for the next hour. Mayhap Mieka had been right in the first place, and his moodiness was because of the girl.

Worst Namingday ever.

They slept, if one could term it that, in the coach that night. And the next night. They were allowed out five times each day: in the morning for breakfast, at noon for lunching, around five for tea, after dark for a late dinner, and—grudgingly—about midnight when the horses were changed yet again. That their liberation from the coach was entirely due to the horses, without any thought at all to their own comfort, was made obvious on the very first day: Rafe asked the driver to stop so he could get out and have a piss, and he was told to hold on to it for another three hours until the switch to another team of horses and another driver was made. Rafe responded by taking a cue from Mieka's flouting of Winterly Circuit regulations, and relieved himself out the window.

By the third day, Rafe had had enough of trying to fold his big body into a bench seat, and demanded they stop at an inn. Mieka tugged the woolen cap down over his ears before he climbed out, and stepped into a pile of horseshit left in the yard, and thought seriously about maiming someone. Jeska, for preference, who fell about laughing as Mieka tried to scrape the slime from his boot.

"Shut it!" he snarled, and dug his hand into the mess, and threw a clod at the masquer. He missed. This infuriated him even more, and he went for Jeska with both fists.

When he woke up, draped across a wooden bench in the stable yard, Cade was approaching with a bucket of water. "You just never learn, do you? At least all your teeth are still there. Jeska must be mellowing in his old age."

Mieka pushed himself upright and groaned. The only source of pain was his jaw, and it was further humiliation that Jeska had evidently felled him with a single contemptuous punch. He stuck both hands into the bucket to wash them, and opened his mouth to complain.

"For the love of the Gods and Angels, stop whining!" Cade snapped. "Haven't I enough to worry about without listening to you snivel?"

Mieka didn't speak to him, or anyone, for a whole day.

Finally they arrived back at the port town, and back on board their ship he immediately climbed up to the top bunk and got out his roll of thorn. The other coach, the one full of servants, was decanted onto the ship that would carry Princess Miriuzca to Gallantrybanks. They could clean it with a toothbrush or burn it to the waterline for all he cared. All that mattered to him was the paper twist marked in red, and the little glass thorn in its nest.

"Don't even think about it," said Cayden as he walked in the cabin door. "We're rehearsing this evening."

"For what?"

"The show we're giving tomorrow night. They *do* have theater here, Mieka—well, not exactly a theater, more like a town banqueting hall for important feast days—but we're performing."

"Still wanting to show the yobbos what a real play looks and feels like? I thought we didn't want to frighten them."

"See my face?"

"You mean the 'I don't give a shit' face? Fine. Wake me when it's time to go to this theater."

The thorn roll was taken from his hands. "Get up. Do your job."

He considered refusing. But Cade was indeed wearing a *face*, and there was a flash in his gray eyes, and anyway it would get him out of this cabin for a bit. Hells, it was something to do.

The "theater" Cade led them to had seen plays performed before. There was, in fact, a backstage full of costumes and scenery, none of it up to Mieka's standards but, he supposed, serviceable enough for the kind of amateur theatrics people did at home. No magic involved, no intensity of sensation or emotion beyond what the actors brought to the piece. A few of these amateurs had gathered in the otherwise empty hall, and one of them gathered up the courage to approach Touchstone.

"We—would it be good if we watch?" His heavy accent made the words nearly unintelligible.

Cade loathed strangers at rehearsal. So Mieka blinked several times with surprise when he nodded and smiled, and gestured to the chairs stacked around the edges of the space.

"They'll tell their friends," he explained when Jeska asked. "Full houses for the next three nights."

"Not much pay," Rafe interpreted, "but plenty of trimmings."

It was a relief to think about nothing except the staging, the timing. "Troll and Trull" wasn't a demanding piece, but Mieka always enjoyed the silliness of it. He used the withies Cade had primed with just enough for a quick run-through, and even these hints of the full magic had their small audience gasping. Afterwards, one of them came up to him and reached out a shy finger to the glass twigs.

"Oy, let those be," Mieka warned.

"I only—"

"Best do as he says," Rafe drawled. "He hates anybody touching his toys. They loom large in his legend."

Mieka stuck his tongue out at him.

That evening, Rafe and Jeska went out drinking. Cade stayed in the cabin with Mieka, and together they sampled a bit more of Auntie Brishen's thorn. The packet they used was marked with black and green and a splotch of red. As Cade prepared the glass thorn and Mieka mixed the powder, they talked over the reactions of the evening.

"Don't seem as wary of the magic, do they?"

"They're too curious. Besides, what we do is what they do— oh, stop that, you'll have to clean the thorn all over again if you snurt all over it! What I meant was that the basics of theater are familiar to them, so we're not threatening. They can understand what we do."

"But they can't *do* it."

"But they'd *like* to—and that's our way in. I don't know why I didn't see it before."

"Oh, you mean the way you didn't see the King's real reason for sending us?"

Cade looked up.

"You want to have a care about that," Mieka counseled. "You hang your jaw open like that in winter, your teeth will freeze. C'mon, Quill! We're here to impress everyone with what King

Meredan has at his beck and call. *Magic*. There'll be no fleets sailing up the Gally River to watch from me little lair in the tower."

"It—it would mean using magic as a weapon of war," Cade breathed. "Nobody's stupid enough to do that again, or even threaten it!"

"If you say so."

"Mieka… where does that come from? When you bounce about like that, I mean."

He shrugged. "I guess it's just the way me brain works. You pick everything apart to find out what makes it the way it is—and see if you can change it," he added with a shrewd sidelong smile. "I just see what I see." After a moment, wondering if he dared, he said, "And I don't like seeing you sad over Lady Vrennerie."

"I'm not. Not exactly, anyways." He held out the thorn. "And even if I am, here's a cure for it, right?"

A few minutes later, they lazed together in the lower bunk, Mieka's back against one end and Cade propped on pillows against the other, long legs bent at the knees.

"They're afraid of us already, so why did the King bother?" Cade said suddenly.

"P'rhaps they've got used to what little magic there is here, and need reminding that there's other, and more, and stronger. Who cares?" He stretched, the luscious sensations seeping through him.

"This Guild I heard about," Cade insisted. "One of the things they do is *stop* magic. They're afraid of magic—afraid of light—" He broke off, his long fingers twitching.

Mieka knew that nervous signal by now: he wanted pen and paper. "Those things in the water—"

"Cayden, don't you bloody dare put them into my head!"

"I was thinking about the man who controls them. Or guides them, whatever he does. He prob'ly took a big chance, talking to us. They need him and what he can do, but they're afraid of it…

light, they're afraid of the light… they use these people when they're useful, and then forget about them."

"When was the last time you invited a fishmonger to dinner?"

Cade shut his eyes. "It worries me when you make sense. Or when I think you're making sense." A stifled giggle. "What'd you say the green was again?"

"Like it, do you?"

"C'n you imagine a splinter that suddenly decides to make itself into a building? *There's* something I can use and you could have fun with!"

He sighed and scratched his ear where the woolen cap had irritated his skin. "I s'pose those things would swim anyways, right? I mean, this way, they're useful."

"Thought you didn't want to think about thinking about them."

"Then tell me a story, Quill."

He sat bolt upright, panic in his eyes. "The Treasure! I keep forgetting about the Treasure!"

"It's a boring story. I don't want to hear a boring story. If you're to be boring, I'm going elsewhere. Unless you're about to have an Else*when*, eh?" And that reminded him. "Why'd you look like that when I said about the house?'

"What house?"

"*My* house."

Greenthorn seemed no match for the emotion that came into his eyes. "I–I just—I don't want things to change."

"Why would things change? Rafe got married."

"But everything'll be *different*, and I don't want you to change."

"You're always tellin' me to grow up."

"'S not what I meant." He slumped miserably into the pillows and closed his eyes again. "I dunno what I meant. I didn't mean anything." Whatever he'd meant, and he had meant something, Mieka was sure of it, there'd be no getting it out of him. Within moments, he was asleep. Mieka sighed again, and nearly fell off the bunk when Cade spoke once more.

"Rafe said. It's not just me. Rafe says, too. I'm not crazy."

"Yeh, you are," Mieka whispered. "Dream sweet, Quill." Which for him meant not dreaming at all.

Mieka wanted to knock their audience back on its collective bum. Cade had something more understated in mind—if that was the right term for a clowning farce like "Troll and Trull."

"They're used to words—those and a few costumes and backdrops are all they have to work with, yeh? So we don't give them any words at all, or at least as few as possible. We do it all with the sights and sounds and smells and things."

Jeska's moans of protest weren't so emphatic as they might have been. He'd learned, performing for a court that by and large understood almost nothing he said, that as useful as the words and his voice were, he could produce almost the same effects just using his face and body. He'd said something once, Mieka recalled dimly, about all the facial and physical cues that people registered whether they knew it or not. It was up to Mieka and Rafe to play on those with magic, so the people in the back experienced the same things as those at the front, even if they couldn't see every fine distinction of expression and gesture.

Stripped of its wordplay—much of it comprised of puns a non-native speaker wouldn't understand anyhow—"Troll and Trull" was mainly a lot of visual jokes and broad physical comedy. At the first appearance of the Troll, there was a nervous murmuring through the audience, and Mieka's lip curled. Magic again, magical folk, what was wrong with these fools? But as he danced lightly behind a couple of chairs on which he had arranged the glass baskets, plucking up withies and feeling like a god as he sent magic out for Jeska to play with and Rafe to command, he heard giggles become howls and then roars of laughter and knew that the pair of them had decided to milk it till it mooed.

Rather like old times, he thought, that first show in Gowerion when he'd startled and amazed them all, and found willing partners in the fun. The serious pieces challenged his skills, and he was craftsman enough—Cayden would say *artist* enough—to want them as perfect as he could make them. There was a deep satisfaction that came to him after a really great performance of "Doorways" or "Caladrius." Still, gratifying as the serious pieces were, there was no more direct route to an audience's admiration than laughter.

Like old times, as well, when the coins started piling up onstage. Mieka vaulted over the chairs to help Jeska collect the trimmings, and knew that he had more than enough for the shopping he'd thus far neglected. Bracelets, earrings, necklets, *what*? He hadn't even thought about it until he'd received her letter. But with the coins in his pockets and his hands, and the letter tucked into his jacket, he could think of nothing else.

A few rounds of drinks distracted him. By the time they were back on board ship, and he hoisted himself up to the top bunk, he was as happy as if the greenthorn were still gliding through his veins. When Cade threw a nightshirt over his face, he laughed and threw it back at him.

"We were good tonight!"

"We were," Cade affirmed.

"Why do I always feel better after a show?"

"Because you devour applause. It's not just food and drink— and thorn and fucking. You're a glunsh for adoration."

Mieka sat up, bumped his head on the ceiling, and looked around for something else to throw. Cade was grinning at him.

"And you aren't?" he accused.

"Oh, you wanted the *serious* answer! All right, then. You're happy after a show, first, because it's over. Second, because we did well. Third, because you love doing what you were meant to do. Fourth—"

"Why aren't you the sort of person who can just say, 'I dunno' and leave it at that?"

"You asked."

"And you always have to answer."

"Do you want to hear the rest of it?"

"Say on, O Great Tregetour."

"Fourth, because you need to work."

"Because I feel good after."

"No, because you *need* to work."

"Good Gods! This *is* the serious answer!"

"I repeat: You asked. Everything I give you in those withies, you combine it with your own sort of magic and—it's like you cribble out all the things that bother you, all the stress, get rid of it. I didn't really realize it until just recently. But it's why I could never be anyplace near as good as you are at glisking. You put so much of yourself into it."

"So do you, into the withies."

"But I'm not *using* it. That's the difference. I don't know how else to explain it. I think it puts you back in balance with yourself and everybody else."

He thought about that as he stripped off jacket and shirt. "But doesn't the same thing happen to you with the words? When you write, I mean?"

"Sometimes. If I'm lucky." Cade dragged his nightshirt over his head and flopped into bed. "And if I'm not lucky soon about the Treasure—"

"It'll come. It always does, right?" Craning over the side of the bunk, he asked, "Want some more of that thorn on our way home?"

"If there's any left. I had a look in the roll, Mieka. Like I said, you're a glunsh."

"Hardly the way to talk to the man with the means to make all your dreams come true, Master Silversun!" But he laughed as he said it, and then wriggled out of his trousers and dropped them onto the floor. "Second night out, then."

"Hang those up. If I miss my aim at the piss pot in the dark, you won't have anything to wear tomorrow when you go into town."

"Want to come with?"

"Not if I've written my initials on your pants."

"All right, all right!" He slid down, groped around for his clothing, and flung it into a corner. "Happy? And how did you know I'm going into town tomorrow?"

"You have money. You'll spend it. Good night."

"You're a snarge when you're smug."

"I know."

The shops were a fascinating, if frustrating, experience. He found a million things he wanted, and many things he bought for his family, but nothing that suited his needs. Trouble was, he wouldn't know what those needs were until he found out what *she* wanted. He'd planned to bring home pocketfuls of gemstones and silver and gold and let her take her choice, and now he wasn't even sure if she'd choose him. He fingered the letter he kept in his pocket as a talisman, and could almost taste her scent on his fingers. Renewed despair sent him into a tavern—with the woolen cap pulled firmly down over his ears.

Several drinks later, he emerged blinking owlishly into the bright summer sunlight. He hadn't gone ten paces down the street, looking morosely for more jewelry shops, when a hand tugged at his elbow.

"Please," whispered a voice. "Please, talk?"

"About what?" he snarled, yanking his arm away.

A boy of about fifteen stood before him, three friends of about the same age huddling nearby, staring anxiously. "Please—"

"What is it?" he asked more gently.

"I want to doing as you doing."

"You're too young to drink," he said, conveniently forgetting that he'd first got into a keg of beer at fourteen-and-a-half. His father had been cross, but agreed not to tell his mother—he'd pleaded for hours, for it had been Jed and Jez's keg, and he'd convinced Fa that he didn't want them to get into trouble for leaving it where he could find it. Well, more accurately, leaving it locked in a cupboard barely two days after Jez had taught him how to pick locks.

"Not drinking." Leaning closer, in a whisper: "Magicking."

Oh, shit.

He glanced round. Nobody on the street but casual shoppers—men and women of all ages, children, everything perfectly innocent. Still...

He crooked a finger at the boys, and they followed him around a corner into an alley that served the shops. He could see the street, but they were effectively isolated from passers-by.

"I can't teach you magic," he said abruptly. "You have it or you don't, understand?"

Another of the boys stepped forward. "I have!" he announced, and from beneath his jacket produced one of Touchstone's own withies, six inches long and tinged a faint purple.

"Where the fuck did you get that? Never mind—give it here!" He snatched it and stowed it up one sleeve. "Thought you'd steal some magic, did you?" he demanded, part of him panicking that he and Cade had got so casual about counting up withies at the end of a show. "Waving one of these about don't make you an Elf, nor a Wizard, neither—nor a player. It's got to be in here." He tapped his own temple. "And in here," he added touching his chest. "Understand?"

"But—we were seeing, yesternight—"

How did he explain it to these boys? He could scarcely explain it to himself. All he really knew was that for them, lacking the magic, it was hopeless. They could never be what they wanted so much to be. It wasn't in them. And even if it was, they'd never be allowed to use it. Not here.

He understood Cayden's anger now. His sadness.

It occurred to him that even lacking a withie, he could influence them with a bit of magic to give up their dreams. He'd worked a gentle easing of Blye's grief last year, the sort of manipulation he didn't use very often anymore. But their longing would only come back. There was nothing he could do to make it clear to them how hopeless it was, except to tell them the brutal truth.

So he pulled off his cap to show them his pointed ears.

They blanched, and stared, and two of them turned tail and ran.

"This is what you need to be," he said to the pair who were left. "And you're not. It ain't inside you. So forget about it, eh?"

The boy who'd stolen the withie looked defiant; the other one looked crushed.

"You *can't!*" Mieka snapped, frustrated, regretting the cruelty, knowing how he would have felt if someone had said the same things to him. "Go be merchants or hack drivers or anything else you like, because you can't be this!"

He left them there in the alleyway. He returned to the ship, and wouldn't tell Cade why he was so upset. He let him think it was because he'd found nothing in any of the jewelry shops. And he didn't share his redthorn after their show that night, because he needed the oblivion of sleep.

20

Only one thing remained clearly in Mieka's memory from that voyage home. The furore of the Princess's arrival, the loading of her baggage, the incredible noise of the farewells as the ships sailed out of the harbor—these things he ignored. Or slept through. Or noticed, in the one case, only because the blast of the cannon salute disturbed him from a lovely daydream. He wasn't seasick this time, and he didn't even drink very much. All he wanted was for these interminable days at sea to be over, and to be home, and to find her, and to make her his and his alone.

Only one thing did he recall, and it happened the final night of the trip. Reasoning that he needed to be alert and at least somewhat sober on the morrow, he stashed his thorn-roll in his satchel that evening after dinner, set clean clothes and the netted bag of presents for his family on his bunk, and went up on deck to let the night air clear his head.

And there it was: moonglade.

He watched for hours, it seemed, listening to the slap of waves on the hull and the rustle of sails in the wind, staring spellbound at the crumpled ribbon of silver spreading across dark water.

"I knew you'd be here," Cayden's soft voice said behind him.

"And I knew you would, too—sooner or later." He felt

the warmth of Cade's arm where he stood close beside him, and leaned a little nearer. "Where've you *been*?" he demanded, wishing he didn't sound so much like a petulant child. "I haven't seen you hardly at all, this whole time."

"I thought p'rhaps you needed your tower, or as close as could be to it."

"I've never seen a moonglade from the tower."

After a moment, Cade murmured, "Home tomorrow. At long bloody last."

"Quill… did we do right by going?"

His answer was frustratingly oblique. "It'll work out, Mieka."

"Seen it, have you?"

"No. Not my choices to make."

"You'll never tell me what to do, will you? With my life, I mean—" He chuckled. "For certes, you tell me when and how to *breathe* when it's to do with one of your plays!"

"And you do as you fancy anyhow, have from the very first, so why do I even try?"

Mieka heard the smile in his voice. "You an' me, we're alike that way, y'know. Can't nobody tell us nothin', eh? Not that we heed, or even much listen to." He watched the light on the water for a while in silence. Then: "Make me one, Quill. When you do your piece about people being afraid of the light, of magic— make me one of these."

"How did you know?"

He bounced a few times on the balls of his feet, delighted that he'd guessed right without even being aware that he was guessing. Instincts again, he told himself gleefully, his instincts that would never steer him wrong. "Oh, I'm a wonder, I am!"

"Shy and modest, as well."

"And there's another way we're alike!" He bumped Cade with a shoulder. "I know something else. You'll never put on view where the light leads. Like in 'Doorways.' Not your choice to make, what comes of following the moonglade."

"Care to write it for me?"

"You're not peeved with me, so don't pretend. Vered Goldbraider wants people to think. Rauel Kevelock, he wants them to feel. But Cayden Silversun wants them to make their own choices."

A little while later, Cade said abruptly, "We never used the thorn, that second night out."

"Sorry for that. I can send some along with you home, if you like."

"Beholden. I keep meaning to ask. How did you first find—I mean, when did you begin—?"

"I was about thirteen, fourteen. Shocked? Don't be. Fa had a name for me. Little Lord Ascian, the one without a shadow, because I never stood still long enough for the sunlight to catch me." He smiled and shook his head. "I drove poor Mum stark staring mad. We couldn't afford a physicker, but they took me to one anyways, and he said I was just contrary enough to warrant a contrary type of remedy. Bluethorn."

"But—doesn't bluethorn—?"

"Yeh, I know. *More* energy? But it worked. 'Twas only now and then, just when I got really outrageous. It lets me concentrate, if you can credit it. By then it was past hoping it'd do me any good in school, of course. I knew what I wanted to be, though, and it took me through lessons in glisking."

"I'm not understanding. How can something that quickens the way bluethorn does let you focus on fewer than a thousand thoughts at once?"

"You know better than to ask me how or why something works," he chided. "For me, it's enough that it does."

Cade seemed to think this over, then said, "The rest of you catches up with your brain, is that it? Like catching the current in the river and going along with it, instead of trying to fight it all the time."

Mieka shrugged. "Could be."

When the ship's bell rang the hour, they both flinched.

"It's late," Cade muttered. "And chilly."

"Just a while longer, Quill, please. I'll be wakeful half the night anyways."

So they stayed, and before the next bell the captain shifted their course, and the moonglade was behind them. Far off, just visible as lights like stars floating in formation on the sea, the Princess's ship slid into view.

"I wager she doesn't sleep much tonight, either," Mieka said.

"Who? Oh—the Princess."

"Well, and Lady Vrennerie, too." He glanced up and sideways, and could barely make out Cade's forceful profile. "You've decided about her, haven't you? Don't tell me it's her decision to make. You could have her if you want her. The ways she looks at you—and you do want her, Cayden."

"Not enough."

"You won't let yourself."

"Leave it be, Mieka."

Warning in that tone, and in the rigidity of his muscles. "I think you're wrong."

"And I think you don't have the first fucking clue what you're talking about." He pushed away from the railing.

Mieka caught at his arm. "I'm sorry, Quill—truly, I'm sorry. Don't be cross with me."

Thin shoulders slumped a bit. "I'm not. I'm angry with myself—well, and with you, too, for being right. Come on, it really is cold up here."

It felt to Mieka as if he'd only just closed his eyes to sleep when shouts and cheers and the booming of cannon woke him. After bumping his head on the ceiling for what he swore would be the very last time, he scrambled out of bed and bumped into Cayden. They washed quickly, dressed, and were up on deck to see a magnificent sight: hundreds and hundreds of boats, all come out to welcome the new Princess home. Sailboats of every size, rowboats, fishing trawlers, pleasure barges, anything that plied the Gally below the Plume or ventured out to sea, they swarmed like bees at the river's mouth and set the captains of the King's ships to frantic lowering of sails lest they plow right into the jostle.

Mieka laughed, and waved at the people crowded onto the boats, and felt his heart stutter with the thought that mayhap *she* might—but no, her mother would never allow—

And then they were at the docks, and completely ignored for the other ship, and he danced impatiently at the railing and squinted into the welcoming throng. Surely her mother would let her come to greet him, surely she would plead and beg that she had to see him as soon as may be, she simply *had* to see him—

He caught sight of his family: the tall figures of his eldest brothers, Jezael with Tavier on his shoulders, Jedris with a protective arm around Blye, who was barely visible beside Mum and Fa and Jinsie. For a moment he was surprised that he'd never before thought of Blye as family, but now of course she was—and then the warmth iced over as he saw his twin sister and wanted to strangle her for her interference in his life, for wanting to make his choices for him. He found Rafe's parents nearby, with Mistress Bowbender, but no Crisiant, and that worried him. Nobody expected Cayden's parents to come welcome him home, but Derien had evidently hitched a ride with Jed and Blye, for there he was, right out front, jumping up and down and waving both arms.

No, wait—Crisiant was there, just hidden briefly by Petrinka and Cilka. She looked… thinner. All at once Mieka knew what had happened, and turned to Rafe in anguish. The fettler had seen, too, and understood; he rubbed both hands over his face and beard, then shook back his hair and pasted on a smile.

Mieka tugged at Cade's arm, and tiptoed to whisper, "Crisiant lost the baby." Cade stared down at him, shocked. "Do we say anything?"

"Is there anything to say? Take up your cue from her and Rafe."

Elsewhere there were trumpets and shoutings, and royal ceremonies, and uniformed guardsmen queued up in bright array. When he finally set foot on the dock, Mieka fell into his parents' embrace, hugged Blye, pretended Jinsie didn't exist, and before he knew it, they were all in hire-hacks going home to Wistly Hall.

All of them, including Cade and Dery, Jeska and his mother, and the four Threadchasers. Mistress Mirdley, he was told, was there supervising the come-home feast. The only thing Mieka wanted to do was catch the next public coach to Frimham—after he murdered Jinsie, of course—but for the rest of the afternoon and on into the evening he was trapped.

Aware that this was not a gracious way of looking at things, he exerted himself to be his usual self. Only Cade seemed to know what the effort entailed; every so often Mieka caught a wry, sympathetic glance from gray eyes. But this was his family all round him. He couldn't disappoint them—not just the Windthistles and Blye (who'd become family long before she married Jed, he realized all at once), but Cade, Dery, Mistress Mirdley, Jeska and his mother, Rafe's parents—and he hurt anew for Rafe and Crisiant's loss every time he looked at them. They relied on him, all of them did, to tell the best stories and make the funniest jokes. It was his responsibility to them as surely as it was his responsibility to be the best glisker in the world for Touchstone. There was food and drink to be shared, and presents to be found and opened and exclaimed over, and if anybody noticed that he'd brought absolutely nothing home for Jinsie, it was lost in the tale of how he'd acquired the carpet.

His father and siblings roared with laughter. His mother covered her face with her hands. Mieka glossed over the tricky bits, making the barkeeper rude instead of threatening, leaving out entirely their flight from the tavern and Cade's curtain of magical fire. He caught a searching glance from Blye, and promised himself he'd tell her the whole of it some other time. But for now he had to be Mieka—*clever and mad*, as she'd called it—and he'd had years of practice at playing fast and loose with the truth if it made for a better story. Or, of course, if it kept him out of trouble.

He slipped only once. Cade had atoned for Mieka's neglect by giving Jinsie a beautiful beaded coinbag. She was nearly in tears when she saw it, and cast Mieka a look of furious hurt before flinging her arms around Cade's neck and kissing him on both cheeks. The subsequent teasing might have embarrassed everyone, except that right then Rafe called for Tavier's attention and asked if he still had any interest in a dragon's egg.

Gods only knew when or where he'd found it. He'd said nothing to Mieka. It turned out to be a fat oval of tin painted white, invisibly hinged on the inside. Open, it revealed a tiny pottery dragon, crimson wings spread, talons touched with silver.

"I couldn't find a real one," Rafe apologized. "But I hope this will do until I can."

Tavier nodded solemnly and put his small arms around as much of Rafe as he could, and hugged tight. Again Mieka was heartsick, realizing how wonderful a father Rafe would be, and what he and Crisiant had lost.

Shortly thereafter the party began to break up. It was still light outside by the time the last hire-hacks departed Wistly, but much too late for the last coach to Frimham. After waving farewell to Cade and Dery and Mistress Mirdley, Mieka took a bottle and glass out to the back lawn and sat in the least rickety of the garden chairs. He'd been there, watching the late afternoon traffic on the river, for only a few minutes before he heard his twin's voice behind him.

"You're a right shit-head, and well you know it," Jinsie told him, and plunked down onto the grass with her back to him. She was fingering the beadwork on the bag Cade had given her.

"Shit-head? Look in the mirror," he retorted. "I know what happened to my letters."

"Cade said. He even tried to apologize for you." She snorted. "Much good any of it did me, so I'll only say this once and have done with it. I don't like her."

"I don't care."

"If you're fool enough to ask her, and she's fool enough to have you, I still won't like her, and I won't pretend to."

"Did you go deaf while I was gone? I just said I don't fucking care!"

"But as it seems you're determined to marry her, and you'll find this out soon enough, I'll tell you. Her mother took work at the Palace, making gowns for Princess Iamina. They have lodgings—"

"Didn't Mum and Fa ask them to stay here?" he demanded.

"They did, and were refused. As I was saying, they have lodgings over in the Hestings, round a couple of corners from the Palace." She turned her head, adding viciously, "And just up the block from the Guards' barracks. I'm sure she finds it convenient."

His chest clenched so tight that he couldn't breathe.

"I assume," she finished, "you'll want to hurry over there right now for a dog's match."

They hadn't fought it out with their fists since they were twelve years old. Mum had raged while she took care of bruises and black eyes; Fa had told him later, very solemnly, that he wasn't a child anymore and any man who hit a woman was no man at all. Thus Mieka settled for kicking his chair over as he stood up.

"Don't ever speak to me again."

"Mieka—"

"Ever!" And he ran back up to the house.

"No, sorry, never met them."

"What's that name again, lad? Plenty of seamstresses hereabouts. After all, so many fine ladies to keep in petticoats and silk underdrawers!"

"Dunno. Don't much care."

"Hells, boy, do I look that stupid? If I knew a girl that pretty, I'd be keeping her for meself!"

It was growing dark and Mieka still had not identified which amongst all the grace-and-favor flats was the right one. He didn't even know which building. There were half a dozen of the five-story structures, made of leftover brick and stone from various Palace expansions, arranged around a central square, where lesser servants (he winced at the very notion) were allowed to live rent-free. Their pay was accordingly reduced. Free lodging and the distinction of serving the Royals and their retinues was considered recompense enough.

At first he'd asked using their name. Considering that each building had at least twenty flats of varying sizes, odds were that unless he happened upon one of their near neighbors in the street he'd never find them at all. So then he tried a reference to her mother's profession. No help there, either. A single attempt at a verbal sketch of her produced chortling mockery. (Well, mayhap he'd been a bit lyrical in his description.) At last he stood in the little square of summer-parched lawn, furious and frustrated. There were people all round him and none of them was the right one. He couldn't have felt more alone and foreign if he'd been back on the Continent surrounded by those whose language he didn't speak and whose eyes unerringly found his ears and whose prejudices instantly judged him dangerous. Soon the Elf-light in the streetlamps would ignite, and he was about to make a complete fool of himself by standing in the square yelling her surname when he saw her mother coming round the corner from the Palace.

"You!" she exclaimed as he skidded to a stop in front of her. "What are *you* doing here?"

"Me? What about you? Leaving her all alone in the flat all day—are you insane?"

"Who says she's alone?"

Staring into her smirking face, for the second time that day he came close to striking a woman. If he'd had Cade's talents and Wizardly training, he would have incinerated the old bitch on the spot.

"You've a nerve, you have, coming round after all this time!" Shouldering past him, she gasped when he grabbed her arm to stop her. "Leave be! I'll call the constables, I will!"

"Where is she? Who's she with?"

"And why should I tell you a single word of it? Vanished, didn't you, for months, gadding about all the way across the sea, off with your playmates, all whiskey and wine, while we're here scrabbling to make ends meet! Never a thought to her, never a word—"

"I—my letters—"

"Oh, and dozens of them there were, too! Meantimes she's crying her eyes out every night, no matter that I'm telling her over and again that I knew you were no good, no use, just a pretty little boy who doesn't know how to be a man—"

"Tell me where she is!" he bellowed.

A small crowd had gathered by now, attracted by this very public entertainment. It wasn't the sort of show he was used to giving, and not the way he liked being watched. It was too... honest. He didn't know what to do. Jeska would have held his temper and charmed the old woman and been invited in for tea. Rafe would simply have stared her down with those cool blue-gray eyes until she wilted. Cayden—oh, Cayden would never demean himself by shouting in the street to provide a scandal and a relishing for the neighbors, but then again, Cayden didn't have the balls to go after the girl he wanted, either.

"Tell me," Mieka said at last, trying to control himself and failing. "Tell me, or I'll rip down every fucking door from here to the Palace—"

"Mieka! Oh, *Mieka!*"

It was everything he wanted to hear in the only voice he wanted to hear: startled delight, longing, eagerness, giddy excitement. He spun on one heel.

The man by her side was an off-duty guardsman. The stiff brush-cut of his hair, the height, the square-shouldered bearing, all were familiar to Mieka from providing these things, plus uniform, for Jeska onstage. Handsome in a sun-browned, carroty-haired way, he was frowning and he dared clasp his hand about her waist.

The guardsman was almost a foot taller and at least sixty pounds heavier, and Mieka went for him with both fists. He even landed a punch, right in the man's rock-solid stomach, before a clip to the side of his head sent him reeling. He was stupid enough, enraged enough, to go back for more. He kicked and connected, and the guardsman staggered back, clutching his groin, before opening his mouth in a roar that rattled the glass streetlamps. A moment later, Mieka was on the ground with no very clear notion of how he'd got there until the agony began in his belly.

"Stop it—oh, please, stop!" She knelt beside him, hands fluttering over his face, his shoulders.

"Sniveling little Elf! Get up and take it!"

Mieka stumbled to his feet. She stood in front of him, weeping, and he pushed her aside.

"She's *my* girl now, Elferboy," the guardsman taunted.

"No, I never—Mieka, *please!*"

He'd never been much good at Elfenfire. The blood smearing his vision wasn't helping. Nothing so disciplined as actual thought directed the sudden ragged sheet of yellow-gold light that rippled in the air between him and the guardsman. Someone screamed.

"I'll have the law on you!"

Mieka's lip lifted in a sneer. "Big strapping guardsman like you, scared of a bit of magic?"

The water-blue gaze regarded him with revulsion before shifting towards her. "She ain't worth it," he announced, and took himself and the remnants of his dignity off to the Palace.

Abruptly exhausted, and understanding why Cayden had been so knackered after a similar demonstration, Mieka let the pale glitter fade—or, more precisely, he watched it flicker and die. Using the magic inside a withie, and using that withie to focus that magic, was one thing. Creating it all on his own was quite another.

"Mieka—"

He turned slowly, wiping blood from his eyelids and cheeks. "It's not true, is it?" he whispered. "You're not—?"

"Never! It's only—I didn't hear and didn't hear and I didn't know where you were until Mum saw in the broadsheet about Touchstone—I had to, Mieka, I had to write on the chance you'd get my letter and—"

"I've been out of my mind with worrying—"

"Tell me you still love me, please tell me you still love me—"

"*Love* you?" He caught her close in his arms and covered her face with kisses.

And then a roar of applause and a shrilling of whistles reminded him that they had an audience. A shouting match, a brief fistfight, a display of magic, and now a lovers' reunion: this was better than paying to see a play. They'd talk about it for weeks.

"Where can we go?" he asked urgently.

"Our flat—"

"You can't take him up there!" her mother cried. "It's not decent for a young girl to—"

"You!" Mieka yelled. "Shut it and stay out!"

She folded her arms and glowered. At the entryway of their building, he glanced back and caught a look of smug satisfaction on her face.

There was more swift, incoherent, tearful explanation on their way up seemingly endless flights of stairs. They'd been in Frimham when Princess Iamina and her ladies arrived for a fortnight seaside, and that had led to a Court appointment as seamstress, because Princess Iamina needed new and beautiful clothes for all the festivities surrounding her nephew's wedding.

He listened, incredibly weary, barely taking in the tale of being seen at a tea shop with a friend—a *girl* friend, she quickly added—by one of the Princess's ladies. The very next day a footman had come to the door with a Royal Command. She had gone with her mother to model the clothes.

"The cut didn't much suit me, nor the colors," she went on artlessly, "not on any of the gowns. But Mum knew what she was about, oh she for certes did! There's a jewel the Princess wears—"

"I've seen it, yeh. Let me guess. All the dresses were made to flatter that jewel."

"Wasn't that clever?"

The yellow flower was spectacular. He could readily understand how Princess Iamina would be desperate to cut as magnificent a figure as possible, considering she was many years older than the new Princess. To build a wardrobe around the theme of her fabulous jewel of yellow pearls and diamonds—yes, that was a cunning move, well worth the risk of investing in silks and velvets and lace to make up some tempting samples.

"Here," she said softly, and unlocked the door.

One room. Huge windows. Thick, dark wooden floor; brick walls; two chairs, a table, a standing wardrobe, and a single bed almost wide enough for two. They'd used leftover material to make curtains, with incongruous frills of lace at the hems, and a bright quilted counterpane and pillows.

"Mum asked for this one specially," she said. "The windows."

He walked the eight steps to them and looked out. Rooftops, the building next door, and a glimpse of a Palace tower.

"There's light enough to see all day long for sewing, without having to stoke a fire."

In summer, the heat from a fire bright enough to sew by would be unendurable—not that the hearth was big enough to hold more than a few sticks of wood or a handful of coal. He turned, and the sight of her exquisite beauty in this shabby attic made his heart hurt.

"If you could have anything you wanted," he heard himself say, "what would it be?"

"I want you."

"You have me. What else do you want? What shall I give you?"

She hesitated, still standing by the open door. "I—I want a drawing room, Mieka, a real drawing room, like in the best houses—with pretty chairs and velvet—and curtains with silk tassels. Blue silk tassels."

He smiled. She really was a darling. "Just a drawing room?" he teased. "Not a whole house?"

She caught her breath. "Of our own?"

"Just for us." He saw a flicker of dismay cross her face, and gritted himself, and added, "And your mother, too, if she likes. She'll be company for you while I'm on the Circuit."

"And—" Shyly, eyes downcast, she whispered, "And she can help me with the baby."

He saw it then. She had a roundness to her, a fullness to her cheeks, a lushness to her figure. What Rafe had wanted so much and lost, he would have without even having thought much about it.

He didn't know what to do. What to say. She bit her lips together and shifted slightly, her skirts whispering.

"A nursery, then, as well," he managed at last. "And it'll have curtains with blue silk tassels, too."

She looked at him with radiant eyes—such amazing eyes, the rich purple-blue of irises. "Are you... are you pleased?"

"Yeh. Yeh, I am." She was the most beautiful thing he'd ever seen, and she was his, and yet here she stood in this squalid little room, and suddenly he couldn't stand it. "You can't stay here. I won't let you stay here." He moved to the bed and plucked up the counterpane, tossed it onto the table, opened the wardrobe and started grabbing clothes. "You're coming home with me. Right now, right this instant."

"But—Mum—"

"*My* mother will take care of you. We'll be married by next week—" He realized he had no tokens to give her, no necklet or bracelet or anything at all in the collection of presents he'd bought on the journey, only some trinkets, a shawl, a pair of gloves. And no toys for the baby, he thought—no, that was wrong, he had a box full of them, intended for Rafe and Crisiant's child. He and Cade had picked them out.

"Next week?"

He returned to the more important point. "Nothing grand, and I'm sorry for it, but—"

"But with the baby coming at Wintering, we ought to hurry." She nodded. "I don't mind. Truly, Mieka."

He left off piling clothes onto the counterpane and moved to take her in his arms. Holding her close, feeling the softness of her, the fullness of her belly, he wondered how he could have not known until she told him.

All at once he laughed, and kissed her, and together they

knotted the counterpane around her clothes and started down the stairs. They met her mother halfway down, and the outrage in the old woman's eyes swiftly became smirking complacence again, once she learned there would be a wedding. Mieka didn't care. Let her think and say and do as she fancied.

He didn't care about Jinsie's stunned exclamation, either, when he flung open the front door of Wistly Hall. He gave her a look to char beefsteak, and called out, "Mum! Fa! We're home!"

21

Sagging with weariness after so many weeks of travel, Cade felt as if they'd already been on a circuit tour. But they'd played only a few shows on the Continent, that last three of them for naught but trimmings, and Jeska was right when he said they were rusty. They had to work, and work hard, before the Winterly.

Cade had too much to do. He was too tired and, contrarily, too restless, to do any of it. As far as the practical matters of his profession were concerned, there were the pieces to be decided on for the Winterly Circuit; conferences with Kearney Fairwalk regarding itinerary, accommodations, days off, and pay; withies to be counted and ordered, and glass baskets to be checked for damage; clothing for the stage and for warmth to be sorted and cleaned. Personally, he still had a double handful of Elsewhens to organize and label inside his own head. And then there was the nagging problem of "Treasure."

And Lady Vrennerie.

And Mieka.

The very first on his list of things he didn't want to do was helping Mieka decide on a house.

He was roped into it a week following their return. It was not in Mieka's power to surprise Cade with the news of his marriage;

he'd known it was coming. Simple knowledge of Mieka, not an Elsewhen, had warned him in advance. Neither was he surprised about the child, although this, too, involved no special foresight on his part.

Mieka had left it to Blye to inform Cade the day after the ceremony.

"Mishia sent word round to invite us to dinner," Blye fretted. "We didn't expect a wedding!"

They were seated in the kitchen at Number Eight, Redpebble Square, over cups of a hot mocah spiced with cinnamon. Cade had brought back a large box of it for Mistress Mirdley, along with half a dozen kinds of tea and a copper cloak-pin in the shape of a kettle, which had amused her even as she scolded him for spending his hard-earned money on her.

"Just as well nobody knew," Cade said. "None of us could be there anyways. Jeska's helping his mother move, Rafe and Crisiant—" He broke off and sought refuge in a gulp of mocah that tingled on his tongue. Rafe and Crisiant were in seclusion, in mourning.

"And as for you," Derien accused, "once you got home, you slept for two days and then disappeared into the Archives! I haven't hardly seen you at all."

Neither had anybody else, especially not Lady Jaspiela, who had made several attempts to corner and interrogate him about the new Princess. Cade had avoided her, just as he had avoided Wistly Hall. He had been in no mood to watch Mieka marry the girl he knew would turn out to be his ruin. He shrugged, ruffled his little brother's hair, and replied, "You can come with me to inspect the house Mieka wants to buy."

The ceremony had been a small one, just family one evening in the torchlit garden, but Mieka had promised a grand party once he found a house. To that purpose, he'd vanished each day for a week, armed with a list of properties for sale and to let, doing it all on his own until he discovered a house that was almost perfect, he informed Cade (in a note as scrawlingly illegible and badly spelled as ever; some things would never change).

"What's he want to go live out in the wilderness for?" Dery asked. "He's a Gallybanker, not a farmer! We'll never see *him*, either!"

Blye smiled. "When you don't inherit a house, you take what you can afford, where you can afford it."

"But I thought Touchstone was swimming in money!"

"It isn't out in the wilderness, smatchet," Cade teased. "It's but an hour upriver. And talking of rivers, I never had the chance to hear about your wedding trip, Blye."

"I already asked when they got home," Dery told him. "There's nothing to tell about where they went or what they saw—" He danced out of reach of Mistress Mirdley's wooden stirring spoon before finishing, "—because they never left the barge the whole time!"

Blye turned crimson. Cayden nearly strangled trying not to laugh. And Mistress Mirdley, who could move a lot faster than anyone gave her credit for, rapped Derien sharply over the knuckles.

"Keep a civil tongue between your teeth or you'll spend the day in your room!"

"But Cade says I can go with him to Mieka's new house!"

"Have fun," Blye said. "Beholden, Mistress Mirdley, but I ought to get back now. Jed should be finished with the drawings by now for Mieka's wedding present."

"It's a cabinet," Dery said. "With beveled glass windows."

"Rikka's uncle is doing the hardware," Blye added. "I'll ask about your new cauldron when he brings them along, Mistress Mirdley." And she betook herself off to the glassworks.

"Go put on a clean shirt," Cade advised Derien. "And comb your hair. And try not to say anything stupid, right? No matter how hopeless this house of Mieka's looks."

When he raced upstairs, Mistress Mirdley eyed Cade sidelong. "Don't let that Elf do anything stupid," she said. "By which I mean make sure there's a decent kitchen in this *almost perfect* house."

"I doubt he's even looked to see that there *is* a kitchen."

But he had, and there was. Not a very big one, and it wanted the warm gleam of copper and a hearthfire and some comfortably cushioned chairs, but a nice kitchen all the same.

Cade was glad he'd asked Derien along. Mieka and the boy kept each other entertained on the long drive upriver and inland. Dery had brought a map of the Home Province, and traced their route diligently while Mieka pretended that his new house was somewhere off the page, in a village so tiny, it wouldn't be on any maps. Dery eyed him askance.

"Everything in the world is on a map, so that you can always know where you are!"

"Is that all it takes?" Mieka asked whimsically. "A map? Did you hear that, Cayden?"

"I made a map of all the places you went on the Continent," the boy went on. "Tobalt Fluter published one in *The Nayword*, but he was wrong about the days and distances. Being on the river made you get there a lot faster. So *my* map is right."

Cade caught Mieka's swift glance at him; they both remembered the river only too well.

"I'd like to see it, this map of yours," Mieka said. "I'm not sure I always know where I am, and I'm *really* confused sometimes about where I'm going, but it'd be nice to have some certainty about where I've been!"

Once they reached the house, at the end of a lane that backed onto open fields, the pair of them leaped from the hire-hack and Cade was glad of that, too, for he suddenly knew what was about to happen to him.

The instant he saw the house, he knew it was coming. The

outlines of roof and windows and doors were the same, even though the last time he'd seen the place it had been night. There was no mistaking the tilt of the chimney, the broken stones of the front walk.

Gulping a deep breath, he got out and told the driver to wait, and hoped he'd be able to cover the Elsewhen once it beset him. Better still, he'd be alone when it came. But he couldn't count on that.

"Needs a bit of sprucing," Mieka said, unlocking the front door.

"A bit?" Dery echoed as one of the hinges came loose.

Making a face at him, Mieka gestured grandly and bowed them inside.

Cade could actually feel it, sense it, hovering at the edges of his mind. He took one step, then two, barely hearing as Mieka enthused about the spaciousness of the drawing room, the four bedchambers upstairs (two that overlooked a tributary of the Gally river), the possibilities of the kitchen.

They went there first, down the narrow hall, and Cade managed to say something about how pleased Mistress Mirdley would be that there was actually a place to cook. He felt the Elsewhen ease off, for there were no echoes in this room, which he had never seen before. He'd resisted glancing to the left while in the entry, wary of the room where firelight had glowed while pages were ripped from a folio and burned.

Mieka urged them back through the passage and raced Dery up the stairs, dust whirling in their wake. It was then that Cayden made his mistake—or perhaps the real error had been in bringing Derien along. He glanced up, and saw his little brother's face peering from between the railings, and heard him call out, "Cade! Hurry!" In the next instant he glimpsed another face. Only memory—and although for one of the few times in his life he was prepared for when it came, it wasn't what he'd expected to see at all.

{Empty.

He walked slowly through the door. Paused a few steps from the hall into the drawing room with its cold hearth and scarred wooden floor, remembered the rustle of pages and the flaring of fire as they burned, one by one. Whatever chairs or tables or cupboards had been here once, they were gone now.

Empty.

He climbed the stairs wearily, not touching the oaken banister so thick with dust, almost as dirty as the first time he'd actually been in this house, scratched and splintering now with the many impacts of fists and fire irons and broken glass and Mieka's drunken thorn-sullied staggering body. There was no carpet anymore to bunch and trip on, no framed Trials medals on the walls to fall and shatter. Just the worn, dirty wood underfoot, and broken railings.

Empty.

He bypassed the bedchambers and went to the end of the passage, opened the door of Mieka's hideaway, hearing the familiar creak of hinges that had needed oiling for so long that to oil them now would seem like anointing the dead. She had kept them noisy to warn her when her husband had surfaced from immersion in alcohol and thorn.

It was not quite empty in here. A tall oaken cupboard still stood in the far corner—a fine piece of furniture once, with beveled glass set in the doors. Wedding present from Jed and Blye. One of the doors had been kicked in, wrenched almost off its upper hinge, the sole remaining pane of glass a splintered spiderweb.

A breeze through a window left open to the rain—there were water stains on the floor, and the casement had warped— fluttered something on a bottom shelf. He crossed the small, narrow room, deliberately not remembering the two deep velvet chairs where he'd sat so often with Mieka, the small cabinet between them with neat racks of glass thorns and paper twists, the tray of fine whiskeys and brandies and a set of Blye's most elegant goblets. Crouching before the broken glass door, he squinted through the dust and recognized without much surprise a copy of their first portfolio, the one they'd used that first Winterly Circuit. The pages had been tied with a purple ribbon. He reached for them, steady-handed, and undid the knot.

"Dragon." "Sailor's Sweetheart." "Silver Mine." "Troll and Trull." "Hidden Cottage." He turned pages, seeing the color-coding and private symbols he and Mieka had worked out together, and cramped scribbled notes on performing.

More here—make them feel it! and *Green shirt NOT red* and *Anger fading to regret* and *Make sure Quill gives me enough for this—*

—and all at once seeing that name in Mieka's handwriting brought tears to his eyes.}

"Quill?"

There were tears in his eyes. He knuckled them away and smiled down into the worried face, and managed a cough and an exaggerated sniffle. "I'd better go outside before I start a sneezing fit—with a nose like mine, I'd break all the windows."

"It's a bit dusty," Mieka admitted. "But it'll be a good house, once it's polished up and furnished—don't you think?"

"You really want to buy it?"

"I want to know what you think."

"I think the only thing holding those timbers together are the worms curling up in them."

"That's why the Gods gave me two brothers who work construction." He peered up into Cade's face, suspicious. "Did you just—?"

"Can we have lunching on the back porch, Cade?" Derien yelled from upstairs.

"Why don't you run get the hamper?" he called back.

"Quill," Mieka said warningly.

"Doesn't take an Elsewhen to know that the chimney will come tumbling down in the first stiff wind. And I'm surprised that with those ears you can't hear the mice in the walls."

"You hate it," Mieka said, crestfallen.

"I hate to think how much it would cost to put everything to rights. Why don't you find a place that doesn't need so much work? Brothers or no brothers, it'd be months before you could move in here."

Mieka walked into the drawing room, over to the cold and empty hearth. Cade followed uncertainly, watching as he ran his fingers over the stone mantel.

"You're right," Mieka announced abruptly. "I'd do better to spend it all on something that's ready now."

"You can make changes to whatever you buy," Cade suggested, trying not to sound relieved. "Put your own hallmark on it. This one's just a little too much to deal with, innit?"

He sighed, and nodded, and Cade reminded himself to spend part of this evening relegating the Elsewhens about this house to the *Never Will Be* portion of his mind. Though he knew others would take their places, he could only hope that none would include wandering through a house Mieka had abandoned. It had been like picking over a corpse.

They ate the meal Mistress Mirdley had packed for them, then gave in to Derien's plea and told the driver to take the long way round back to Redpebble Square. It was the last day of school holidays, and he was determined to stretch it out as long as possible, for he had a pile of books waiting for him at home in preparation for his first classes on the morrow. Cayden knew that as a good, conscientious elder brother, he ought to get the boy home in time to do some work, but it was a lovely day and he was so grateful about the house that he, too, wanted to make the afternoon last.

Of such fond and innocent indulgence of a younger brother were Elsewhens created.

It lacked three hours before twilight, and they were still eight or ten miles outside the edges of Gallantrybanks, when Derien pointed to a stooped old man pounding a sign into the dirt. The sign read SELLING AUGHT. Beyond it was an oddly sprawling fieldstone cottage: one level, a central square with slightly shorter wings to the left and right, thatched roof, two chimneys, a trellis above the lych-gate overrun with climbing yellow roses. Surrounded by a three-foot fieldstone wall, the property included a wooden outbuilding almost big enough to qualify as a barn. Bricks that matched the chimneys were set in a swirling pattern from the gate to the front door. Windows gleamed in the afternoon sun, dazzling Cade's eyes.

{He had no idea what he'd find here—well, no, that wasn't strictly true. Mieka would be here. Exactly how drunk or thorned-up he'd be was the uncertainty. He told himself to prepare for anything. As if that were possible, with Mieka Windthistle.

Everything looked normal, even charming under the light dusting of snow that glistened the winter morning. Tidy stone wall, trellis arching above the lych-gate, brick walkway and chimneys, stone cottage with shining windows, wooden "Lodge" as Mieka had named it when he turned the little barn's hayloft into a hideaway reminiscent of his tower lair at Wistly. Cade descended from his carriage and told his driver to come back in an hour. He waited until the clatter of hooves and wheels faded up the road, then pulled his cloak more closely around him and opened the gate.

He was halfway up the walk before he heard noises from inside the Lodge. Yes, that was where Mieka would be: hunched in one of the velvet chairs, filthy and unshaven, bottle in one hand and thorn-roll in the other as he tried to decide what to use next.

Biting both lips together, Cade strode through the cottage yard and was within steps of the Lodge when its door burst open and Mieka hurtled into him.

"Quill! Run for it!"

He was laughing, a maniacal grin splitting his flushed face, those eyes bright and wild. Cade was dragged along by an elbow to the front of the cottage, where Mieka pressed him against the wall and peered around the corner.

The Lodge exploded.

"Ha!" Mieka roared, clapping both hands together. "Brilliant! C'mon, Quill, let's do the rest!"

"The rest—?"

Mieka dug into the pockets of his greatcoat and within moments Cade's hands were full of trailing coils of fuse rope and packets that trickled black powder onto the snow. The Elf held up an elegant engraved silver flint-rasp and clicked it a few times, sniggering as Cade spluttered and backed off in case the sparks hit the powder. "Come *on*!"

"Mieka—you can't just—"

"Can't I? Watch me! Everything worth anything is gone. Whatever's left, I still own it—for the next few days, until the law courts come after me—and I can do as I fancy with it—"

"And you've a fancy to blast it all to bits?"

"I always knew you were a bright lad, Quill! I'm glad you're here—it would've taken *hours* to set up all by meself."

"Mieka, I won't—"

"Yeh, you bloody well will!" Merriment turned to fierce rage with a swiftness that startled even Cade, who was long used to Mieka's reckless emotions. "Drove all the way out here to see if you could do anything to help, didn't you? Well, *help* me!" Another dizzying swerve, another dazzling impudent grin. "Look at it this way—help me do it right, and you won't have to worry about picking random bits and pieces of me from the wreckage!"}

Mieka had left the hire-hack and was talking animatedly with the old man. Derien had climbed atop the fieldstone wall, polite enough not to run about where he hadn't been invited but itching to leap down and explore. As Cade caught his breath and subdued the queasy wambling of his stomach, he saw a grin break like sudden sunlight across Mieka's face.

He'd helped Mieka stash the powder charges and light the fuses. He knew he had. He remembered feeling a sudden upsurge of turbulent joy in potential destruction. And in this Elsewhen, plotting the annihilation of his own house, Mieka was *alive*.

So when Cayden climbed down from the hire-hack, he was able to smile when Mieka yattered on about how this house was made of stone so there wouldn't be any mice, and the thatch was only a year old, and weren't the roses beautiful, there were three bedrooms and a sitting room and a big kitchen, and the price is just about what the other one was, and let's go inside and take a look, Quill, shall we?

The village lawyer was sent for. Rafe could have haggled the price down much better than Mieka or Cade, and it didn't help that Derien was racing all over the place, begging them to come see this or that marvel, especially the view of the woodlands descending into a dell at the back of the house. Cade knew he ought to caution Mieka to have his brothers come out and take a look at the place before he actually agreed to purchase it. Perhaps something impetuous remained inside him from the sight of all that black explosive powder. This wasn't the other house—it was all he could think, that this wasn't that other house. He'd help Mieka buy this one because sooner or later he'd help him get rid of it, and whatever mutilation of a life he'd live here with her.

By the time they got back into the hire-hack, the local Minster chimes had rung five, and Mieka was the rapturous new owner (provisionally) of a rambling cottage, an almost-barn, and half an acre of land. Moving in would have to wait until the old man had packed up all his belongings for the relocation to his grandson's house outside Lilyleaf, but that would also provide time to purchase and deliver a few basics of furniture.

Cade wasn't at all surprised when Mieka directed the driver to head for the shops near Redpebble Square. He was puzzled, however, when the Elf ignored all the furnishers in favor of a draper's shop, just about to close up for the night, and came back out within five minutes chortling over a dozen blue silk tassels.

Amazingly, Mieka and his new wife moved into the house within a fortnight. Each day was spent in packing, organizing, shopping, and preparing; almost each night was spent at the Kiral Kellari, the Keymarker, or another tavern playing a show, which meant that the shows themselves had to serve as rehearsals. They had precious little time left before the start of the Winterly Circuit.

Cade spent his days in his room or at the Archives. Kearney had ordered relevant books from his Fairwalk Manor library sent to Redpebble Square, and provided the equivalent of a Royal Writ, signed by some functionary indebted to His Lordship, for free access to whatever mouldy old tomes and documents Cade thought might aid him in writing "Treasure."

It wasn't going well.

On the nights Touchstone wasn't working, Cade sought inspiration in thorn. He dreamed, right enough, but they were *dreams*, not visions, and cumulative frustration made him surly.

For some reason known only to the recalcitrant inner workings of his mind, almost all he could think about was the old man seated at the prow of that barge on the Vathis River, conjuring purple-gold light that teased and taunted those massive monsters surging through the water.

Praise be to the Lord, the Lady, all the Angels, and the Old Gods that he didn't dream about *that*. But he couldn't stop thinking about it. Often, and usually in the middle of copying down a few possibly relevant sentences from some worm-eaten volume it had taken an archivist three hours to find, he'd see the hulking yellowish shapes and the light that goaded them, or hear the echo of their screams.

Should he try to merge the two concepts in some way? Use the image of *vodabeistes* and what he was increasingly sure was the reality of Fae regalia together somehow? He had to write "Treasure"; he had a commission; if he didn't write it, he and Touchstone were fucked. Yet the luring swirls of fire kept nagging at him.

The others weren't any help. After a show, Rafe went home to Crisiant. Jeska went out prowling. Mieka went home to Wistly—and this was another sore point. His new house was too far to make the round-trip every time they had a booking. So he'd turn up just in time (and more often late), sleep at his parents', stay for the show the following night, then the next morning return to Number 39, Hilldrop Crescent. This went on for more than a fortnight, until he flatly refused to make the daylong journey to Sir Teveris Longbranch's country home for a private performance.

"We have to go," Cade said. "It's a day there, and a show, and a day back, but—"

"Fine," Mieka snapped. "I'll be there—for twice the fee."

"Twice!" Kearney squeaked.

"We're Touchstone," Mieka said flatly. "We may still be on the

Winterly, but everybody knows we were bully-rooked and deserve the Royal. The Princess herself wanted *us*. Not the Shadowshapers, not the Crystal Sparks, not Black fucking Lightning. So Sir Thingummy can bloody well pay for the privilege."

"But—but—the fee was agreed, it's in writing, don't you see—"

"Then unwrite it. Rewrite it. I don't give a rat's fart. I've a wife and mother-in-law to support and I want the money."

The old woman had moved in with them. She was out of a job, Princess Iamina having decided she had enough frills and furbelows for Court festivities. Cade had silently wished them joy of her presence and looked forward to the day when he and Mieka would detonate the whole house, wiping her and her daughter out of their lives forever.

But as he listened to Mieka argue with Kearney, he stayed silent, too, about a thing he was thinking: that it had been Mieka who'd insisted that Touchstone must apologize in person to those tavern owners they'd disappointed by their absence on the Continent. That sort of thing didn't seem to matter to him now. Nothing mattered but his wife. And the money. Cade took Kearney aside and murmured that he'd forgo his own share of their pay in order to accommodate Mieka. Thus was the matter settled.

"Bad enough I'll be gone when she has the baby," Mieka said later.

"If we'd got what we earned, the Ducal or Royal, we'd be off on the Circuit *now*, and I could be there with her *then*. It's Fairwalk's fault, and he can mend it."

"I understand." He also understood something else: that the work meant less to Mieka, and even aside from the danger that posed to Touchstone, it was perilous for Mieka's own well-being. What he had realized so suddenly about the Elf while talking with Lady Vrennerie was even truer than he'd known at the time. Mieka needed to perform. Jeska loved it, Rafe found satisfaction in it, Cade craved it—but Mieka *needed* it.

22

Expected back in Gallantrybanks to perform (at great expense) for the public celebrations of the royal marriage next spring, Touchstone began the Winterly Circuit two weeks early. Places where they had played five or six shows last year, they would do only four. If the schedule of performances was relentless, the travel was brutal. Had their horses not been hired (at massive expense) from Romuald Needler, they would never have made it. It turned out that whereas one of these huge white monsters fit between the shafts of the King's coaches, two would not; so Touchstone had ended up (at colossal expense) hiring the Shadowshapers' wagon, long since refitted to accommodate these horses.

The first time Mieka stretched out on one of the bunks, knowing it would be his alone for the whole trip, he announced, "*Definitely* I want one of these!" Kearney assured him that with all the money they'd be making, he'd be able to order one built for them by next summer. They still hadn't been paid the balance of their fee for the trip to the Continent, but Kearney was working on that, and they dreamed up their design accordingly.

It became their project for at least two hours of every day they spent in the wagon, and it soon seemed that the only time they weren't in the wagon was when they were onstage or collapsing into beds upstairs at an inn. Gallantrybanks to Shollop, Shollop to Dolven Wold, on to Sidlowe and Scatterseed—people wanted to see Touchstone, and Touchstone gave everyone what they wanted to see at an accelerated pace, and if they hadn't been nineteen and twenty and twenty-one years old, they wouldn't have lasted a fortnight.

Thorn helped.

Bearing in mind that Mieka was leaving his pregnant wife behind, he was in remarkable spirits. This puzzled Cayden, who had expected him to be surly and fractious. But after the first fortnight or so, he realized that it was further confirmation that Mieka *needed* to perform. Lacking that emotional outlet, the Elf was unmanageable. Behind his glisker's bench, though, Mieka could use everything that was in him, focus it on the work. Nothing distracted him from creating his distractions, as it were. In the strangest way, this made their friendship one of equals. It never showed up more clearly than onstage: the magic Cade primed into the withies, the imaginings and dreamings and coldly calculated effects, Mieka used with an immediacy and intensity that left audiences gasping.

Snow came early and heavy that year. It bothered the huge horses very little. Within the wagon, the firepocket and Auntie Brishen's whiskey kept Touchstone warm enough. Their coachman, on the other hand, was constantly exhausted. Nephew of last year's driver, he was barely thirty and powerfully built, but even his abundant young muscles wore out controlling these horses. So when they reached Homage Knoll, just the wrong side of the Pennynines where a blizzard had closed the pass and the weathering witches hadn't yet cleared the road, he took to his bed for two solid days.

It was said there were attractions to Homage Knoll not readily discernible to the transient visitor. The only thing it had ever been known for, as far as Cayden knew, was that on a hillside nearby (nobody recalled exactly which hillside, and thus all the local landowners vied for precedence, though none could substantiate his claim), a hundred or so rebellious nobles assembled to pledge fealty to King Somebody-or-other, who had defeated them in battle. That he had promptly lopped off all their heads had given rise to the tale that Lord So-and-so's hillside was the authentic site, for there were about a hundred more-or-less skull-sized boulders strewn about the field below. All of His Lordship's competitors were certain that some ancestor of his had collected the rocks and salted the field with them in secret, then claimed to be astonished by the "discovery." Whatever the truth, whichever miserable, windswept, snow-clogged mound it had been, this was Homage Knoll's sole claim to historical note.

Yet its residents persisted in praising its other virtues. They said quite seriously that one had to linger a while to appreciate the place. By the third day of Touchstone's involuntary residence, Cade had yet to discover anything worth looking at or doing, or even worth asking about looking at or doing.

This might have been a consequence of his current petulance. Well, his ongoing petulance, truth be told. He just couldn't seem to make "Treasure" cooperate with what he had already decided it must do. At Sidlowe he had asked around again about local legends, and especially about a lake—unsure if it was a real clue but taking the chance anyway—and been frustrated at every turn. Having Rafe point out that getting stuck like this was usually his own damned fault helped not at all. He was tired of everything's being his fault. He was tired of being responsible for everything from making sure Mieka actually got out of bed in the morning to making sure Jeska was in his assigned bed at night. They needed Kearney Fairwalk to be here instead of in Gallantrybanks, here to sort things so that Cade could get on with his work. How could he liberate his mind to create when daily life kept a stranglehold on him? He was an *artist*, damn it.

Mieka's mood, on the other hand, could not have been cheerier. Yazz had appeared out of nowhere their second night here, and the Elf and the Giant had been happily exchanging news, rambling the snowy hills, and visiting Yazz's local relations. They made the oddest possible pairing, Cade thought as he watched them set off that third morning. Yazz had another purpose to his visit besides congratulating Mieka on becoming "rich an' famed" (relatively speaking, anyway): He was courting a distant cousin. The romantic rituals attendant on the process included a lavish outdoor picnic—even in the middle of winter. Mieka had certainly dressed for it, having commandeered Rafe's new wolfskin coat and Jeska's thigh-high boots, adding a badger-fur hat borrowed from the coachman. He looked like a fat, fuzzy, overgrown puppy as he gamboled along beside his huge companion. For a man who loved his comforts as much as Mieka did to be braving a luncheon in the snow was a tribute to his affection for Yazz. That, or he'd been promised excellent food or fantastic liquor or both.

Cade turned from the windows of the taproom and wondered what he was going to do with himself all day. Rafe was writing yet another letter to Crisiant; Jeska was off chatting up the local shopgirls. He could hear their coachman coughing in an upstairs room. Bored, restless, and knowing that nothing would come out of his pen today but additions to a rather obscene series of ballads, Cade wrapped himself up in every woolen garment he'd brought with him, tunic to socks, and threw on his father's old gray overcoat and a cloak atop it for good measure before setting out to walk off some of his funk.

He deliberately chose the exact opposite direction taken by Mieka and Yazz. Nothing more uncouth than intruding on a family party. Slogging up a hill about two miles out of town, hoping that the summit would provide an inspiring view, he dug his gloved hands more deeply into his pockets and watched every breath cloud in front of his face. He was freezing and irritated and lonely and unhappy, and anybody who knew him could have seen that he was enjoying every moment of it.

He supposed the view was lovely, if one liked white. Snow-covered hills to his left, snow-covered Pennynine Mountains to his right—he could do this sort of thing in his sleep, prime a withie for white and cold and the clean sharp scent of the breeze. He spread his arms and shut his eyes to imagine it onstage—

—and tumbled down a grass-covered hill into summer.

He landed at the bottom of the hollow in an inelegant tangle of limbs and coat and cloak. He blinked several times, but the green didn't turn to snow. Grass, ferns, a pear tree heavy with fruit, a hawthorn hedge. Bright flowers bloomed like strewn carpets. Seated in their midst was an elegant, spindle-boned young woman busily tapping at flowerheads with a single finger, making them turn different colors. Her hair was green, a shade that reminded him of sunlight shining through leaves. She looked up from idly changing the colors of the flowers, and didn't seem at all surprised to see him.

"I was wondering who it was I kept sensing," she said. "Waited for you this whole day, I have, and boring it's been, as well."

"Sorry," he said mindlessly as he untangled himself from the cloak, which seemed determined to throttle him. A thorn-dreaming was this? The abrupt slide into summer was like to the Treasure dream where he'd been a Fae.

"I may have got it right—what do you think?" She gestured to the flowers all around her, and as she did they burst into a spiral whirl of colors.

It was beautiful and impossible, and he memorized it hungrily for future use onstage. As she turned to judge the effect, he saw the delicate, silver-veined iridescence folded neatly across her shoulders and back.

Wings.

Cade lost his knees again and sat down hard in the grass. "You're Fae. You're actually *Fae.*"

"Of course I am, ridiculous boy. Green Summer Fae, to be precise." She faced him again, folding her long, slim hands in her lap, and tossed the hair from her face. Her bones were too sharp for beauty, and her ears came to extravagant points, and her eyes were green with flecks of gold. "You ought to know that," she went on. "You ought to have remembered."

"Sorry," he said again, not sure what he was apologizing for.

"I suppose it *has* been quite a long time, by your standards. It always is, I find. I've given over taking offense." She leaned forward a little, squinting at him. "Though I must say, you haven't aged a bit. Most unusual, for a Human."

"I wish I knew what you were talking about. We've never met."

"Of course we have! Met, and more than met! We—" Her eyes went wide and she caught her breath. "Oh! But it isn't you at all!"

"I'm beginning to think the same thing," he muttered. It was hot, here in the summer sun. He unbuttoned his father's coat and the top-most two sweaters. "Who did you think me?"

"You expect me to remember *names*? And it's not my fault I mistook you for him. You're very alike." She began counting on her fingers, stopped, frowned, began again, paused again, and finally shook herself with a ruffle of gleaming wings. "Four generations, mayhap five. I never had any use for numbers. But—yes, with as many years as you count them gone by—five generations it must be. Well, these things show up oddly in you Humans—eyes, noses, and the like."

"I'm mostly Wizarding blood," he told her.

"Not all, boy. Not all, by any means."

As she watched him, mild amusement in her eyes, he suddenly wondered just how stupid he would prove himself to be, in the end. She was Fae; she'd sensed his presence in the area; she'd waited for him; he looked familiar to her.

"It was you," he whispered. "I got it from you."

If this *was* prompted by thorn—and he hadn't sought his private supply in days—his imagination was working it for all it was worth.

She regarded him with vague interest, the way she might look at a shawl or book that had belonged to her own great-great-grandmother. An artifact, a curiosity of no real relevance, momentarily intriguing.

"How—I mean, what happened that you—that I'm—that you and he—?"

"I had a fancy to a Human lover," she said with a shrug. "He wasn't handsome, but he was the first I'd met in a long while who had enough Wizard in him to see me clear. He was rather sweet, as I recall—and he could make me laugh. Of course, I didn't think it was all that terribly funny when I discovered there'd be a child! But I was young, and curious to see what it might turn out like. I ought to've known. Positively the ugliest thing I've ever seen, and I've been in the presence of purebred Trolls. Everything Human about it—and it hadn't even a hint of wings."

"So you left it with some family or other." Frostcroft, the name had been, of the girl who'd married a Watersmith and brought Fae and madness into the Silversun bloodline.

"It cried such an awful lot, and it really was ugly. Their baby was sickly and about to die, and they'd neglected the usual defenses against changelings—"

"Bells, red ribbons, daisy chains, ashes," he recited dully. He'd always paid attention in school whenever anything to do with the Fae was discussed.

"Not even a single steel pin sewn into the child's clothing!" She sniffed her disdain of such careless folly. "So it was hardly my fault. They got a healthy baby, didn't they? So they've nothing to complain of."

A healthy baby in place of a dying one… to which they gave their name and their love, never knowing it wasn't their child at all.

"I was the one endangered," she went on petulantly. "Their house was near enough to a Minster to hear the bells, but I didn't even know that until I'd switched the babies the night theirs died, and took theirs to the burning ground. I gave it a decent fire— I'm not a barbarian!—but then some tiresome old man climbed the bell tower early in the morning, and of course I had to leave before the thing burned completely to ashes."

"The child was a girl," he reminded her.

"Was it? Yes, I suppose it was. And before you ask, I don't recall any names and I never saw the baby again. Why should I?" She paused, and smoothed the folds of her dark green skirt across her knees.

"Their baby girl had red hair when she was born—"

"Well, of course she had red hair," interrupted his great-great-great grandmother. "It's those we're drawn to, when we have to do such things. But it grew out black, after she got well."

"Just like her face began to change until she didn't look like either of her parents?" he suggested, already knowing the answer but wanting to hear it from her.

"That was the shape-shift wearing off, and very slowly. I'm good at subtlety. You may sit there all stiff and disapproving as you like, boy, but I have *never* neglected my spellcrafting!"

"No, you just neglected to care for your own child. She lived a very long time, you know."

The Fae smirked and shrugged her shoulders. "She would, though, wouldn't she?"

"She was my great-great-grandmother."

She counted on her fingers again, and nodded. "So I *was* right! Five generations from me to you!" Pleased with herself, she twirled a finger in the air and the flowers began their color-dance again, dizzying him.

"Stop it. Please."

"But it's beautiful!"

"It's making me feel ill."

"Beauty sickens you? With a face like yours, I'd think you'd want to look at beautiful things as much as possible." She sighed, and shrugged her wings again, and the rioting colors settled to quiet. "What did I give you? You said you got it from me. What is *it*?"

"The futures."

For an instant she looked delighted. Then she squinted into his face again and her fists clenched on her knees. "Why haven't you thanked me, then?"

"It's different for me. You—all of you—the prophecy is there, but nobody can trust what you say because you report only what pleases you."

She looked bewildered. "Why make everyone unhappy by telling them about the ugliness that will come?"

"It's not honest. It's not the truth."

Anger sparked in her eyes. "Are you calling me a liar, boy?"

"It's not *all* of the truth," he amended. "And anyone who believes the future will bring nothing but joy and sunlight and love—anyone who believes that is a fool."

"Just because you've *seen* the nasty bits doesn't mean you have to *succumb* to them." She leaped to her feet and held out a hand, and one of the pears obligingly took flight into her open palm. "You're a dull boy," she announced, "and I don't much care for your criticism. Truth is always beautiful, and anything ugly needs to be avoided and ignored. What's the use of it? All it does is make one unhappy. You know you agree with me every time you look in a mirror. But I'll give you a token to remind you, shall I?"

She tossed the pear at him. As it arced gracefully towards him, it changed from green to gold. He caught it, nearly dropped it—because it was very heavy. It had turned to real gold.

"It's beautiful, isn't it?" she challenged.

He looked at her. "Yes."

"And it's *honest* gold." Mocking him now.

"Fae gold," he said. "It'll change back once I've left here."

"It's real enough right now, and real enough to me, and it ought to be to you as well! But if you've no use for my gifts, you ungrateful clod—" She snapped her fingers, and the pear became soft and brown and rotten in his hand.

Deliberately he clenched his fingers around the stinking, putrid fruit. It oozed out of his hand, dripping onto the blue and yellow flowers. "Sometimes I wish it could be this easy to be rid of your other gift."

"Now who's the liar? What would you do if you could no longer foresee? You'd live your life like every other ignorant, silly Human, blundering blindly from year to year—"

"At least I wouldn't have to look at the ugliness! I wouldn't have to know what kind of pain is coming!"

"Haven't you worked it out yet? Yes, we can see the future, the wicked and awful things as well as the sweet. But we speak only of the good, and you still don't understand why. If we told what we know about the evil to come, who would have the strength to face it? We *choose* to reveal what's beautiful. Are the wonderful things any less true than the horrors we choose *not* to reveal?"

"But—"

"Oh, close your mouth, you stupid boy! If all you want to do is gripe about the dreadful bits, do it somewhere else!"

"Don't you understand? People *die!*"

"Of course they do! That's the silliest thing you've said yet!" She tossed her hair over her shoulder and sighed her impatience. "Admit it, why don't you? You love the inheritance that comes from me, because it gives you the power to choose!"

"My own choices. Not other people's. I can't make their choices for them."

She gave a shrewd little laugh. "But I'll bet you keep trying, don't you?"

"How do I know what's right? How do I know what to do?"

"You wait for the next vision. You do what you can, and you wait." She cocked her head and smiled maliciously. "And how does this make you different from the rest of your dreary Human world?"

Cade stared down at his hands. There'd be no contending with her; everyone knew the Fae had an answer for everything, whether it was understood or not. He supposed he ought to count himself lucky that he wasn't completely bewildered. This was probably because he was part-Fae himself.

All at once he asked, "He didn't matter to you at all, did he? Your Human lover."

"Why should he?" Her dainty little face scrunched up as if she'd bitten into a sour apple. "Oh, you mean I didn't *love* him. How silly!"

"Do you even know how to love?"

"Do you?"

"Yes," he said at once. Thinking of his brother, his friends, and Lady Vrennerie.

"Ever had a woman?"

"Yes!"

"More than one? Amazing! I trust they all kept their eyes shut. Did you love any of them?"

He took just a fraction of a second too long to answer, and she giggled.

"You see? Love's nothing to do with who you want to lie with. You see someone, you want her, you bed her, and there's an end to it."

"But—but it's supposed to *mean* something."

She gave another impatient shrug. "Is the bed warmer, are the sheets smoother, if you're wildly in love with the girl?"

"It's supposed to *mean* something," he repeated stubbornly.

"Come back in a dozen or so years and tell me if you still think the same thing. It's really all very simple, you know. Bodies are bodies. Hearts and minds only complicate the matter."

Now he knew where he'd got the cynical cast to his character.

And then it hit him with the force of a cannonball in the stomach: She was *Fae*. And so was he. And in the midst of winter here he was in sudden summer.

No, nothing to do with thorn, or his imagination. This was real. She was real. He eyed her sidelong, a smile of anticipation quivering at the corners of his mouth. "Tell me about the Rights."

Her jaw dropped open and her wings rustled nervously along her back. "How could you possibly know anything about the Rights?"

"I do, though," he said, not bothering to keep the smugness from his voice. "I know somebody took them, and hid them, and they're still where he left them. I've a fancy to go looking."

"The Rights." She narrowed her gaze. "Tell me what they look like."

"A necklet and a crown. Glass, with gold and silver threaded inside. Diamonds on the crown." He paused, frowning. "Mayhap a bit dirty these days, underneath all that rock and mud for so many years."

"If you're thinking to use them, think again! The magic's gone from them, boy. There'll be no throning, no ruling—"

"I don't want to use them, I just want to know where they are. And why," he added, unable to help himself.

"If you listened to the part of you that's me, you'd already know that!"

"Tell me anyway."

"The Crown of the Fae King... the Carkanet of the Queen..." Her wings arched and then folded tight. "The Human king wanted them. They got lost."

"I say they were deliberately hidden."

"They're gone, and their magic with them, so why bother?"

"What happened?"

She was silent for a long moment, and then started to speak. He would never know how long it took her to tell the tale. Time had no meaning in her world. When she finished, she arose without further comment or any attention to his questions, shook out her skirts, reached around to smooth the edges of her silver-veined wings, and walked away. She vanished between the pear tree and the green sloping hill. There was no doorway, no portal, no shimmer of magic. She simply walked into nothingness.

And he was sitting and shivering on packed snow, and if he hadn't felt the pulpy rotted fruit still on his fingers, he would have thought he'd dreamed the whole thing.

He washed his hands in snow and pushed himself to his feet. It was very late in the afternoon now, though of the same day or a dozen years in the future, he had no way of knowing. He struggled up the hill and began the long trudge back to the village, shivering, all his bones feeling as if they'd been separately bruised by his tumble down the slope into the Fae world. His mood whipsawed between elation and dread, smug triumph and appalled foreboding. If he wrote this, and Touchstone performed it—if all the Kingdom knew what he now knew—

"Quill! What are you doing all the way out here? We've been searching for *hours!*"

Mieka, splendidly drunk on homebrew, all bundled up in furs.

"Went for a walk," Cade mumbled, frozen hands deep in his pockets.

"Halfway to the topmost Pennynine, by the weariness of you. Come on, back to the inn. We'll have to shout for Jeska and Rafe along the way, they're out looking for you, too." Mieka linked elbows with him. "Yazz is triumphant! The fair Robel has accepted him, and when he has steady work they'll be wedded—

and that remembers me, I think once we have our new wagon we'll have need of a driver, and Yazz would be perfect!"

Cade nodded.

"I knew you'd agree! It won't be until summer, but she's wearing his token and even had one ready for him, sly chit! Lovely bracelets they exchanged, too." He held out his own left arm, though the chain of heavy silver links his wife had given him was hidden beneath many sleeves. "Ever notice how all that sort of jewelry is circular? Bracelets, necklets, rings—"

"Maybe that's because fingers, wrists, and necks are usually sort of round, y'know?"

"All the promising things, they're *unbroken* circles. Used to be they were crafted with magic, not just fused by a bit of magic like you did with Jed and Blye, but we live in decadent times. Mum has a lovely ring that's come down in Da's family for generations now—white gold, pink gold, and gold gold strands woven round and round—"

"But if it's sealed with magic, how can it be handed down?"

"It unseals at death."

"Or divorce?"

"Or divorce," Mieka admitted. "But that's a nasty bit of magic needs to be done, if divorce happens, and leaves scars—only not on the fingers."

Cade nodded. He didn't mention that Mieka and his wife wore matching bracelets, not rings. But he did wonder if, to an Elf, there were levels of commitment.

As if hearing his thought, Mieka went on, "There's married, and then there's bonded, for Elves. It doesn't happen much these days, which is why you've never heard of it. Mum and Fa were wed almost ten years before it happened for them."

"Before *what* happened? If you don't mind me asking, of course."

"Dunno," he replied cheerfully. "To hear Mum tell it, one

morning Fa just looked at her across breakfast and they both knew neither of them would ever look at anybody else ever again."

Cade laughed his skepticism. "Don't even try to tell me that before that morning either of your parents had ever—"

"*Everybody* looks, Quill," he said sagely. "Doing something about it is another question, o' course. That's choice, or good manners—or sheer terror of getting caught!" He laughed and kicked at a snowbank. "But not even *looking* at anybody else, not ever again—"

"Can't imagine it, personally."

It was an invitation to describe the state of his own marriage. Not that Cade had much doubt; Mieka's conquests weren't quite so numerous as Jeska's, but conquests there had been on the Winterly this year just as there had been on the last. It was tempting to think that perhaps Jinsie had been right, and there was magic at work on Mieka that relied on proximity. Then again, he'd never known the Elf to deny himself.

Mieka said, "Fa says he knows full well when a girl's pretty—he ain't blind!—but he ain't interested, either. I think it's—it's knowing that nothing anybody else could offer could ever compare."

Cade thought that over. It didn't exactly harmonize with what the Fae had said. But it reassured him that he was right: It *was* supposed to mean something.

Mieka had darted off to climb a hillock and yell for Rafe and Jeska. Cade scrubbed his fingers with snow again. His palms still felt sticky.

"Your hands aren't cold enough?"

Glancing up at the bemused face, he admitted, "It'll take some explaining."

23

Looking a right fool, Jeska showed up on one of the gigantic white mares. Cade gratefully climbed up behind him, escaping Mieka's excited questions, while Mieka backed away so fast that he slipped and landed in a snowbank. He walked along at a respectful distance from the horse, still demanding that Cade tell him everything. Rafe came upon them about a half mile later, and—merely for the sake of the mockery, for he wasn't terribly fond of horses either—clambered up behind Cade. The horse didn't seem to notice, and there was plenty of room. The final insult came when Jeska persuaded the animal into a trot.

"Fuck-wits!" Mieka yelled after them. He arrived back at their inn a whole pint behind, and by the time he'd shed his furs and settled in their corner of the taproom, they were another half a pint ahead.

"Letters," Jeska told him, tossing two across the table, neatly missing the steaming cauldron of soup but not the platter of fresh bread.

"How'd they know to send here?" Mieka brushed crumbs from his letters. "We're s'posed to be at least halfway to New Halt by now, ain't we?"

"My wife," Rafe announced, "is a brilliant woman who can

read a map."

"And predict a sickly coachman who's kept us in one place for three days?"

"Instructions to the Royal Post in Dolven Wold to keep an eye on the weather and the mountain passes, and forward the packet accordingly." Rafe raised his glass. "Gentlemen, to my wife."

"Crisiant," Cade toasted, and drained his glass, and went back to his own letter.

Mieka tore into the one from his wife and ignored their teasing—something about how no one and nothing but her could make him neglect his first drink of the evening, and that the scent applied to it had seeped into all their letters as well. He read through it once, hiding his smiles, and tucked it into his pocket to savor later on. Then he opened the one from his father.

> *Everyone is well. There is, however, a difficulty with the bank over payments on your new home. The first, second, and third installments were paid timely, but it seems there are no funds for the next and will not be until Touchstone is paid for the Continental journey.*

"Did we get paid?" he demanded of Cayden.

"Paid for what?"

"Months of misery! My father says I'm skint."

"Kearney's negotiating, or so his clerk told me," Jeska said. "After all, wasn't our fault they went into a snit and canceled us at the last instant. They engaged us to perform, and we performed. They owe us the money."

Cade was frowning at Mieka. "You didn't spend *that* much on the house. I was there when the price was agreed on, and the payments scheduled."

"There should've been enough, even after paying Jed and Jez. Listen." He read aloud from his father's letter.

Lord Fairwalk is trying his best, but there's no saying when the money will be available. Not wishing you to lose the house, I've made the following arrangement and I hope you won't mind too much but it's the only way to continue regular payments to the former owner. I have let the place to Sakary Grainer until the spring.

"Spring!" exclaimed Jeska.

"Chirene's pregnant, hadn't you heard?" Cade folded his letter, looking secretive.

As you may know, his wife is expecting their first child, and they desire a quiet location away from the bustle and noise of Gallantrybanks until her confinement and for a few weeks after. The Shadowshapers have arranged their bookings so that he may be with her for a fortnight or two, then stay in town for a week, and so on. He can of course afford servants to care for her during his absences.

Mieka winced.

Your mother and I will be delighted to have our new daughter-in-law back at Wistly. We'll take the very best care of her, please don't worry. Her mother has been engaged by the new Archduchess—

"New *what*?" demanded Jeska. "When did this happen? Who'd he marry?"

"Lady Panshilara," Rafe said. "Crisiant mentions it."

Cade nodded. "It was a few days before the official wedding on the Princess's eighteenth Namingday, so she could strut about being called 'Archduchess' and being extremely important."

"And how do you know this?" Mieka asked, then answered

his own question. "Lady Vrennerie! Your letter was from her! How did she know to send a letter to you through Crisiant?"

"She didn't. She had it delivered to Redpebble, and Derien passed it on."

"Letters from unmarried ladies," Rafe said, shaking his head. "It's a shocking flirt you are, Cayden Silversun."

"Shut it and let Mieka get on with what his father says."

Her mother has been engaged by the new Archduchess as a dressmaker, and so will be living at the Archduke's house upriver starting next month, but will come to Wistly as often as she can. Again, I hope you approve of these arrangements. Your mother and I were at wit's end trying to think what to do before Jinsie had the idea to let the house and contacted Master Grainer.

Jinsie's idea? And why had she thought of Sakary? Mieka kept on reading.

The rent is enough to cover the payments until spring, at which time I trust that you'll be able to reclaim the house for your own. All the family send their best love, and your mother reminds me to tell you to keep an eye out for Yazz, who, Brishen says, is traveling in the area of Homage Knoll and will find you if he can.

Mieka put down the letter and took a long pull at his ale. "Why haven't we been paid?"

"I'll write to Kearney and ask." Cade glanced around the taproom, filling up now with regulars, and lowered his voice. "I've things to tell you, and it has to be in private. Let's head upstairs after we've eaten, right?"

Mieka caught Jeska's regretful glance at the barmaid—a very pretty girl indeed, and the one Mieka had had his own eye on for the evening's entertainment. It seemed neither of them would be enjoying her tonight. It sounded to be one of Cade's talk-until-dawns.

An hour later they took the discussion upstairs, threading their way through the crowded tavern and up to Cade and Mieka's room. Their coachman, just down the hall, shouted for them, and when Rafe opened his door informed them from his bed that even if the pass had cleared by tomorrow, they'd be staying at least another day. The very thought of reining in those horses made him tired and sore all over again.

"We've bookings—" Cade began.

"Yazz can start early," Mieka said at the same time. He gave the coachman his most endearing smile. "Friend of ours. Part Giant, drives for me auntie. We've ordered up a wagon even bigger and better than this one for next year—"

"Suits me," the young man said. "If you've got somebody to take my place, I'm done."

"You can't," Jeska told him. "You've been hired—"

"—to drive a coach, not that bloody great ship on wheels!" He pushed himself up in bed, groaned, and sank back down. "My uncle got me the job, and he can damn well have it back!"

"Just stay on until we're across the mountains," Cade coaxed. "We'll double your fee—"

Mieka whined his distress.

"Over the pass, then," the coachman grumbled. "But there's no amount of money or threats from the Stewards will make me go all the way back to Gallybanks the way I've come. Those aren't horses, they're dragons with their wings chopped off!"

Touchstone shared a glance and a shrug, and left the man to his misery. On their way down the hall to their own rooms, Mieka couldn't help but whisper, "Double?" to Cade, who made a face and no answer.

"So what's the revelation?" Rafe asked as the door shut and he claimed Mieka's bed and pillows for his back.

"I—er—I had rather an adventure today."

Eventually Cade managed to stumble and stutter through the whole tale of his encounter. Mieka watched as Jeska's eyes widened with each sentence, and Rafe looked frankly skeptical. Mieka believed every word of it. What he didn't quite believe was that the puzzle of the Treasure was nearly solved. Once it was, mayhap Cade would give over his moods. They were becoming wearisome.

"She could tell me the whys and whens and whatfors, but nothing about the *where* of it," Cade finished, elated and frustrated. "I know now what it was, and why it was valuable, and even how it was lost, but—"

"It'll come to you," Mieka soothed. With proper use of thorn, it would come to him. He had every faith in Cayden. "But look, we've the outline of what really happened—and won't *that* cause a fuss!—so you can write it all up for us and we can get started learning it, yeh?"

"We won't know how to play it until we know where it happened," he said stubbornly.

"We have the whats of it. Enough to work with. Midwinter, bitter cold, and a lot of rain. A stone wall falling down, setting sun through the chink in the rocks—so not as much rain as I'd thought, or else wind blows most of the clouds away. We can decide later. A hill, open space, a lake, mayhap a few trees for perspective, and there's the scenery sorted. Wind—"

"You said that already," Rafe pointed out.

"—and if it's sunset, there'll be Minster bells, and people yelling as they give chase, and that's the sounds. As for the look of the man—he's Fae, innit he? A lot taller than Jeska—"

"Shit-head," the masquer replied amiably. "Do I have wings?"

Mieka leaned forward from his lounging pose against bed pillows and poked Cade in the spine. "I've never done proper Faerie wings, Quill. Can we give Jeska Faerie wings? Please?"

"Setting, sound, person," Rafe enumerated. "Some earth and mud smells, but nothing more than that. Keep it fresh, Mieka," he warned. "None of your authentic shit stinks, like with the pig."

"But that's just it!" Cade cried. "Until we know exactly where it all happened, it *won't* be authentic! It won't be real! They won't believe it!"

"Innit that what we do best—make them believe in it?" Rafe smiled as he poured out more whiskey.

"What he means," Jeska said with a sigh, "is that they won't believe he's solved it."

"We can hand out a printed guide to your research notes before the performance," Rafe said with every evidence of sincerity. "Authentication. Scholarship, even."

"That won't do!" Cade objected at once. "If they read it beforehand, they'll know what I—! Oh. You're trying to be *funny.*"

"He's not tryin' very hard," Mieka said consolingly. "Face up to it, Quill, you can't tell people exactly how you learned it all. *That's* what they'd never believe."

"But—" Then he slumped a bit. "All right."

Mieka listed the points. "Sight, sound, scent, feel—no tastes, I think, unless you want a hint of wine or somesuch just to show we can. Would he have taken a drink or two before going out in the cold? Prob'ly so."

"There, you see?" Jeska snatched up the pages of Cade's notes. "Now all you need do is write it, just like the Fae lady said, and we're done!"

"All I need do is write it," he echoed in disgust.

"And I need to learn it." He sorted through to the two versions of the poem. "Chuck the old text right out me head, make sure I don't remember anything… about… it…"

Mieka had learned long ago that Jeska had trouble reading. He was brilliant with numbers—though Touchstone was earning enough now that he didn't have to supplement his income anymore by doing the books for various businesses—but words came to him only with difficulty. At the moment he looked as if he'd never seen a written word before in his life. Just as quickly his expression changed to the sort of righteous enlightenment usually associated with Angels in a Chapel window.

"What?" Cade demanded.

"Oh, nothing much," he drawled. Rising from the floor with fluid grace, he set the two pages on the bed beside Cade and Mieka. Then he carefully covered almost all of the new poem— or, rather, the old version of the poem that to him was new— with the blank side of the second page. "Try this."

> No night bedarked as soonly
> As athwart the crumbling wall
> Cold stone a-tumbling fell
> Klunshing and climping all
> Ere morning brighted the field
> Regal bells had pealed
> To wrongly doom a thief
> Condolement there be none
> Long shadows scrape the throne
> O'erset and e'er cast down
> Spun carkanet and crown
> Ever hidden, never found.

Mieka peered over Cade's shoulder as the words slowly disappeared beneath the blank paper. Rafe came to join them, and read the remaining letters aloud.

"*N-a-c-k-e-r-t c-l*—'nackert close'? *Nackert?* What kind of word is that?"

"Knackered?" Mieka asked.

"No *K* to start. But it's very clearly *Close*—like in Criddow Close, you think?"

Cade snorted. "An 'exhausted' street with only one outlet? Do me a favor."

"Nackert," Mieka kept mumbling, and spelling it out loud, listening to the sounds. *"N-a-c-k-e-r-t*—Nackerty! It's one of Uncle Breedbate's words, I've heard him say it—Quill, find your books, look it up, I don't remember what it means!"

A wild carouse through every book in or out of the crates he'd insisted on bringing with him on this trip finally yielded a definition.

"'A field with many corners'!" Cade exclaimed. "Nackerty Close!"

"There's no *Y* in it," Rafe objected. "It's more likely a wrong spelling of *knackered*."

Mieka was biting his tongue between his teeth. Suddenly he burst out, "Didn't you say that *clunsh* is always spelled with a *C* and not a *K*? Somebody changed it deliberately in that poem, Cade. Jeska's right—this is deliberate!"

"What was *knacker* originally?" said Cade, and answered himself, "The man who put down horses."

"But all these other words," Mieka reminded him, pointing to the text, "they're all the same sort Uncle Breedbate uses, so it can't be *knackered*, that doesn't make any sense."

"The street where the knacker lives makes more sense than a field with a lot of corners with only one outlet," Rafe persisted.

"But that doesn't match the rest of it. It wants a field, and a stone wall. And a lake." Cade read it aloud, adding after each line the interpretations he and Mieka had worked out months ago.

The shortest night of the year. The sun going down over a wall that tumbled apart, begriming what was below it. At dawn across the field—and here he arched a brow at Rafe— bells rang, somebody was killed for the theft even though he was innocent—

"There's a line missing," Mieka interrupted. *"Wall—all.*

Field—pealed. But there's nothing rhymes with *thief.* That's where the *Y* line ought to be! That would spell *nackerty!*"

"I couldn't find any version with a line starting with *Y,* not even in *Lost Withies.*" All at once he wore the same dawning-sunlight look as Jeska. "No *complete* version—" And once more he went scrambling through the books, and then his notes, papers flying. "Here! 'Y-cladden in his grief' comes right after the line about the thief, only in this rendering there's no rhyme—but that's right where it should be to spell out *Nackerty!*"

"Nackerty Close," Rafe mused.

"Y-cladden?" Mieka asked.

"It means—"

He interrupted Cade. "I can figure what it means, beholden all the same!"

Rafe was still frowning. "Why can't it still be *knackerty* with a *K*? That would make more sense."

"None of this makes much sense," was Jeska's opinion.

Cade rounded on him. "Of course it does! You throw all the versions together, pick out the ones that give clues—like the *golden light* of the hidden Treasure, and from the glimpse I got it *was* golden, and silver, with diamonds—"

"Hold on a tick! Where does it say anything about diamonds?"

"I—I saw it."

"How?" When Cade merely looked at him, Jeska chewed his lip.

"Oh."

"Put it together," Rafe said, "with what the Fae told him, and we've got it. We just don't know exactly where."

"There can't be that many places called Nackerty Close, can there?"

Jeska asked. "I mean, it's not a common word, none of us recognized it—"

"*I* did!" Mieka reminded him. "And I can tell you something else, too! Wherever it is, it'll be on lands the Oakapple family once owned!" He grasped Cade's shoulders from behind and shook him gently. "Where are we scheduled to be on Wintering Night?"

"We can't go on a Treasure hunt."

Mieka propped himself on an elbow, watching as Cade got ready for bed. Honest to all the Gods, the man was just ridiculously skinny—exactly what Jeska had once called him (though not in Cayden's hearing): a nose on legs. "We don't have to tell anybody when we find it. Let's just go make sure it's there, Quill."

"We won't be anywhere near any of the former Oakapple lands on Wintering Night. And it's s'posed to be someplace near Sidlowe, remember?"

"You are *no* fun."

"And besides, if we did find it, we'd have to admit how we worked it out."

"Like Rafe said—scholarship. Think of your bettered reputation! You can give Tobalt Fluter an exclusive interview and tell the tale the way you want it told, and not have to admit a thing."

"If you say so." After a few moments of silent washing, Cade slipped into his nightshirt and climbed into bed. He hesitated before putting out the candle. "Mieka…"

"What's got you anguishing *now*?"

"You don't seem worried. About renting out the house, and—and everything."

"What can I do about it? Not a damned thing. And anyways, Mum will make sure she's cosseted. That's what mums are for."

"A disappointment to her, though," he suggested, "having to leave her new house so soon after moving into it."

"We'll go back in the spring, and it'll be ours outright. I'm wondering why Sakary, though. It's not as if he likes me, or would go out of his way to do me any favors. Jinsie must know something we don't."

"Oh, we all know it, I think." Cade eyed him sidelong. "At Blye and Jed's wedding. Alaen came over all agroof in Chirene's exquisite presence."

"So *that's* why he sent Briuly in his place!"

"How did you—? Oh, never mind." He paused. "Clever of Jinsie, though, to think of Sakary and Chirene."

"Mmm. I may actually forgive her one of these years."

Cade smiled and leaned over to pinch out the candle flame. A bellow from outside in the stable yard startled him so much that he nearly knocked the candle over.

Mieka sighed and reached for his trousers. "Yazz," he explained. "He said he might come by later. Absolutely no sense of time, that one. Give him a shout down, won't you, before he wakes the whole village!"

A couple of hours and more than a couple of pints later, Mieka saw Yazz stashed in a corner of the kitchen. He was still smiling as he climbed the stairs. His friend was elated at the immediate prospect of a job, and Mieka had the bruised ribs to prove it. The emphatic hug of a part-Giant would snap Cayden right in two; he'd have to remember to tell Yazz to take it easy with the gratitude tomorrow.

Everything would work out; he knew it would. Mum and Fa would take care of her and the baby, Yazz would be able to marry Robel sooner than planned, they'd get the house back in the spring—and there was that barn, he told himself, it might make a nice home for Yazz and Robel—and, of course, Cade would find some obscure reference somewhere to Nackerty Close, and—

He knew an instant before he opened the door that something was wrong. Cursing in the darkness as he stumbled over a chair, he lunged for the candle and lit it. Cade was turning fretfully in bed, mumbling, and there were tears on his cheeks.

"Cayden!" Mieka sat beside him, took the long-jawed face between his hands. "Quill! Wake up!"

He did, gray eyes wide and staring. "Mieka?" he whispered.

"The one and onliest. Want a drink? You look like you need one." Cade shook his head. "I'm all right."

"Another one about me, eh?" At least Cade had learned not to lie to him. As he nodded slowly, Mieka tapped his nose with a chiding finger. "I think what you ought to do is *choose* not to pay attention to suchlike anymore. Don't tell me it doesn't work like that, you've brain enough to make whatever work that you want it to work."

"I'm sorry," Cade said. "It's just—sometimes I can't tell what's real. I can't tell what's the dream—Gods, the *nightmare*—"

"Quill, look at me. This is real. You and me. I'm here, I'm real, and whatever you saw, it won't happen. I promise."

He shook his head again, biting both lips between his teeth. "Damn it all, will you stop? My word's not enough for you?"

"It's—it's me," he managed. "I keep telling you—it's what *I* choose, what *I* do or don't do—"

"So you're in charge of the whole sodding world and everything in it? Gods, Cade, I knew you were conceited, but this is the outside of enough! *Look* at me! Whenever something like this gets into your bloody brilliant stubborn stupid head, just *look* at me. I'm here. We're real. Ain't nothin' more real than us."

He hesitated, then admitted, "I keep telling myself it's not my responsibility. Not my fault. Like with the Princess. If we hadn't done 'Hidden Cottage'—but then Ashgar didn't have to pretend to cry, did he? And she didn't have to decide on the basis of that alone that he's a wonderful man."

Mieka regarded him thoughtfully. "That's one of the few sensible things I've heard you say about the Elsewhens, ever.

Whatever anybody else does, it's not your fault because it's not your decision to make. And anyway, look at what's happening with Yazz. Perfect, right? He's dead chuffed, by the bye, and wanted to run all the way back to his uncle's place and wake everyone up to tell them he's a job as of tomorrow!" He laughed softly. "The time it took me to persuade him elsewise! He's curled up on the kitchen floor next the fire, and won't the cook have a shock in the morning!" There: he'd got Cade to smile a little. To encourage it, he added, "Of course, she'll hear him long before she opens the door—snores like a whole pack of hounds belling on the hunt, he does. Poor Robel!"

"I'm glad we can help him—glad it worked out."

"It'll always work out—that's what I'm here for, innit? Since that first night in Gowerion. Now, get back under the blankets, you're frozen." He tucked Cade up to the chin and fussed with the covers, and sure enough, there was another smile. "Back to sleep with you. No more nasty dreams tonight."

"I wish I could be sure of that."

"Haven't you learned yet, Quill? You don't hardly ever have really awful dreams when you're sleeping near me. And if you do, I'm always here to talk you out of them."

He looked thoughtful, then relieved. "You may be right."

"Of course I'm right. I'm Mieka Windthistle. Sweet dreaming, Quill."

24

"Lads," Mieka said as he packed the glass baskets, "d'you know how long we been at this? Seventy-nine days."

"My felicitations," Rafe said. "You can count."

"Only another fifty left," Jeska reminded them, then called out to the servants, "Oy! You missed a spot, over that way!"

Cade leaned on his lectern, watching brooms hurry glass shards into dustpans. Mieka had been rather more enthusiastic than usual tonight in shattering withies. That meant he was getting bored. He'd solemnly sworn to Cade when they started the Winterly Circuit that he'd brought along not a single grain of black powder (though Cade had gone through his satchel anyway, just to make sure), so at least that manner of mayhem was denied him. But a bored glisker was a dangerous glisker.

Not to mention a glisker who wouldn't shut up.

"There's a reason they call it *playing*, right? It's s'posed to be *fun*, innit?" He finished shutting the crates and sat on the velvet bench.

"This is a slog and a drudging and I'm tired."

Rafe seated himself on the edge of the stage and inspected his fingernails. "Your pardon, gentlemen, I'm about to weep."

"I mean it! I used to be young! Any day now I'll be plucking gray hairs out me head!"

"And then you'll go bald," Jeska said sweetly, "and have to wear a wig, like Sir Kyler."

"Does he?"

Rafe snorted. "You didn't notice that furry thing perched at the top of his face?"

"I thought it was a hat." Mieka considered. "Or maybe that his beard got confused about where to put itself."

Sir Kyler Crushberry had engaged them for three nights at his new and lavish country home for the entertainment of guests who'd lingered for a week or so after Wintering. Having been part of the delegation sent to fetch the Princess, Touchstone had been besieged from all quarters since their arrival at Bramblings; everyone from the titled lords and ladies to the kitchen maids seemed indecently eager for any gossip they could get. The pay was almost worth the constant harassment.

Cade waited, and waited some more, until all the servants had left and the doors were shut. Then he cleared his throat gently, and the three turned to look over their shoulders. "Thought you might be interested," he said, and used a withie he'd been keeping in his lectern to conjure a map on the back wall. It had been a while since he'd done any glisking, and this was naught but a picture—nothing fancy, no flourishes, though he couldn't help it if a bit of his triumph seeped in.

The effect was everything he desired.

Rafe spun round on his bum to stare. Jeska caught his breath and reared up like a startled horse. Mieka leaped to his feet and began to dance.

"You found it, you found it! I knew you would, Quill, I *knew* it!"

For on the map, Cade had placed a single glowing golden dot and two words: NACKERTY CLOSE. He grinned at the jubilant Elf. "Thought you were feeling all elderly and decrepit!"

"You found it!"

He let the magic fade, and tucked the withie into his jacket pocket. "It's nowhere close to anyplace we're going, and not even near Sidlowe as the rumors have always had it, but at least now we can drop some hints."

Mieka stopped midstep and nearly took a tumble. "Hints?" he echoed. "But—we'll go looking for it, we have to! Don't you keep saying that unless we find it, nobody will believe—"

"What I *said* is that finding out exactly where makes it authentic. I never said we had to unearth the Treasure, or let on we know where it is."

Rafe pushed himself to his feet. "And who's the lucky sod who'll be hearing these hints?"

"Alaen and Briuly, of course." Jeska sat back down and hugged his knees, looking superior. "Not Lord Oakapple," he explained, "he shits gold coin these days, what with his coal mines and all, and it's not as if he was any help to us. But Alaen and Briuly, they're players, like us—sort of, anyways—and need the money—"

"Very much like us!" Mieka put in resentfully. "So why should they have the advantage of us?"

"They're connected to the family," Jeska went on. "So they've a right to the Rights, as it were. And didn't you talk long and hard with Briuly on board ship, Cayden?"

"He provided a few ideas. And before we left Gallantrybanks, I bought Alaen a few drinks at the Heel Tap. An outstandingly seedy establishment," he added with a wince, "but conveniently round the corner from the Archives. The family stories Briuly didn't recall, Alaen did."

"So they get the hints, and we don't?" Mieka glanced at the back wall as if the map would reappear at his whim. "Where exactly is it, Cade? Come on, tell!"

Rafe laughed at him. "Twenty years old this coming summer, and can't read a map!"

"Cade!" he whined.

"Since I'm confessing," he said, "it helps that my little brother is a fiend for maps and things. I had him do one up for me of all the old Oakapple lands, from what I could learn at the Archives. Taught me a lot about scale and contouring," he mused, just to see the frustrated jut of Mieka's jaw. "Not to mention how words get mangled over the years, and sounds shift about."

"Cade!"

"Before we left Gallybanks, I begged an afternoon with the High Chapel Chronicler—for a while he thought I was applying for a job—"

"Where is the bleedin' thing?"

"—but eventually I got a list of all the Chapels sponsored by kings and queens and what-have-you—for the bells, y'know—and then it was a matter of plotting them out on the same map, so I set Dery onto it and—"

"*Cayden!*"

Jeska shook his head. "You want to go claim it for yourself? Not bleedin' likely!"

"Why shouldn't we?"

"Cade did all the work."

"Helped along by thorn!"

"You're a one to be talking," Cade couldn't help but say. "I've seen how little you've left in that roll."

Mieka rounded on him, sneering. "One word from me, and Auntie Brishen won't remember your name!"

He didn't know how they'd gone from smiles to snarls so fast. They seemed to be doing that a lot lately, so much so that he was expecting Rafe and Jeska to do the usual, and quietly remove themselves from the skirmishing field. Instead, someone intruded upon it.

"Master Windthistle?" The footman hesitated in the doorway, came forward, hesitated again as Mieka turned a furious scowl on him. "Your pardon, but this just now arrived for you, by special courier."

"Give it here, then!"

"Beholden," Jeska said, and the boy made his escape.

Mieka ripped open the letter. Cade saw the purple wax seal, and knew it must be from Wistly Hall. And then he remembered: Mieka's son was due sometime around Wintering. He'd forgotten—but Mieka hadn't. Scant wonder the Elf was so nervy these days.

Mieka sat down very suddenly on the stage, as if his legs had turned to porridge.

"Well?" Jeska asked. "Nothing's wrong?"

He shook his head, stunned. "A girl. A little girl. Born on Wintering Night. Looks like me, Mum says. My ears, anyways. And the hands." He looked up at Cade, then looked about him as if wondering how he'd ended up on the floor.

A daughter? Cade felt almost as bewildered as Mieka. A swift glance at Rafe revealed not a trace of a flinch, only a broad smile, only genuine pleasure.

"Well done! What's her name, then? Or can't you tell us?"

"Hmm?" Mieka sorted through the meaning of the words; it was almost funny to watch him do it. "Oh. Jindra. My sister and I, we agreed back when we were little to name our firstborn after each other—"

So he'd forgiven Jinsie, Cade thought. Or perhaps he'd mentioned it to his wife months ago, before the wrangle, and forgot to unmention it.

And then it really hit him: a girl. Not a little boy who looked through the railings as his parents hit each other. He'd had no glimpse of that Elsewhen for a long time, and felt a fool when he realized why. That future had been possible, but once the baby was conceived, had become impossible. Which meant that Mieka could have bought that house after all, because there would be no little boy to stare down from upstairs. *"So you're in charge of the whole sodding world and everything in it?"* Nothing to do with him. Not his responsibility.

"You should find the courier," Rafe was saying, "and give him a bit for his trouble."

Jeska nodded. "And we should drink the baby's health—and her mother's, too." He paused, frowning. "Awkward, not having a name to drink to. Is it just you who knows it now, or the rest of the Windthistles, now that she's family?"

Cade heard the crackle of hearth flames.

Rafe laughed again. "Are you wondering which of them to bribe into telling you?"

Not like the other Elsewhen, in that house—not a large fire for warmth, but a small one, made just for the purpose of burning paper to ashes.

"They don't know," Mieka was saying. "And neither will you! She's 'Mistress Windthistle' to you lot!"

Only one sheet of paper. Not a whole folio. Only one page.

{She was a beautiful woman, beautifully dressed, with black hair cascading in rich waves down her back. Wide ribbons of sea-green and brown fluttered as she crumpled a letter in both hands—her father's hands, small and slender, the ring and little fingers almost the same length. She crouched beside the hearth, waiting for the flames to build.

A young girl, perhaps fifteen and perhaps not, came into the room. "Mum? I heard a courier come to the door—"

"The King is holding a ceremony."

"What sort of ceremony?"

"At the Palace. It's been twenty-five years, and the King wants to remind everyone about the summer he took the throne."

"And we're *invited*? Mum!"

"We'll not be there," she snapped, and threw the letter into the fire.

"But—"

Rising, she whirled on the girl. "D'you think I intend to sit and simper while people make speeches about what a wonderful man your grandsir was? How he and Touchstone changed theater, how he was so brilliant and creative—"

Defiantly: "He *was*!"

"Listen to me, and mark what I tell you. Your grandsir was a selfish, spoiled, heartless bastard who cared about drinking, fucking, and thorn. He never gave a damn about your grandmother nor me. He did whatever he pleased with whomever it pleased him to do it with, without a thought to anyone else—"

Dark eyes the color of irises regarded her with cold cunning. "If you hate him so much, why do we live on his money?"

"My money! He owed it to me—all the Gods know he never gave me anything else!"}

"—and a Namingday gift for the baby, something pretty—"

"Crisiant will see to it," Rafe said, soothing the anxious father. "Cade? Come on, there's a bottle waiting upstairs to honor Jindra and her mother with!"

They were over at the door, Rafe with his lectern, Mieka and Jeska with crated glass baskets. How had they got way over there? He was too stunned to understand.

That future—how could it have anything to do with him? How could it be his fault that Jindra ended up hating her father? And—twenty-five years since the King took the throne? *Took* it? Not *inherited*—not Ashgar, then? The girl—woman, really—she'd looked to be about thirty, but Elves didn't show age the way most people did, so she could have been half again that old. The scene whirled in his head, Jindra and her daughter—good Gods, Mieka's granddaughter!—and a King who'd taken the throne and a celebration of when he'd done it and Jindra loathing her father and—

"Cade!"

He swallowed hard, lifted his own lectern—which seemed unreasonably heavy all of a sudden—and called out, "Yeh, coming!"

He stopped using thorn after that. He didn't want to dream. He didn't want to see. He went back to his old standby: enough alcohol to put him to sleep without giving him a hellacious hangover the next morning.

From Sir Kyler Crushberry's house outside Lilyleaf they traveled to Castle Biding. He avoided all the echoes there, especially the top of the tower where he and Mieka had watched the moonglade, though in truth there wasn't much else to remind him of last year. There was no Fair spreading bright booths and awnings across the fields, no encampment of tents. The place looked naked and forsaken without them. And with naught but the castle and town to provide audiences, they played only two shows and moved on.

Their original driver had gladly deserted them at New Halt. Yazz was the perfect coachman, so good with the horses that Mieka teased him that he couldn't possibly have any Giant's blood in him, and did Robel know she was bespoken to a fraud? Yazz only growled affectionately. He was perfect, too, in the unspecified but necessary duty of carrying the Elf upstairs some nights and downstairs some mornings, for Mieka had combined a renewed dedication to drink and thorn with his yearly head cold. He mostly slept through his misery between Castle Biding and Frimham.

Now—and quite suddenly, too—the Winterly was over. In

less than a month they'd perform at the wedding celebrations, and Cade had spent all this time avoiding the actual writing of "Treasure." When he finally sat down in his usual room at Fairwalk Manor to work, he felt as if his brain had been prised out through one ear, put through a meat grinder, and spooned back in not quite its original configuration.

The usual five-shows-and-a-day-off had not applied on this whirlwind Winterly. Travel, arrive, set up, play, drink, sleep, play, drink, sleep in the wagon while traveling, drink in the wagon while traveling, arrive, set up, play... only twice, at Shollop and New Halt, had they done five consecutive shows and then been allowed a day to rest. Their last few performances had got sloppy, and they all knew it. Now the Circuit was over, and they were taking a few days at Fairwalk Manor to collapse. There was plenty of money in their pockets after their bookings at Sir Kyler's and a repeat of last year's one-person-audience at that strange mansion outside New Halt, another night that had given them all a lingering case of the weirds. Mieka had enough for the spring and summer payments on his house, and not only had Jeska bought the seaside cottage for his mother, but he was no longer in arrears in supporting his daughter. Rafe and Cade intended to bank the lot. Kearney was reassuring about the remainder of the fee for the trip to the Continent, due any moment now. They would be paid lavishly for the Court performance, and there was the money promised by Lord Oakapple for "Treasure"—if only Cade could finish the poxy thing.

He stayed at Fairwalk Manor a few days after the others left, so frustrated that he risked thorn again. It gave him the same sequence as last spring: a race to find the Rights, the suddenness of summer, the tumbled wall, the belling hounds, the thundering hoofbeats, and capture. His ears were still the pointed ears of a Fae, and the tips were still numb in the cold. But he learned nothing new.

He was still unable to decide whether it was a foreseeing, a product of his imagination, or a backseeing, as it were. Never in his life had he experienced something out of the past. Thus it had to be all the reading he'd done, and all the pondering, added to his writer's mind, producing this blending that had, after all, turned out to be true.

Or as true as he could trust a Fae to be.

What she had revealed to him had been shocking enough. Very different from his Elsewhen, prodded out of her when she discovered he knew what the Rights looked like—Mieka was right, and there'd be a real shit-storm when Touchstone performed "Treasure." Probably not the wisest choice of plays for the whole Court, and at wedding celebrations into the bargain, but Cade didn't even have to think about whether or not they'd do it.

If only he could get the bleeding thing finished.

Everyone else was in Gallantrybanks. And everyone else who'd been invited to play the celebrations was rehearsing, whether strictly in private (the Shadowshapers) or noisily in public (Black fucking Lightning). With every worthwhile group now resident in town, there were no bookings to be had, not even for Touchstone.

He heard from Crisiant, a dry little missive expressing her gratitude that her husband had returned to her in the appropriate number of pieces and reasonably sane. She mentioned how well Derien was doing in school, that Jeska's mother was delighted with her new seaside home, that Mishia and Hadden Windthistle were thrilled to have their only grandchild living in the big old house, and Jinsie and Petrinka adored taking care of the baby. This was Crisiant's way of saying that neither Mieka nor his wife spent much time with their daughter. Crisiant quite clearly didn't approve; Cade didn't have an opinion one way or the other. In his experience, admittedly limited to his little brother, a baby didn't get interesting until it started learning how to talk, at which point one could teach it all sorts of words guaranteed to shock the adults. He wrote Crisiant back with the observation that as long as Tavier didn't decide to experiment with feeding worms to the child in hopes it might transform into a baby dragon, everything would be fine.

He knew where he was going with "Treasure." He just couldn't quite figure out how to get there. He saw the ending scene in his head: the shadow of a man on a wall, hanged by the neck, dead. He knew that this man was Fae, and that he'd just barely managed to hide the Rights beneath the wall. He knew the shape of the throne, the rough-hewn rock that nobody would ever guess was so hallowed a place, and now he even knew where it all was. His original guess had been confirmed: the "Regal bells" had belonged not to a Royal residence but to a small Chapel established by a long-ago Queen. A Chapel beside a lake. With the Oakapples' disgrace, the Chapel had lost patronage, and eventually been unconsecrated and sold, converted to a private home. The bells were long gone by then, of course. But it was more proof that he was right.

Yet he had no theme for the piece, no overarching idea, to weave through the story and make it eloquent.

"They had it in mind to claim the Fae Rights as well as the Human, as they'd done with the Elves and Wizards and all other inferior folk. But it didn't really happen that way at all."

He could still hear her spiteful little laugh, the satisfied rustle of her wings. He reminded himself to give Mieka magic to make wings with, made a note, stared at the otherwise empty page, and went to bed with a bottle of Kearney Fairwalk's best Colvado brandy.

With Crisiant's letter had come a note from Derien. Why wasn't he home, what was he doing, didn't he understand that everyone was trying out their new pieces and perfecting their best old ones in the competition for the top place on the schedule? It was worse than Trials, or so Jeska had mentioned when he came to tea at Redpebble Square, and Dery had cozened Mistress Mirdley into giving him a huge meal because what with selling the old house and buying the cottage for his mother and supporting his daughter he was living Lord and Lady only knew how. Cade stifled laughter, admiring his brother's innocence—Jeska had a long, long list of ladies who did more than make sure he got a good meal. He wrote back to say that Touchstone would be just fine with whatever placement they received at the celebrations, and he was working, and he'd be home soon.

Kearney showed up eventually. He showed admirable restraint in waiting a whole day before presenting to Cade a whole inventory of reasons why it would be a frightfully marvelous idea to agree to the Archduke's proposals about a new theater. Cade heard him out, and when he finally reached the end of his arguments said, "No."

"But—"

"He won't be owning us. We can't be bought. Anybody else, if they're stupid enough or venal enough, but not us."

And then he had it.

People who thought they could buy other people—own them—possess and rule them—

He knew.

—people who thought to put you in debt to them so that one day you were compelled to pay back in coin of their choosing—

"Mine he is, and mine he stays." He'd said that himself, hadn't he? But the reason Mieka was his—their—glisker was because Mieka knew just as well as he did, as Rafe and Jeska did, that with no one else would any of them ever find the fusion that made Touchstone truly great. If Mieka was his, theirs, then Cade belonged to Mieka and Rafe and Jeska just as surely, for just the same reason. They'd chosen one another, all four of them. They'd

made the decision to belong to Touchstone, to create of their four disparate talents and personalities this one singular thing, the first group in theater that wasn't named by a plural.

But everyone had the right to decide for himself. Nobody had the right to coerce, threaten, bribe, entice, suborn—or make rebellious war. The Rights might belong only to the Fae, but *rights* belonged to everyone, the *right* to decide. To choose.

And so he had it, and he knew.

He left Kearney spluttering with despair and indignation in the drawing room and returned to his chamber and wrote. Someone brought him food, tea, brandy; he assumed he ate and drank at some point during the day, because by nightfall he became aware of an urgent need for the garderobe. He changed into a nightshirt and one of Kearney's brocade dressing gowns, much too short for him, and continued to write. Long past midnight he collapsed across the bed with a smile on his face.

And the next morning he drove with Kearney back to Gallantrybanks.

His Lordship spent the first few hours of the long drive trying to worm information out of Cade, who kept changing the subject, which Kearney would change back again.

At last the nobleman flounced in his seat with frustration. "How am I to prepare Oakapple for what he'll see if I don't know what's to be seen?"

"He can be amazed along with everyone else," Cade replied carelessly.

"He's *paying* for it!"

"Talking of that, has the Palace sent along the rest of our money yet?"

"Let me worry about that. Can't you give me the slightest clue? I really do have to know, don't you see, Cayden. I have to know at least who the real villain is!"

Leaning forward to get a better view from the window, he

remarked, "Nice day for it, this drive. Spring's come early this year. What's the old saying? 'The sooner the winter, the sweeter the spring'?"

"Cayden, please!"

"And plenty of flowers about, had you noticed? That remembers me—where can I buy some flowers to take to Wistly tomorrow?"

"Cayden!"

It was approximately the same whining tone that Mieka often used, but it didn't make him laugh.

They arrived very late at Redpebble Square. Cade sneaked silently up to his fifth-floor room and slept without dreaming until Derien pounced at about noon the next day.

"You're home! Why didn't you say you were coming home?"

Cade grunted as the boy sat on his legs. "Get off, or I'll cancel your surprise for helping me with 'Treasure.'"

The soft mouth rounded in a silent *Ooh*.

"You did, y'know."

"I did?"

"Your map was invaluable."

"You solved it?"

"I did. With your help. And today I'm going over to Wistly, and we'll start working out the details."

"Is that the surprise?"

"You go over to Wistly whenever you like, that's no treat."

"Not anymore, it ain't."

"*Isn't*, and why *isn't* it?"

Dery shrugged. "It just isn't, not anymore. Everybody dotes on the baby. It's pathetic. She doesn't do anything, just lies about and sleeps and cries and makes a stink."

"That's what babies do, smatchet. That's what *you* did!"

He responded to the teasing with a frown. "But—you liked me anyways, didn't you?"

Cade wanted to wrap his arms around the boy. Instead, he drawled, "You weren't too bad, I s'pose."

"What's the surprise?"

"Then again, you did get rather stinky at times…"

"Cayden!"

Preposterous, the way everybody seemed to be saying his name in that tone of voice these days. "I'm not telling. Except p'rhaps to say that you might keep an evening free about a fortnight from now."

Derien frowned, making the calculation, then gave a shriek of delight. "The Palace, you're taking me to the Palace to see Touchstone!"

25

On the whole, taking everything into consideration, opening the front door of Number Eight, Redpebble Square, was a bit more than Mieka felt up to doing. Within waited the rest of Touchstone, Lord Kearney Fairwalk, and one of the Trials Stewards. They were gathered to decide where Touchstone would be placed in the order of performances. That the Shadowshapers would come last on the final night was a given; that Black fucking Lightning had the advantage in the competition to immediately precede them was also a given. The unfairness of last year's Trials could still roil Mieka's guts, and he was fully aware that in his present state nothing good could come of his appearance at the meeting.

So he walked round to Criddow Close to call on his brother and sister-in-law.

"You're looking prosperous," he told Jedris as he walked into the shop. "Plenty of work, old son?"

"Miek!"

Jed left off cleaning displays of glassware and hugged him. A hug from Jed or Jez was a bone-crushing experience for almost anyone, but Mieka always rated a lift into the air and a squeeze that forced the breath from his lungs. It had been that way since they were children. So, too, the yelp of protest, the wriggling, and the plea to be set down before he lost consciousness or actually died.

Ritual completed, Mieka made sure of his footing and then rubbed his ribs pointedly. "The very least you could do is offer me a drink."

"You know where everything is. And don't use any of the good glasses."

"I'm still waiting for the invitation to dinner where you bring out all that plate Fairwalk gave you."

"You'll wait a while."

"No great cook, is Blye? I thought you looked a bit thinner. You could hire Mistress Mirdley for the evening."

"If I'm thinner, it was all that running forth and back to that house of yours. Whatever possessed you to buy something in the middle of nowhere? And have you finally decided what you want to do with the barn? It's a nice bit of building for all its age."

"I was thinking mayhap Yazz and Robel might want to live there. Only with a loft up top for me, with an outside stair."

"Hmm. I'll have Jez put some designs together."

Drinks poured, they settled on tall stools behind the main counter and toasted each other. Mieka said, "You're lucky I didn't buy the other one. You'd be busy until your grandchildren have grandchildren. Have you work you're actually being paid for?" Because it had occurred to him, much belatedly, that the Archduke might take out his annoyance at Touchstone's refusal to be owned by crookeding the dealings of Touchstone's friends and relations.

"Big new summerhouse at one of the town mansions," Jed replied, thereby relieving Mieka's worry. "Jez and I are doing the framework, Blye's making the panes."

"And boring me witless it is, too," came Blye's voice from the glassworks doorway. "Naught but squares of clear glass. Flat, stale—but decidedly profitable."

Mieka jumped up for a hug and kiss, but Blye waved him back and began brushing the glitter of glass dust off her clothing with exaggerated care. "Mustn't spoil your frustling! How can we bear the honor of his condescension, Jed, having the great Master Glisker here in our humble little shop?"

Her husband intoned, "We shall seek to struggle on, regardless of our unworthiness to breathe the same air as the mighty glisker—"

"Oh, shut it!" Mieka growled, and caught her up in his arms much as Jed had done to him.

"Aren't you supposed to be at Cade's about now?" she asked when he set her down. "Great and weighty talk about the celebrations, and all. Cade was nervous all yestereven about it at dinner."

"He gets to come to dinner and I don't?"

"He has better manners," Jed told him. "Come to talk of it, he *has* manners."

"I love you, too, Jed." He felt a nudge against his feet, and reached down to scratch Bompstable's silky white ears. "They can yatter on quite charmingly without me, I'm certain sure. Another glass?" He held up the empty one in his hand. "Where's your 'prentice?"

"Shush! Don't mention that word!" Jed grinned as he poured out more ale.

"She's not my apprentice. That would be illegal," Blye seconded virtuously. "Rikka cleans the shop and glassworks, and waits on customers. And that's all." The twinkle in her eyes belied her words. "It's her half-day, so she's out interviewing chirurgeons who specialize in teeth."

Mieka whistled through his own. "Made that much already, has she? So you'll be losing her soon."

"Not if I can help it," Blye said. "But, as I said before, she's *not* my apprentice."

"After her teeth are put together the way she wants them," Jed added, "nobody will recognize her. She's done something with her hair, and grown up a bit as well. There's a young man or three up Beekbacks way who'll take note, and then we'll lose her anyways."

"Not if I can help it," Blye repeated.

She finally convinced him that it really was important for him to be at the meeting. He felt better about it as he slipped in through the kitchen door of Redpebble Square. Two drinks with Jed had helped. They gave him the self-assurance he needed to carry through a certain plan.

After bestowing a smacking kiss to Mistress Mirdley's cheek, he sailed into the parlor with a cheery, "Greetings, all!" and sat himself down on the carpet near Cayden's chair. "Frightfully sorry to be late. Is it tea time already? Jeschenar, worthy son of your wonderful mother, be a dear and pour me out a cup, won't you? Ever so beholden!"

"Nice of you to join us," growled Cade, but Mieka didn't turn to look at him. If he did, he'd break into laughter before he'd done what he intended to do.

"We were just discussing things, don't you see," said Fairwalk, looking nervous—but didn't he always? "Lord Broadflock was giving his opinion—"

"And valuably, I'm sure," Mieka interrupted, recognizing the Steward as one of those who'd been most in favor of Black fucking Lightning last year at Trials. Good; that would make this more fun. He accepted a cup from Jeska, whose face was a study in conflict. Amusement, uneasiness, a spark of eagerness in his eyes at what Mieka might be planning, for Jeska knew him well enough to be certain he was planning something. From this expectancy Mieka judged that Lord Broadflock had not made a favorable impression. He glanced quickly over at Rafe, whose lips were twitching beneath his beard; further encouragement. Not that he required any.

"As I was saying," Lord Broadflock harrumphed, "much depends on the nature of the plays presented. Their length must be such that three groups can perform in one evening, and as there are three nights of celebrations, culminating of course in the performance of the Shadowshapers on that last evening—"

"Of course!" Mieka said brightly.

"Brief but powerful is what you're looking for," Fairwalk interjected. "Lively, amusing, thought-provoking, demonstrating all that Touchstone is known for—"

"We promise not to shatter anything expensive," Mieka contributed, and reached into his jacket pocket.

"Beholden," said Lord Broadflock in a forbidding tone of voice.

Fairwalk said, "I was just informing His Lordship that Touchstone's will be an entirely new piece, and I don't yet know what its length might—Cayden, have you timed it out yet?"

Mieka uncorked a squarish, flattish blue bottle and poured some of its contents into his tea. Then he set the bottle on the carpet so that its white label was clearly visible to Lord Broadflock, and took a long swallow from the cup.

Only Cade couldn't see the label, though Mieka was sure he'd recognize the bottle by its shape and color; almost everyone knew this brand, either from having used it or seeing it advertised or passing by its manufactory down past the Plume. He had a quick look at Jeska, whose elegant brows had arched, and the crown of Rafe's head as he bent to hide his face. Fairwalk looked paralytic. The Steward seemed to have something caught in his throat.

Mieka used The Eyes. "Oh, I'm so sorry—I do cry your pardon—did you want some? Shocking bad manners not to share, me Mum would string me up by me ears." Leaping to his feet, and with his most winsome smile, he poured a bit into the Steward's teacup and sat back down again on the floor.

Lady Jaspiela, he reflected, would not approve of her best porcelain being rattled so on its over-hasty way to a tabletop. If not an actual break or crack, surely a chipping might result. He hadn't considered that. Ah well. She'd forgive him. He sipped from his own cup again, and when it became clear that no one else was possessed of the powers of speech, said, "We were talking about Touchstone going on directly before the Shadowshapers, weren't we? Excellent! And quite an honor, innit, Cayden? Beholden to Your Lordship!"

"Before th-the Shadowshapers," Lord Broadflock managed, and got to his feet, and within moments was out the door, Fairwalk trailing along behind.

Mieka was unable to believe his luck. This had worked even better than he'd intended. Delighted, and grinning from one side of his face to the other, he finally turned to Cade.

"What's in it?" Cade demanded.

"What's in what?"

"The bottle."

"What bottle?"

"*That* fucking bottle!" Cade roared.

He peered at the label. "Blacksaddle's Equine Liniment? I thought it tasted odd." All at once he coughed, then choked, and clutched at his throat, and was about to topple artistically onto the carpet when Cayden kicked him. "Ow!"

"Whiskey," Rafe said in a strangled sort of voice. "It'd have to be whiskey."

"Of course it's whiskey!" Mieka sat up, rubbing his leg where Cade's boot had got him. "And it worked! I got us placed right before the Shadowshapers!"

Jeska said, "You did, that. C'mon, Rafe, let's go tell Crisiant."

It wasn't until the pair were in the vestibule that they finally started to laugh. The door slammed shut behind them, and Mieka turned a wounded look on Cade. He suddenly understood why the others had left in such a hurry. He'd never seen Cade this angry. This cold.

"You *clown*," he said in a low, lethal voice. "You think you're so fuckin' funny—you never take a breath unless it comes out as a joke. You think everything is just one huge prank, all of life is only there to be laughed at. Well, take me off the list of things you make fun of. I'm done!"

"Oh, settle down! Stuffy old twiddlepoop like that, he needed taking down a peg. Besides," he said, earnest now despite himself, "the Stewards cheated us at the last Trials, giving the Ducal to Black fucking Lightning when everybody knows Touchstone deserved it. And he was in their favor, you know he was! So I mucked about with him a little, just to get some of our own back."

"And what if he'd left? Did you think of that? What if he'd got fed up to the back teeth with waiting for you to get here, and crossed us off the list altogether? What if he'd been so offended by what you said—leave alone what you did!—that he—"

"Not in a million years. The Princess likes us."

"And the Archduke hates us, or as near to as makes no difference!" His voice began to rise in pitch and volume. "You and your damned jokes—is there anything in the world you take seriously?"

Mieka suddenly heard himself saying things he'd never said to another living soul.

"You think I don't know why I am the way I am? The audiences—onstage and off!—they want the laugh. They don't want real. That's the business we're in, innit? Making unreality. I told you a long time ago, somebody has to teach these people how to dream. Show 'em there's more to life than goin' to work and goin' for a pint and goin' home—they don't want real from us, they get enough of real in their own lives. We go to work, too, only we work in places that don't exist. For them, *we* don't really exist."

"That's not true! What we do—it's real when it's onstage and—"

"And who had to argue you into being honest in your work,

into putting more of yourself into it? You don't want them to see who you really are any more than I do!" Mieka sprang to his feet again and started to pace the carpet. "What you do when you write, and prime the withies, there's so much more of you than there used to be—d'you remember when we talked about that? But there's not many who truly understand what they're seeing and hearing onstage—Tobalt, maybe, he's a bright lad—Gods damn it, Quill, they don't *want* real!"

"Mieka—you have to be real to *someone*—"

"Not to them. And it's easy for me, y'know. Look at me. How many people like me are rollin' round the Kingdom? I'm all Elf to look at. Tall enough to be Human, and me teeth came out squared off instead of pointed, but the rest is Elf to me fingertips. They see me walk onstage and they *know* something mad and clever's about to happen. But I'm the first thing they see that isn't real to them. They don't want me to be real. I'm a laugh when I'm there and the echo of a laugh when I'm gone. And that's the way I want it. Except—" He paused, and wrapped his arms around himself, and shook his head. "Except sometimes I do that to me friends, the people I care about, the ones who don't want just a laugh, they want *me*. Just like I am. Well, sometimes I lose that, I forget that. The walls go up all by themselves and I forget how to get round them. I forget sometimes that there's people as want who I am. It scares me. *You* scare me. The thing about you is that the walls might as well not be there. To you, they're invisible. I can't do anything about that and it scares me even worse. So if I end up throwing a couple of bricks in your face, that's why."

Cade sat there staring at him, gray eyes blank with shock. Not the Elsewhen kind, but honest fist-to-the-guts gobsmacked. Furious with himself for revealing so much, Mieka shrugged and turned for the door.

"Send round when you want to rehearse. I'm done here."

"Do you know what scares *me*?" Cade whispered, and Mieka

stopped cold. "That one day, all that's left will be the echo."

This infuriated him anew. Those damned Elsewhens. Cade still didn't trust him to make his own decisions. He could have recited example after example of his instincts guiding him correctly. Instead, he swung round on one heel. "Don't you want to know where I'm going? I'm for the shops—to buy me a yellow shirt." He had the satisfaction of seeing Cade turn white to the lips. Unable to resist, he taunted, "What was the exact color again? Lemony, or p'rhaps more of a buttercup? Daffodil? C'mon, Cade, give us a hint! Oh, but you don't *do* that, do you? That would be *telling*. Well, I'll just have to use me own judgment, then—but that scares you even worse, doesn't it?"

"Go on, then!" Cade shouted. "Go drink yourself cross-eyed! Go stick thorn in your arms until you kill yourself! I don't fucking care!"

"Yeh, you do," he jeered. "You're afraid of that more than anything else, and we both know it. Every time you have an honest feeling, you turn tail and run like it's a dragon with poison dripping from its teeth! Look at that girl you wanted, and she wanted you, only you started feeling things for her, didn't you? Real things—honest things! So she's set to marry somebody else now, and all because you were too scared—"

"What?"

He froze. "I—I thought you knew." It had been in the broadsheets, and when he'd read it he'd felt both sorry for Cade and angry with him. But the news had appeared while Cade was at Fairwalk Manor. "It's—she's bespoken to Lord Eastkeeping— I'm sorry—I thought you knew—"

"Get out." The long body unfolded from the chair, and even from a dozen feet away Cade seemed to tower over him. "Now."

He turned and fled.

* * *

It was warm in the springtime darkness of the river lawn, and he felt himself to be wrapped inside one of his own creations. He could feel the cool damp of the grass beneath his bare feet, and the slightly splintery arms of the chair. City sounds reached him only vaguely from across the water. Wistly Hall was quiet. A few crickets, birds flying past with a chirp or twitter. There wasn't light enough from the lamps along the riverwalk or the boats plying the river by night; he would have added a half-moon to emphasize the scene. He wasn't onstage, though, and this wasn't a scene, and Jeska wouldn't be stepping from the shadows to recite his opening lines. But it wasn't reality, either, naked and unadorned. It was him, and a chair, and the wet grass, and a mostly empty bottle. And whatever had been in the thorn he'd used earlier. He didn't remember, and didn't care.

Whatever it was, it made the Elf-light lanterns across the water dance in rainbow colors. Quite pretty, really. A while ago, a few of them had bloomed like flowers, and that had been even prettier. Rather like a more benevolent version of the thorn Pirro Spangler had slipped him way last year. He liked this sort. It was pretty.

"Mieka?"

He didn't glance round as his wife spoke his name. He heard her footsteps hissing through the grass.

"It's late, dearling," she whispered, and knelt at his side, her beautiful hands clasping his knee.

There really ought to be a half-moon. The faint shine of lights from the opposite bank and the drifting boats didn't gleam as they ought to on her hair.

"There's a chill in the breeze. Come up to bed."

He upended the bottle over his glass. "When I'm ready."

"What troubles you, dearling?"

"It's not my fault the girl's marrying someone else."

"I don't understand."

"Cayden!" he spat. "Master Cayden bloody great Tregetour!

Thinks he's the best thing to hit the Kingdom since—since—"
He couldn't find the words. Small wonder. He wasn't the bloody
great tregetour, was he—just the glisker, the one who used the
magic but couldn't prime it into the withies.

"Mieka, what's wrong?"

He shrugged. "Oh, everybody sayin' how fuckin' brilliant
Cade is, how clever—figurin' out 'bout the Treasure an' all—" He
squinted to see her in the darkness, the pale and perfect face, the
gorgeous eyes. "Y'know what, about Master Cayden bloody great
Tregetour Silversun? I was there when he saw it! I gave him the
thorn! Without me—" He snapped his fingers and felt her flinch.

"Dearling," she said again, "why don't you come up to bed
now?"

"*Dearling,*" he mimicked cruelly, "me glass is fuckin' hollow,
innit!"

"There's more in the dining room—"

"Then go get it!"

While she was gone, he glowered at the river. The pretty
lights were just lights now, yellow and boring. Cayden bloody
Silversun, most brilliant mind ever to grace the theater, best
writer in a generation—two generations, three—

He raised his glass in a spiteful toast, and was both infuriated
and glad that there was no drink to drink. He opened his mouth
to shout for her, but she was there beside him all at once, a bottle
in her hands.

"All he ever does is *stand* there," he snarled. "Who is it does all
the work, eh? Who is it ends up wrung out every fuckin' night?"

"I know how hard you must work, Mieka," she whispered.

"But you *don't* know, do you, because you're not allowed to
watch! No women in the theater! I'll do something about that, I
will," he vowed, and gulped more brandy.

She knelt beside him again. "They need you, they need you
so much, they wouldn't be where they are if not for you."

"Too bleedin' right! And Cade wouldn't have the first notion about the Treasure if not for me! D'you know how he got it figured? All those books, that's how they think he did it, reading himself half-blind, and then piecing it all together, and a story from the Fae—" He snorted. " 'Twas thorn what did it, thorn I gave him! He *saw* it, like he sees a million other things—not that he ever tells me! I always know when it's about me, there's a look he gets—but he never says a fuckin' word. Have to make the decisions, he says, live me own life, can't choose for me. In one of them, he hated me. He saw what's to come and he *hated* me—and he won't even tell me what I did to make it like that! An' there was another, only this was a good future, it was his Namingday and we'd got old and I was there—I was still there—"

A boatman called from the river, and she flinched again, her head turning, and the faint glow of the Elf-light across the water lit her face. He could see in her eyes that she didn't understand.

"He knows what will happen," Mieka told her, speaking very clearly so the words would be the right ones. "He dreams it. He sees what will come. Never breathes a word of it—but he knows. He *knows!*"

"Mieka—"

"It's how he knew about the Treasure! Gods in glory, girl, are you thick in the head? *He sees the futures*—all of them, hundreds of them!" He drained his glass and hurled it across the lawn. With it went the last of the thorn and his energy. He couldn't seem to move. "I'm tired," he mumbled. "Gods, I'm so tired…"

"Come up to bed, dearling."

He was muzzily aware of hands helping him up, guiding him, half-carrying him back up to the house. There were lights burning in the family dining room, and from somewhere he heard a baby crying.

* * *

The Keymarker had got Touchstone cheap, because every other important group was back in Town and that meant every important place was booked. The Palace still hadn't come through on payment for the trip to the Continent. The Keymarker wasn't a step down, but it wasn't the Kiral Kellari, either. That stage was currently graced three nights a week by Black fucking Lightning, at half again as much as Touchstone would get for the Keymarker. But they needed money, and the Keymarker had offered, and here they were.

A new sign had gone up. No words, just a huge iron key hanging over the sidewalk. Master Ashbottle had been busy inside, as well. There was a great metal key painted gold on either side of the stage, and one up over the bar, and Rafe was worried about the bounce of the magic. Mieka didn't care about that. He was angry that they weren't all made of glass so he could shatter them.

The artists' tiring room backstage was more nicely appointed than he remembered, with a selection of nibble-food and their favorite beverages. Mieka downed a glass of very good whiskey—Auntie Brishen was right to be worried about this new distillery—as he took off the boots he'd walked over in and prepared to pull on the soft-soled leather knee-boots he preferred for work.

And then he caught Cade looking at him. *That* look. The Elsewhen look.

Just a flash, just a brief turn, but Mieka was at his side and grasping his arm before it was over. Roughly he yanked Cade outside into the corridor, through the Artists Entrance, into the back alley.

"Unless you tell me exactly what you just saw—"

"I–I can't—"

"Gods fucking damn you, Quill!"

"No, Mieka, I mean I don't know what I saw, it wasn't clear—"

"Tell me! All of it!"

He seemed to wilt. Evidently fierce treatment while he was still stunned was the line to take. The others had coddled him far too long.

"You—we'd just finished—you jumped over your bench—" He frowned. "You stumbled, like your right leg had gone out from under you, and I caught you—Gods, you were white as bleached linen—like all the blood had drained out of your face—"

"Was I wearing a yellow shirt?"

Cade stared at him as if he'd gone completely out of his mind.

"The yellow shirt!" he repeated impatiently. "Was it that Elsewhen? The one where you hated me?"

"N-no… it was…" He looked Mieka down and up. "It was tonight," he breathed. "Not even an hour from now—"

"So whatever it was, I got through the show?"

Cade nodded. "But you were hurt, your right leg—"

"I'm fine. Stop worrying."

"It was tonight," he insisted. "You had on exactly what you're wearing now—except—except—"

"What? Tell me!"

He looked down at Mieka's bare feet below the hems of white trousers. "The soft boots," he mumbled. "You were wearing the soft boots."

"I always wear—" Peering up into Cade's face, he blew out a long sigh and said, "Why didn't you just say so in the first place? I'll not wear them, not tonight. Will that do?"

"I don't know. I never know." He pulled away and opened the door. "Do as you like. I have to check the withies."

Mieka followed him silently. Back in the tiring room, he stuck his feet back into the boots he'd worn over here. Stiff leather, not supple like the others, but if it kept that look from Cade's eyes…

"So you finally learned," teased Rafe as Mieka emerged into the little corridor next the stage. "Those tall black boots are all right for the black trousers, but with the white they cut you off at the knees and you look even shorter than Jeska."

Hearing him, Jeska shot back, "At least I'm not getting as wide as I am tall!" and gave him a playful shove with one shoulder. Rafe bumped into Mieka, who jumped to one side. A servant girl, passing nearby with a tray of used glassware, tried to backstep, and the glasses fell shattering onto the brick floor. And Mieka, recovering his balance, crunched his right boot onto the wickedly sharp shards.

"My lords, gentlemen—"

Had he been wearing the soft leather, he would have sliced his foot wide open.

"The Keymarker has the honor to present—"

Scant wonder Cade had seen him white-faced. He'd finished the performance, while bleeding into his boot for more than an hour.

"Touchstone!"

He looked up and saw Cade, gray eyes huge with shock. Dredging up a smile, Mieka said, "That's a first, then, innit? First time we've broken the glassware *before* the show."

26

Unhappily for Cayden, but ecstatically for *The Nayword* (the next issue sold out in two days), he ran into Tobalt Fluter that next evening. It happened in the Bag o' Nails, the tavern that had taken over much of the Downstreet's business but never quite managed the feel of the old place. The excitement here was whom you might see at the bar, not what you might see onstage.

Cade was alone at a small table in the back, drinking himself stupid. It wasn't that he regretted telling Mieka about the Elsewhen. Unless he was prepared to endure the boy's pestering and whining forever, he'd been pretty much compelled to start sharing his Elsewhens. That was what he told himself, at least. And in the end he didn't truly mind that it had been forced out of him. It had to happen sooner or later.

What horrified him, and kept him flicking a finger in the air to signal the barmaid for another round, was that for just an instant—for less than an eyeblink of time—he'd thought to himself, *What if I tell him, and it changes things, and he doesn't finish the performance?* After all, even if he'd been unsteady on his feet and pale as a ghost, the show had been successful. Everyone had applauded madly, and thrown buckets of coins onto the stage.

Had he really been willing to sacrifice Mieka's well-being just to get through a show?

What sort of monster was he?

During the first two pints he analyzed the Elsewhen itself in light of what had occurred in the hallway. Mieka's right foot had come down on the broken glassware; it was simple enough to assume that the soft-soled boots had been no match for the shards, and he'd cut himself, and spent the show slowly bleeding. The leather was tight enough that he hadn't actually bled to death, and he'd managed to finish the performance, but—

Cade realized then that with only two days left to their booking at the Palace, it was entirely possible that Mieka could have been either too weak from blood loss or too immobilized by the injury to do his job. And that wasn't even to consider infection and fever or even permanent damage to his foot, or—

What sort of monster *was* he, to think for even an instant about not warning Mieka?

The next pint was devoted to self-condemnation.

He began the fourth with a silent toast to the Elf, for he'd also realized that in the Elsewhen, as much pain as he must have been in, as increasingly dizzy as he must have felt, he had done his job. He'd not let them down. He knew how essential he was to them, how their success didn't depend just on Cayden's words or Jeska's brilliance or Rafe's strength and subtlety. The four of them together, they were *Touchstone*, a singular thing, and they had to work together or—or—

{"You can't do this to him, Cade," Rafe said quietly.

"No?" His mouth stretched in a thin smile that felt like a scar across his face.

Mieka strolled into the empty tavern. Late, as usual. Cade glanced at Rafe, then Jeska. They weren't going to help him; he could see it in their faces. The masquer's jaw was set and after a long glare at Cade, he turned his head away. Rafe—he wasn't just glaring, he was clenching his fists as if ready to use them.

Cade felt his lip curl. If he had to do this himself, he would, and be damned to them. He turned to Mieka, sickened once again by those glazed, lightless eyes, the ruin of that once-beautiful face. He held himself from a flinch as those eyes focused blearily on him, as a cunning little smile stretched his lips and emphasized the creases framing his mouth.

"Good t'see you, Quill," he said, his voice rougher, raspier, the drink and the thorn coarsening his voice just as they had coarsened his face and his body.

"Are you sober enough to understand this, and remember it?"

He blinked. "What? What're you—?"

"You've one chance," Cade said in a dangerously soft tone, "and one chance only. You drag yourself out of whatever gutter you're wallowing in, you stop drinking, you get rid of the thorn—*all* of it—and you prove to me that you can still do your job without putting Jeska or Rafe at risk. You do that, or you're out. Understand? Clean yourself up, or go to whichever hell will take you in. I mean it. If I think you're a danger to us, you're sacked."

He was white to the lips, and for a moment looked as if he might topple with the shock. Betrayal, pain, anguish, shame, terror—so many things in that damaged face, in those lightless eyes. But then he lurched to his feet and stood there, gripping the table, swaying slightly before stiffening his spine.

"You fucking bastard," he whispered. "You wouldn't be anything if it wasn't for me. You'd be licking boots at Court, the way your mother planned—wed to some puling idiot of a girl—" He laughed, a harsh and grating sound. "You think *I* drink too much? How many bottles do *you* get through each night? If it wasn't for me, you'd be on your face or on your knees for anybody with liquor or thorn to offer you—"

Cade wasn't aware of getting to his feet, or of drawing back his hand. He knew that he'd slapped Mieka—open-handed, a deliberate insult, the way he'd slap a whore—only when he heard the crack of his fingers on flesh, and felt the sting on his palm, and saw him stagger.

"You been wantin' to do that for years," Mieka hissed. "Felt good, did it? Why not do it again? I'm too drunk to mind much, have to hit me a lot harder to really make me feel it! C'mon, Cade! All the times you wanted to, here's your chance!"

"You think you can't be replaced? You think we need you so much, we'll put up with this shit forever? I could walk outside and find a dozen gliskers I'd trust more than I trust you!"

"G'on then, and try!"

When Cade raised his arm again, Rafe stood up and grabbed Mieka, pulling him out of reach. "Stop it! Go home and sleep this off—both of you!" he snarled over his shoulder at Cade. "Nobody's getting sacked—come on, Mieka, he didn't mean—"

"He—he *did* mean it—" Tears spilled down his cheeks, rage and drunken self-pity that sickened Cade with disgust. "He *meant* it, Rafe—"

"At last you understand," Cade said very softly. "Be at the theater tomorrow by noon, and be there sober—or I swear I'll never work with you again."

Rafe dragged Mieka out of the tavern. Jeska stayed, silent, then slowly raised his head and looked up at Cade.

"You know I don't meddle. I masque what you give me, I do the work, and I'm bloody good at it. Whatever's between you and him is your concern, not mine."

"So what's your point?"

"That I've never said anything like this before. And you'll

never hear anything like it from me again."

"Say what you have to say, and then get out."

A spark of anger flared in his limpid blue eyes—and Cade remembered suddenly the vicious street fighter of long ago. He hadn't seen that Jeska in years. But the rage was gone as quickly as it had kindled, and his voice was very soft when he spoke.

"I want to know if you're aware what you just did."

"What d'you mean?"

"You just threw him away with both hands."}

"Cade? I thought that was you. Oy, what's been, old son?"

The chipper greeting, the companionable slap on his shoulder—he raised his head and met Tobalt Fluter's abruptly worried gaze. He knew what must be scrawled across his face. Composing himself, he waved to the chair opposite and as Tobalt sat down, Cade drained the fourth pint down his throat and beckoned for another. The ale washed the sickness and anger out of his mouth. He needed more.

"How many bottles do you get through each night?"

"This one's on me," Tobalt said as the barmaid brought their drinks, and flipped her a shiny coin.

"Professional visit, then," Cade observed. "Article to write, have you?"

"Only if you agree in advance." He lifted his glass and took a swallow. "There's rumors dancing from one edge of Gallantrybanks to the other about what Touchstone will perform."

"Why don't you go bother Vered, or Rauel? There's rumors about the Shadowshapers, too."

"They're all locked up together at Chat's house, rehearsing."

Cade grinned mordantly. "Which, by implication, is what we ought to be doing, but which, by further implication, we don't need to do because we've got it all done and dusted."

"Do you?" Tobalt asked with innocent sincerity.

"Would I tell you if we did?"

"Probably not. But there's plenty else to talk of, y'know."

He considered, then shrugged. "Quote me accurately, that's all I ask."

Tobalt looked hurt. "When have I ever not?"

"Theater, in the right hands, can change lives. And if you change enough of them, you change the world."

I point out that this is ambitious, even for Cayden Silversun.

"Think about it. The Shadowshapers do! They've taken theater to a whole new place, where the audience comes not just for a good time, a few laughs, maybe a tear or two while nobody else can see—what they do, it's feeling and thinking and encouraging people to consider their lives. Mayhap without realizing it, but it happens all the same. It's never just the same tired old playlets. They work new ideas into them, even the trite old things people have seen a thousand times."

I mention that I've heard it said, by those who denounce theater in general and the Shadowshapers—and Touchstone, and Black Lightning—in particular, that it's no good rousing emotions, stirring things up that way, and even less use to do it through the imagination. That it's encouraging illusion.

Silversun disagrees.

"The emotion born of imagination is just as real as any other. You can't laugh at the man in charge to his face—but you can laugh yourself silly in a theater, and I'm thinking now of the farce plays, you know the ones I mean. The ones where the head man always ends up in muck of one kind or another. Same with weeping, you know. Can't cry, mustn't cry, unmanly to cry. But I've seen grown men, stone-faced farmers and tough sailors and men of business who'd sell their own grandmothers, they weep buckets over something like 'Silver Mine' or 'A Life in a Day.' It's a safe place to go, the theater. You can feel and dream and think without fear of the consequences. Without fearing yourself, that what you think and feel and dream will run away with you, the reason so many people keep themselves to themselves in their daily lives."

I ask if this is what he means about changing the world.

"I know where you're going, and that's not what I mean at all. During the performance, people see and hear and experience what we want them to. It's one purpose of Art to cause a reaction. The Artist has a purpose in creating, and one of those purposes is to bring about a reaction in the audience. But there are other objectives, and the most important of them is to have people think about what they've just experienced."

Where does beauty fit in?

"A very wise person once said to me that when we see the truth, no matter how painful, there's beauty in that. The courage to see and acknowledge the truth is always beautiful— but things that are beautiful aren't always true."

And what do the rest of Touchstone think about this? Your glisker, for instance.

"Mieka! I know exactly what he'd tell you if you asked— that thinking only gets in the way."

"You never know when to shut up, do you?" Blye asked.

"Splash a bit more vinegar on it, won't you?" Cade invited.

"It wasn't that bad," Dery soothed. "You didn't mention women in theater this time."

"Should have." He stared into his teacup, wishing he dared spike it with a dollop of whiskey. Mistress Mirdley had sent up her best hangover remedy this morning without his even having to ask. It had mostly worked.

They had gathered as usual in the kitchen, where the Trollwife was pointedly ignoring him while she pounded her big fists into a pile of bread dough. With every blow came a little puff of flour. He imagined the dough to be his brain—it had certainly felt as thickly inert this morning—and the puffs to be thoughts of the arrogant sort he'd recklessly blithered to Tobalt Fluter last night. She'd have to pound harder to get them all.

"So you're bidden to the Palace by the Princess herself," Blye said. "Quite the honor."

"You should've seen Mother when the note arrived." Dery grinned. He skipped over to the door, then turned, and Jeska couldn't have done a better job at imitating Lady Jaspiela. "Whyever would Her Highness want to see *you*? I trust you recall everything I ever taught you about addressing Royalty." He strode over to the workbench, looked up at Cade, and went on, "Hire one of those boats. And bring a gift. Nothing presumptuous, mind. Flowers would be appropriate. And for mercy's sake, wear your best jacket! And brush your hair! And clean your teeth! And do your schoolwork—" He broke off with a comical frown. "Oh, wait, that's what she says to *me!*"

Cade bowed, shaking with laughter. "As you say, Mother dear. Much beholden, Mother dear." He supposed he oughtn't to encourage the boy in such disrespect, though it was scarcely his fault if Lady Jaspiela was a snob.

"Why a boat?" Blye wanted to know.

"So nobody at the Palace titters behind a glove that the wife of the First Gentleman of the Bedchamber can't afford her own carriage, of course," Cade told her. "She was right about bringing a gift, though—I am beholden to her for that."

"But not flowers," Derien said. "And that's where you come in, Blye."

Cade nodded. "That little box of yours was such a success, I know there's something else amongst your work she'd like."

"And there might be a Royal Warrant in your future!" Dery concluded.

"And that dragon's egg of Tavier's will hatch any day now," she retorted. "Well, come on, then, Cade—let's go see what's in the shop."

After much deliberation, they settled on an exquisite three-inch-high candleflat swirling with white and forget-me-never blue, and at two precisely that afternoon Cade presented himself at the Palace's rivergate after a lazy drift downriver below the Plume. This was the oldest part of the compound, built nobody knew quite when. The sand-pale riverstone walls were five feet thick and filled in with rubble, which made for an interior of seeping damp only partially mitigated by several miles of tapestries. Cade had been here once before, during a littleschool outing, and he could swear that the same frowning guardsmen who had been on watch back then glared disapproval at him now. He and Rafe had escaped their group and the guards, and played swordfight all the way to the top of the stairs before they were caught. He was vastly tempted to give these sentries the slip now, but there was no one to play with.

He'd no idea why they were looking at him like that. It wasn't as if he hadn't dressed for the occasion: his best pewter-gray brocade jacket, whisper-fine white shirt, boots polished to a mirror gleam, and the little silver falcon pin Derien had given him. He would in no wise disgrace himself, his family, or Touchstone. Yet when Lady Vrennerie came to greet him in the reception hall, he suddenly felt as ragged and motley as a crow-keeper in a wheat field. He'd forgot how pretty she was, how good she smelled, how her nose scrunched up a bit when she smiled. In the months since he'd last seen her, he'd taken advantage more than once of what was on offer after a show; it wasn't that he felt guilty, now that he was taking her hand again, it was more that being with those girls was… expected of him. Monotonous. Even, once the immediate pleasure had passed, dismal.

"Master Silversun! How glad am I to see you!"

"Lady Vrennerie," he responded, and bowed over her hand, seeing the silver bracelet circling her wrist. She was wearing peach silk today, the slim-cut gown she'd worn to the masked ball. Since returning from the Winterly, he'd not noticed any ladies wearing gowns similar to hers. How like her, he thought, to wear what suited her and shrug at fashion.

She suggested a walk through the gardens. He nodded and followed. Once they were away from the building and out in the open where no one could hear, she said, "It was me sent the note. I asked my lady to sign it because I didn't think you'd come if you knew it was me asking."

"Of course I would have! We're friends."

Her look of relief was quickly replaced by a wide smile. "Then why did you call me Lady Vrennerie?"

"Because you called me Master Silversun," he retorted, and they smiled at each other.

"I wanted to tell you that I appreciate that you didn't put a name to me in that article."

"What can you be thinking, to read that exceedingly low and vulgar broadsheet?"

"I read *everything*," she said flatly. Then another grin decorated her face. "You'd be surprised how my vocabulary has expanded!"

"I'd be shocked, is what you mean." They walked together through a knot garden fragrant with new spring growth. "I didn't name you, because my mother always told me that a true lady is mentioned only once in her life in print, to announce her marriage." He looked her in the eyes, letting her know that he knew. "I wish you very happy, Vrennerie. I've heard excellent things about Lord Eastkeeping."

"He is a good man," she agreed. "Do you really think I'm wise?"

Aware that she wasn't referring to his characterization of her in Tobalt's article, he smiled. "Yes, I do."

"Beholden, Cade."

"How does your lady? Is she happy?"

"She finds nothing in Gallantrybanks that is not pleasing her."

An answer that was not quite an answer. He waited a moment before asking, "And outside Gallantrybanks?"

She gave him a sidelong smile. "You're quite clever enough to change the world, you know. Yes, the only matter for displeasure is at the moment outside Gallantrybanks, but will be here tomorrow for the start of the celebrations."

"The new Archduchess."

"You were gone all this autumn and winter, so you didn't hear, I suppose. First there was the matter of the dowry. The Tregrefin sent the proper number of fleeces, but Lady Panshilara put it about that they were of the third quality, not the first. This wasn't so serious—it turned out she was wrong, and they were exactly as they should be—but before it was settled, she began saying—she—"

"Just tell me," he encouraged gently.

In grim tones, she said, "I traced it to her maidservants. They were whispering that there needn't have been that foolishness on the night of the wedding at home, because anybody could have—could have had her, she'd not been virgin since her fifteenth year! I was so afeared the King would send my poor lady back."

Cayden whistled soundlessly through his teeth. Surely the girl couldn't just be returned, as if the shop had sent the wrong wine.

"I wish you'd been here, Cayden," said Vrennerie.

What she thought he could have done about it, he'd no notion—and then it hit him. His father. She was thinking about his father's position in Ashgar's household.

"But the marriage happened," he said roughly. "And not a complaint from Ashgar, I'd take my oath on it." Looking anywhere but at her, he finished, "Knows a virgin when he has one, does the Prince."

She said nothing for several paces. Then: "I told you this because the Archduchess found an ally."

"Let me guess. Princess Iamina."

She stopped walking and clutched at his arm. "How did you—?"

"Because as little as they like each other personally—and it takes no wit to guess that—they're both threatened by the Princess—or, rather what the Princess will eventually produce. An heir. Gods save me from Court trickeries! If you're truly wise, Vrennerie, you'll have Lord Eastkeeping take you off to his country estates and never set foot here again if you can possibly help it."

She shook her head. "But then I would be of no use to my lady."

How could he ever have thought she might have been the woman in the Elsewhens, who'd been bored by his work and cared for noting but the money and prestige it brought her?

"The alliance did not last," Vrennerie went on, with a bleak satisfaction.

Cade snorted. "How did you manage it?"

"Who said it was me?"

"Who else?" He grinned.

She chuckled acknowledgment. "All I did was make a mentioning of how talented Princess Iamina's dressmaker must be, to make her look so much thinner and younger than she really is. They're both of them vain as vain ever could be, and not even a common cause of disgracing my lady could survive Panshilara hiring the woman."

Women. Naught but conceit and folly, treachery and spite. It was worse than one of those mawkish playlets Mieka so adored playing for laughs.

And with thought of the Elf, it came crashing into his head. The fingers plying a pen across a page. The words *a secret knowledge about Master Silversun* glimpsed before the page was folded by hands he recognized, only this time the sealing wax was orange and the flames used to melt it had a reddish glow, little licking flames unlike the green of a Goblin's making or the yellow-gold of an Elf, the blue of a Wizard, even the purplish gold of the old man who had controlled the *vodabeists*. He knew the hands, and who had made the fire, and who was about to betray him.

But with what knowledge?

Oh, so simple. So obvious. His secret.

How had she learned it?

What choice of Cade's own had led—would lead—to the writing of that letter?

"I—I have to leave now," he said, feeling helpless and not liking it.

Bewildered, Vrennerie began a protest. "Cayden—"

"I have to leave," he repeated, and without another word started for the white brick path he knew led to the outer gates, the ones into Gallantrybanks and not to the river, and once outside he flagged down a hire-hack—

And sat in it for long minutes, unable to give an address. Because he knew now that there was only one person who connected him and his secret to Mistress Caitiffer. If he went to Wistly, if he confronted Mieka, demanding to know why—

He couldn't. It would be the end of them, of Touchstone.

He could go to the Archduke's mansion instead. He could find the old woman and—and—

And do what? Bribe her? Threaten her? Beg her not to tell?

What must he do or not do to prevent this?

And then he almost laughed. Who would believe it? *Cayden Silversun can see the futures.* Nonsense. There was no proof. No evidence. She could write what she pleased to whomever she pleased. *Cayden Silversun has dreams, and they come true.* Complete fantasy. No one would ever believe it. The only people who knew for sure were friends or dead, like Sagemaster Emmot. He was safe.

The hack lurched forward slightly. The driver settled his horse with a cooing sound, then turned his head to look at Cade.

"Number Eight, Redpebble Square," Cade said at last, and leaned back into worn leather. As he did so, he felt the little box in his pocket, the one containing the candleflat. He'd forgot to give it to Vrennerie for the Princess. He was reminded suddenly of the gifts Blye had made for Mieka's eighteenth Namingday, long before the girl and her mother had invaded their lives.

He wished he'd known at the time that things would never be that good again.

He wished he'd had the courage to warn Mieka.

It was all his fault, in the end. Nothing—not him, not Touchstone, not anything in the world—would ever mean as much or be as important to Mieka as she was. She'd leave him one day, or he'd leave her, it didn't really matter. The damage would already have been done. And Cade would stand in the doorway of his house with a note in his hand from Kearney Fairwalk, and he'd say, *"But I'm still here,"* and Mieka would be dead.

"You just threw him away with both hands."

That wasn't true. Mieka's was the betrayal. Mieka's was the responsibility.

"You don't trust me!"

Neither did he trust his own pride and anger and hatred and fear.

"I think I hated you."

But it was just Mieka being Mieka: careless, thoughtless, impulsive—clever and mad—

"Well, then, I'll just have to remember never to buy a yellow shirt."

Of course it was just the yellow shirt. That would make

everything all right. None of it would happen if Mieka chose never to buy a yellow shirt.

"You wouldn't be anything if it wasn't for me!"

He could still remember the first time he'd looked down into those eyes. The ratty bar in Gowerion, the front and effrontery, the rage when Mieka played "Sailor's Sweetheart" for laughs, the knowledge so grudgingly admitted that this mad and clever little Elf was their completion, their missing piece.

But he also remembered the Elsewhens, all those times he'd battered Mieka's face to a bloodied ruin. If he went to Wistly Hall to confront Mieka, he'd end with blood on his hands and he'd see it there forever, even after he'd washed it away—like in the long, hideous vision where he'd sat in the garden of Clinquant House waiting for Mieka's corpse to burn and stared at his hands and wondered why the blood didn't show.

"When the Cornerstones lost their Elf, they lost their soul."

Cayden had changed that. They weren't the Cornerstones, they were *Touchstone*, that singular thing they made together and could never have been without Mieka. He'd changed it, but it hadn't been enough.

"When Touchstone lost their Elf, they lost their soul."

Whatever he did, it would never be enough.

And yet… and yet, when he had slogged up to his fifth-floor room, mercifully unseen by Derien or Mistress Mirdley, and collapsed exhausted onto his bed, he dreamed the dream where Mieka's hair had gone silvery, and there was a bottle of sparkling wine on the bar and a bowl of mocah-dust berries, and a teasing voice challenged, *"You didn't remember, did you?"*

When he woke, he did remember. His Namingday. His forty-fifth Namingday. *That* life, and none other.

But if he wanted it, he would have to fight for it.

The gilt-columned corridor outside the Palace's great hall was packed with people—all of them male, which was a pity because Mieka could have used the sight of a pretty girl or six to distract him from nerves. Everybody was doing a brand-new piece, specially created for the occasion; everybody was anxious. Even Black fucking Lightning, Mieka was pleased to note. Pirro Spangler was clenching and unclenching his twitching fists. The fettler, Herris Crowkeeper, had taken up pacing as a hobby—not that he got far, not in this crowd. Kaj Seamark started at every noise. Thierin Knottinger actually looked ill.

Mieka concentrated on lounging against a convenient wall, talking with Chattim Czillag. The Shadowshapers would be doing a mad little piece about a frustrated poet trying desperately to get his work printed, and some of the poetry was so bad that Chat confessed he had a horrid time not falling over laughing.

"Proves Vered has a sense of humor, then?" Mieka asked.

"Rommy Needler told us we had to do something funny, we were getting known as the Grims. By the bye, he also says he's never seen his horses looking so sleek. You took good care of them on the Winterly, and of the wagon."

"Muchly beholden to you for the favor," Mieka said sincerely, though they'd paid quite a bit to hire the wagon and horses. "Yazz treated those beasties like they were his own children. Brushing them down for hours a night—for a Giant, or mostly so, he's the best with horses anyone's ever seen. And no, you can't hire him away from us! We'll have our own wagon by this summer, and he's to drive it."

"Play nice, little one." Chat grinned. "It's still our horses you'll have to hire!"

"And what will the Grims be doing tonight, then, at Master Needler's piteous plea?"

"Well, we all got drunk one night at my place, and this popped up." He leaned closer, lowering his voice, although there were so many people milling about that he could have shouted and not attracted any attention. "Rauel and Vered competed, as always, but this time to see who could come up with the most repulsive rhymes. Me, I think they dug into their own childhood efforts and just won't confess it. But some of it truly is foul. Real chankings."

"Stuff of the 'she doesn't love me, I'll have to kill myself' and 'what's the meaning of life' sort?"

Chat nodded, the lock of prematurely gray hair falling over his eyes. "'My knees are meant for crawling on / Crawling to your door' and such like. All that lovely pompous torment one goes through at fifteen or so. Rauel masques the poet, and Vered all the different publishers he visits. But the real fun is Alaen."

Mieka blinked a question at him.

"He's offstage, of course—couldn't get him to come on and be masqued. He starts playing a tune, and Rauel hears him in the street, and the next thing you know Rauel's warbling the poetry set to music!"

"The same poetry?"

"The same *bad* poetry. And then he's onstage, and a whole bank's worth of money being thrown at him. The point being, of course, that you can get away with a lot of bilge when there's music backing it up."

"Not a very nice poke at the songsmiths."

"Well, no. But the funniest part is that Alaen doesn't realize it. He agreed to do it only if he could add a couple of the songs to his own folio—once we've done them here, of course."

"He plans to do them as jokes?"

"That's the funny part. He's absolutely dead sincere about them."

"Telling all our secrets, now, are you?" came Vered's voice from nearby. He was jostled, snarled a bit over his shoulder, and Mieka and Chat made room for him against the wall. "What about Touchstone, then? I've heard dire things from the Stewards."

"Really?" Mieka smiled.

Vered cuffed him lightly on the arm. "Mucking about again with one of the Sacred Thirteen," he intoned through his long, narrow nose. "Simply shocking, young man, simply not done! Once, with the Dragon, was bad enough—but *twice*! You wicked, wicked boys!"

Chat took up the scold, wagging a finger in Mieka's face. "There'll be no more of the 'Treasure' at Trials anymore, not the good old familiar version they can judge against all others they've seen for the last thirty years! No, not a thrilled man in the lot, Master Windthistle, not a single one."

Mieka shrugged. "You'll just all have to learn Cade's version—as if anyone else could ever do it the way we do!"

"Humble, isn't he?" Vered observed to Chat.

"If the Stewards have half a brain amongst them," Mieka insisted, "they'll take it out altogether and leave it at the Twelve."

"Quite the difficulty Touchstone has caused. And pleased to do so, I'm sure." Vered looked about him, then leaned down and whispered, "Give us a hint, won't you? What's the real story?"

"Watch and learn." He deployed The Eyes on Chat. "Those withies working for you?"

"Brilliantly. Tell us, Miek!"

"Any word on what Black fu—Black Lightning will daze and amaze us with?"

"Mieka!"

"I hear the lovely Chirene has had twins—or was it triplets?" Vered said, "Just twins, boy and girl. And now I'm intended to ask about your daughter, all nice and polite, so the subject's changed?"

"Nobody expects you to be polite, Vered," Chat soothed. "Did I tell you, Miek, my own girl's in pig again, our second son, we hope. Who stole the Treasure?"

Mieka smiled his sweetest. "A dry spring this year, what? Could do with a sprinkle of rain to help the flowers along."

Chat took him by the scruff of the neck and shook him playfully.

Laughing, Mieka made his escape, slithering through the crowd, trying to find space to breathe.

"Mieka! Have you seen Jeska?"

He turned to find Kearney Fairwalk shouldering his way—with multiple apologies—towards him. "Haven't seen him!"

Usually one would only have to go looking for the prettiest girl in the place, and there Jeska would be. But in this sea of men, finding one rather short masquer would be a problem.

"Rafe and Cade are over there, by that column with the red flowers," Fairwalk panted, having reached Mieka's side. "Do go and join them, won't you? Must keep you all together, don't you see—outrageous crush—a scandal that the Stewards allow it—"

Mieka began the long push to the indicated column. Cade and Rafe had their backs pressed to it. As Mieka neared, Rafe risked the swarm and took a few steps, grabbed him by the arm, and hauled him out of the throng like a puppy from a kennel cage.

"This is ridiculous," Cade announced. "I can't hear myself think. Come on!"

"We ought to stop here," Mieka argued. "How will Kearney find us?"

Cade shrugged irritably. Rafe tapped Mieka on the shoulder and said, "Don't mind him—Lord Oakapple turned up earlier. He can't decide whether to be in raptures or in hiding."

"So he doesn't know?"

"Not even a hint!" Rafe grinned maliciously. "Dead chuffed that Cade figured it out, terrified of what the true story might be."

"As long as he pays up, who cares?"

Cade stumbled against him. "Lord Oakapple can go fiddle with himself. The truth is the truth—"

"—and therefore beautiful?" Mieka laughed up at him. "We all read the article, Quill!"

Fairwalk, with Jeska in tow, struggled through to them. "This way!"

A few minutes and a few bruises later, they were in a room scarcely larger than a broom cupboard. Rafe slammed the door and leaned his spine against it.

"Gods!" Jeska exclaimed. "That's a relief! Who let all those people in?"

"Good job we didn't bring Dery in this way," Rafe said.

"I'm regretting that we brought him at all," Cade fretted.

"There's three Windthistles—two of them six-foot-five— and a Threadchaser looking out for him," Mieka soothed. "Did I forget to say beholden for the tickets, Kearney?" He looked around. "Kearney?"

"If you think I'm opening this door to let him in, have another think about it," Rafe warned.

Eventually the noise outside died down. Rafe cracked the door open a bit, nodded, and they eased out of the room. The hallway had depopulated dramatically, and they knew why when, from the great hall there echoed a shout of, "Your Gracious Majesty, Your Royal Highness, Your Grace, my lords, and gentlemen—Black Lightning!"

"Oh, splendid," Jeska muttered. "Anybody seen Alaen to warn him to pay attention to us?"

"He won't be heeding anybody but the Shadowshapers tonight," Mieka said. "I had it from Chat himself—"

"I should talk to him all the same," Cade decided. "We've half an hour of—" He waved a contemptuous hand towards the great hall.

"—*that* before we're on."

He had scarcely left when Fairwalk fluttered over to them. "Lord and Lady and Angels above—I thought I'd never find you again! Where's Cayden?"

"No idea," Mieka said. "Any hope of a drink round here?"

"Not that I've seen," said Fairwalk, though his gaze shifted to the right, which Mieka took to be an involuntary indicator that there were indeed drinks to be had.

"Make it three," Rafe said. "Cade can get his own."

"Mieka! You can't—please don't—"

"Won't be a tick of the clock," he promised.

Three columns down there was an alcove, and in it was the sad sight of a hundred or so upended bottles in a gigantic tub of melting ice. Mieka growled low in his throat and wondered how he could possibly have missed this on the way in. He turned, spotted a half-open door leading from the alcove, and started for it.

"Just listen for a moment, won't you?" Cade's voice said. "Alaen, this is vitally important—"

Mieka nearly pushed the door open to add his insistence to Cade's, but the anguish in Alaen's voice stopped him.

"I told you—unless it helps me with Chirene, I'm not interested!"

"Oh, for fuck's sake, Alaen!"

"I can't help it, Cayden, I—"

"Just *listen*! You have to watch everything we do onstage tonight, understand? Watch and remember, you and Briuly both—"

"I don't care! I can't think of anything but her. I'm in love with her, Cade."

"Does Sakary know?"

"Gods, I hope not—I don't think *she* knows."

Derisively: "She's a woman. She knows."

"What am I to do?"

"Why are you asking *me*? What do you think I could do?"

"You—but I thought you'd understand! You want somebody you can't have—you know how it feels, seeing that person and—and—"

"Shut it!"

Mieka winced. After the initial white-faced shock at hearing she was bespoken, Cade hadn't shown a morsel of feeling one way or the other about Lady Vrennerie. Ah, but that was Cade, wasn't it, right down to the ground.

"But, Cade, I've seen your eyes when you—I just thought—"

"Not very good at thinking, are you? Didn't do any before you fixed on her!"

"I don't see her that often, and never alone, but I love her, I want her—oh Gods, she's the most beautiful thing I've ever seen—"

"Is that the criterion, then?"

"Wh-what d'you mean?'

"The most beautiful *thing*, you said. Like she's a tapestry to display on the wall, or a lute you can possess—"

"Fuck you! That's not how it is! The first time I ever saw her, I knew. I haven't stopped thinking about her since. It's been all hells, her living at Mieka's house, I don't dare go all the way out there, someone would see me, someone would find out—"

"You showed that much sense? I'm amazed."

Alaen didn't seem to have heard him. "When I play, she's the one I'm playing for, singing to, even though she's never there—if there was any hope, any hope at all—"

"Hope? There's none, Alaen. No hope in the world."

Suddenly Mieka wondered which of them he was speaking to.

"But there has to be! If I could just be near her, alone with her, for a few moments, I could tell her, and—"

"And then what? You'd fall into each other's arms and everyone would be happier than swine in shit?"

Alaen's tone turned vicious. "Is that what *you're* hoping for, Cayden?"

Time and past time he interrupted this. Plastering a carefree grin onto his face, he swanned through the door, calling out, "Quill! Where've you got to? Oh! Here you are! His Lordship's blithering about something that only you can mend, you'd best go smooth his fruzzles. Alaen, old son, you wouldn't happen to know where there might be a drink about, would you? I'm perfectly parched!"

Cade wore that blank expression he used when he wanted to be a thousand miles from wherever it was he currently stood. Mieka threw him a grimace of a smile behind Alaen's back, just to let him know he'd heard enough to understand, and pulled the musician out of the alcove and down the corridor, babbling amiably all the way. At the far end he glimpsed Vered Goldbraider's distinctive white-blond hair, and steered Alaen towards the Shadowshapers. They were as grateful to have him back as Mieka was to get rid of him.

"No drinks left," Mieka reported when he found the rest of Touchstone again. "I knew I should've brought me own bottle! I—" He broke off as a sudden gust of emotion hit him like a slap in the face. He didn't just want a drink, he wanted to laugh hysterically, and dance on corpses, and drag some girl into a corner and fuck her until she screamed—

Just as quickly as it happened, it was muted. He dragged in a gasping breath. "Gods almighty! What *was* that?"

"Black fucking Lightning," Jeska muttered, and wiped sweat from his forehead. "Subtle as a shipwreck!"

Mieka looked up at Rafe. The fettler's gray-blue eyes were unfocused, his lips bitten in a tight line. He was deflecting the backwash from the performance, and he didn't stop for long minutes, until applause thundered through the great hall.

"Beholden," Mieka whispered when Rafe's face cleared of strain. "More than I can tell you."

"Crowkeeper couldn't control his own farts, much less his glisker," Cade said. But he looked unaffected, as if nothing had touched him—and that, Mieka told himself, was Cade, too. Right down to the ground.

"It's time," Fairwalk said suddenly, and Mieka wondered where he'd come from. "They're about to announce you."

Cade shook his head. "Give it a few minutes. The audience needs to recover from that."

Mieka understood instantly that he was worried about Rafe, not the audience. Gods, for some bluethorn right now, just a bit of it to get that look out of Rafe's eyes. But in the next moment rage replaced the fettler's exhaustion, and the jaw beneath the thick black beard set stubbornly, and he met Cade's eyes with a curt nod.

All the same, Mieka told himself to be very careful with the magic tonight, adjusting it himself as much as possible so that Rafe didn't have to work so hard.

Sakary Grainer approached, his usually impassive face flushed with anger. "Did you feel that?" he demanded of them all. "Stupid fools oughtn't to be allowed on a stage!"

"We're all right," Rafe said. "You?"

"He's in luck that I didn't send it all right back at him."

"We'll have to try that sometime." Rafe grinned.

"Name the day." Sakary glanced round as Rauel called his name. "Here's to it—we're sneaking in at the side to watch."

"Enjoy," Mieka said, and winked, and within moments heard the Steward cry, *"Touchstone!"*

Mieka concentrated on the place first, just as they'd planned. A cold twilight, cold clouds, cold sun hanging listlessly in the sky. A second withie gave him the wind, the footsteps, the ragged breath. A third guised Jeska as a tall, becloaked man, hood up over his head, pausing to look back over his shoulder in terror.

"No night bedarked as soonly—as soonly—" He stammered out the words of the poem, and the wall swirled into view ahead of him. "Crumbling wall—athwart the crumbling wall—yes! Here!"

Gently now; a throne coalescing into recognizable shape from what had seemed at first to be a simple stone wall. Triumph threading through the sight, and urgency, and defiance. That last was the most important, Cade had said. Without the insolent disdain, what followed would mean nothing.

Jeska collapsed onto his knees and from his cloak there fell a wrapped bundle that spilled diamonds and gold-and-silver-threaded glass into the mud. He moaned in dismay at the sacrilege—and then started with terror as he heard the galloping hooves and the howling dogs. (A nice touch, that; saved Cade having to provide and Mieka having to conjure the actual company of cavalry and hounds.) Scrabbling at the wall, he shoved the bundle deep and staggered up to his full height, lifting both arms, his hooded cloak slipping to the ground, revealing the pointed ears and iridescent wings of a Fae.

The audience gasped. Mieka spared attention enough for a brief glance over at Cade, who wore a harsh little smile.

Lightning blasted from the Fae's fingertips, toppling the

wall atop the Treasure just as the last rays of the sun seemed to reach for the glimmering crown. He stood straight, let his arms fall, and as night swept across him the pursuers caught at him, billowing cloaks throwing wild shadows in the darkness.

The spinning shadows resolved with painful suddenness into a castle hall blazing with torchlight. Dozens of shifting sinister shapes lined the walls, their faces hidden beneath hoods. Chained by iron at wrists and ankles, he kept his feet despite the wounds that bled from his shoulders, arms, thighs. Crimson dripped from his bruised lips. As he drew himself straight again, his wings quivered across his back.

"The Rights are not yours, will never be yours," he cried. "Be Liege of all you fancy, let all others bow their heads to you. But not us. Never us!" Nasty, spiteful, this was not the romanticized Fae of noble bearing and quick caprice. "We are the true rulers of this land! You are the usurpers—all you craven Elves and traitorous Wizards, cowardly Sprites, conniving Gnomes, deceiving Goblins and faithless Pikseys and arrogant thieving Humans! The Rights belong to the Fae and if we cannot have them, no one will!"

A low murmuring flowed through the audience. Into it, Cade's voice said, "Mayhap we are all these things, and more, and worse. But *you* broke the peace. *You* brought this war upon us all. *And you lost.*"

It was Rafe who spoke the Fae's doom: "Hang him." And his deep, powerful voice sent a tremble through the great hall, from the front rows of seats where the Royals sat to the balcony where carved wooden screens hid the ladies.

Bells rang out, deep mismatched notes that hurt to hear. Sunlight flared through the windows. When the dazzlement faded, the Fae was naught but a shadow on the far wall: dangling by a noose, turning slowly, dead.

Jeska, himself once more, walked silently to the center of the stage. When the bells ceased, he said, "Those who make war, those who break the peace, those who take that to which they have no right—these are the thieves. The Treasure they steal is life, and *that* belongs to us all."

Cade had worried that not everyone would recognize those words. Mieka had told him to use them anyway, because the people who needed to hear them would know them by heart: the King, whose father had spoken them, and the Archduke, whose father had been condemned by them.

Jeska lifted his hands, and between them Mieka conjured with delicate care a gleaming necklet and a splendid crown of glass spun with threads of gold and silver, the diamonds sparkling as the Rights turned slowly, in time with the hanged man's shadow on the wall. And instead of shattering glass withies or glass windows or glass candle-shades, the glass crown and necklet disintegrated without sound into tiny dazzling broken shards that lingered in the air like stars.

Mieka had no idea when the applause began, or who began it. The next thing he knew was that he'd obeyed what had by now become instinct, and had leaped over his glass baskets, and he and Cade and Rafe and Jeska stood with linked arms and took their bows.

"*Touch*stone!" someone yelled, and the chant was taken up from the marble floor to the wooden rafters. "*Touch*stone!"

Mieka looked up at Cade, and tightened an arm around his waist, and laughed.

Very late that night a conversation took place in a Gallantrybanks mansion.

"Your Grace must recall that I didn't find him until he was almost thirteen."

"Rather late."

"Not really. He had to want it, you see. That fribbling fool of a father, that Harpy of a mother… not many friends, and of course looking the way he does… this is exquisite wine, Your Grace."

"You mean that he had to want it the same way I had to want it."

"Precisely. Another year or two and it might either have been crushed out of him or driven him mad. He is of a temperament that it could have gone either way. But when I came for him, he was ready."

"I suppose that, like me, he was spilling over with questions."

"Not at all. He was so eager for what I offered that he asked almost nothing. In some ways, he's very innocent, and remains so. I taught him as I taught all my other students, though mayhap I made him work a little harder for it. It was later, when he trusted me, that the questions came—"

"But by that time he did trust you, and the answers you gave. May I refill your glass?"

"Beholden, Your Grace."

"So now it is confirmed, or so you say."

"He could not have known what the Rights actually were, and looked like, unless he had seen them. Yes, it is confirmed, although I never required any proof, myself."

"Why didn't you bring him to me? Why did I have to discover him on my own?"

"Your Grace knows the answers."

"I know *my* answers. I should like very much to hear yours."

"And why I steered him towards the theater?"

"That would seem to be one of the more important questions."

"It is *the* most important. As for the others—you recall, I'm sure, what it was like, being seventeen years old and eager to prove yourself."

"I recall that you cautioned against doing anything of the sort. Good advice."

"For you, yes. But for him it was necessary to demonstrate

to his parents that he's not the mistake they think him to be. To show himself gifted. To strive for independence, to make his mark. All the usual fevers of adolescence."

"I remember."

"You were constantly in the public eye. You had to be careful. But he had to try his wings."

"And now that he's taken flight…"

"He has confidence, made a name for himself. At almost twenty-one, he possesses the fame, the money, the respect, and the acclaim he craves. Not that any of it will ever be enough for him, of course."

"One might almost think you feel sorry for him. Are fond of him."

"I do pity him, yes. But he's not the sort for whom one feels fondness. I admire his talents, and I'm gratified that he fulfilled my expectations. But he isn't a person one likes. A prickly and difficult character, Cayden Silversun. From what I have observed, one either loves him as he is, or accepts him with a shrug."

"Devotion or indifference?"

"Once curiosity is satisfied. There is no charm about him, Your Grace."

"Unlike his glisker."

"Ah, yes. The Elf. He is fiercely protective of his 'Quill' because he feels everything with the wild intensity of his kind. This will work to your advantage, of course."

"Better if he had chosen to feel fiercely indifferent."

"Elfenfolk don't 'choose.' But what you must understand is that to break the one will be to break the other."

"Naturally, I want a lesser shattering for Silversun."

"He is the stronger, certainly. He could not have survived his gift otherwise."

"You might have confirmed it sooner."

"Your Grace's life has been one of difficulty and dissembling.

You have stepped with caution around lies and liars since your childhood. Would you truly have believed in what Cayden is if it had not been thus demonstrated to you?"

"How dare he use those words tonight—the very words that doomed my father—"

"Arrogance, which will also work to Your Grace's advantage. But to return to the point, his gift has been independently corroborated—"

"That old woman will be trouble."

"Such women always are. She can be appeased. Accommodated."

"I wonder why I ought to bother."

"Because she may accomplish the necessary without your having to lift a finger. The Elf is, as I say, devoted and protective. If he is separated from Cayden Silversun in a manner totally removed from any hint of your involvement, so much the better."

"Caitiffer… I'm surprised they kept the name."

"No one remembers the word these days. One of the proud old Witchly clans from the Durkah Isle. The Gods only know how she's lived here so long without being spotted. But the fact is that she's here, and her daughter with her, and they will in their doing undo what's between the Elf and Silversun. I give it two years. Mayhap three."

"Why can I not simply—"

"Have you a son or daughter yet, Your Grace?"

"Have I ever mentioned how deeply I loathe that sweetness in your voice like poison?"

"You have always understood that this was a long game. Why so impatient?"

"If Silversun can reveal possible futures to me, why should I not discover what's in store and adjust my moves accordingly?"

"Several reasons. He doesn't yet know that you are aware of his special talents. He doesn't trust you—that abortive move regarding the glassworks was incredibly foolish, unworthy of you."

"It was my calculation that owning his glasscrafter would be a step towards owning him."

"The Elf is not the only one capable of fierce devotion. Cayden loves the Cindercliff girl—or, I should say, Mistress Windthistle—as much as he is capable of loving anyone."

"And yet he didn't marry her."

"Do you love your favorite hound the way you love your wife?"

"My wife is not a subject for discussion."

"She was a clever move, you know."

"I would not have married her otherwise. I admit I'm pleased you approve of her."

"Of herself, her person, I neither approve nor disapprove. What I appreciate is her ambition. And what I deplore is the proposition you made to Touchstone regarding a theater. The idea itself is not without merit. But the timing was all wrong."

"I might have succeeded, if the Wordturner whelp had done his job."

"That's debatable. Cayden respects Fairwalk in many ways, but not enough to counter his own instincts. As exceptional as his intellect may be, he would not be able to do what he does in priming the withies—which Mistress Windthistle makes for him, *specifically* for him and the Elf, knowing and loving them both—if he lacked equally significant emotional depths. You've come to know his mind a little. You must understand his heart before you can use him as you think to use him."

"His heart is of no use to me."

"That's where Your Grace is mistaken. Passionate as the Elf is, he would have little to work with if Cayden did not provide. Their partnership is what all tregetours and gliskers aspire to: a connection that amounts to a communion. If what I've heard is true, it was that way with them almost from the first. This was an extraordinary stroke of luck for you, of course."

"And why may I not take advantage of it now, rather than wait?"

"Recollect, please, his ancestors."

"I remember Lady Kiritin quite well."

"You remember her. I *knew* her."

"But you never told him that you did?"

"Of course not. He's ashamed of her ruthlessness, though in secret I believe he rather admires her power. But more to the immediate purpose for Cayden, and to the longer purpose for Your Grace, the grandsire, Cadriel, was a Master Fettler. Power of a different kind, but more importantly, power in an environment where Cayden, too, could find success. The other Silversuns... there was a great-grandmother who was quite mad, but it was through her that he inherited the potential. She was one of the last Watersmiths. Not just an Elfen bloodline, but Fae. Cadriel was her only son. Of his two sons, Zekien is a charming fool and the other, Dennet, went mad during the late war."

"Is Cayden likely to follow them into madness if pushed too hard?"

"That is where the grandsire comes into it. Consider the fettler's role onstage. *Control.*"

"Then we needn't worry too much about shattering him?"

"There is always the possibility. But in my estimation, he's resilient enough. To resume. Where the poetry came in, I've no notion. Once I saw it, I encouraged it, of course. Because I knew—slowly, it's true—but I knew what he could become."

"I must confess that I still don't see what the one has to do with the other. What his need to write and perform plays has to do with my need to know."

"There is something else you must understand about him, and about his gift. He sees only those things which he has the power to change. To express it differently—when no choices or decisions of his will affect a particular future, he will not see it in

advance. Doubtless he has seen nothing of Your Grace's future—
or I should say futures—because what you choose to do or not
do is not Cade's to influence. Any contact between you therefore
must be carefully restricted until he is ready to—"

"Are you telling me that this scribbler of playlets can *decide*
my future?"

"Gently, Your Grace, I have not finished. As I have been
explaining, in him are power, intellect, emotion, and above all
control. He doesn't want to become like his great-grandmother
or his uncle, so he is accustomed to self-examination and self-
discipline. I taught him much in this line. He balances his fear
against his arrogance, his heart's pain against his mind's authority.
He knows that he sees only what he has the power to change.
Heed me well, Your Grace. He must be broken, his balance
overset. His pride and his intellect must work together without
encumbering emotions. He must *want* to bring about the world
Your Grace envisions. And before you ask, it has everything to
do with what he does onstage. Did you not feel the power of it?
More importantly, did you not read what he himself said?"

"Read? Read what?"

"One of the broadsheets. What he said was this: that theater
in the right hands can change lives—and that if you can change
enough lives, you can change the world."

"Why do you laugh? What's so funny about that?"

"I laugh because he knows, and yet he doesn't know. Such
an innocent, for all his posturings! Your Grace, believe me when
I say that there is more to be used of this magic of his than the
ability to look into the futures. There is so much more."

LIST OF TERMS

agroof flat on your face; "knocked all agroof"

aroint found only in the imperative mood, get thee gone

ascian (ash-ee-in) a person without a shadow

blash weak or watered-down beer

breedbate someone who likes to start arguments or stir up quarrels

bully-rook a bragging cheater

Caitiff witch

carkanet necklace

chankings food you spit out

chavish the sound of many birds chirping or singing at once; the sound of many people chattering at once

cheverel kid leather

claum to handle with dirty fingers

climp to touch a clean, shiny surface and leave smudges of dirt or grease

clinquant glittering

clumperton clownish, clumsy lout

clunsh mixture of mud and dung

crambazzle worn-out, dissipated old man

cribble to pass something through a sieve; colloquially, to put sombody through the wringer

crizzle flaws in glass

cullion rude, disagreeable, mean-spirited person

dog's match a quickie

eesome pleasant to look upon

efter thief who robs theater patrons during a performance

feazings the frayed or unraveled ends of a rope

fliting an exchange of invective, abuse, or mockery, especially one in verse set forth between two poets

fribbler foolish, fussy man; also a *fribble; to fribble* as a verb

frustling shaking out and exhibiting feathers or plumage

gammon to trick or deceive, especially by talking nonsense

giddiot *giddy* and *idiot*

ginnel a narrow passage between buildings

gleet slime, sludge, greasy filth

glunsh to devour food in hasty, noisy gulps; by extension, a glutton

grouk become gradually enlivened after waking up

hest command

on tick goods received on credit

quat a pimple; used in contempt of a person

rumbullion an old term for rum

smatchet impudent, contemptible child

snarge a person no one likes; a total jerk

snup to snap up something of value that someone else has discarded or is selling for a bargain price

snurt expel mucus in sneezing or snorting

tiring room from *retire;* a private chamber

twiddlepoop foolish, fussy man

wamble the rumble, gurgle, or growl made by a distressed stomach on the verge of nausea; adj., wambling ("a wambling belly")

yark vomit

ABOUT THE AUTHOR

Melanie Rawn is the author of the bestselling Dragon Prince trilogy and of the Dragon Star trilogy. She graduated from Scripps College with a BA in history, and has worked as a teacher and editor. Rawn lives in Flagstaff, Arizona.

ALSO AVAILABLE FROM TITAN BOOKS

GLASS THORNS

MELANIE RAWN

TOUCHSTONE

Cayden Silversun is part Elven, part Fae, and part human Wizard. After centuries of bloodshed, in which Cade's Wizard kin played a prominent role, his powers are now strictly constrained. But in the theatre, magic lives.

Cade is a tregetour, a playwright who infuses glass wands with the magic necessary for the rest of his troupe, Touchstone, to perform his pieces. But alongside the Wizardly magic that he is sure will bring him fame and fortune on the stage is the legacy of the Fae within him. Troubled by prophetic visions of not only his future but the fates of those closest to him, Cade must decide whether to interfere, or stand back as Touchstone threatens to shatter into pieces.

"A captivating tale of magic, theatre, politics, and love... Rawn's storytelling mastery, ability to create unforgettable characters, and fresh approaches to world building and magic theory make this a must-read." *Library Journal*

TITANBOOKS.COM